EVA

NOVELS BY IB MELCHIOR

EVA
THE TOMBSTONE CIPHER
THE MARCUS DEVICE
THE WATCHDOGS of ABADDON
THE HAIGERLOCH PROJECT
SLEEPER AGENT
ORDER of BATTLE

EVA

Ib Melchior

DODD, MEAD & COMPANY

New York

To Cleo—now and always

Copyright © 1984 by Ib Melchior
All rights reserved
No part of this book may be reproduced in any form
without written permission from the publisher.
Published by Dodd, Mead & Company, Inc.
79 Madison Avenue, New York, N.Y. 10016
Distributed in Canada by
McClelland and Stewart Limited, Toronto
Manufactured in the United States of America
Designed by Claire Counihan
First Edition

Library of Congress Cataloging in Publication Data:

Melchior, Ib.
  Eva : a novel.

  Bibliography; p. 323
  1. Braun, Eva—Fiction. 2. Hitler, Adolf, 1889–1945—
Fiction. I. Title.
PS3563.E435E9 1984   813'.54   83-27492
ISBN 0-396-08294-7

Acknowledgments

The author wishes to express his appreciation for the valuable assistance given him in the research for this book by:

The San Pedro Boat Works, San Pedro, California
Dr. Leif Melchior, New York, N.Y.
The U.S. Army Information Service, Los Angeles, California
The Veterinary Medical Association, Los Angeles, California
The Modern Military Branch, Military Archives Division, National
  Archives and Records Service, Washington, D.C.

EVA is a work of fiction. All characters in the work, with the exception of the historical personages who are mentioned, are fictional. Any similarity to actual persons is purely coincidental.
                                                                    —Ib Melchior

---

"Thirty-six years after the Second World War fresh mystery has arisen over the fate of Eva Braun, Hitler's mistress and wife for one night. According to an eminent American scientist the body the Russians identified as that of Fraulein Braun was probably someone else."

The Times, London, July 3, 1981

Contents

PART I
April 26-May 4, 1945
1

PART II
May 31-June 14, 1945
135

PART III
June 20, 1945
309

Appendix   315
Abbreviations   321
Bibliography   323
About the Author   327

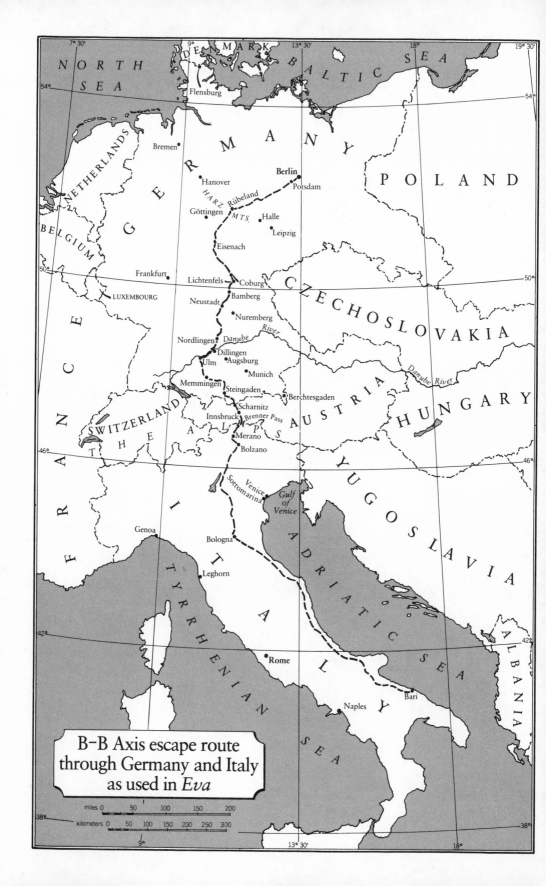

B-B Axis escape route through Germany and Italy as used in *Eva*

NORTH SEA

DENMARK

BALTIC SEA

Flensburg

NETHERLANDS

GERMANY

POLAND

Bremen

Hanover

Berlin

Potsdam

BELGIUM

HARZ

Göttingen

Rübeland

MTS.

Halle

Leipzig

Eisenach

LUXEMBOURG

Frankfurt

Lichtenfels

Coburg

CZECHOSLOVAKIA

Bamberg

Neustadt

Nuremberg

FRANCE

Nordlingen

Danube

River

Dillingen

Danube River

Ulm

Augsburg

Memmingen

Munich

Steingaden

Berchtesgaden

AUSTRIA

HUNGARY

Scharnitz

Innsbruck

Brenner Pass

THE

A

L

P

S

SWITZERLAND

Merano

Bolzano

Venice

Sottomarina

Gulf of Venice

Genoa

Bologna

YUGOSLAVIA

ADRIATIC SEA

Leghorn

ITALY

TYRRHENIAN SEA

Rome

ALBANIA

Bari

Naples

miles 0   50   100   150   200

kilometers 0   50   100   150   200   250   300

PART I

———•◦•———

April 26 – May 4, 1945

1

─── •◦• ───

HE FELT A SHARP BLOW to his right foot. He looked down. His boot was ripped open and crimson blood was welling out from the ragged gash. He knew his foot was shattered. He felt no pain—only surprise. He tried to move his ankle. He could not. He knew what had happened. A shell fragment or a bullet from the small arms fire below had torn through the unprotected floor of the slow-flying Fieseler Storch and struck him. He felt the little reconnaissance plane shudder. He was losing control.

"Hanna!" he cried. He did not recognize his own voice. "Take over. I've been hit."

He glanced out the window. A haze blurred his vision as the blood drained from him and the shock began to dull his senses. Less than fifty feet below lay the battered, burning ruins of Berlin—a city crumbling in the agony of its death throes. Through the debris-strewn streets, running like open scars between the gutted, battle-scorched buildings, little black figures scurried aimlessly. Russians? *Wehrmacht*? Refugees? No matter. They all looked like frenzied ants in an anthill, raked over and put to the torch. His mind was numbed. He had not realized the totality of destruction.

He felt the woman, crouched in a half-standing position behind him in the single-seater plane, reach across him and grab the controls from his hands. A red haze closed in—and *Luftwaffe General* Ritter von Greim lost consciousness.

Flying at roof-top level the Storch dipped and recovered sharply as *Flugkapitän* Hanna Reitsch fought the controls from her awkward position behind the comatose man. She felt his head flopping insensibly between her outstretched arms. She willed herself to ignore it. In lightning-fast succession her flying stunts through her years as a test pilot raced through her mind: the near fatal crashes; the first jet planes; flying the live V-1 aerial bomb. But nothing like this.

She could reach only part of the controls. She stretched her slight five-feet-two frame as far forward as she could. She clenched her jaw in angry determination. She would make it. Hitler had summoned them. On a vital matter. He needed them. And she would not let her Führer down.

She looked out. She had to get her bearings. They had left Flughafen Gatow on the far bank of the Havel River west of the Chancellery only a few minutes earlier, beginning their sixteen-kilometer flight to the center of Berlin. They had crossed the river and the crater-dotted expanse of Grunewald Forest. On her left, to the north, through the reddish haze of smoke and dust she could make out the proud, imposing structures of the Olympia Stadion. She peered down at the gutted and scorched buildings just below. She knew where she was. Over the Charlottenburg district—better than halfway to the makeshift landing strip on the East-West Axis beyond the Victory Monument.

Suddenly the little single-engine monoplane shuddered and banked as shrapnel or bullets from below slammed into a wing. The starboard wingtip brushed a tall ruin as Hanna struggled to right the craft. Dammit! she thought viciously. Another four, five kilometers. Dammit! Not now! Not after flying all the way from Munich to Rechlin Luftwaffe Base in Mecklenburg, 150 kilometers northwest of Berlin, and from there to Gatow—with half their twenty-plane fighter escort shot down during the flight. Not after finding the Storch at Gatow Airfield—the only plane they could possibly hope to fly in to the beleaguered Chancellery—and taking off under enemy artillery fire. She would not be shot down.

Not now!

She threw a quick glance at the damaged wing. Gasoline was pouring from the wing tank.

Two more kilometers.

The firing from below had stopped. She passed over the Tiergarten—the Berlin Zoo. She banked, lined up the plane with the Charlottenburg Parkway, and came to a lurching, bumpy landing just before the Brandenburg Gate.

A dust-streaked military Volkswagen careened toward the plane.

A lighter colored, dirt-free circle on the sloping hood between the frog-eye headlights bore witness to the fact that the spare tire had recently been removed. The canvas of the convertible top usually gathered behind the rear seat was missing, leaving the naked metal struts folded up like the legs of a dead spider.

The little vehicle skidded to a halt next to the Storch. A young SS officer was standing next to the driver, holding on to the windshield. He gave a smart *Heil Hitler* salute.

"*Obersturmführer Knebel, zu Befehl!*" he snapped. "At your orders!"

Hanna leaned from the cockpit. "The General has been hit," she called. "Help me get him down." She uncoiled herself from her cramped position, ignoring her protesting muscles.

Greim had regained consciousness. His face was chalky and drawn. He winced as they wormed him from the cockpit. His foot dripped blood.

"I have a staff car waiting for the General," the young SS officer said. "Over there." He pointed. "I am to—"

"Forget it," Hanna interrupted him. "Just help me get him into the Volkswagen. Now! I want to get him to the Bunker Lazaret at once."

The driver piloted his little Volkswagen along the shell-pitted, debris-strewn Unter den Linden, making as much speed as he could. The young *SS Obersturmführer* stood beside him, clinging to the windshield, peering ahead, calling directions and warning him about obstacles. In the rear seat sat Ritter von Greim, rigid in pain, scrunched into a corner, as Hanna tried to cushion his injured foot against the bumps and lurchings of the vehicle.

Shocked, appalled, they stared at the destruction around them. As far as they could see a suffocating shroud of dirty gray dust and smoke hung over the city, splotched with reddish fire balls from burning buildings, licked by blood-red fingers of flame reaching into the darkened sky.

Their progress was slow through the ravaged avenue, strewn with the cracked and splintered trunks of the once proud and famous linden trees, snapped like bones on a torture rack, littered with toppled lampposts and the wrecks of abandoned, burned-out cars. They drove past the scorched and gutted buildings, pockmarked by shrapnel, their blackened, empty windows watching the little Volkswagen's journey through this forecourt of hell. And playing an ominous obbligato to the infernal phantasmagoria, the awesome sounds of distant battle, the shelling, the rockets, the artillery fire and the wails of fire engines and ambulances—from time to time blotted out by ground-shaking explosions.

They turned into the nearly deserted Wilhelmstrasse, past the once-splendrous Adlon Hotel, most of it still standing, battle-scarred and fire-scorched. The once great thoroughfare—center of government offices—was filled with rubble, shattered glass, and broken masonry from the demolished buildings; only a narrow lane remained open through the wreckage. Muddy water, burst from broken mains, flowed past the piles of debris, swirling in mini-maelstroms where partly clogged drains or cracks in the pavement led to the sewers below.

The driver threaded the vehicle precariously between one such whirlpool and a blackened half-track, still burning. In the oily pool floated a disemboweled dog, slowly circling in the eddying water, rhythmically dipping into the vortex and resurfacing—too big to go down through the drain.

Bleakly Greim looked at the devastation around him. Defeat lay over the mortally wounded city like a blanket over a corpse. He knew he was witnessing the end of a great metropolis. The death spasms of the vaunted Third Reich. Like that wretched dog, he thought dismally. Dead, but not willing to go down.

They jolted past the badly damaged, long since abandoned Old Chancellery Buildings, a huge bomb crater blasted out in front of it, filled with ash-coated water slowly swirling as it bled into the subterranean cavities below, and past Goebbel's Propaganda Ministry, its blackened façade echoing its purpose—poised across from one another like a doomed Scylla and Charybdis.

Skirting a disabled Jagdpanzer they turned the corner into Vossstrasse. The New Chancellery directly on their right was still standing, but air raids had blasted gaping holes in the walls. And makeshift barricades had been erected at the imposing entrance.

Grimly they stared at the ravaged buildings where deep in the bowels of the earth below the bleak ruins lay the Führer Bunker of Adolf Hitler. From the roof above, pointing toward the heavens, as if in accusation, the haughty flagpole stood naked, stripped of the Führer's personal standard with its steel and flames and its swastika—the *Hagenkreutz*—set in a field of arabesques, which always flew over the Chancellery when Adolf Hitler was in residence.

Idly Greim wondered if the naked pole was an attempt to fool the enemy air raiders into thinking that the Führer was elsewhere, or to prevent the suffering Berliners from storming the place, demanding relief. Or was it simply an oversight?

The Volkswagen came to a halt.

General Ritter von Greim and *Flugkapitän* Hanna Reitsch had arrived at the Bunker.

The hospital bunker deep under the complex, connected to the even deeper Führer Bunker through a series of underground passages, was teeming with activity. It was a little before 1900 hours. Ritter von Greim was lying on a stretcher while a doctor was attending to his wounded foot. Hanna stood by his side.

Suddenly a familiar, raspy voice spoke behind them.

"*Mein lieber* Greim! *Gnädiges Fräulein* Hanna!"

In the doorway to the Lazaret stood Adolf Hitler.

They both turned toward him.

Hanna was shocked. Her beloved Führer had changed, aged alarmingly since last she saw him. In a birdlike stoop he stood smiling at them. His complexion was unhealthily sallow with a chalky appearance, his cheeks sunken. His hair had turned gray; making his distinguished little mustache, which she found so attractive, look darker than ever in his pallid, waxen face. But his deep-set eyes still burned with the familiar fire. His right hand clutched his left before him in a vain effort to check its constant trembling, a reminder of the assassination attempt at the Rastenburg Wolf's Lair in July of the year before, when a bomb had demolished the conference room in the Lagebarrack. She felt the pressure of a deep sadness build in her chest. The Führer. Adolf Hitler. The greatest man Germany had ever produced, having sacrificed himself for his beloved fatherland, was as much a ruin as was the city in which he had chosen to make his gallant last stand.

In a hunched shuffle, dragging his left foot, Hitler moved over to Greim. He beamed down at him.

"Miracles can still happen, *mein lieber* Greim," he rasped. "You and *Fräulein* Hanna are here." He looked at them. His eyes suddenly flashed in rage. "*Reichsmarschall* Goering has betrayed me!" he shouted. "Deserted the Fatherland! The coward made contact with the enemy behind my back and I have given orders for his immediate arrest!"

He stared down at Greim, lying mesmerized on the stretcher.

"I hereby name you, Ritter von Greim, the *Reichsmarschall's* successor," he intoned solemnly. "Commander in chief of the

[7]

Luftwaffe with the rank of *Feldmarschall!*" His eyes bored into them. "Nothing is spared me," he said hoarsely. "Nothing! Disillusionment. Betrayal. Treachery. Heaped upon me. I have had Goering stripped of all his offices. Expelled him from every party organization." His voice rose steadily as the fury built in him. "He is a traitor! A deserter! I have been betrayed by my generals. Every possible wrong has been inflicted upon me. And now this! Sold out by my oldest comrade!"

Abruptly he stopped. Neither Greim nor Hanna said a word. Hitler turned to the doctor.

"I want the *Feldmarschall* moved to the Führer Bunker," he ordered curtly. "I want *Standartenführer* Stumpfegger to perform any necessary surgery personally. I want the *Feldmarschall* fit and able to fly out of here in four days!"

He turned on his heel and left the Lazaret.

Even under thirty feet of earth and sixteen feet of concrete the bunker had trembled and shaken when later that night the Russian heavy artillery units for the first time since the onslaught on the city had hurled their explosive shells to strike the Chancellery itself. Until now only aerial bombs from enemy aircraft had been able to reach the heart of Germany—the place Hanna Reitsch reverently looked upon as the Altar of the Fatherland. The Führer Bunker.

But now the Russian hordes were only a few kilometers away.

Adolf Hitler sat at his desk alone in his study, under the oval painting of Frederick the Great, the Prussian warrior king who was his idol. It was the only wall decoration in his bunker study. It was painted by Anton Graff. Hitler had bought it in Munich in 1934 and it had been with him ever since. It had become a fetish. A symbol of his own greatness. Now a thin film of cement dust that had sifted down during the bombardment dulled the surface of the oil painting.

He could not sleep. It was dawn, Friday, April the 27th. No one in the bunker knew what kind of day it was above. During the night, elements of the U.S. 3rd Army had crossed the Danube, outflanking the city of Regensburg. The vital channel seaport of Bremen had been taken by divisions of the British 2nd Army, and the Baltic port of Stettin had fallen to Marshal Rokossovsky's 2nd White Russian Army. But Hitler had no thoughts for these defeats. Only for the paper he held in his trembling hands.

The message.

The message from *Standartenführer* Otto Skorzeny.

Absentmindedly he brushed the thin covering of cement dust off his desk. Once again he read the message, brought to the bunker only hours before by an SS officer courier:

GHEIME KOMMANDOSACHE
Sonderkampfgruppe Skorzeny   *den 24.4.45*
Feldhauptquartier   *Nr. 177-4/45 g. Kdos chef.*

Cheffache!
Nur durch Offizier!

GEHEIM   *GEHEIM*   *GEHEIM*
Betr. Sonderdienstpersonal   *Führersache*

SECRET COMMAND ACTION
Special Battle Group Skorzeny   24 April 1945
Field Headquarters   No. 177-4/45 g. Com staff

STAFF BUSINESS
Officer Courier Only

SECRET   SECRET   SECRET
Re. Personnel for Special Duty   Führer Action
1. In response order this command, *Obersturmführer*
LÜTTJOHANN, WILLIBALD; SS # 3.309.288; Knight's
Cross, Gran Sasso Mussolini Rescue; Oak Leaves, Knight's Cross,
"Operation Greif"; detached this unit as of date. Ordered report
Reichschancellery, Berlin, 27 April 45.
2. Service record attached.
3. Above officer recommended unconditionally.

Heil Hitler!
Skorzeny

Standartenführer Otto Skorzeny, Hitler reminisced. One of his very best officers. *Ein prima Kerl!* And an Austrian. As he was, himself. Had he only had more officers of Skorzeny's caliber, he thought bitterly, things might have been different. The man had made an excellent impression on him at their very first meeting, he remembered. At the Wolfsschanze. In July, two years before. When he was searching for a daring young officer of unquestioned loyalty to lead the rescue mission to free Il Duce. He had put Skorzeny in charge. Skorzeny's action had been both brilliant and audacious. For a moment Hitler let himself savor one of the really heroic operations of the war. Well guarded, Mussolini had been held captive on top of a totally inaccessible mountain. Gran Sasso. In the Abruzzi range. With a handful of paratroopers Skorzeny had surprised the Italian troops guarding Mussolini and freed him. And to get the Duce off the mountaintop Skorzeny had crammed himself, a pilot, and the Duce into a tiny Storch and literally taxied the plane off the mountain top over the edge of a 3,000-foot drop, barely gaining enough flying speed to keep the overloaded plane from crashing. And he had brought the Italian leader to safety in Germany. It had been a magnificent feat. The entire world had been in awe of German courage and ingenuity. Otto Skorzeny was an officer he could trust. One of the few. A man of enormous imagination, personal courage, and great resourcefulness. He nodded slowly in remembrance. As with "Operation Greif." What the Americans had called the "Jeep Parties." Only last year. Captured American jeeps with Skorzeny's specially trained, English-speaking troops in U.S. uniforms, roaming freely behind enemy lines, playing havoc, turning road signs around, cutting communication wires and setting fires. Skorzeny's handful of special commandos had created such panic that vast numbers of enemy troops were immobilized searching for them. Eisenhower himself had been kept a virtual prisoner at his own headquarters. He smiled to himself. *Standartenführer* Otto Skorzeny was a *real* officer. A *real* German.

He grew sober. But now, when the most vital, the most crucial of all missions was at hand, when once again he was searching for a daring young officer, Otto Skorzeny could not be the man. He had wanted him. But he had realized that the officer would stand out far too much. Six feet, four inches tall, with a scar running the length of his left cheek, the man would be too recognizable. An absolute impossibility for the present mission. Besides, Skorzeny was of the greatest importance to the final preparations of the Werewolf Organization and the National Redoubt—the *Alpenfestung.* So he had asked him to recommend his best, his most loyal officer.

He flipped the page and peered at the *Lüttjohann Personalienakt* attached:

LÜTTJOHANN, WILLIBALD
SS Obersturmführer, # 3.309.288
Born: Göttingen, 21 June 1914
Hitler Youth, Group: Center, 1929
  Promoted: *Gefolgschaftsführer* 1931
SS 1933
  Assigned RSHA 1936
  Assigned *Sonderabteilung Ausland* 1937
  Agent Provocateur, U.S.A.
    German-American Bund, N.Y., 1937/38

Hitler smiled a thin, self-satisfied smile. The German-American Bund under that buffoon, Fritz Kuhn, had still been an excellent operation, astonishingly successful and effective considering it had to be carried out on a large, highly visible scale in a foreign country. He recalled the many news stories of violent rallies in open support of the German cause; the American Stormtroopers— sometimes outdoing their German brothers in their brutality and zeal; the fine propaganda films and the riots in the German part of New York City. Yorkville, it was called, as he remembered. Yes, the Bund had done much for the Nazi ideology, much to weaken the internal security of the United States. Of course, only in a decadent democracy could such actions be allowed to take place. It had been to his gain. The Bund had been important in recruiting patriotic spies and saboteurs who had served the Fatherland well through the years. He looked at the *Personalienakt*. Largely because of the efforts of such men as *Obersturmführer* Willibald Lüttjohann. The young officer chosen by Skorzeny seemed an excellent choice. He would know the enemy well.

He read on:

> *Waffen SS* 1939
>   Campaigns: Warsaw, Poland 1939
>   Belgium/France 1940. Dunkirk
>   Promoted: *Stabsscharführer* 1940
>   "Operation Barbarossa," Russia 1941
>   Field Commission: *Untersturmführer* 1941
> *Sonderkampfgruppe Skorzeny* 1942
>   Knight's Cross, Gran Sasso, 1943
>   Promoted: *Obersturmführer*, 1944
>   *Jagdverband*, Denmark, 1944
>   "Operation Greif," 1944
>   Oak Leaves, Knight's Cross
>   Werewolf Training Ctr., Neustrelitz 1945

Hitler frowned. The Werewolves. Why had he heard nothing? Krueger should be in position by now. He clenched his fist. It still twitched uncontrollably. The enemy would quickly learn the deadly perils of occupying German soil once the Werewolves were let loose. *They* would be the ones to make the invaders cringe in fear. He had at once approved the formation of the organization when Himmler had approached him with the idea. *Unternehmen Werwolf*—Operation Werewolf. Dedicated young men and women; from the SS; from the Hitler Youth; civilians, who would gladly lay down their lives in the performance of their duty, a duty which was to inflict death and terror on the invaders. Like their medieval namesakes. Himmler had put Prützmann, an SS General, in charge. And, of course, there was Skorzeny. When the time came they would be the backbone, the living spark of the continued resistance from the Alpine Fortress. He frowned again. He made a mental note to order Bormann to find out why there had been no word from Krueger; the general should be ready to go into action in a few days. He suddenly felt impatient. Nothing ever went the way it should. He could rely on no one but himself. And yet he had to.

He returned his attention to the service record of Willibald Lüttjohann. It was imperative that *that* young officer be unfailingly reliable. He read:

    Vital Statistics
        Height: 6 feet
        Weight: 180 pounds
        Hair: Blond
        Eyes: Blue
        Complexion: Fair
        Identifying Marks: None
    Special Capabilities
        Languages: Fluent English; some French, Italian
        Expert Marksman, small arms
        Expert, Close Combat
        Parachutist

He pushed the papers aside. He had asked Skorzeny for the best. He had not been let down. For once.

Willibald Lüttjohann. A young man he had never seen. A young man who soon would be carrying the future of the German Reich in his hands.

Abruptly Hitler gathered up the papers and put them away. Squinting for the keyhole he unlocked a drawer in his desk. Two large identical envelopes embossed with the state seal and thick with papers were lying side by side. For a moment he sat staring at them—unseeingly. Then he picked up one and stood up. Dragging his left foot he shuffled toward the door.

In the little chamber off Dr. Stumpfegger's examination room across the hall from Hitler's study, *Feldmarschall* Ritter von Greim was asleep. The shock had worn off and his injured foot had begun to hurt. Stumpfegger had given him a sedative to help him sleep. An orderly was just placing a small tray with a carafe of water and a glass on a table next to the bed. He straightened up and stood at attention as the Führer entered.

For a moment Hitler hovered at the door, watching the sleeping officer. "Wake him!" he rasped, without looking at the orderly. He walked to the foot of the bed.

The orderly at once stepped up to the sleeping Greim. Gingerly he took hold of the officer's shoulder, gently shaking him.

"Herr Feldmarschall," he said. *"Bitte. Bitte aufwecken!"*

Greim stirred fitfully. The orderly became more insistent. He shook the patient. "Wake up, please!" he said loudly. "The Führer wants to speak with you."

Slowly Greim opened his eyes. With difficulty he focused on Hitler, standing at the foot of his bed. He screwed up his eyes in an effort to clear his drowsy mind. *"Mein . . .* Führer," he whispered, his voice husky.

The orderly helped him to sit up, banking his pillow behind him. Hitler nodded to the man. "Leave us," he said.

The orderly left. Hitler pulled up a chair next to the bed. Heavily he sat down. For a moment he stared solemnly at the groggy man in the bed.

"Greim," he said portentously, "I want you to know exactly why I summoned you here."

Greim started to speak. Hitler silenced him with a wave of his hand. "Just listen to me," he said. "I promoted you to *Feldmarschall* because I need you," he continued. "But that is *not* the reason I had you come here in person. I could have done that more efficiently by telephone. Obviously I would not have subjected you to the danger you faced, if that had been the sole, the real reason for wanting you here." He smiled cynically. "But it will serve convincingly enough as my reason for those who would question my motives. And they are legion, believe me, *mein lieber* Greim." He looked soberly at the officer. "There is another reason," he said gravely. "A vital reason—a top secret reason—which made it imperative that I see you in person. Do you understand?"

Greim nodded. Fighting Stumpfegger's sedative, he still found it difficult to concentrate.

"Before you leave here," Hitler went on, "you will be given official orders. But your *real* mission will be given to you by me. Personally. Now! I want you to have time to prepare yourself for it. There can be no margin for failure!"

Greim stared at the hunched-over old man sitting next to his bed. The Führer. The leader of the German nation. The German people. His commander in chief. He knew something of great importance was happening, and he struggled to focus his attention. "I . . . shall do my utmost, *mein* Führer," he said, his speech slurred. "As I have . . . always done."

Hitler nodded. From his pocket he brought out the large envelope he had taken from his desk. "In this envelope are some documents," he said, his voice strangely tense. "Others will be added before you leave." He paused. He looked at the envelope with an undecipherable expression on his haggard face, then back at Greim. "Your mission," he grated. "Your mission will be to carry this envelope and its contents to safety and to see that the instructions contained in it are carried out faithfully." For a moment his hooded eyes grew glassy. "Left here," he said hoarsely, "it will only fall into—into the wrong hands."

He handed the envelope to Greim. "I want you to read the documents. Now!" he said. "I want you to realize the vital importance of your mission."

Greim took the envelope. He opened it. It contained half a dozen documents, all imprinted with official seals and stamps. He began to read. Hitler sat immobile, watching him.

And suddenly the drug-induced haze that swaddled Greim's mind was torn away. At once he was fully alert. Mesmerized, he read on.

Finished, he let the papers sink down on the bed. Obviously shaken, he stared at Hitler.

"*Mein* . . . Führer . . ." he breathed. "I . . ."

Hitler silenced him. "Only you and I know the contents of those documents, Greim," he said soberly. "*Reichsleiter* Bormann will be told. And one other—but you need not know who." He looked at the *Feldmarschall*, his eyes burning. "You understand what is required of you?"

Greim nodded. "I do, *mein* Führer. I shall not fail you."

Hitler nodded. He had picked the right man. "And you realize that until the proper, the designated time, the knowledge you now possess must remain strictly secret?"

"I do."

"The documents must under no circumstances fall into enemy hands. If such a course is inevitable, they must be destroyed at all costs."

"Understood, *mein* Führer."

Hitler's eyes bored into the man.

"And should you be captured, *mein lieber Feldmarschall*," he said softly, "should you be interrogated in such a way that you are in danger of revealing what you know—and the enemy may employ means you cannot resist: torture, drugs—you will protect the secret with your life! Even if you have to take that life yourself!"

"I will, *mein* Führer!" Greim picked up the envelope. For a moment he stared at the embossed seal on it. The swastika, held in the claws of a German eagle.

Or was it a Phoenix?

Hitler nodded slowly. He took the envelope. It rustled faintly in his trembling hand. He stared at it.

It had begun. Phase One. The Greim mission.

Phase Two, the most crucial, the most important part of *Unternehmen Zukunft*—Operation Future—would begin when Skorzeny's young officer arrived in the Bunker later that day. One *Obersturmführer* Willibald Lüttjohann.

He wondered what he would be like.

Everything would depend on him.

The future . . .

2

A CLOUD OF SATIATED FLIES rose in alarm from the carcass of a dead horse as *Obersturmführer* Willibald Lüttjohann skidded to a halt on the dirt road. Sitting astride his BMW R750 motorcycle he was aware of its power throbbing beneath him. He was glad he'd chosen the cycle for the trip to Berlin from the Commando School in Neustrelitz rather than the offered half-track and detail of SS men. He liked to depend on himself, and he'd figured he'd get through alone on the bike a helluva lot easier than with a half-assed escort. And he'd been right. Taking back roads and cutting across country he'd been able to evade enemy patrols and the crush of refugees and military traffic. It did not matter that the trip of about a hundred and fifty kilometers had become twice as long. He gunned the bike. He liked to hear the deep, controlled growl of promised power.

He raised the goggles from his grime-streaked face, revealing two circles free of dirt around his eyes. He peered ahead. It was beginning to grow dark. The back-country road in front of him was empty. He pulled his map from his brief tunic. He was wearing his commando outfit. He was approaching Berlin toward Spandau, having skirted Nauen and Falkensee. It was the only approach still open into the city, surrounded by Russian assault troops. On the horizon a red haze reached up into the sky from the city which was now the front line. The deep-throated rumble of distant battle filled the air, and it seemed as if the very clouds above were aflame.

He quickly oriented himself on the map. According to the intelligence given him there was a narrow gap in the Russian lines south of the Charlottenburg district—between Charlottenburg and Wilmersdorf—still held by friendly troops. He'd have to cross the Havel River—he hoped he could find a bridge still standing; he'd hate to have to abandon his bike—and head for the Tiergarten. The Chancellery was just beyond. He studied the map closely. Wilhelmstadt seemed his best bet.

Briefly he wondered again why he had been ordered to Berlin. Urgently. To report to the Führer himself! The thought once again filled him with excitement. He suppressed it. Get there first.

Again he gunned the motorcycle. His *Blitzrad*—his Blitzbike— as he liked to call it. He felt it was almost part of him, and he considered it lucky. The first two numerals of the license number, WH 219514 were his birthday, the last two his birth year. *Had* to be lucky.

He lowered his goggles and adjusted them. He gunned his bike and sped off toward the distant hell.

Once again Adolf Hitler unfolded the map of Berlin. He had carried it along all afternoon and it was rapidly disintegrating from the perspiration on his sweaty hands.

Where was Skorzeny's man?

Where was *Obersturmführer* Willibald Lüttjohann?

He should have reported to the Bunker hours ago. He spread the map out on the conference table in the lounge hall. He stood staring at it, fixedly. He looked up as Hanna Reitsch came out from Ritter von Greim's room. He motioned her over.

"*Mein liebes Fräulein* Hanna," he said solemnly. From his tunic pocket he fished out a little glass phial sealed with copper. "It is cyanamide," he explained meticulously. "Dr. Stumpfegger assures me it acts instantaneously. One bite—and you will not have to fear anything." He looked at the phial in his hand with a strangely morbid look in his eyes. "We all have them," he said. He handed it to her. "It is not what I would have liked to give you as a farewell present, *meine liebe* Hanna."

Moved almost to tears, Hanna was about to speak, when across the hall a door opened and Hitler's personal valet, *SS Standartenführer* Heinz Linge, came out from the Führer's quarters. He left the door open. Through it Hanna could see a young woman sitting on the sofa, engrossed in a photo album with an ivory-colored leather cover.

Eva Braun.

For a brief moment Hanna's eyes rested on the girl. She had

been astonished, and a little jealous, when all the rumors about the little assistant to the Führer's official photographer, Heinrich Hoffmann, who had become the Führer's mistress, turned out to be true. Even during the short time Hanna had been in the Bunker she had seen the influence the girl had on the Führer. She looked at her. She was attractive. Blond. With a pleasant face and a good figure, perhaps a little on the plump side, she looked younger than her thirty-three years. Clad in a close-fitting gray suit she sat on the sofa unconscious of Hanna's scrutiny. As she turned the pages in the album her little diamond-studded wristwatch glinted in the light. Hanna wondered if it had been a gift from the Führer. No doubt, she thought, again with a twinge of jealousy. But she could not dislike the girl. Eva Braun had been unfailingly friendly toward her, and grudgingly she admired her. Eva was by far the calmest and most composed of the women in the Bunker. And the most pleasant. Together she and Eva had tried to entertain the six Goebbels children, telling them stories and teaching them to yodel—to the dismay of their parents. She sighed. She, Hanna, would leave the Bunker.

Eva Braun would stay.

Hanna looked away. She wondered what would become of the Führer's mistress.

She looked at Hitler. She could not speak. She merely smiled and took the offered phial.

Hitler once more turned his attention to the map spread out on the table. Deeply disturbed he studied it. He had entered on it every scrap of information received about conditions in the city outside. He knew it was still possible to get into the city from the west, although the Russians were driving hard to close the ring around the Chancellery. And they had been pressing their attack at Spandau. It worried him. He had issued urgent orders that the bridges across the Havel were to be held at all costs. Axmann, the one-armed *Hitler Jugend* leader, had deployed his Hitler Youths all along the river and he had them man street barricades and fortifications protecting the gap, along with the *Volkssturm*. He hoped they would hold.

Long enough.

Again he folded the worn street map. It was rapidly coming apart at the soggy seams.

Where was Lüttjohann?

Willi Lüttjohann was making his way through a rubble-strewn street approaching Kaiserdamm. It was getting dark but the many fires, most of them raging uncontrolled, lit the harrowing scene confronting him. The destruction was terrible to behold. Most of the buildings were in ruins, and those still standing showed the ugly, raw scars of bombings and shellings.

He had crossed the Havel on a bridge held by a detachment of Hitler Youth, led by a seventeen-year-old. Boys, thirteen to fifteen years of age. He had been shocked. Had it come to this? Did the Fatherland have to be defended by children? They had been efficient. They had examined him and his papers thoroughly before letting him go on. Reluctantly, he had thought.

There were few people abroad. He saw a couple of men rummaging through the mountainous piles of foul-smelling garbage heaped against the ruins. One boarded-up store had been broken into and a dozen or so ragged people were busily looting its stock. Several women brandishing knives were carving chunks of meat from the haunches and flanks of a dead horse, still harnessed to a demolished wagon. Lying between the wagon poles the head of the animal was wrenched around, its dead eyes open, sadly watching the women at their grisly task.

Willi felt sick. The city was disintegrating. And its people. It tore at him even more than the sights of villages he'd passed through, every window hung with the white sheets of surrender—waiting for the enemy.

He turned a corner, skidding in the mud cover left by the shattered masonry and mortar and the broken water mains. The street before him was empty. About a hundred meters ahead a barricade of rubble and sandbags built around an overturned streetcar blocked the entire thoroughfare. He began to work his bike through the debris.

Wolfgang Schiller was two days shy of his thirteenth birthday. He was already a *Fähnleinsführer* in the Hitler Youth. And he was proud of his responsibilities. He poked his friend Helmuth, almost six months his senior.

"Look," he whispered. "Someone is coming. On a motorcycle."

The two boys peered fearfully down the stretch of darkened, deserted street in front of the barricade. Automatically they moved closer together. They were alone at their post.

"Should—should we get Herr Brauner?" Helmuth whispered, clutching his MP40 submachine gun. "And the others?"

Wolfgang shook his head. "He said not to disturb them unless it was important," he whispered back. "He said they hadn't slept for two days—and better they sleep now than when Ivan comes."

He bit his lip. He knew it was up to him. *He* had the rank. *He* had to decide if it was important. Or not. Was it? One lone soldier? He wished he could decide. If it *wasn't* important and he alerted the men from the *Volkssturm* unnecessarily, he would surely be ridiculed. But what if it was? And he handled it himself? He would show himself to be a real soldier then, wouldn't he? If he could only make up his mind . . .

Helmuth peered out through the barricade. He looked frightened. The strange man on the motorcycle was slowly coming closer. He turned to Wolfgang. "Who do you think it is?" he whispered, hoarsely.

"I don't know."

"A . . . Russian?"

"I don't know."

"Do you think he is one of ours?"

"I don't know. He doesn't look like it. His uniform looks funny."

"What—what'll we do?" Helmuth's voice quavered.

Fähnleinsführer Wolfgang Schiller said nothing. He did not know what to say. He took a firmer grip on the Panzerfaust poking out through an opening in the barricade. He knew it could knock out a tank, if it hit just right. He had seen it done. It would certainly destroy a motorcycle. And the man on it. He had fired a Panzerfaust once before. In training. You just aim it. Be sure no one stands behind you. And pull the trigger. It was like a rocket.

The man on the motorcycle was steadily coming closer. Wolfgang could see him clearly now. He did not recognize the uniform. And the helmet did not look like the ones he knew. He began to tremble.

"Oh, God," he prayed. "Let me be brave. Not—not like the last time." And softly, full of fear, he whispered the Hitler Youth oath to himself, his dry lips moving with the words: "I promise in the Hitler Youth to do my duty at all times, in love and faithfulness to the Führer, so help me God . . ."

The motorcycle was halfway to the barricade. What should he do? Was it a Russian? A Russian scout? Would they come in force? Or—was it a German soldier? He *had* to make up his mind. The tears began to run down his cheeks. What should he do? Shout to the man? And what if it *was* a Russian, he would be warned. And start shooting. Oh, dear God, what should he do? What? . . .

His finger was on the trigger of the weapon. He began to tremble. His hands shook. And suddenly . . .

Willi more sensed than saw the flash. Instantly he knew what it was. And even as the realization streaked through his mind to reach his conscious thought he reacted instinctively. He catapulted himself from the moving bike. The violent shockwave from the blast when the Panzerfaust warhead hit the bike, disintegrating it in a ball of fire, slammed into him, hurling him into the rubble. He felt a piece of shrapnel rip through his crash helmet savagely tearing it from his head. He let himself go loose as he hit the rubble of broken masonry and chunks of shattered concrete. With detached wonder he realized he was unhurt except for a numbness of his limbs and a ringing in his ears from the explosion. He pressed himself down among the broken bits of stonework. Cautiously he raised his head.

"Idioten!" he screamed. "Hold your fire!" His shout was at once drowned out by the staccato rattle of submachine-gun fire from the barricade.

Willi was mad. What the hell did the *verschissene* bastards think they were doing? He kept down. Snaking his way between chunks of masonry and shattered brickwork he reached the ruined wall of a demolished building. Using all his skill of infiltration and concealment he made his way through the wreckage until he flanked the makeshift barricade. All was quiet. He drew his Walther P-38. Slowly he raised his head and peered out over the barricade position.

Behind the roadblock, at a small opening, a lone soldier was crouched. One lone soldier. Willi was surprised. The man below seemed to be watching tensely, a Mauser rifle aimed down the street toward the burning motorbike.

Quietly Willi stood up.

"You idiot!" he called sharply. "You could have . . ."

The soldier at the barricade whirled toward him. He raised his rifle—and fired.

Willi felt the bullet whizz by his right cheek. He hit the ground. He had a flash view of a white face under a large helmet. His P-38 flew into position in front of him. And he fired. Two rounds. A trained reflex action.

At the barricade the soldier fell. Backwards. As if pushed by an invisible fist.

Warily Willi got up. He ran down to the fallen soldier. He looked at him, the bile rising in his throat, burning it.

A tiny figure in a uniform two sizes too large for him. A boy. His downy, grimy cheeks still wet with the streaks of tears. His dead eyes looking at his killer with a child's surprise. And around his neck an Iron Cross. Second Class.

There was a sound behind him. Footsteps. Hurrying. He whirled on them, automatically falling to one knee, his P-38 locked before him.

There were six or seven of them. All elderly men clad in a mixture of uniforms and civilian clothes. But the red armbands with the black stripe and white letters—*DEUTSCHER VOLKS-STURM WEHRMACHT*—and the two *Hoheitsabzeichen*—the German eagle with the swastika—worn on their sleeves proclaimed who they were. The people's army. The defenders of Berlin. Along with the boys.

Willi rose as they walked up to him. "I am *Obersturmführer* Lüttjohann," he snapped. "Report!"

One of the men stepped forward. "I am Brauner," he said, "Alois Brauner." He stared at the dead boy. "You—you killed him," he said tonelessly. "Little Wolfgang. You—killed him . . ."

"He fired on me," Willi said curtly. He was surprised how harsh his voice sounded. "He blew up my motorcycle with a Panzerfaust. Damn near killed me!"

Brauner did not hear him. He knelt down beside the dead boy. With infinite sadness he closed the questioning eyes. Gently he touched the Iron Cross.

"Only a week ago," he said quietly. "On the Führer's birthday, it was. The Führer himself gave him this. In the garden of the Reichschancellery." He looked up at Willi, accusingly. "For destroying a Russian tank."

"I did not know he was just a boy," Willi said defensively. "He fired at me. I called to him—but he fired at me. I had no choice. His bullets would have killed me just as damned dead as if he'd been your age!"

The men all stared at him. Brauner stood up.

"He was frightened," he said wearily. "Just as he was when that Russian tank suddenly came around the corner and bore down on him. Up near Moabit, it was. The boy froze. He could not run. He just stood there. Watching the tank. Coming closer and closer. I was there. I saw it. Then suddenly he threw away the Panzerfaust he had been holding and ran. The Russian tank kept coming. It ran over the charge—and it exploded. It blew off a track." He looked down at the boy. "Wolfgang got the Iron Cross. Second Class. I—I guess he was trying to live up to it."

Willi was suddenly angry. "And what the hell was he doing here? Alone? On a military roadblock. A child! Where the devil were you?"

Brauner peered nearsightedly at him. "The Russians are still many blocks from here," he said tiredly. "We haven't slept for days." He sighed. "They—they sent us a couple of boys from the Hitler Youth to—to . . ." He let the sentence trail off.

"He was alone," Willi said.

Brauner nodded. "There were two of them," he said, not really caring whether the SS officer believed him or not. "The other one, Helmuth, must have run off. Home, I guess . . ."

He looked at the tiny, still form of Wolfgang Schiller, *Fähnleinsführer* in the Hitler Youth. "Wolfgang," he said. "He stood his ground. This time." He looked at Willi. "And you—killed him . . ."

Willi glared contemptuously at the *Volkssturmer*. "His blood is on *your* hands, old man," he growled. "*You* live with it!"

Angrily he turned on his heel and stalked off. He had to make it on foot to the Reichschancellery. It would take time. Children, he thought bleakly. Children and old men. Frightened children and foolish old men, neither of whom should be concerned with the harsh realities of war.

He disappeared into the blackened ruins.

Behind him, sprawled in death, lay Wolfgang Schiller, Hitler Youth, son of Fritz, who had been killed on the Russian front, and of Hilde, who was waiting for him at home with a wonderful birthday gift. A briefcase. For his studies at the *Hochschule*. Real leather. So very hard to get.

She would never see him again.

From Kaiserdamm Willi cut through the Tiergarten. There would be less chance of running into another barricade, he thought. And the Reichschancellery was located just east of the park.

He quickly regretted his choice. He had not been prepared for the harrowing sights that met him.

The Tiergarten had been mercilessly bombed. The cages and runs were all damaged, the ones holding the dangerous animals shored up with timbers from the ruins and reinforced with wire fencing. Some were burned and gutted hulks—the charred carcasses of the wild inhabitants lying like discarded toys on a smoldering city dump.

The pitiful howls and bellows of the maimed and dying animals pierced his ears and he found himself welcoming the occasional shot that abruptly stilled a piteous scream.

He was startled when a large crane, most of its feathers scorched off, flapped across his path, the remains of one leg flopping awkwardly beneath it.

At the tumbled-down wall of a brick building he passed a man, obviously an attendant, sitting on the ground, staring at a badly mangled, big red kangaroo, a dead baby dangling from its pouch. The tears were streaming down the man's face.

He passed by the Aquarium—totally destroyed. And the reptile house. At the broken fence of the deer run a doe stood motionless, watching his approach, her glistening guts hanging from a gaping wound in her abdomen. Suddenly she took alarm and leaped to get away. Her thrashing hoofs got tangled up in her entrails and she fell heavily to the ground, unable to get up. Looking at him with huge brown eyes filled with pain and dread, she waited.

He shot her.

And he was sick.

If there was a hell for animals, he thought, it would be like this.

Finally he stood before the sandbagged, guarded entrance to the New Reichschancellery. The officer in charge of the guard detail examined the sealed envelope Willi held out to him.

"From *Sonderkampfgruppe* Skorzeny," Willi said. "Urgent. For the Führer's eyes only."

The officer glared at him. He motioned to a non-com. "Take this man to *Reichsleiter* Bormann," he ordered.

Obersturmführer Willibald Lüttjohann had arrived at the Bunker.

Unternehmen Zukunft—Operation Future—was ready to be launched.

3

——◦•◦——

"HEY, MORT! Heard the latest scoop? They got that bastard Himmler!"

CIC agent Woodrow Wilson Ward came barging into the office of Major Mortimer L.—for Lucius—Hall, Commanding Officer of Counter Intelligence Corps Detachment 212 at Iceberg Forward in Schwarzenfeld, where XII Corps Headquarters Forward had moved into a nondescript housing development at the edge of town on April 26, two days before.

"What the hell are you doing back here, Woody?" Hall scowled at the young man. "I thought you were with Jim on the Kratzer case. In Steinach."

"I was," Woody said airily. "We got Kratzer. He's on his way to AIC. Case closed."

Hall eyed the young CIC agent who nonchalantly had draped himself over a chair. Woody was one of his best operatives. Intelligent. Imaginative. Resourceful. And stubborn as hell. But he got results. Many a time Hall had had to pull his service record to add an accomplishment, a recommendation, or a decoration. Purple Heart. Bronze Star. By now he knew that record by heart.

Woody was born in San Francisco on September 17, 1920. A Virgo, with all the supposed traits of that sign. His father, Peter Ward, had met his mother during World War I when he served in the U.S. Expeditionary Force in Europe, and she was a Red Cross volunteer. A Swiss, Lucinda something-or-other. They had married as soon as possible after the war was over and named their boy after Peter's hero, President Woodrow Wilson. After graduating from Berkeley, Woody had studied International Law at the University of Neuchâtel in Switzerland with the idea of joining his father's law firm, Wenton, Ward & Zimmemann, in San Francisco as an expert in that field. Woody was in Switzerland in 1939 when the war broke out, and he returned at once to the States. Since he had traveled extensively in Europe, skied and climbed in the Swiss and Bavarian Alps, and spoke fluent German and some Italian, he had been a natural for the U.S. Military Intelligence Service when he volunteered just after Pearl Harbor, and he'd ended up in the Counter Intelligence Corps. A Staff Sergeant, he had more than once turned down a field commission. "Too damned busy to take time off for that crap," he'd said. Hall thought he knew the real reason: the three-year extra hitch that automatically went with the commission. And Woody— however bang-up a job he was doing—just wanted to get the war over with and go home.

"You came all the way back to Corps to tell me something I can read in tomorrow's *Stars and Stripes*?" Hall asked sourly.

"Not—exactly," Woody admitted disarmingly. "Actually, I want to talk to you about the latest latrine rumor. About the point system for going home."

Hall raised an eyebrow. "How the hell do you know about that?" he asked archly. "The War Department hasn't issued any directives yet."

"Ran into a guy from G-1," Woody explained. "Pumped him a little. He said they got the advance poop."

"Let's hear it."

"It's a four-point system, Mort," Woody said eagerly. "You get credits for length of service, service overseas, combat service—and for having kids." He leaned forward. "Here's how it's supposed to work. You get one point for each month of service plus one point for each month overseas. You get five points for each combat decoration and for each battle star, and you get twelve points for each kid you've got!"

"Got any?" Hall asked drily.

"Who the hell knows," Woody said, shrugging mischievously. "Nothing that'll give me twelve points, that's for sure." He grinned. "But get me home and I guarantee I'll start on it right away!"

"I don't doubt it."

"Anyway, a guy's got to have eighty-five points to be eligible to go home." He glanced sideways at his C.O. "An *enlisted* man, that is. Officers have to have more. Sorry." There was a hint of self-satisfaction in his voice. "They call it the Adjusted Service Rating Score." He looked earnestly at Hall. "Listen, Mort. This waltz is pretty near over. I don't want to get stuck doing lousy occupation duty in Kraut country. I want to go home. I counted up my points. I've got an ASR score of seventy-six. Seventy-six points. Including my five battle stars and that Purple Heart I got at the Bulge. And the Bronze Star for that *Reichsamtsleiter* case in Meiningen." He looked disgusted. "I'm a lousy nine points short."

"T.S.," Hall commented drily.

"Yeah. But it doesn't have to be tough shit, Mort." Woody looked earnestly at his C.O. "All I need is two more months and a cluster to my Bronze Star. And I'm home free."

"And you want me to write you up for one? On what grounds? Being the first to figure out how to beat the point system?"

"Shit, no, Mort." Woody sounded offended. "I'll *earn* the damned points. All I need is a case that'll give me a chance to do it. You know—a 'glamour' case. Some big-shot deal. Something that'll be noticed. You know."

"You usually pick your own damned cases," Hall commented acidly.

"Sure. I know. But I thought you might know of something. Throw it my way." He looked guilelessly at Hall. "How about it? A lousy five points."

Hall leaned back in his chair. He steepled his fingers beneath his chin and contemplated the young man sitting across from him.

A "glamour" case. He didn't know of any. And if he did, would he assign it to Woody Ward? Probably. Nobody would be better qualified. A pain in the ass sometimes. Too damned much of an individualist. The kind of guy who never bowed to authority, just touched his fingers to his cap. Anywhere but in the informal atmosphere of the CIC where everybody was pretty much on his own, he'd have spent the greater part of his army career in the stockade. But as a CIC agent he was top drawer. He shook his head.

"I've got nothing in the files, Woody," he said. "Not a damned thing." He nodded toward an olive drab filing cabinet, the one that rode with him in his personal vehicle every time Iceberg Forward moved to a new location. "You're welcome to take a look."

Woody looked disappointed. "Hell, Mort," he said, "I believe you."

He stood up. "I'd better get back," he said. "See what's cooking at 2nd Cavalry." He started to leave.

The telephone rang.

Hall picked it up. "CIC," he said crisply. "Major Hall." He listened for a moment. He looked startled. He glanced at Woody, who had stopped and stood watching him. He frowned, and tried to speak. "Who is . . ." He was obviously not able to interrupt whoever was talking on the phone. Hastily he scribbled something on his pad. "Listen," he said firmly. "Who is this?" There was a click. Hall looked angrily at the receiver and hung up.

"What the hell was that all about?" Woody asked.

Hall scowled at the phone. "Beats me," he said. "Some joker—German, judging from his accent—got himself patched through." He shook his head. "Damnedest thing I ever heard."

"What?" Woody was intrigued.

"This Kraut says to me"—he looked at his pad—"count your soldiers, Major. And if you are one short you will find him lying at the side of the road to Albersdorf. Dead." Hall looked disgusted. "What kind of melodramatic claptrap is that supposed to be?"

"Albersdorf," Woody said, his interest at once aroused. "I know the burg. Off the road to Vohenstrauss. We've held that real estate for a week."

His mind raced. Who was the dead "soldier"? How was he killed? Why? By whom? And who was the informer? Could it be a Werewolf action? Like those werewolves who murdered the Mayor of Aachen about a month ago because he cooperated with the US forces? Sure sounded like it. They'd advertised themselves enough with that corny radio program of theirs. They certainly were talked about. If he could get a line on them, crack the Werewolf Organization, get enough information to make a real dent, he might just have his "glamour" case. Get his cluster. His five points. Even if it was some other subversive action, it might do it.

"Look, Mort," he said eagerly, "I'll take the case. I'll get over there right now. Take a look. Okay?" He was halfway out the door before Hall could call after him:

"Not alone, dammit! That's an order!"

"Sure," Woody called over his shoulder. "I'll pick up a driver at the pool."

"Find somebody who speaks the lingo!"

And Woody was off.

Hall looked after him. He glanced at the note on his pad. *Count your soldiers, Major.* He shook his head. It might well be a wild goose chase.

Then again, it might not be.

An hour later Woody and a corporal named Tony Fossano turned their jeep off the main road between Schwarzenfeld and

Vohenstrauss and barreled down a forest-lined dirt road toward the village of Albersdorf, visible in the distance. Fossano, a street-wise kid from lower Manhattan spoke a smattering of German, learned in a high school course he'd elected to take in the school's foreign language program to spite his old man who wanted him to learn Italian. His knowledge of the language wasn't enough for him to have been "raided" by the CIC for use as interpreter but enough for him to get along.

As long as things stayed simple.

Suddenly Woody sang out. "Hold it! Stop!"

Fossano stomped on the brake and the jeep skidded to a halt.

"Back up," Woody said. Fossano did. Woody pointed. "Bingo!" he said.

In the middle of a small clearing a few yards off the obviously seldom-traveled road a neat white wooden cross had been pounded into the ground. And next to it lay a large bundle wrapped in a solid brown tarpaulin.

The two men got out. They walked up to the bundle. Woody was puzzled. Who the hell had put up the cross? The whimsical informer on the phone? "Give me a hand," he said grimly. "Let's see what we've got."

Fossano looked dubiously at the tarpaulin-wrapped bundle. They were supposed to be looking for some dead guy, weren't they? Uneasily he shifted his feet. He glanced at Woody. He tried in vain to find the agent's insignia of rank on his uniform. There was none. Only two officer's US emblems on his collar tabs. Nothing else.

"Say—eh . . ." He paused. "What *is* your rank?"

Woody looked at him. "I'll give you the official spiel, corporal," he said evenly. "The SOP answer given by *any* CIC agent to anyone who wants to know—from corporal to colonel!"

He glared at the soldier. "It goes like this: My rank is confidential, but at this moment I am not outranked." He jutted his face close to the corporal. "And that sure as hell goes for right now," he snapped. "So hop to it!"

"Yes—eh, Sir," Fossano stammered.

Together they unwrapped the bundle.

The sight that met them turned their stomachs.

The soldier had been dead two or three days, Woody thought. He was an American, dressed in field uniform except for his boots, which for some unknown reason had been removed. The cause of death was easily established. A deep cut on the left side of the man's neck had severed the jugular vein. His uniform was blackish-red with dried blood. A rope was tied around his left arm.

But it was the man's face that held the eyes of the two men riveted in horror and revulsion.

It wasn't there!

Someone had carefully and methodically obliterated it. Beaten it to a sickening, unrecognizable mass. There were absolutely no features left, nothing which by the wildest stretch of imagination could be called a face. The nose was flattened. All the teeth knocked out. The eyes two sunken pits of crusted gore.

For a moment the two men stood staring at the gruesome sight, fighting to control the sour bile that rose in their throats. Finally Fossano turned away, his face ashen.

"The bastards," he muttered, shaken.

"Let's—let's find out who he is," Woody said, his voice sounding tight in his throat.

Systematically, struggling to overcome their queasiness, they searched the mangled body. When they had finished Woody knew with grim realization why the victim had no face. Someone had desperately wanted to conceal the identity of the mutilated corpse: it had been stripped of all identification—dog-tags, wallet, papers; the uniform pockets were all empty; and the soldier's unit shoulder patch had been ripped from his shirt-sleeve. That was also why the boots were missing, Woody realized. The soldier's serial number must have been stamped or inked into the leather.

Woody stood up. He rubbed his hands along the sides of his pants, rubbed and rubbed—unaware of doing it. Something was nagging at him. Something didn't fit . . .

He looked around. The little clearing was littered with trash. Straws from bottle sleeves, US Army ration wrappings, a few rags which appeared to have been torn from a woman's dress, a broken wine bottle, two pieces of blue chalk, a torn page from a newspaper. Woody picked it up. It was from an Ohio tabloid dated March 15, 1945.

He turned to Fossano. "Pick up everything you can find," he told him. "Pile it up over there. We'll make a list of it."

"What for?" Fossano demurred.

"Just do it!" Woody snapped. He didn't explain. Perhaps it *was* a little farfetched to expect the refuse to contain some kind of clue. But—shit! He had to try. He turned back to the body. Carefully he covered it with the brown tarpaulin. Then he went to help Fossano gather up the junk that littered the clearing.

The feeling that he was missing something wouldn't leave him. Something *was* out of kilter. He was certain of it. He had long since come to trust his hunches.

Suddenly he knew what it was that was bothering him.

Why would some vengeful German bastard want to hide the identity of his victim? There was no obvious reason. Was there a hidden one? It didn't make sense. But he didn't know what to make of it.

When they had picked the place clean Woody inspected the pile of trash. Not a thing in it gave him any ideas. It was just a heap of rubbish.

"Put it in the back of the jeep," he ordered Fossano. He looked toward the village only a couple of hundred yards down the road. "Let's go see what they know in that burg," he said.

The closest farmhouse had a direct view of the area with the clearing, and Woody decided to start his investigation there. If anyone in Albersdorf had seen anything, the people there might be the ones.

Woody got into the jeep. He turned to Fossano. "Listen, corporal," he said. "A couple of words to the wise. Keep your eyes peeled. Always be ready for anything—but don't look apprehensive. The Krauts will accept that you're in charge if you *act* that way. Remember that. If you see anything suspicious, or find anything, let me know. Don't try to handle it yourself. Is that clear?"

Fossano shrugged. "Sure," he said. "I'm just along for the ride. It's your damn show."

The village of Albersdorf consisted of perhaps two dozen farmhouses. Woody and Fossano drove into the yard of the farm they had picked out. A huge, burly man with a weather-beaten face, close-cropped graying hair and fists the size of small hams was cutting and stacking wood near a small shed. He stopped his work and looked up with a hostile glare.

Fossano stayed in the jeep as Woody jumped out and strode up to the farmer.

"Is this your farm?" he asked crisply.

The big man nodded.

"What is your name?"

"Huber," the man answered sullenly. "Werner Huber."

Woody watched him closely. "There is the body of an American soldier lying in the woods only a short distance from here," he said. "Do you know about it?"

"Yes," the German answered, an almost imperceptible note of mockery in his voice. "And so does everyone else in Albersdorf!"

"Then why did you not inform the American authorities?" Woody asked angrily. "There has been a Military Police office in Vohenstrauss for days."

The farmer shrugged. "We thought it was none of our busi-

ness," he said. "We are farmers in Albersdorf. Not soldiers."
Somehow the man gave the impression of enjoying himself.

Woody felt a deep anger build in him. He controlled it.

"How long has the body been there?"

Again the farmer shrugged. "Two—three days," he answered.
He put a beefy, dirty fist to his nose and rubbed it. "Yes—three
days it was."

"Three days!" Woody exclaimed. "And nobody reported it!"

The German looked at him, the hint of a smirk on his face.
"We thought surely the Americans knew," he said.

Woody wanted to hit the bastard in the face. Instead he asked:
"Who else lives here?"

The farmer scratched his head. "There's old Anton," he replied. "And my daughter." Sudden hate flared in the quick glance
he shot at Woody. "My wife was killed," he rasped. "In Regensburg. She had gone to buy some clothing for us. It was an air
raid."

"Where are they?" Woody asked coldly.

"Anton is in the stable. It is the day we clean for the cows,"
the farmer said. "My daughter is in the house. It will soon be
time to eat." He looked at Woody, a mocking smile on his lips.
"You should talk to her, *Herr Offizier*," he drawled. "She saw
what happened."

At once Woody turned to Fossano. "Corporal!" he called.
"There's an old man working in the stable. Get him. Bring him
to the house." He turned to the farmer. "Move!" he said.

The *Bauernstube* of the farmhouse—the combined kitchen-liv-
ing-dining room which is the hub of all Bavarian farmhouses—
was simple and pleasant. Blue-and-white checkered curtains at the
windows, a large wooden table with chairs and benches around
it, and the inevitable big black, wood-burning stove.

The farmer, Huber, his daughter, and the old farmhand sat stiffly
on a bench against the wall, warily watching Woody and Fossano.

Woody glared at them. He turned to Fossano. "Take a look
around," he said. "Anything out of the ordinary, let me know.
And, be careful."

"Okay." Fossano ambled off. Woody fixed the farmer's daughter
with a cold stare. The girl, a pleasingly plump blonde in her early
twenties, watched him fearfully.

"Okay," he said crisply, "start talking. What did you see?"

The girl looked at him with wide, frightened eyes. Instinctively
she moved closer to her father.

[32]

"From the beginning," Woody said. He softened his voice. No need to scare the girl into silence. "Just tell me the whole story." He pulled over a chair and sat down, his eyes on her level, no longer looming over her. Little by little she relaxed.

"It—it was three days ago," she began timidly. "Early in the morning. I—I saw them from my window. I saw them throw the bundle next to the road."

"Who? Did you get a good look at them?"

The girl nodded.

"Do you know who they were?"

Again the girl nodded. She looked frightened.

"Who?"

"They were—they were American soldiers," she whispered.

Involuntarily Woody started. "American!" he exclaimed. "How do you know?"

"They—they were in uniform."

Woody's mind raced. American uniforms. Were enemy saboteurs operating in American uniforms? Like those Jeep Parties during the Bulge? Werewolves? Or, *had* the men actually been Americans? Bleakly he knew that could well be the case. He realized that was what had been bothering him. The whole thing hadn't been consistent with a German strike. Grimly he looked at the girl. "How did they get the body—the bundle there?" he asked.

"They came by truck. Not many trucks come to Albersdorf," she said. "So—I watched."

"Describe the truck."

The girl did. Woody's face grew sober. It had been a US Army ¾-ton. The description was unmistakable.

"What did they do?" he asked.

"The two soldiers opened the canvas in the back of the truck and took out the bundle. They put it in the clearing. They—and the two girls."

"Girls?" Woody frowned. "What girls?"

"There were two girls riding in the truck. With the soldiers."

Four of them, Woody thought. Two men—Americans or Germans—and two girls. How the hell were the girls involved? He had no immediate answer. He filed the puzzle in his mind.

"There is a number painted in white along the hood of the truck," he said. "Did you see it?"

The girl nodded. "Yes."

"Do you remember it?"

She shook her head. "Only the white star," she said.

[33]

"Did you see anything else?"

"No." She stopped. "Only . . ."

"Only what?"

"Only some boxes. Stacked in the back of the truck. I saw them when they took the—the bundle out of there."

"What kind of boxes?"

The girl described them to him. He felt bleak. From her description the boxes could well have been US Class I supplies. Ration cartons. Dammit! It looked more and more as if this were not a CIC case at all but a case for the CID, the Criminal Investigation Detachment. Not his ball park at all.

Fossano sauntered back into the room. Woody turned to him.

"Nothin'," the corporal shrugged. "I didn't see nothin'."

"Go out to the jeep," Woody told him. "Raise somebody— anybody in Vohenstrauss—on the radio. Have them send an ambulance. We'll meet them at the clearing."

"Sure. Why not?" Fossano left. Woody looked at the girl sitting quietly, apprehensively watching him. He'd asked her the jackpot question and come out with one big fat lemon. Some "glamor" case. Shit, he could kiss that five points good-by for sure. He had a good idea what had happened. Three horny guys and two willing *Fräuleins*. A fight—that turned out a little too violent—and a frantic attempt to conceal it by destroying the identity of the victim and putting the blame on the Krauts. If that wasn't the exact scenario, it would do till a better one came along. But it sure as hell wouldn't earn him his cluster, even if he did solve the damned case. He might as well chuck it and look for greener pastures.

He contemplated the girl sitting tensely before him. He felt uneasy about her. That crazy hunch that every CIC agent developed. That feeling at the edge of the mind that something was being missed. What else did she know? He swore to himself. Hell, he couldn't just drop the case. He was involved. He was there. And, dammit, he'd asked for it. He might as well follow through. It *was* his job. Of course, he could turn the case over to the CID. Ultimately he'd probably have to. Should he do it now? Bail out? Or, once started, follow through? What the hell, he'd take it a little further. Reluctantly, somewhat cynically, he admitted to himself that he was hooked. What the hell *had* happened? What *was* the bottom line? He looked at the girl.

"What happened after the men . . . ?" He couldn't get himself to say Americans. Not yet. ". . . after the men put the body in the clearing?" he asked.

[34]

"They drove away."

"With the girls?"

"No. The girls walked. Back the way they had all come."

Figured, Woody thought. Trouble—drop the broads.

"How did you know the bundle contained a body," he asked.

"I—we did not know," the girl said. She glanced at the farmer. "My father went to take a look. He told us."

Woody nodded. Fossano came back into the *Bauernstube*. "They're sending a wagon," he announced. "Be there in about twenty minutes."

Woody nodded. "What do you know about all the trash in the clearing?" he asked the girl.

It was her father who answered. "The *Amis*"—he used the derogatory German expression for Americans—"the *Amis* threw it there. When they first came to Albersdorf. More than a week ago."

So much for the Sherlock Holmes clues, Woody thought wryly. He glanced at Fossano and caught the smug look on the corporal's face. Screw him! It had still been the right thing to do.

"And the cross?" he asked. "The white cross. Who put that up?"

The Germans shook their heads. Woody watched the girl. She looked apprehensive. Guilty. Was she hiding something? What?

He looked at his watch. The ambulance would be at the clearing any minute. He turned to the Germans. "You stay here," he ordered. "I'm not through with you yet. You wait right here. Understood?"

The farmer glared at him. "We have chores to do," he grumbled sullenly. "A farm does not run without work."

"Do your chores," Woody snapped. "But don't leave the farm."

He motioned to Fossano. Together they left the *Bauernstube*.

The ambulance had left, taking with it the grisly bundle. Woody stood looking at the now strangely empty clearing. Knocked askew, the white wooden cross still stood in the trampled grass. Woody was bothered by it. Who had put it there? Why? He had a hunch that if he could find out, a big piece of the puzzle would drop into place. He had examined the road shoulder. He didn't really know what he was looking for. Tire marks? Boot prints? Anything. He had found nothing.

He looked around at the surrounding woods. The undergrowth was quite dense except in a spot just opposite the road. Here a forest meadow about fifty feet away could be seen through the trees. A narrow path winding through the underbrush led from it to the clearing. Woody walked down toward the meadow. As he neared the open field he noticed animal tracks in the dirt. Hoofs. And little hard, brown pellets scattered about. Goats.

Fossano was rooting about in the trees close to the clearing. Suddenly he shouted to Woody. "Hey! Look at this." He pointed toward the ground. "Pretty weird."

Woody hurried back. A trail running parallel with the road crossed the path to the meadow. A few feet down the trail Fossano was squatting, looking at something on the ground. Woody looked down.

There, scratched in the dirt, was a bizarre, strangely disturbing design. It could be the head of a goat, grotesquely, repulsively distorted, or it could be the evil face of a devil with fangs and horns and tufted ears.

Woody crouched down beside Fossano. He looked toward the clearing. Although he, himself, was hidden by the brush he could see the little white cross clearly. He grinned at Fossano. "Bull's-eye!" he said. "Give that man a cigar!"

"Yeah?" Fossano sounded suspicious. "What for?"

Woody pointed to the macabre design traced in the dirt. "That," he said. "Mean anything to you?"

Fossano shrugged. "Nah," he said. "Just some kooky scribble." He squinted at the repugnant image. "Means nothin' to me."

"Means nothing to me either," Woody said. "But that's not the point. Who drew it, and more important *when,* that's the point."

"Okay. So—when?"

"The body has been lying in the clearing for three days," Woody said. "We know that. Since Wednesday. Early morning, Wednesday. It rained Tuesday, well into the night, so this whatever-it-is must have been drawn since that time or it would have been washed away." He looked at Fossano. "Whoever drew it must have seen the body." He looked down at the ugly devils' face scratched in the dirt. "I wonder what he was watching while he sat here drawing this thing," he mused.

"Yeah. If anything."

"If anything," Woody repeated thoughtfully.

Fossano looked at Woody with grudging respect. He'd never had much use for the CIC boys—the Christ-I'm-Confused boys—living the life of Riley. But this guy could use his noodle. "Maybe he's the joker who put up the cross," he volunteered, surprised at himself.

"Could be," Woody agreed. "I think we'll have another little talk with friend Huber and his daughter."

Once again the farmer, the girl, and the old farmhand were assembled in the *Bauernstube*. Woody had automatically looked the place over. All was as before. The three Germans had apparently not as yet had their meal, but a loaf of bread and two large sausages had been placed on an old newspaper on a small table.

"Once again," Woody scowled at them. "Once again I ask you: Do you know who put up the cross in the clearing?"

The girl glanced apprehensively at her father, but no one answered.

"Who tends the goats around here?" Woody suddenly asked.

Involuntarily the girl drew in her breath. Her father gave her a quick, angry glance. He sat stony-faced on the bench. Woody fixed his eyes on the girl.

"Well?" he asked.

Suddenly the old farmhand, the man Huber had called Anton, spoke up. "That would be Szarvas," he said.

Huber shot him a murderous glance. Woody was startled at the icy depth he saw in the man's eyes. The farmer turned to him.

"Szarvas is a Hungarian," he said contemptuously. "He does not speak German well."

"What is his full name?" Woody asked. "Is Szarvas his given name or his family name?"

"It is not his name," Huber said stonily. "It is the name we call him. It is the name of his hometown. Where he was born. He is always talking about it. We do not know his name."

"Where is this Szarvas now?" Woody asked.

Huber did not answer.

"With the goats," Anton said. "In the field."

"Do you know where?"

Anton nodded. "Today it is the Ziegler field," he said. "Not far from here."

Woody turned to Fossano. "Go with the old man," he said. "Bring this guy, Szarvas, back here."

"Yes, Sir," Fossano said.

"I will not have Szarvas in my house," Huber said heatedly. "He is a Hungarian. He was in a KZ Lager—a concentration camp."

Woody looked at the man, his eyes cold. "Too bad, Huber," he said. "*I* want him here. And he *will* be here!" He nodded to Fossano. "Get going."

"Come on, old man," the corporal said to Anton. "Let's go find the damned goats."

They left. Huber glanced after them. "Szarvas," he spat. "He is *damisch*—an imbecile!"

The girl turned to her father, her eyes suddenly ablaze. "No, Father, he is not!" she said with unexpected fervor. "Once he was a great artist. In Budapest." She turned to Woody. "Things went bad for him," she said. "He was sent to a—a camp. It made him—old. And it is—difficult for him to—to express himself. But he has not forgotten. He is not an imbecile. He still draws. Often. And sometimes beautifully." She turned to her father. "You must not say Szarvas is an imbecile. He is a kind man."

Woody stared at her. A goatherd. An artist making drawings. Often. Here was the creator of the devil in the dirt.

But why the obvious reluctance to reveal his existence?

Twenty minutes later Fossano came back with Anton and the enigmatic goatherd.

Szarvas was a middle-aged man, small of stature with graying hair, who looked years older than his age. His long, slender fingers toyed with a cigarette Woody had given him to win his confidence. He had taken it, but he did not light it. His German was halting and limited to words strung together without structure. But gradually Woody got his story.

Szarvas had indeed put up the cross for the dead American comrade. He had been dozing in the woods early in the morning, when he saw the American soldiers unload the bundle. After they left, curiosity had gotten the better of him and he had looked to see what was in the bundle. He had been sad—and he had made the cross.

Woody made him repeat his story. Over and over. In an attempt to catch the man in a contradiction. He made none. He was telling the truth. In dismay Woody pieced the whole story together. From what the girl had told him and from what Szarvas had seen . . .

Wednesday morning, April 26, at about 0645 hours an American ¾-ton truck, covered, had driven up to the clearing on the road to Albersdorf. Two soldiers in field jackets and without leggings, and two civilian girls had disembarked. All of them helped unload a large, tarpaulin-covered bundle from the rear of the truck. In the truck had been eight to ten large cardboard boxes fitting the description of ten-in-one US rations. As soon as they had dumped their burden the soldiers had driven off in the direction of the Schwarzenfeld-Vohenstrauss highway, and shortly thereafter the girls had walked away in the same direction. According to Szarvas's description one of the soldiers had been a corporal. The other had no stripes.

Szarvas was perhaps not very bright, but like a true artist his power of observation was keen.

Gloomily Woody examined the case in his mind. It fit. There was no doubt about it. It was a case for the CID, not for him. Dammit to hell!

Oh well. Back to the lousy files.

He looked at the goatherd. Too bad. Here was an eyewitness, and a good one, who unerringly could pick out the murderers from any lineup. Hitch was—they had no lineup. They couldn't very well parade the whole damn army before him.

Suddenly he sat bolt upright. Of course! They *did* have a lineup. An unusual one, but a lineup nevertheless.

Quickly he turned to the girl. "I need some paper," he said urgently. "And a pencil. Can you get it for me?"

She nodded, puzzled. She hurried off. Presently she returned with paper and pencil.

For the next several minutes Woody was busy imitating Szarvas, the artist. When he was finished he had a series of twelve US Army shoulder patches—from the big *A* of Third Army and the windmill of XII Corps to the Second Cavalry Group—plus a couple of imaginary patches thrown in for good measure.

He looked at the Hungarian.

"Did the American soldiers wear patches?" he asked. He touched his left shoulder. "Here," he said. "Shoulder patches?"

Szarvas looked puzzled. He touched his own shoulder, uncomprehendingly. Suddenly he grinned. "Yes," he said. "Yes, yes, yes! Picture. Beautiful picture. Pretty colors." His eyes sparkled.

Woody showed him the patches he'd drawn. "Pick it out," he said tensely. "Which one?"

Szarvas's eyes searched the line of amateurishly drawn insignia. Suddenly he jabbed a slender finger at one of them. "There!" he cried. He put his hand on his left shoulder. "I see," he said.

It was the patch of a small unit stationed in the Corps area!

Woody was elated.

With the leads he could now give CID the case was solved. All they had to do was locate a corporal and a private in a certain known unit stationed near Vohenstrauss, who in the morning of 25 April, 1945, driving a ¾-ton truck, had been drawing rations for a small number of men. It would be a mere matter of looking it up in the Orderly Room Detail Report of the outfit!

Tooling along down the road from Albersdorf Woody felt good. He was driving himself. He was too keyed up not to be doing something. So, it hadn't been the kind of case he'd hoped for. He had solved it. Without ever learning the name of the victim. Or his killers. Hot damn! In the back of the jeep sat Szarvas, eagerly

[39]

testing the wind as they sped down the road. Woody had decided to take him back to Corps. The little guy deserved better than a bunch of mangy goats—and Krauts. Perhaps repatriation to his hometown, when the time came. Reunion with his family. He'd do his damndest.

Fossano, sitting next to him, gave him a sidelong glance. "That patch trick was pretty damned smart," he said. He yawned. "Huber sure was an ornery bastard. I wonder what the other guy would've been like."

"Anton?"

"No. The other guy in the house."

Woody stopped the jeep. He stared at Fossano.

"What other guy?" he asked sharply. "You didn't tell me you saw someone else in the house!"

"I didn't. I just figured there'd be someone else. Out in the field, maybe. How the hell should I know?" He sounded suddenly defensive. Had he screwed up? He hadn't thought it important. Shit!

"Why do you think there was another man in the house?" Woody asked, his voice measured.

"Well, I was poking around in Huber's bedroom. You told me to take a look. There was a big wardrobe, kind of. It was full of clothes. Huber's mostly. But some of them were a lot smaller and more dress-up like, I guess. I thought they'd have to belong to some other guy. But didn't *see* nobody!"

At once Woody turned the jeep around. He barreled back toward the Albersdorf farm.

"Why the hell didn't you tell me?" he snapped. "You heard that shithead, Huber, tell me only he, his daughter, and the old farmhand lived at the farm."

"The hell I did," Fossano said defensively. "He must've told *you* that. He didn't tell *me* nothin'."

Woody clammed up. He suddenly realized the corporal was right. He had still been sitting in the damned jeep when Huber made his statement.

"I didn't think it was important," Fossano said sullenly. "Anyways, I thought you got everything you wanted."

Woody kept quiet. He cursed himself. It was his own damned fault. He'd been stupid. He should have remembered he wasn't working with a trained investigator but with a driver from the motor pool. It wasn't Fossano's fault. It was his. All of a sudden it all came together. Huber's reticence. The girl's apprehension. His own nagging feeling. Shit! He hoped he wasn't too late.

He stopped the jeep outside the farmyard. Gun in hand, followed by Fossano, he quickly ran to the door.

For a second he listened. Then he kicked it down. There were four people in the *Bauernstube*. Huber, his daughter, Anton—and a slightly built man in his forties, standing in the process of putting a sausage wrapped in newspaper into a rucksack.

Startled, they stared at the Americans.

"Up against the wall!" Woody ordered sharply. "Hands on top of your heads. All of you. *Move!*"

They scrambled to obey.

Huber looked furious. He turned angrily to Anton and his daughter. "I told you not to bring that imbecile into it," he snarled. "He told them."

"Szarvas told us nothing," Woody said. "*You* did. With your gorilla bulk and your ham-sized fists. And a bunch of clothes in your closet four sizes too small!"

Huber glared malevolently at him. He said nothing. Woody looked at the stranger.

"You might as well tell me who you are," he said.

The man drew himself up. "I am *Sturmbannführer* Franz Gotthelf," he said. Though he was obviously frightened, his voice was firm. "I am not a military man. I am a dentist."

"What are you doing here, Major? House call?"

The quip went over the German's head. "I—I left Berlin," he said. "The Russians are closing in. I thought—I thought I could hide out in a small village. Until it is all over. I knew my—my rank in the SS would make it difficult for me, if I were captured." He nodded toward the glowering Huber. "This man put me up. I needed a place of refuge. He needed the money I paid him."

"I bet," Woody said. He looked at the SS officer. "Major," he said, "have you ever had a ride in a jeep before? If not, this is your chance." He motioned with his gun. "We are taking you back to Corps."

"You've been busy," Major Hall said. He looked at Woody, draped over a chair before him. "Would you like another case— or is one a day enough for you?"

"Hell, Mort," Woody said. "It all came together. The damned case solved itself."

Hall picked up the Corps directory. "I'll get the CID boys on it right away," he said. He started to look for the number.

"Courtesy of CIC." Woody grinned.

"What about that dentist pal of yours?" Hall asked.

"I've got him stashed in the local jail. The MPs have taken it over. He'll go back to Army detention tomorrow."

"Did you question him?"

"What for? He's just a dentist. The only reason I pulled him in is because his SS rank is high enough to qualify for mandatory arrest."

"Get a statement."

"Oh, shit, Mort! A lousy dentist. They can do that at AIC."

"I don't care if he is an undertaker. We hooked him and I want an interrogation report."

"Okay, okay. Don't get your guts in an uproar."

"Get what you can. The research section likes that sort of crap," Hall said. He grinned. "Anyway, I thought you were all fired to hell to get this case! Go see what you can extract from your dentist friend."

"Oh brother," Woody groaned. He uncurled himself from the chair and, sighing deeply, left the office.

SS Sturmbannführer Franz Gotthelf had obviously resigned himself to his fate and had decided to be cooperative. It was easy for him. He had nothing to hide. He had answered every question Woody had put to him. Fully and candidly. He had told his interrogator his entire life story and career as a dentist, from dental school to when he began to work for the Führer's personal dentist. A great honor, of course.

Woody was vaguely interested. Perhaps the man could come up with something of interest after all. Somebody was sure to be excited about Hitler's teeth.

"Did you work on the teeth of Adolf Hitler yourself?" he asked.

"No, no," Gotthelf protested quickly. "Only *SS Brigadeführer* Blaschke did that. He was the Führer's personal dentist. The General did all the work on the Führer's teeth himself. I—I was not involved in that at all."

"What did you do?" Woody asked.

"I assisted. On the dental work done for many of the high-ranking party members. And the military. The Goebbels family. Dr. Goebbels. He had some problems with his maxillary left molars. And I sometimes worked on the children's teeth. *Feldmarschall* Keitel, of course. And *Reichsleiter* Bormann. I worked on a gold crown for his right bicuspid in the lower jaw. Very successful. And Eva Braun. We made . . ."

"Who's Eva Braun?" Woody asked.

Gotthelf looked embarrassed. "*Fräulein* Braun is—eh—the Führer's special friend," he said lamely.

"His mistress, you mean?" Woody was intrigued.

Gotthelf nodded.

"Well, well," Woody chuckled. "Will wonders never cease? Nice-looking chick?"

Gotthelf blushed. "I do not know—chick," he said stiffly. "We worked on a bridge for *Fräulein* Braun," he continued. "I was to have fitted it myself. But it was finished too late. The fitting never took place. The bridge still lies in the laboratory in Berlin. And there was work for the secretaries who worked for the Führer. *Fräulein* Junge and *Frau* Christian. And I made a crown for . . ."

"Did you assist on any work made for Hitler, himself?" Woody interrupted. Would the man never stop talking? He wasn't remotely interested in Goebbels' kids or Hitler's girl friend. But maybe Adolf himself.

"No." Gotthelf shook his head. "*Brigadeführer* Blaschke had his personal technicians. Fritz Echtmann and Käthe Heusermann. They did all of the Führer's work. But there were many others . . ."

And on it went, until Gotthelf had run out of both steam and information.

Woody typed up a brief interrogation report. A damn waste of time. Whatever tiny hope he'd still nurtured that the interrogation of *Sturmbannführer* Franz Gotthelf would yield *something* of importance was snuffed out.

The coveted extra five points looked farther away than ever.

He brought the report to Major Hall.

The C.O. looked up brightly, as Woody entered the office. "Hey," he said. "The CID just called. They got the two men. And they confessed. It was pretty much as you'd figured it. That rope around his arm, incidentally, was meant to make it look as if the poor bastard had been tied up. Kept prisoner. Cute touch."

He leaned back in his chair, steepling his fingers under his chin. "The CID boys said thanks for a job well done."

"Charge," Woody said sourly. "That's a great help."

Hall looked at the report. "Well," he said, "did you learn anything earth-shaking from your friendly neighborhood dentist?"

Woody shook his head.

"No," he said. "Nothing. Not a damned thing."

[43]

4

---◆◆◆---

A SOUR SMELL OF DEFEAT AND RESIGNATION permeated the Bunker, now that it had become common knowledge that the Führer had decided to take his own life. It struck Heinz Lorenz, Reich Press Representative to the Führer, forcefully as he came hurrying down the stairs to the lower level of the Führer Bunker. It was the foul, debilitating breath of *Götterdämmerung*. The end was truly near. An ignominious and terrifying end. True, he thought, Hitler's grim decision to end his life in the Bunker had not been unexpected. For days he had been talking about it and making preparations. But hearing it finally voiced as an irrevocable resolution had still been a shock to him.

He walked rapidly through the far corridor past the machine room and the guard room. He always felt uncomfortable in the Bunker. This time more than ever. The Bunker moles had become so jaded to the grotesque that they did not see the morbid incongruity in the fact that the Führer in almost the same breath he announced his decision to commit suicide had also announced his intention to marry his mistress, Eva Braun. Lorenz could not help being appalled. The wedding ceremony would be that night.

Fräuleine Gertrud Junge, Trudl, one of the Führer's personal secretaries, had taken great delight in telling everybody who would listen that she had actually been present when the Führer had proposed to *Fräulein* Braun. She had actually *seen* the historic moment! The Führer had walked up to his beloved and whispered in her ear. She had drawn back in astonishment and she, Trudl, had heard a distinct little gasp. The Führer had then hurried from the room and *Fräulein* Braun had come over to her. Her eyes had been moist with unshed tears, and she had whispered: "*Meine liebe Trudl,* tonight we are certainly going to weep!"

Her first reaction had been one of grief, she'd stated dramatically, for she had thought *Fräulein* Braun was referring to the Führer's death. But she had quickly learned that she meant tears of joy.

Lorenz hurried through the door to the conference corridor and walked toward the Führer's quarters. Despite all the gallows-courage preparations for the wedding he felt an air of resigned despair that seeped into every corner of the Bunker. Even the gloomy, depressing corridor that connected the Propaganda Ministry with the underground concrete warren that was the Führer Bunker seemed cheerful to him in comparison, the yellowish, domed lights that studded the ceiling at regular intervals almost festive.

It was shortly after 1900 hours, and Lorenz bore ill-starred tidings.

A few minutes before, sitting at his radio transmitter-receiver in his little cubbyhole of an office off the Propaganda Ministry tunnel he had intercepted a German language broadcast from Radio Stockholm. Quoting a BBC Reuters report. It had shocked him deeply.

Behind the Führer's back *SS Reichsleiter* Heinrich Himmler had offered the Allies an unconditional surrender!

Lorenz was disturbed. He knew the Führer was apt to deal harshly with harbingers of unwelcome news. The bulletin he clutched in his hand might well hold disastrous consequences for himself. But withholding it might be even worse.

At the door to the Führer's quarters Hitler's valet, Heinz Linge, stopped him.

"The Führer is not to be disturbed," he said.

Lorenz drew a sigh of relief. He handed the bulletin to Linge. "Urgent," he said. "Please give it to the Führer as soon as possible." And before there could be any discussion he turned and quickly walked away.

White-faced, livid with rage, Hitler stormed into the little hospital room. For a brief, heart-stopping moment, shaking in uncontrollable fury, he stood staring at the startled Ritter von Greim and at Hanna Reitsch sitting at his bedside.

Brandishing the Reuters bulletin over his head he screamed at them, his voice hoarse with hatred, his face distorted in such frenzy that it was barely recognizable, the blue veins standing out in his neck, bloated with rage.

"Himmler is a traitor!" he shrieked. "*Der treue Heinrich hat mich verraten!* Behind my back the despicable double-crosser has offered to deliver the Reich—the German people—*me!*—into the hands of the enemy!"

His venomous paroxysm of fury threatened to choke him. He shook the bulletin at Hanna and Greim who sat watching him, aghast.

"Must all great men suffer a damnable betrayer?" he screamed. "Caesar his Brutus. I—*Himmler!*"

In berserk agitation he began to pace the little room, ranting his rage at the traitorous Himmler.

Profoundly shaken, Hanna watched her beloved Führer gripped in the throes of his violent agony. Her heart went out to him. Was he to be spared nothing? Even now? She knew he had always valued and believed in the loyalty and devotion of Heinrich Himmler, his trusted, ever faithful supporter and ally. Who now, in the eleventh hour, had stabbed him in the back. She knew how deeply the wound must hurt. It was the most cruel blow of all. She knew. But she knew not what to say.

"Goering was always a contemptible opportunist. Corrupt," Hitler mouthed venomously. "But Heinrich! Worse! Pretending to be loyal!" He suddenly whirled on Ritter von Greim. He shook a trembling fist at him. "A traitor must *never* be my successor as Führer of the German people," he shouted. "You! Greim! Arrest him! See to it that he doesn't succeed in his treachery!"

With burning, bloodshot eyes he stared at Greim, his look going through the man and beyond.

"The Russians are about to assail the Reich Chancellery," he rasped. "You must leave the Bunker as quickly as you can."

Abruptly he turned and stalked toward the door.

"Report to me as soon as you are ready," he ordered.

And he was gone.

Time had run out. There were other pressing matters that had to be attended to.

Now!

Feldmarschall Ritter von Greim looked down at his bandaged foot. The wound was far from healed. He swung his leg out over the bed. Painfully he stood up, supported by Hanna Reitsch.

The Führer had given him an order to be carried out.

It would be done.

The coldly penetrating, unblinking eyes of Frederick the Great watched the two men sitting in Hitler's study.

There *is* a resemblance, Bormann thought. It is in the eyes. You cannot escape them. He wondered what it was the Führer had wanted to talk to him about so urgently. *Im strengsten Vertrauen*—in the strictest confidence. Somehow he felt vaguely uneasy. The Führer had summoned him personally, seeking him out in the Bunker. There was an air about the man he had never seen before. The Führer seemed uncharacteristically stoic, as if he were looking at the world with the eyes of a man already dead. That was it, he thought. It was undoubtedly the fact that death by his own hand was imminent. He dismissed his uneasiness.

Hitler fixed his deputy with a steady gaze. "It is time," he said quietly. "It is time I told you, Bormann, that *I know*."

Bormann stiffened, his instinct for self-preservation instantly alert. "Know what, *mein* Führer?" he asked guardedly.

Hitler sighed.

"Argentina."

Bormann sat bolt upright. The shock exploded through him. Hitler's eyes never left him. "Your plan to escape the Bunker and the Russians," he said. "Your secret plan, Bormann, your preparations. Made long ago."

Bormann's mind raced. Adrenalin pumped its reinforcement to every nerve end in his body. How had Hitler found out? *Um Gottes Willen!*—how? Who had talked? It was impossible. No one could. He had seen to that. He suddenly felt a cold shudder twitch through him. Fegelein! *SS Gruppenführer* Hermann Fegelein. Married to Eva Braun's sister, Gretl. Himmler's special liaison officer to the Führer himself. Only hours before, his execution, ordered by Hitler, had been carried out. Fegelein had left the Bunker clandestinely. Hoping to escape. He, too, had had an escape plan. But the Gestapo had caught up with him. And he had been shot. He, Bormann, had been present when the bullets from the firing squad cut the poor devil in half. Was this what Hitler had in mind for him?

He was suddenly acutely aware of his Walther 7.65 in its holster on his belt. His beautifully ornamented *Ehrenwaffe*—Honor Weapon—presented to him by the Führer himself. Could he kill him? And claim the Führer had shot himself? Everyone knew he intended to take his own life. He quickly rejected the idea, however tempting. There was no way he could get away with it in the power struggle that would follow. Wait. He would wait. Wait to see what would develop. Use the Führer's own axiom: As long as one lies in wait like a cat and takes advantage of every moment to deal a sudden blow or make a sudden parry, one is not lost. Possibilities will always arise. He threw up his hands.

"*Mein* Führer," he protested. "I do not . . ."

Hitler impatiently waved him to silence.

"Stop it, Bormann," he said. "There is no time for empty denials." He placed both his hands on the table. The left one shook uncontrollably. He leaned toward Bormann. "I *know*," he said flatly. Accept it. I have known for some time. About the old abandoned sewer system. The hidden supplies. The disguises. The suddenly missing workers. All of it."

Bormann clenched his jaws. He stared at Hitler sitting quietly, contemplating him. He was right. The time *was* past for being evasive. For lies. He looked steadily at Hitler.

"How?" he asked.

Hitler waved a trembling hand at him. "Unimportant," he said. He stood up. For a moment he paced in a laborious shuffle before the painting of Frederick the Great. He turned to Bormann. "Important is," he said, unsuspected authority in his voice, "important is that your plan fits in exactly with my own!"

Bormann was thunderstruck. The Führer! Had he decided to leave the Bunker after all, now that it was too late to fly him out? In the last possible moment.

"*Mein* Führer!" he exclaimed. "Are you—are you planning to—break out?"

Hitler turned to look at his deputy with disdain. "*Sei nicht dumm*," he chided. "Don't be foolish." He stopped his shuffling gait. He looked at his trembling, withered arm. "You know my decision. It is unalterable. I shall die here. In the heart of my city. My Fatherland." Angrily he grabbed his shaking arm. "I am half dead already!"

He fixed Bormann with baleful eyes. "No," he said firmly, "I shall not attempt to leave here. I will not take the chance of suffering the disgrace of being captured. The Bolsheviks shall not parade me in a cage through the streets of Moscow!"

Bormann had a twinge of self-disgust. He should have known. Hitler would simply have taken over the operation now that he had the facts. Not have asked to go along. Anyway it was obvious the Führer was not physically able. And every man, woman, and child in Germany would recognize him. It was not the same as with him. Very few people were familiar with the appearance of *Reichsleiter* Martin Bormann. Certainly not the enemy. Then what did the Führer mean?

Hitler stared at his deputy sitting in shocked silence before him. "No, Bormann," he said, "I shall not go with you. And I will not stop you. In fact, I have already made certain arrangements to help you. To ensure the success of your escape."

Bormann was stunned. For once in his life he was totally unprepared for what was happening. He was at once leery. He had long since learned that in the inner circle around Hitler nothing ever was what it seemed to be. The first question he always had to ask himself in any situation was: Where is the trap?

"I—I do not understand," he said, playing for time to think. "How . . . ?"

Hitler gave a crooked little smile. He knew exactly what his deputy was thinking—and doing. So be it.

"I shall be perfectly frank with you, Bormann," he said soberly. "I expect the same from you. I know of your plan to escape from the Bunker—and from Berlin—and to head for what I have been told is so colorfully called the Flensburg escape hatch. That you hope to take refuge in Denmark—at a certain hospital, I understand—and there wait until you can safely make your way to South America." He sat down at the desk again.

He gazed at the silent deputy. He shook his head. "I have made better plans for you, *mein lieber* Bormann," he said. "In a few hours *Feldmarschall* Greim will leave the Bunker. He will fly to Admiral Doenitz's headquarters. He will hand him sealed orders from me, personally, instructing the Admiral to place at your disposal when you arrive in Flensburg—a submarine. Type XXI, ocean going, *Schnorchel*-equipped. Its very existence there has been kept secret. It will take you to South America. Argentina."

Bormann stared at the Führer. If it was true, if such arrangements had in fact been made, his successful escape to South America was virtually assured.

"Now," Hitler said firmly, "I want you to tell me, in detail, how you expect to leave Berlin."

Bormann thought quickly. He decided. It might all be a trap to make him divulge his plans. But he had to take that chance. He had a gut feeling that Hitler was being honest with him. Had the Führer wanted to, he could have had him shot summarily. Without any preponderance of proof. Like Fegelein. He nodded.

"An escape route *has* been prepared, *mein* Führer," he began. "I came upon certain blueprints when the Bunker was being constructed." He told his story carefully. "In 1936, when the new Olympic Stadium complex was built for the Olympic Games it was necessary to construct an entire new sewer system to serve the area. Some of the existing system was enlarged and rebuilt but most of it was abandoned."

He licked his suddenly dry lips. It was not easy to have to disclose his most secret scheme. "The blueprints I acquired showed this abandoned system," he continued. "One main conduit ran from the Tiergarten in a straight line to the west, skirting the Olympic site and dipping under the Havel River to the suburb of Wilhelmstadt."

He paused. Hitler sat silent, listening, studying him.

"I inspected it," Bormann went on. "I ordered every access to it walled up securely. Except two. I had . . ."

"Where located?" Hitler interrupted.

"One in a Tiergarten building directly across from the underground bunker garages approximately two hundred meters inside the park. The other in Wilhelmstadt. At those two places I had the access sealed and rigged with a built-in explosive that, when detonated, would reopen the passage."

Again he paused. Hitler looked at him. "And the people who performed this work?" he asked tonelessly.

"Foreign laborers, *mein* Führer," Bormann answered. "They were—eliminated."

"Supplies? Equipment?"

"Stored inside the Tiergarten access," Bormann replied. "Everything that will be needed. Sufficient for a party of four."

"And the blueprints?"

"Destroyed."

Hitler nodded, satisfied. But he withheld his approval from his face. For a moment he gazed at his deputy. "I could give you my help, Bormann," he said slowly, "or I could have you shot."

For a while the two men sat staring at each other as the tension built in the little room. Then Hitler sighed.

"But—I have decided to help," he breathed. "However, there is one condition."

"What is it?" Bormann was at once on guard again.

"You must take someone with you," Hitler said. "Someone I will choose. Understood?"

Bormann was intrigued. Who was that important to the Führer? No matter. He would agree, of course. It would be easy to get rid of whoever it would be that the Führer would saddle him with. When the time was right.

"Who?" he asked.

Hitler looked straight at him, his eyes suddenly ablaze.

"Eva," he said.

Despite himself, Bormann looked shocked. Eva Braun! He knew the girl had pledged to die with the Führer. Everyone in the Bunker knew. When Hitler had decided to die by his own hand in the Bunker, Eva Braun emphatically had vowed to join him in death.

"But—Eva!" he blurted out. "I thought—I thought *Fräulein* Eva had decided to end her life here."

Somberly Hitler nodded. "And that is how it will appear," he said. "To the world she *will* die with me." His voice suddenly rang with a strange, fanatic determination. "But she *must* live! She *must!*"

Totally mystified, Bormann stared at the suddenly agitated Hitler. "I don't understand," he said. "Why?"

For a moment Hitler looked at his deputy. "Because of what Dr. Haase told me," he said gravely.

Bormann's thoughts were awhirl. Professor Werner Haase. A brilliant physician. Tall, in his fifties, and already silverhaired, Haase was dying of tuberculosis. He had only part of one lung left, which often caused him to gasp for air. For the last several weeks he had been Hitler's physician having replaced Dr. Brandt, arrested for some nebulous reason he no longer remembered. Haase? True, he *had* seen Hitler and Haase engrossed in intense, whispered conversations. He had assumed it had to do with the coming suicides. What *had* been said? He did not even know how to ask.

"*Mein* Führer?" he said.

"Soon the German Reich will be without its Führer," Hitler intoned solemnly. "The world without Adolf Hitler." Some of the old fire returned to his voice. "But it is imperative that my seed, my genes, live on. A Germany in my image *must* endure for the ages." He paused. He looked at Bormann—a burning, piercing gaze. "Eva Braun is carrying a child," he said. "*My heir!* To be born into the world in less than five months."

Bormann was too stunned to speak. He merely stared at Hitler.

"Eva Braun, whom I this night take to wife, will bear my son," Hitler finished.

Bormann tried to collect his racing thoughts. The wedding. Of course. That was why Hitler wanted to marry that insipid little snip of a photographer's assistant. That was the real reason for the ridiculous eleventh-hour wedding. To make their union legit-

[51]

imate. To give the Führer's son his name. Son? He frowned at Hitler.

"Son?" he said. "How . . . ?"

"The stars decree it," Hitler said. "The signs all predict the child will be a boy. My son."

Bormann stared at him. He had never shared the Führer's mystical belief in astrology. Stupid nonsense, of course. But he had an uneasy feeling that this time—this time it was true.

Eva Braun *was* carrying the Führer's son!

"It is clear to you now, is it Bormann, why Eva *must* leave Berlin and *must* be brought to safety?"

"Of course," Bormann affirmed at once. "And I pledge to you I shall do my utmost to ensure the safety of *Fräulein* Eva and her unborn child."

Another promise, easy to break, he thought. Once out of Berlin he could do as he pleased. *Fräulein* Braun—or *Frau* Hitler—would have to fend for herself.

Hitler nodded. As if reading his deputy's mind he continued: "It will, of course, be in your own interest, Bormann, to keep Eva from harm, until she is safe in South America."

Bormann frowned at him. What did he mean?

Hitler gave him a thin smile. "Let me explain, *mein lieber Herr Reichsleiter,*" he said, a hint of mockery in his raspy voice. "I have amassed a vast fortune, Bormann. My royalties from *Mein Kampf* alone." He spread his hands eloquently. "Unlike so many others, this was not done for my own personal benefit, but to ensure that our National Socialist ideals will never die!" He looked shrewdly at Bormann. "I do not exaggerate," he said quietly, "when I tell you this fortune now runs into billions of *Reichsmarks*. It is hidden, of course, in accounts in international banks, most of it in Switzerland." He looked steadily at Bormann. "And Eva, and only Eva, knows where and how to find it. *She* is the key. The sole key. The key to a vast and secret treasure, Bormann, that can become yours. That can help the survivors of this last battle ultimately to win the war. You, and others like you, who will flee to safety. Mengele. Eichmann. Stangl. Müller. You know the list as well as I." He fixed Bormann with a piercing stare. "Eva *must* be kept safe. She *must* reach asylum in South America. Argentina. She *must* give birth to my son! And you, Bormann, must assure her safety. If. If the treasure I offer you is ever to be yours."

Bormann thought fast. He had, himself, gathered quite a fortune. He had, of course, had access to the special funds hoarded in a secret account in the Reichsbank in Berlin. Realized from the jewelry, the currency, precious stones, and other valuables confiscated from the Jews before they were sent to extermination camps. And from the gold extracted from their teeth, once there. He had been able to dip into this fund, secretly, and build a fortune for himself. A great fortune, safe in Argentina.

But nothing like the wealth Hitler was offering him.

He drew himself up.

"I would protect *Fräulein* Braun and her child with my life, *mein* Führer. Whatever the circumstances," Bormann pledged fervently.

"Of course."

Bormann was elated. If Eva Braun knew the locations of the accounts and had the key to obtain the funds, it would not be difficult to get that information from her. Not at all.

"And so that you will know all the details, *mein lieber* Bormann," Hitler continued, "each of the banks holding my accounts—in a variety of names, of course—each has been sent a photograph of Eva and a sample of her signature. Only she *in person* can make disposition of the money."

He was amused to see the tiny glint of chagrin that flitted through Bormann's eyes. He knew his deputy. He also knew he would now do his utmost to safeguard the girl. And the fortune . . .

"You may rely on me completely, *mein* Führer," Bormann said earnestly. "I shall not let you down."

Again Hitler nodded. "There is one more thing," he said. Laboriously he got up from the desk. He shuffled to the door and opened it. His valet stood in the corridor outside.

"Linge," Hitler said to him, "send *Obersturmführer* Lüttjohann to me. At once."

Willibald Lüttjohann was awed, being in the presence of *Reichsleiter* Martin Bormann and the Führer himself. But he was a soldier. He kept himself from showing any emotion. He stood ramrod straight as the Führer spoke about him to the *Reichsleiter*.

"*Obersturmführer* Lüttjohann is a graduate of Skorzeny's elite commando school, *Herr Reichsleiter*," he explained. "He has distinguished himself with Skorzeny in the service of the Reich. He has been taught every possible military art and commando trick—and I am informed he excels in them. He speaks English, French, and Italian and he is a superior officer in every way, of unquestioned loyalty."

Bormann glared at the young officer in his commando uniform. Instinctively he knew he meant trouble for him.

"Loyalty must be stamped on your heart, *mein* Führer," he said. "Not merely on your belt buckle."

Hitler smiled. "And I am reliably informed that it is, *Herr Reichsleiter*," he said. He glanced at Bormann. "*Obersturmführer* Lüttjohann will accompany you and Eva. Just in case . . ."

He smiled to himself. It was his final safeguard to ensure Bormann's performance. He had thought of everything. He turned to his desk. From the drawer he took one of the two large envelopes. He walked up to Bormann.

"Read this," he said. He handed the envelope to Bormann. "You will carry it with you when you leave here. Guard it with your life. You will give it to Eva when you get to South America. It contains all the documentation she will need to prove conclusively that her son is the heir of Adolf Hitler."

He returned to his desk. "And Bormann," he said, "you should know that I have also made arrangements for a—a *smokescreen* to be laid down for your protection. Conflicting reports as to *when* you were seen leaving the Bunker. That you managed to escape, or that you were seen killed on the streets of Berlin, or that you defected to the Russians." He smiled thinly. "There will be reports that you were seen taking refuge in the Bavarian Mountains. In Denmark. In many different places, in fact. All to confuse the truth, of course."

Bormann was gratified. It was the only thing he, himself, had been unable to arrange. It would have caused suspicion. But he knew how important it could be, and he did not doubt the effectiveness of Hitler's efforts. No one could equal the Führer at mixing truth with falsehood in exactly the right proportions to make the whole sound convincing. His motto—the bigger the lie, the more easily it will be believed—had become a truism.

"And now, *mein lieber Herr Reichsmarschall,*" Hitler said. "You and I will brief *Obersturmführer* Lüttjohann. Together. So he may know exactly what is demanded of him."

And they did.

Finally Hitler rose. He looked gravely at the two men. "What has been said here," he warned, "must stay with the three of us. No one else—I repeat *no one*—must know. The secret must remain with us." He fixed them with compelling eyes. "Swear it! On the sacred oath you once gave to the Reich—and to me."

Solemnly they swore.

"Now go," Hitler said. "And prepare."

[54]

In unison the two men threw up their arms and cried *"Heil Hitler!"*

Bormann was halfway out of the door, Lüttjohann behind him, when Hitler called: *"Obersturmführer* Lüttjohann! *Ein Moment."* He beckoned the young officer to return. "I have some further instructions for you."

Bormann, turning in the doorway, glared at the young man. He had been right, he thought angrily. Skorzeny's *Spitzbube*—Skorzeny's young brigand—would bear watching. Already the machinations were beginning.

He closed the heavy metal door less gently than he had intended.

Willibald Lüttjohann returned to the desk. Smartly he came to attention. *"Zu Befehl!"* he snapped. "At your orders!"

Hitler looked at the young man. He liked what he saw. Instinctively he knew the officer could be trusted with the special and far-reaching orders he, and he alone, was to be given. Slowly, grimly he began to talk . . .

Fifteen minutes later it was done, and *Oberstühmfuhrer* Willibald Lüttjohann left the Führer's quarters fully briefed.

For a moment Hitler sat quietly at his desk. His shoulders drooped. He let his arm twitch without attempting to control it, and his face sagged.

It was done.

The two men in whose hands the future of Germany, of Adolf Hitler, now rested, had been given their all-important orders. He reflected on the momentous differences between the two. One, mature, greedy, and powerful, shrewd and devious and totally untrustworthy, concerned only with himself; the other, young and idealistic, loyal and eager to serve his Fatherland—and his Führer.

He sighed.

Stiffly he got up from his chair. He shuffled to the door to Eva's dressing room. It stood slightly ajar. He pushed it open.

"You heard," he said. It was a statement rather than a question.

The man who stepped into view in the doorway was perhaps forty years of age, although his powerful, athletic build made him seem younger. Rugged, yet lithe, he gave the impression of danger about to be let loose. *SS Sturmbannführer* Oskar Strelitz had been with Hitler from the start. He had marched with him in Munich in 1923 as a member of *Stosstrupp Hitler* and he had cheered himself hoarse at the Nürnberg rallies. He would lay down his life for the Führer—no hesitation, no questions asked.

And Hitler knew it.

"You heard it all," Hitler repeated.

"I did," Strelitz said grimly.

Hitler looked at him. He put his hand on his shoulder. "You know your mission, Oskar," he said. "You know how important it is to me. To us. Our common cause. To Operation Future."

Strelitz nodded.

"Follow them, Oskar," Hitler continued earnestly. "Protect them. From any dangers. Pursuit. Betrayal. Protect Eva with your life."

Again Strelitz nodded. It was self-evident.

"I will give you whatever written authority is needed. It will be total. But do not interfere as long as things go well. Do not make your presence known to them. Only in total secrecy lie your own safety and protection. Do nothing, unless it becomes imperative. Then, if necessary, you will take over Bormann's task, or Lüttjohann's duties," he said earnestly. "You understand?"

Sturmbannführer Oskar Strelitz looked into the burning eyes of Adolf Hitler. He placed his own hand firmly on the trembling hand of the Führer resting on his shoulder. "I do!"

5

EVA ANNA PAULA BRAUN opened the wardrobe in her room adjoining Hitler's quarters in the Bunker. She looked critically at the meager selection of plain dresses. What should she wear? It was April 28, 1945, the most important day of her life, the day she would become the wife of Adolf Hitler, Führer of the German Third Reich, and she wanted to look her best.

She lit a cigarette. She knew Adolf strongly objected to her smoking—to anyone smoking, for that matter—and she never did in his presence. But she needed something to calm her excitement.

She held out a dress. Should she wear the pretty blue one with the white collar and cuffs? She knew it was becoming to her. She rejected it. Just not festive enough. She let a stray thought flit back to her fantasies of long ago. She had always wanted to wear her grandmother's brocade dress when one day she'd be married. But, of course, that was not possible. The dress was still at Berchtesgaden. The flowered one? No, she had worn that one a lot in the Bunker. She liked it, though. It was very much like the one she had worn the day she had met Adolf. Sixteen years ago. It had been in the photographic shop of her employer. Heinrich Hoffmann. She had been standing near the top of a ladder taking down some supplies when Adolf Hitler came in. She had been aware of the man, whom *Herr* Hoffmann had called *Herr* Hitler, watching her, and she had deliberately stretched to reach something on the very top shelf, although she did not need it. She knew her dress would ride up, and she wanted *Herr* Hitler to see a little more of her legs. She had good legs.

She finally selected the black silk taffeta. It had a high neck and a full skirt. It was the most festive one, and it was one of Adolf's favorites. It fit her tightly. For a moment she frowned in concern. Would it be too tight? She had already put on a little weight. Had anyone noticed? Had Liesl given her a funny look? Just yesterday? She shrugged off her concern. Soon it would not matter. She shook out the dress. It would need ironing. Liesl would see to that. And do her hair. There was so much to be done. For a moment she thought affectionately of the maid who had served her so faithfully. Liesl Ostertag. She would have to leave her something. Some jewelry. Only she had so little with her in the Bunker.

She put the black dress, which was to be her wedding dress, on her bed.

The morbid appropriateness of its color did not occur to her. She hurried off in search of Liesl.

Adolf Hitler also had last-minute preparations to attend to, although of a vastly more far-reaching nature.

The table in the anteroom to his study had been opulently decorated in preparation for the wedding reception. The gleaming white tablecloth bore the initials A.H. as did the silver dinner set. And the champagne glasses sparkled. Only the flowers were missing. Hitler did not seem to notice any of it as he hurried toward the little hospital room of *Feldmarschall* Ritter von Greim. Just as he took no notice of the fire hoses snaking through the conference room corridor nor the chunks of fallen plaster on the rug. He paid no attention to the two SS officers who stood smoking as they conferred, and did not hide their cigarettes as he shuffled by, and he seemed not to hear the raucous music coming from the general dining area on the upper level of the Bunker. His world was beginning to collapse around him—and he paid it no heed.

In the corridor, Artur Axmann tried to stop him. Only a week before, on the Führer's fifty-sixth birthday, Axmann had brought a group of his Hitler Youths to the Bunker to be decorated for bravery. The youngest had been twelve years old. He had destroyed a Russian tank. In the Chancellery garden above, Hitler had personally pinned the Iron Crosses on the puny but proud chests of the boys.

Axmann looked haggard and deeply worried. His hectic visits to the Bunker were made between battles in the city above when he could leave his headquarters on Friedrichstrasse from where he directed his Hitler Youth boys who defended the city and desperately tried to hold the Havel bridges from the Russian onslaught.

"*Mein* Führer," he insisted, "I beg you! You must leave the Bunker. Leave Berlin! The Russians will overrun the Chancellery within days. Perhaps hours. I will personally take the responsibility of getting you out. Safely and unharmed." He spoke rapidly as he walked beside Hitler who had not stopped. "I pledge to you, *mein* Führer, the life of every single member of my Hitler Youth to get you out to safety."

Hitler brushed him aside. He seemed not to have heard. He entered the hospital room.

Ritter von Greim, leaning on Hanna Reitsch and a cane, was hobbling across the floor. When he saw Hitler he quickly removed his arm from Hanna's shoulder, put his cane behind him and stood erect, placing as little weight as possible on his wounded foot.

Hitler did not notice.

"*Herr Feldmarschall,*" he said, "when will you be leaving?"

"We plan to leave here about 2300 hours, *mein* Führer," Greim answered. "We will attempt to take off around midnight."

Hitler frowned. "Midnight is still hours away," he said shortly. "Why delay?"

"It is the time of least enemy ground action," Greim explained. "The very early morning hours. The only possible way to fly out is in a small, slow, low-flying plane, vulnerable to small arms fire from the ground. A one- or two-seater plane."

Hitler nodded. "Of course. You must give yourself the best possible chance. Your mission demands it." He looked at Hanna. "You will accompany the *Feldmarschall?*" he asked.

"Yes, *mein* Führer," Hanna acknowledged. "Unless you will permit me to stay at your side."

Hitler shook his head. "I told you already," he said shortly. "Both of you. You must leave." He turned to Greim. "You will use the same plane in which you flew in?"

"No," Greim said. "The Fieseler Storch was destroyed. In the Russian artillery bombardment this morning. We have an Arado-96, a light artillery observation plane, standing by. It has already been fuelled. It is ready for takeoff."

Again Hitler nodded. He seemed to hear only part of what Greim said.

"Here are your final orders, Greim," he said. "Your mission is threefold. First—arrest the traitor, Himmler. See that he does no more harm to the Reich. Secondly—as commander in chief of the Luftwaffe use whatever squadrons are available to you to attack the Russian forces that threaten the Chancellery. Keep a corridor open to the west. To link up with the Mecklenburg pocket. Prevent the enemy from overrunning the Chancellery grounds for as long as you can. And third"—he pulled the big envelope from his uniform tunic pocket—"deliver this into the hands of *Grossadmiral* Doenitz. You already know part of the contents. Operation Future. There are also further instructions the Admiral must carry out."

He gave Greim his hand. "I know you will succeed," he said. "You must!"

"*Mein* Führer," Hanna said, close to tears, her voice unsteady with emotion. "I implore you! Leave the city. It is *not* too late. Take my place with the *Feldmarschall*. You *must* live, *mein* Führer. For the German people. The German Reich. You must not die!" Her voice broke.

Hitler regarded her. He was obviously moved. He patted her arm awkwardly. "*Meine liebe, liebe* Hanna," he said quietly. "Death will be a relief for me. I have been deceived and betrayed by everyone—except a few like you."

For a moment he looked at them. "*Hals-und-Beinbruch*," he said. "May you break your neck and your legs"—the traditional German good-luck wish. "I shall not see you again."

He turned on his heel and with a barely noticeable limp walked from the room.

It was late when the wedding ceremony finally got underway in the small conference room. The plan had been to begin the proceedings much earlier, but it was now close to midnight.

First there had been the delay of finding two suitable rings to be exchanged. Neither the groom nor the bride had been able to provide them. And suddenly everyone in the Bunker who had been wearing wedding rings sported naked fingers. Gold was at a premium. It was all they would have left if flight from the city became necessary. Then someone had suggested the Gestapo treasury. The SS officer who brought the rings over to the Führer Bunker had wondered what the Führer wanted with two wedding rings that had been confiscated from some rotten Jews before they were gassed. When he found out he wisely kept silent. And he was only too pleased to get out of the Bunker *Klapsmühle*—the Bunker nut house. The groom and the bride tried on the rings for size. They were too big.

And then there had been the difficulty in finding a magistrate to perform the civil wedding ceremony. Dr. Goebbels had remembered a justice of the peace, one Walter Wagner, who had married him and his wife, Magda, and a search was mounted to find this man. He had finally been located, fighting in a *Volkssturm* unit near the Friedrichstrasse, and was brought to the Bunker.

The small wedding party assembled in the room included Goebbels and Bormann, who were to be the witnesses.

Bormann stood next to Eva as her witness. Eva had been baffled at the sudden, unaccustomed friendliness of the man, who alone among all the Führer's close associates had always held her in contempt—and had often shown it, when Hitler was not present. Now the man, whom Eva considered a loathsome, oversexed toad, had been almost deferential. "*Gnädiges Fräulein,* may I, please?" he'd asked when he took her arm. She had been puzzled and uneasy.

Because of the unusual circumstances, both she and Adolf had requested the special war wedding procedure, so that the ceremony could be performed without the customary waiting time. Both of them had solemnly affirmed that they were pure third-generation Aryans and suffered from no hereditary diseases, facts which were duly entered in the records.

And now they stood before the magistrate. Eva in her black taffeta dress with the gold clasps at the shoulder straps, wearing a bracelet set with tourmalines, her diamond-studded watch, and a topaz pendant. Adolf was, as usual, in his uniform.

To the accompaniment of Russian artillery shells and the rockets from "Stalin Organs" exploding above, the nervous magistrate, who had been told to hurry through the formalities, began the ceremony. He looked awkward in his combat dusty civilian clothes and his *Volkssturm* armband.

The oversized rings were exchanged and Justice of the Peace Wagner looked solemnly at the two people standing before him.

"I come now to the solemn act of matrimony," he intoned. "In the presence of the witnesses here assembled I ask you, *mein* Führer, Adolf Hitler, whether you wish willingly to enter into matrimony with *Fräulein* Eva Braun. If this be so, I ask you to reply, 'Yes.' "

"Yes," said Adolf Hitler.

"Now, herewith I ask you, *Fräulein* Eva Braun, whether you are willing to enter into matrimony with *mein* Führer, Adolf Hitler. If this be so, I ask you to reply, 'Yes.' "

"Yes," said Eva.

"Now, inasmuch as both the engaged persons have declared their intent to enter into matrimony, I herewith declare their marriage valid before the law," Wagner intoned, obviously relieved that his momentous duties were discharged.

Eva felt as if she would burst with excitement. She was the wife of the Führer, Adolf Hitler! At last. She was the rightful *Führerin* of the Third Reich, and no one could deny her. After all those long, long years. She did not even notice that her husband did not kiss her at the conclusion of the ceremony. She was used to his not showing her affection in public. The tears of happiness in her eyes were enough.

Bormann was the first to congratulate her. All smiles, he bowed to her and kissed her hand. It disturbed her, and when the magistrate asked the four principals in the ceremony—Hitler, Eva, and the witnesses Goebbels and Bormann—to sign the marriage certificate—in the proper sequence, of course—she began to sign herself *Eva Braun*. She laughed, crossed out the *B* and wrote *Hitler, geb. (née) Braun.*

It was done. The wedding party joined the other celebrants at the wedding feast to enjoy the good food, the wine, and the champagne.

And, as Hitler broke with tradition and toasted his new wife with a glass of sweet Tokay wine, a small two-seater Arado-96 observation plane raced along the makeshift airstrip at the historic triumphal arch, the Brandenburg Gate.

Hanna Reitsch was at the controls. *Feldmarschall* Ritter von Greim, who had arrived at the airstrip on crutches, sat stiffly in the second seat.

The Russians had fought their way even closer to the airstrip than when they had arrived in the Storch. The stark ruins ringing the area were tinged with a blood-red glow from the fires. Bright searchlights from Russian antiaircraft batteries lanced the night sky. And the cacophonous sounds of battle assaulted their ears.

They had been told takeoff would be impossible. Russian forces lay in wait a short distance from the end of the runway, ready to shoot down any plane that tried.

Hanna had said nothing. She had taxied to the other end of the airstrip and was now streaking down the runway, taking off *with* the wind instead of against it, as the enemy would expect. Fighting the controls, urging the little plane to gain speed. She hurtled straight at the six massive columns of the great arch looming before them, lifted, and barely cleared the giant bronze statue of Victory and her four-horse chariot—the famed Quad-riga—that stood atop the huge gate. She willed the plane to gain altitude. Quickly the Russian searchlight crews found the small aircraft and pinned it in a latticework of blinding beams of light. Hanna climbed as steeply as she dared. Up from the nightmare of fire and smoke, suffering, and terror that was the dying city of Berlin. Up toward a cloud bank four thousand feet above. Tracer bullets zipped in fiery streaks past the shuddering wings. Antiair-craft shells burst in black puffs of destruction and the little Ar-ado-96 slipped into the concealment of the clouds and headed northwest.

Flugkapitän Hanna Reitsch and *Feldmarschall* Ritter von Greim had departed from Berlin.

And with them went the beginning of Operation Future.

In the Führer Bunker Eva, clad in her blue Italian silk night-gown, climbed into bed with her husband.

On the street above, Justice of the Peace Walter Wagner lay dead, killed on his way back to his *Volkssturm* post.

6

Ober<i>sturmführer</i> WILLIBALD LÜTTJOHANN looked at his watch.
It was 1547 hours—Monday, April 30. He sat alone in the little
temporary hospital room which so recently had been occupied by
Feldmarschall Ritter von Greim. He had been ordered to keep
himself ready to leave the Bunker at any time. That had been two
hours ago. But his keyed-up alertness had not left him.

Outside in the conference corridor a macabre spectacle was
about to take place. A small group of people—less than a score—
was waiting uneasily. They had been summoned to bid their last
farewells to their Führer. A pall of depression hung over the scene.

Time had run out.

Everyone tensed as the door to Hitler's study opened. All eyes
were upon the Führer and Eva as they stepped out into the corridor. Both were pale, but composed. Eva was wearing her favorite Italian-made shoes, and once again she wore her husband's favorite dress, the black taffeta. A pink scarf added a touch of color.
Only hours before, the dress had been a wedding gown. Now it
was to be a shroud.

She embraced the women. To Trudl Junge she whispered sentimentally: "Don't forget to give my love to my beautiful native
Bavaria—*das schöne Bayern.*" She smiled prettily at the generals
and officials, Joseph Goebbels, Martin Bormann. And *SS Sturmbannführer* Otto Günsche, her husband's senior SS Adjutant, who
faithfully had guarded his life. Until now. They kissed her hand.
The hand of the *Führerin* of the German Reich. *Führerin* for a
day.

Hitler shuffled from one solemn leave-taker to another. In utter silence he shook their hands, one by one. But he did not look into their faces. Only when he came to his valet, Heinz Linge, did he speak. In a barely audible voice he said: *"Linge, mein alter Freund,* you must escape Berlin—and live."

Startled, Linge said: "Yes, *mein* Führer. Why?"

"To serve him who will come after me," Hitler whispered, his voice strangely constricted. "As faithfully as you served me."

The last one was Otto Günsche. The officer had his orders. He would guard the door. No one was to enter the Führer's study for ten minutes.

And Hitler and Eva went into the study.

With an ominous clang of finality the vault-like steel door swung shut behind them, and Günsche, his Schmeisser machine pistol at port arms, took up his position at the door.

Hitler took Eva by the hand. For a brief moment he stood gazing at the empty spot on the wall where the portrait of Frederick the Great, his favorite possession, had hung until a few hours ago. He had given it to his loyal pilot, Hans Baur. He looked at Eva.

"My little *Tschapperl,*" he said softly, calling her by the banal Bavarian term of affection he so often used. "My little 'honey pie,' now I have nothing but you."

She squeezed his hand.

He looked at the table standing before the blue-and-white velvet-covered couch. On it his Walther 7.65 and a smaller caliber handgun, a Walther 6.35, had been placed—and two glass phials. He turned to Eva.

"Now," he said.

Quickly Eva removed her scarf. She threw it on the table next to the little gun. She began to unbutton her dress.

Suddenly the door to the corridor opened.

Startled, Hitler whirled toward it.

Otto Günsche stood in the open doorway. *"Mein* Führer," he said apologetically, *"Frau* Goebbels insists on speaking with you. She says it is of vital importance."

Behind the officer Hitler glimpsed the woman, Magda Goebbels. She seemed hysterical. She was shouting: "There is still hope, *mein* Führer! You can still reach Berchtesgaden! There is still hope! You must not die! You *cannot* die! . . ."

He was furious. It had been close. Another few seconds. He glared angrily at Günsche. "You have your orders," he growled. "I will not see her. I will not see anyone! You will keep that door closed. For ten minutes. Whatever happens. Is that understood?"

"*Jawohl, mein* Führer!"

Hastily Günsche closed the door.

Shaken, but still under control, Eva began to remove her dress. It had been close.

Hitler quickly strode to the door leading to his private room. "Strelitz," he called hoarsely. "Bring her out."

SS Sturmbannführer Oskar Strelitz walked into the study. The unconscious woman in his arms bore a striking likeness to Eva.

She was without a dress. Hitler merely glanced at her. She was of no importance, a necessary sacrifice to serve his purpose. And the future. He did not know her name. Strelitz had found her. Working as a volunteer in the Bunker Lazaret. No one knew her. No one would miss her.

But she was vital to the success of the operation.

Eva Braun had to die. *An* Eva Braun. Her body had to be found with his. There could be no doubt. No one must have a reason to hunt for her once the Reich had been struck down.

When the time came she knew what to do.

Eva helped Strelitz to put her black dress on the unconscious woman. And her Italian-made shoes. She said not a word, but the tears were streaming down her cheeks.

Strelitz placed the woman on the sofa. He picked up one of the glass phials from the table and put it in her mouth.

Eva looked away as, with a quick motion, Strelitz clamped the woman's jaws together, crushing the phial. Part of the broken glass fell to the floor. A violent spasm racked the unconscious body and left it still in death.

A fleet, almost impersonal embrace—as if both Eva and Adolf found it difficult to express affection in the presence of death— and they stood in awkward silence. Strelitz glanced at his watch.

"*Frau* Hitler. *Bitte*," he said urgently. "The bandages!"

Quickly Eva walked to her own room, followed by Strelitz, who closed the door behind them.

For a moment Hitler stood alone, staring after them. Then he shuffled to the sofa. One last time. Heavily he sat down. Without a glance at the dead substitute Eva at his side he picked up the remaining phial and placed it in his mouth. He reached for his gun and raised it to his temple.

To those waiting in the corridor outside each second was an eternity. The silence was tangible—taut and heavy. The nerves of everyone were tensed to the ultimate. All eyes were on the massive, closed steel door, all ears were straining for the sound of the shot they expected to come. The shot that would take the life of the Führer. The shot they all knew would be impossible to hear through the thick, fireproof, gasproof, and soundproof double door. But still they listened. And the eternal seconds ticked by . . .

Finally Günsche spoke. "Ten minutes," he said. "The Führer's ten minutes have gone by . . ." He spoke to no one. Everyone.

At once Bormann strode to the door. He flung it open. Over his shoulder Günsche, Linge, and the others took in the sight that met them—every detail searing itself on their minds.

Sitting on the blue-and-white sofa were Adolf Hitler and Eva Braun. From a small hole in the Führer's right temple the blood slowly oozed down his cheek. His right hand hung limply over the arm of the sofa and below it on the floor lay his Walther 7.65. His left hand clutched a picture of a woman to his uniformed chest. His mother. A few glass splinters fallen on it from his open mouth glinted in the light. Eva Braun was leaning into the corner of the sofa, her face partly hidden. Her little 6.35 pistol still lay next to her gay pink scarf on the table. It had not been fired. On the floor near her left foot was part of a broken glass phial. Mixed with the acrid smell of gunpowder there was a strong odor of bitter almonds in the room. The cyanamide had done its job.

Hurriedly Bormann walked into the room. Two heavy woolen military blankets had been thrown over a chair. He took one of them and quickly covered Eva's body. Following his lead, Linge took the other and spread it over the Führer.

Bormann motioned to two SS officers. Between them they picked up the blanket-covered body of Hitler. Bormann himself carefully wrapped the blanket around the body of Eva Braun. Only her feet were visible. And on them her favorite Italian-made shoes. He lifted her up—she was heavier than he had expected—and started toward the stairs that led to the garden above.

At the foot of the stairs the six-feet, two-inches-tall Günsche stopped him. For a moment Bormann thought the man was going to pull the blanket aside and look at the body, but he merely took her in his arms and gently carried her up the fifty stone steps to the garden, followed by the grim mourners.

About ten meters from the Bunker exit, amidst the broken masonry, blackened timbers, uprooted trees, and jagged cement blocks scattered throughout the shell-cratered Chancellery garden, a shallow ditch had been dug in the rubble-strewn ground, and nearby a number of gasoline cans had been stacked. Side by side the two bodies were laid in the trench.

As the corpses were being doused with gasoline, a Russian artillery bombardment suddenly exploded around the garden.

Quickly the mourners sought refuge in the shelter of the Bunker entrance. Here Günsche dipped a rag in gasoline, set it afire, and hurled it out onto the gasoline-soaked bodies in the pit. At once they were enveloped in a roar of flames—an eerie obbligato to the thundering Russian barrage. And sooty smoke billowed up toward the red haze that lay over the city. Suddenly one of the SS officers snapped to rigid attention and gave the Hitler salute. Awkwardly the others followed his lead.

For a while Bormann stood with the silent group watching the blue flames eat at the shrouded bodies. Startled, he saw their limbs twitch spasmodically as the heat contracted the muscles and boiled away the tissue. The sickening sweet stench of burning flesh soon engulfed him and he quietly slipped away, disappearing into the Bunker.

It was 1853 hours. The Führer, Adolf Hitler, had been dead less than three hours. In the desecrated garden above, the flames had not yet consumed his body, but his Bunker world below had already disintegrated into a wild, profane bacchanalia.

The Bunker complex teemed with people. Soldiers and civilians seeking refuge from the hell above mingled with the milling Bunker denizens, imprisoned in a different, ungodly hell deep in the earth. The impending doom had severed every normal restraint of reason and decency. Liquor and lust, fear and despair in hellish fusion permeated everything and everybody and reigned unfettered.

No one paid attention to the three people who made their way through the crowded corridors and chambers of the Bunker system. Two men and a woman. The woman's head was swathed in bandages and her left arm was cushioned against her body in a sling. The older of the two men wore a large, makeshift patch over one eye; he kept his head pulled down into the upturned collar of an army greatcoat. The younger man, clad in a tight-fitting black uniform, assisted the wounded woman as they hurried through the Bunker labyrinth.

Led by Bormann, Eva and Willibald Lüttjohann were headed for the underground garages on Hermann Goering Strasse directly opposite the Tiergarten. It was a long way from the Führer Bunker itself. They had to travel in a wide, semicircular arch of corridors and shelters under the entire length of the New Chancellery building. Through the officers' quarters and the huge civilian bunker; through the Lazaret, the hospital rooms, and dental offices; through the mess hall and the SS guards' bunker.

Bright lights were everywhere; if not, they had been turned off for reasons known only to those who lurked in the gloom. Loud, strident music, screams, and laughter combined in a shrill cacophony filled the air. The stink of cigarette smoke and sour human sweat stung their nostrils.

Eva was appalled. In her entire, ordered existence she had never experienced anything to prepare her for the depraved sights and sounds that now assailed her senses. It filled her with loathing. And fear.

The bunker maze was a bedlam—a Dante's Inferno with the souls of the damned adorned with blood-red swastika armbands and silver death heads.

As they made their way through the officers' quarters the atmosphere of sexual saturnalia threatened to overwhelm her. Women and girls who only hours before had fled from basements and shelters in terror of being raped by the Russian barbarians now gave themselves openly and willingly to any German at hand.

One SS officer was shamelessly copulating on the floor amidst a jumble of empty beer and wine bottles and half-smoked cigarettes, drunkenly cheered on by his fellow officers.

A *Wehrmacht* general, naked from the waist down but with a row of gleaming medals on his immaculate uniform tunic, was tearing at the pants of a buxom, giggling teen-aged girl. And next to a gramophone oozing a Viennese waltz, two SS officers, their uniform pants bunched around their feet, were swaying drunkenly to the music in a clutching, orgasmic embrace.

Eva averted her face. She was profoundly shaken. She felt a sourness rise in her throat. She had a fleeting vision of a girl on a blue-and-white sofa. She had been shocked. Then. But nothing, nothing could be more terrible than the horrifying carnality she was now witnessing.

And on through the hellish network of passageways and compartments their obscene odyssey went.

In the Lazaret a half-naked nurse was masturbating a soldier whose legs were lifted in traction—both feet amputated. Madness shone in her eyes as she stared, transfixed, at the swollen penis in her rapidly moving hand, while she sensuously rubbed her own thighs together.

On the adjoining bed an orderly was changing the bloody bandage on another soldier's chest—oblivious to the spectacle beside him—while two nurses, sitting on a gurney, were stuffing caviar into their mouths with their fingers, emptying a can split open with a surgical instrument.

[69]

And in a dentist's office a naked, corpulent woman, strapped awkwardly into a dentist's chair, was being savagely sodomized by a huge SS guard, her ululating shrieks of pleasure knifing through Eva's horrified mind.

She stumbled along, clinging to the arm of Willibald Lüttjohann. She shuddered deep in her soul. A sudden, terrifying thought swept through her. If she were to be seized by those monsters, could her escorts protect her? Would they? Or would she be forced to become part of the monstrous corruption around her? Instinctively her grip on Willibald's arm tightened.

They entered the SS guards' room. Ahead lay the garages.

Most of the men in the room were in a drunken stupor. Bottles and empty food containers were everywhere. In a corner a group of noncoms were holding a naked girl on a table, her legs spread apart. One man was pouring champagne over her, drenching her blond pubic hair, while others, roaring with glee, took turns licking it off. Eva glanced briefly at the group. But she felt nothing. Nothing any more. . .

Grimly Bormann strode on, oblivious to the infernal scenes around him. Eva and Willibald followed. Ahead they could see the underground garages. Ahead were the stairs to the street above. And deliverance.

Despite the sight that met her, Eva felt a surge of relief as they emerged on Hermann Goering Strasse.

The street in front of them was deserted, empty of people, but scarred with bomb craters and filled with debris and disabled vehicles.

The thick walls and earthwork of the Bunker below had not been able to keep out the thundering din of the battle raging above, but the sounds had been deadened and muffled by the noise in the Bunker itself. Here, in the open, the roar of battle slammed into them with physical force.

The city around them was aflame and under heavy Russian artillery bombardment. The red-black sky was crisscrossed with the beams of searchlights reaching for von Greim's Luftwaffe planes, suicidally seeking to stop the enemy from closing the iron ring around the Chancellery, not knowing it was too late. From time to time the constant, ear-rending roar of battle and the crackling of fire were drowned out by a ground-shaking explosion or the crash of a collapsing wall. The distant wails and hoots of ambulances and fire engines punctuated the steady din.

Across the street the splintered tree trunks in the Tiergarten pointed into the sky in naked futility, unable to protect the city, crying out in death.

In a low run Bormann started across the nearly impassable street. Suddenly there was a sharp explosion which uprooted several tree trunks and catapulted dirt and debris into the air. Another. And another. A Russian mortar barrage hit the edge of the park. Bormann ran back to the shelter of the building above the garages.

Huddled together, the three fugitives waited.

There was a lull in the barrage.

"Now!" Bormann shouted.

They ran across the street. They zigzagged around craters, burned-out vehicles, and fallen trees, racing into the devastated park. Ahead, about two hundred meters, through the shattered trees, they could see a stone building. It looked badly damaged.

It was their destination.

Below it was the hidden entrance to Bormann's escape route.

The ornate sign carved in sandstone over the entrance to the small, squat building—which looked even more graceless with the mantle of vegetation around it destroyed—at one time must have read: *PUMPENANLAGE NO. 2.* But shrapnel had chipped away or mutilated most of the letters identifying the pumping station. Shell splinters had also pockmarked the propaganda slogan painted in white letters on one stone wall: *SIEG ODER SIBIRIEN!* (Victory or Siberia!)—a statement as empty as all Nazi slogans.

A direct hit on one corner of the building had blasted away part of the walls and collapsed the roof over the rubble. The windows all gaped: wide-open dead eyes, with long soot marks from the fires that had gutted the building stretching up from them like huge black eyelashes.

In the basement of the little utility building the destruction was minimal. The pumping station had probably been operational until ten days earlier when the electricity in the city finally failed and it became impossible to pump water to the animal exhibits in the zoo that depended on it.

Bormann turned on a flashlight. He removed the eye patch and turned down the collar on his greatcoat. He took out his gun. Anyone they might happen to meet would instantly pay for that meeting with his life. Leading the way, he strode past the looming, silent, and inactive machinery to a small door. It was warped and he had some difficulty in getting it open. Finally it gave way. Behind it was a narrow tunnel containing a mass of pipes and cables. About fifty feet down the corridor a small side passage joined it. Bormann turned into it. Carefully he counted his steps as he went: Twelve—thirteen—fourteen—fifteen. He stopped. He shone his flashlight on the wall. The coloration and texture seemed only slightly different from the rest of the walls.

"Here," he said with satisfaction. "It is here."

While he searched for the soot where the concealed detonation fuse lay hidden under the mortar surface of the wall and chipped away on it with a penknife, Willibald helped Eva out of her bandages.

"I have it!" Bormann called.

They joined him at the wall. He had scraped away a small area of mortar. Behind it was a little niche, and in it—wrapped tightly in waterproof oil paper—a rolled-up fuse.

Bormann freed the fuse and let it hang from the opening. He handed Willibald a box of matches.

"It is a thirty-second fuse," he said. "Enough for you to reach the utility tunnel." He took Eva's arm. "I shall take *Frau* Eva to safety now. Light the fuse and join us."

He and Eva walked back toward the tunnel. Willi looked after them. He smiled a crooked little smile. *Bonzen,* he thought (Brass Hats). He struck a match, lit the fuse, and waited to see that it was burning properly. Calmly he walked to the utility tunnel and turned the corner.

Bormann and Eva were waiting.

"Hold your ears," Willi said to Eva. She did. Willi and Bormann put their fingers in their ears and almost at once an explosion shook the tunnel. In the cramped space the detonation was ear-shattering. A fiery blast of dust and smoke shot into the tunnel from the side passage as the roar of the explosion reverberated down the corridor.

Quickly Bormann walked back to the passageway. He shone his flashlight into it. The beam from it was a pale-yellow streak of light that sliced through the dust-filled air. He hurried toward the spot in the wall where the explosion had taken place. Eva and Willi followed. Bormann played his flashlight on the wall. A gaping, black hole yawned in the beam.

Willi kicked the last few stones and masonry chunks away— and the three escapees stepped into the abandoned sewer.

The air was foul—stale and dank. Eva gagged, and Willi tried to breathe in shallow breaths holding his nostrils closed. Bormann played his flashlight around. The sewer was circular, with a flattened bottom and about eight feet in diameter. The masonry walls were encrusted with the hardened filth of decades and streaked with moisture which gleamed in the light from Bormann's torch. Pools of stagnant, fetid water speckled the bottom of the sewer which was lost ahead in absolute blackness.

Bormann's light came to rest on a wooden plank raised on ce-

ment blocks above the sewer floor. On the plank stood four bulg-
ing rucksacks and four kerosene lamps. Spades, pickaxes, and other
tools leaned against the plank.

"Let's get some light," Bormann said. He shone his torch on
the kerosene lamps.

And as the flames in the Chancellery garden—consuming the
remains of Adolf Hitler and his substitute wife—were slowly dying
down, the bright flames of three kerosene lamps in a foul-smelling abandoned sewer leaped into life, ready to light the way for
Eva and her son on the first leg of their flight to safety.

In the light of the kerosene lamps Bormann and Willi took a
final look at their maps and plans before starting out. Each had
a set. A diagram of the old sewer system and the all-important
area situation map to tell them the approximate positions of the
enemy forces so they could avoid them.

The sewer plan was complicated with tributaries and branch
lines coming in from various directions, creating dead-end forks
and junctions. But it should not be difficult to follow the main
line. The area map, complete with the most recent military information available when they left the Führer Bunker, showed a
narrow corridor between the enemy from the west and the enemy
from the east running from Wilhelmstadt to the Mecklenburg state
still held by German forces. They had about thirteen kilometers
to travel through the sewer. Willi estimated that it would take
them between four and five hours to cover the distance, barring
any unforeseen delays. That would get them to the exit point in
the suburb of Wilhelmstadt between midnight and 0100 hours.

Bormann looked at the SS officer. There was resentment and
animosity in his gaze. The young man looked too damned competent. Too damned confident.

"*Obersturmführer* Lüttjohann," he said coldly, "before we push
off, there is one thing I want clearly understood."

Willi looked at him. What the hell now? "*Herr Reichsleiter?*"
he queried.

"In all matters, at all times, *I* am in charge," Bormann stated
firmly. "Is that clearly understood?"

"*Jawohl, Herr Reichsleiter.*"

Willi began to put his maps away in his tunic pocket. Bormann
imperiously held out his hand. "I will take those, Lüttjohann," he
said. "I will make all decisions."

Willi hesitated for a second; then he began to withdraw the
maps again. It was a foolish request—or, rather, order—but he
had better comply. It was not wise to antagonize a man as pow-

erful as *Reichsleiter* Martin Bormann. He stopped. Powerful? Now, down here, they were on equal footing. The source of *Reichsleiter* Bormann's power lay smoldering in a shallow grave. He pushed his maps back into his pocket.

"With my respect, *Herr Reichsleiter*," he said calmly, "I think not. There is always the remote possibility that we may get separated."

Venomously Bormann glared at him. Then, without a word, he turned and stalked down into the darkness of the sewer.

Willi looked at his watch. They had been moving steadily through the sewer for only half an hour. Judging by the speed they were making he estimated they had covered a little less than two kilometers. They would be out from under the zoo and under the city proper in another fifteen to twenty minutes.

He glanced at the young woman who valiantly trudged through the fetid sludge beside him. He rather admired her. She had not complained. She had simply shrugged into her rucksack and plodded on.

He looked at Bormann, tramping along a few feet ahead of them. He had never before been in contact with any one of the really influential men around the Führer—except for *Standartenführer* Skorzeny, of course, who was a man unequaled. But if *Reichsleiter* Bormann was a representative sample it was just as well. He wondered if the *Reichsleiter* would have joined the debauchery he had witnessed, had he stayed behind in the Bunker. Probably, he decided, although it might be just prejudice—or intuition?—on his part, he realized. He had known nothing of the man before he had been introduced to him by the Führer; he had not known he even existed. But he did not like him. He couldn't get the vile and degrading scenes he had seen in the Bunker out of his thoughts, the sounds of depravity that had echoed through the bunker still echoed through his mind. It had offended him deeply to see fellow officers disgrace and debase themselves in so disgusting and unmilitary a manner. Somehow he equated Bormann with it all. He glanced at Eva. He wondered what she was really like. The wife of the Führer.

Eva deliberately had banished all thoughts of what lay behind her. For now. She simply could not have coped. She had only one goal—to finish the horrible, depressing march through the terrible sewer. She had never, never in her life been in such a dreadful place. The putrid air made it difficult for her to breathe and the claustrophobic confinement of the tunnel threatened her; she felt that only by desperately exerting her will could she keep the filth-encrusted walls from closing in on her. She was eternally grateful for the sturdy, sensible shoes she was wearing, but she envied the two men their high boots. Her feet were soaked and icy with cold. She thought with longing of the pair of warm woolen socks she knew was in her rucksack. She shifted the pack on her shoulders. She never knew woolen socks could be so heavy.

She was suddenly aware that the number of puddles in the bottom of the sewer had increased, and the water was deeper and felt slimy. They were walking through a part of the old conduit where several smaller drains ran into it—more than usual—all with a mere trickle of dirty water dripping into the main; some of them had the remnants of corroded gratings hanging from the openings where they joined the main sewer tunnel about two feet from the bottom. The stench of decay was overpowering, somehow different from before. Footing in the murky water of the pools was precarious, and suddenly Eva slipped. Her foot twisted under her and she would have fallen had she not grabbed hold of Willi.

"What happened?" he exclaimed, startled.

"I slipped. I twisted my ankle."

"Can you walk on it?" he asked, concerned.

"I think so," she said. "If I could just sit down for a moment."

Willi looked around. "Over there," her said. He helped her hobble over to the opening of one of the smaller tributary drains. He bent a rusty bar out of her way, and Eva sat down on the rim of the drain opening.

Bormann had stopped. He stood watching them with a scowl on his face.

"Let me see it," Willi said. He smiled up at her, reassuringly. "I have seen a lot of twisted ankles in my time," he told her. "Parachuting is almost as dangerous as walking through this place!"

Eva laughed. She felt comfortable with the young officer. "My foot is in good hands, then," she quipped. She raised her foot to him. She hung her lamp on the remnant of the rusty grating as she leaned back and put her hands on the bottom of the drain to steady herself.

She screamed!

She snatched her right hand away as if she had plunged it into a pile of red-hot coals. She shrank in panic against the wall of the drain as a long snake, glistening with sewer slime, quickly slithered past her over the edge, dropped down, and disappeared in the gloom below.

Eva sat petrified in terror, her eyes riveted on the spot where the snake had disappeared.

Bormann called out in alarm. "What is it? What happened?" He started toward them.

"Don't move!" Willi snapped at him. "Stay where you are! Stay perfectly still." He was addressing them both.

Bormann stared at him, uncomprehending. But he remained stock still.

"Herr Reichsleiter," Willi said measuredly, "please listen to me. I think I know what has happened. When I looked at the sewer diagram a short while ago I noticed we were getting near the section of the drain that runs under the Reptile House in the zoo above. The snake exhibits. The building must have been hit. The glass in the display cages shattered. And the reptile tanks. Some of the snakes must have escaped and found their way down here."

Eva was listening to him, gray-faced. She was trembling. But she did not move. Willi peered into the semidarkness of the sewer. The dim light from their kerosene lamps, faintly reflected in the murky puddles, made only a feeble attempt at defeating the gloom.

"Herr Reichsleiter," Willi continued, "use your flashlight. Shine it over the sewer bottom."

Bormann turned on his torch. The beam from it glinted on the wet wall of the tunnel. He moved it down to the floor and played it back and forth. Eva gasped.

The sewer bottom was alive with reptiles. Lizards, toads, and frogs. And snakes.

Stirring uneasily in the sudden bright light they scurried and slithered into the litter and the shadows, or slipped into the muddy water puddles.

Aghast Willi stared at the shuddery sight. There must be hundreds of snakes, he thought. Poisonous and nonpoisonous. Involuntarily he shivered. Which were which? It was impossible to know. They would have to assume that every creature crawling or slithering in the darkness could be deadly.

But they had to go on.

"Herr Reichsleiter," he said tightly, addressing himself to Bormann who stood frozen in a puddle on the sewer bottom. "with your permission we will move on, very slowly. The snakes will not attack us unless they feel threatened. They are as frightened

[76]

of us as we are of them." He looked at the ashen-faced Eva, sitting rigidly on the rim of the side drain. "I suggest we make a fireman's seat, *Herr Reichsleiter,* with our hands. And carry *Frau* Hitler between us until we reach safety. Our boots will give us some protection. *Frau* Hitler wears only shoes."

"I will walk," Eva said softly.

Willi looked at her. He recognized the determination in her voice. He did not argue.

"As you wish," he nodded. "We will move out single file." He glanced toward Bormann. "With your permission, *Herr Reichsleiter.*"

Bormann nodded wordlessly.

"I will go first," Willi said. "With the flashlight. *Frau* Hitler will follow me. And you, *Herr Reichsleiter,* will bring up the rear."

He looked around. He needed a stick. A probe. His eyes fell on the rusty iron bar he had bent out of the way for Eva. About four feet long. It would do. He wrenched it loose.

Slowly, cautiously they started out. They kept to the center of the conduit. Willi played the beam of the flashlight back and forth before him and churned the mucky, fetid water with his iron bar. They were aware of quick, furtive movement in the trash and the shadows beside them, and occasionally there was a splash of water as some creature escaped from Willi's probe.

Eva was petrified with fear. She walked stiffly, almost somnambulistically in the footsteps of Willi, disregarding the pangs of pain in her twisted foot. With each step she expected to feel a slimy, writhing snake under her foot and the pain of a poisonous strike. It took all her willpower to go on. She had always had an unreasonable fear of snakes. She knew not why, but the mere sight of them brought her close to panic. She stared at the back of Willi's head. She dared not look aside.

They were there.

She was aware of the heavy footsteps of Bormann behind her. For the first time in her life she welcomed his presence.

She wanted to curl up and cry.

But she didn't.

Suddenly Willi gave a short, hoarse cry. A large brightly marked snake lying at the edge of a puddle, partly hidden by a soaking wet newspaper, lethargic from the cold and swollen with a frog or toad, had not reacted at once to Willi's probe. Startled, it raised its triangular head, drew back, and struck straight for Eva's leg. Willi had whirled around. In the same instant the snake struck he kicked out at it. With a thud the fangs buried themselves in his boot. He got the iron bar under its body, and with a mighty heave he flung the reptile against the sewer wall.

Eva sobbed. She clung to Willi. Without a word Bormann took the flashlight from him. He probed the conduit ahead of them with its beam. Ten—fifteen meters before them the bottom of the sewer looked dry and firm.

And free of reptiles.

"Los!" he said. "Let's go!" And he walked on. Willi looked at his boot. High on the calf were two punctures about an inch apart and from them glistening venom oozed down the black leather.

Eva stared in horror at the boot.

"Did it—did it go through?" she asked.

Willi shook his head. "No," he said. "I would have felt it. And the venom is on the outside."

He took her arm. Together they followed Bormann on into the sewer.

In the yellow light of his kerosene lamp Willi pored over his plan of the sewer system. They had been walking steadily for about two hours. He estimated they'd covered about five kilometers. They should be somewhere under the Charlottenburg district. About halfway to the suburb of Wilhelmstadt. They were taking a much-needed break. The stale air was suffocating and made any exertion difficult. The sewer tunnel had been relatively dry for the last stretch and he was sitting down, leaning against the wall, resting his feet. Eva was seated next to him.

Suddenly she sat up. She peered back down into the gloom of the tunnel. She listened.

Willi looked at her. "What is it?" he asked.

"I—I don't know," Eva answered uncertainly. "I thought I heard something."

Willi looked down the conduit. He listened. He heard nothing. "A bit of loose mortar. Or dirt. Falling from the ceiliing," he said. "Little sounds carry far down here. And seem larger than they are."

Eva looked at him. "Little sounds carry far . . ." Adolf had said that to her. The same words. The first time they had made love in his private apartment on Prinzregentenplatz in Munich. On the big, red-plush-covered couch with the lacework back in his living room. She had moaned with pleasure and he had shushed her. Little sounds carry far.

It was so long ago. Thirteen years. Ever since they had always made love in silence.

She felt the tears begin to smart in her eyes. She looked away. She peered down the tunnel. There *had* been a funny noise.

"I—guess," she said.

Bormann turned to them. "Do you know where we are?" he asked Willi.

"Yes, *Herr Reichsleiter.*" Willi stood up. He pointed to the diagram. "Right about here."

Bormann nodded. "We should be at the exit point in another three hours," he said. "At about two in the morning." He frowned. The trip through the sewer was taking longer than he had anticipated. That damned girl! She had to trip over her own feet. Slow them down. He wanted to get out of the sewer as quickly as possible and on his way through the German-held corridor to Mecklenburg before it was too late. Hours counted. He had, of course, done what he could to safeguard his escape route. He had seen to it that heavy defense forces would be concentrated around Wilhelmstadt and the salient to the north. Crack SS troops. He had signed the top priority orders personally. In the name of the Führer, of course. But time *was* running out.

The stagnant water in a small puddle in the middle of the sewer shimmered into a myriad of concentric wavelets as on the street far above heavy equipment rumbled across. Tanks? German? Or Russian? He turned to Eva.

"*Liebe Frau Eva,*" he said solicitously, "how is your foot?" Even to himself his concern sounded insincere. To the devil with it! he thought angrily. The little bitch was a millstone around his neck. But a millstone he could not afford to throw off. Yet.

"Are you quite ready to go on?" he asked. "We must try to get to Wilhelmstadt as fast as we can."

Eva stood up. "I am ready," she said.

She was far from rested. Her foot hurt. She was nauseated. But she could not bear the hypocritical solicitude of the man. She held back the tears that stung in her eyes. How was she ever going to stand being with him during the weeks—even months—it would take to reach Argentina?

Her train of thought was abruptly interrupted. A distant explosion above shook the conduit. In quick succession two more blasts jarred the sewer.

"Quick!" Willi cried. "Against the wall!"

At once they ran to the wall and pressed against the side of the drain, standing close together. More explosions shook the sewer.

"Barrage," Willi shouted over the thundering rumble from above. "Coming our way. Put your arms around your head."

They did.

More explosions, ever closer, ever louder, buffeted the conduit. The last one seemed right over them. The blast rocked the entire sewer tunnel. Bits and chunks of masonry, mortar, and crusted dirt loosened by the concussion rained down from the ceiling, rattled on the sewer floor, and splashed in the puddles. The flooring shook and heaved as the earth quaked and a broad crack burst open in the wall behind them and zigzagged toward the roof of the drain with a sharp, tearing sound.

Eva pressed herself against the hard, slimy stone. She clamped her arms down around her head and screwed her eyes shut. Any moment she expected the sewer walls to collapse upon her and bury her alive. She was dimly aware of the two men pressing against her on each side, but she had never felt more alone. She waited for the final blast which would obliterate her, but the barrage had let up.

"Come on," Willi urged, "hurry! We must get away from here before they lay it on again."

He ran into the conduit. Eva and Bormann followed. They hurried, half running, down the dark tunnel, their swinging lanterns shadow-painting the sewer wall with misshapen, moving murals.

Suddenly Willi stopped. He stared ahead. In the distance the sewer was filled with a flickering reddish haze.

"What is it?" Bormann asked.

Willi frowned. "Fire," he said grimly.

"Down here? In the sewer?"

"There must be a break," Willi said. "Up ahead. A cave-in. The barrage."

"What—what do we do?" Eva asked.

"We go on," Willi said. He glanced at Bormann. The man said nothing. For a big shot who wanted to make all the decisions, he thought cynically, the *Herr Reichsleiter* was going about it in a peculiar way. He peered into the distance. He did not voice his fears that the break might have blocked their way. "Let us take a look," he said.

They hurried on.

Presently they stopped again and stood staring at what lay before them.

Willi had been right. One of the exploding artillery shells had blasted a large hole in the street above, causing a break in the sewer tunnel below with the devastating effect of a sinkhole. Brick and concrete chunks had tumbled down into the crater, filling half the conduit with burning timbers from a demolished building above. The smoke billowed through the sewer, stinging their eyes, blinding them with burning tears.

Willi quickly assessed the situation. At the down side of the break was a narrow passageway—strewn with rubble but passable. The burning timbers lay close; they would have to get past the blaze as fast as possible.

He looked up. High above—at street level—a huge pile of broken, burning debris from the demolished building hung precariously perched on the rim of the gaping pit. Any moment it could give way and fall into the conduit below, completely cutting them off.

"We have to hurry," Willi said urgently. He turned to Bormann. *"Herr Reichsleiter,* you go first. Then *Frau* Hitler. I will follow. Make your way past the fall-in. Now." He coughed. The acrid smoke was getting thicker. It was becoming difficult to breathe. "Keep your face away from the flames. Look down. Look where you step. Don't fall."

He pulled a handkerchief from his pocket. "Wet your handkerchiefs. Hold them over your mouth and nose so you can breathe. Hurry!"

Quickly both Bormann and Eva took out their handkerchiefs. They bent down and saturated them with the fetid water from a puddle in the sewer.

"Now!" Willi called.

Bormann took off. He ran toward the narrow passageway below the slope of burning rubble. With surprising agility he danced through the debris and the chunks of brickwork and concrete. Willi watched him with detached amazement. It was like watching a fat, clumsy bumpkin, he thought, walk out onto a ballroom dance floor and begin to waltz with unsuspected grace.

He turned to Eva. She was looking up at him intently, as if drawing strength from him, her pinched face awash with the reflected light from the fire.

"Go!" he said.

She turned toward the cave-in—and froze. She stared ahead through the haze. At once Willi followed her gaze.

The rubble at the base of the fall-in had come alive, and came rushing toward them. A thin, high-pitched sound rose faintly above the roar of the flames, chilling their souls.

Rats!

Hundreds of rats!

Falling, leaping, dropping they came tumbling down the fiery pile of rubble in the break, frenziedly fleeing the holocaust raging above, shrieking in panic, some of them aflame. At the bottom of the slope they milled about in frantic confusion and came pouring away from the fire toward the two people staring at them in horror.

Willi at once realized what had happened. Driven from cellar to cellar by encroaching fires, hundreds, perhaps thousands of city rats had converged in the basement of some large building directly above. The Russian barrage had set the building ablaze and blasted open the old sewer below, creating a shaft of escape for the maddened beasts, plunging them into the old, sealed-up tunnel. The realization did nothing to diminish the horror.

The fear-crazed rats were racing away from the fire toward the gloom of the sewer tunnel, coming directly at Eva and Willi. Paralyzed with terror, Eva dug her nails into his arms.

Willi galvanized into action. "Come!" he shouted. Roughly he pulled her along. At their feet the frenzied rats scrambled past. Willi kicked at them. They drew near the searing flames. "Use your handkerchief," Willi shouted, before he clamped his own dripping kerchief across his face.

Eva followed suit. At once her nose and mouth were filled with the foul stench of the sewer water as her rapid breathing drew it into her lungs. She heaved, and vomit spewed from her mouth. She wiped it away with her handkerchief and hurled it at the rats scurrying at her feet.

The flames were scorching hot on her face. Willi tried to protect her with his own body as best he could as they scrambled over the rubble through the mass of desperate rodents. The terror-maddened creatures—their long, savage teeth exposed in fury and fear, tinged yellow-red by the flames—fought them for every foothold among the debris.

Through the smoke Willi saw the hazy figure of Bormann. Like an apparition from hell he stood waiting for them. He reached out and pulled Eva the last few feet away from the fiery fall-in.

Their own frenzy almost as great as that of the rats, together they ran down the sewer tunnel. They were aware of the panic-stricken rats everywhere around them. Tiny pinpoint eyes shone red with reflected light as the beasts stared at them and scurried out of their way into the trash and filth at the edges of the drain.

Suddenly there was a loud, rumbling crash behind them.

They turned to look.

The ruin above had thundered into the sewer, filling the break with burning debris, sealing the tunnel behind them.

It was exactly 0227 hours, May 1, 1945 when they finally stood before the walled-up exit point—two hours later than their estimated time of arrival.

"The fuse is located four feet up from the ground, *Obersturmführer*," Bormann said. "In the center. Behind the mortar. There is a small pickaxe in your rucksack. Use it."

Willi nodded. He shrugged out of his rucksack and pulled the little tool from a side pocket. It was actually a mountain climber's hammer, the long, slender head pointed at one end, blunt at the other. The rucksack contained other items borrowed from mountaineering: matches in a watertight metal cylinder, and, of course, the heavy woolen socks.

Bormann and Eva took cover a short distance down the conduit.

Eva shivered. Now that deliverance from the dreadful place was near, the oppressive confines seemed to press in on her a hundredfold. She eagerly anticipated being able to climb out into the open.

Willi came running back to them. "Cover your ears!" he called.

Hardly breathing, they waited.

The sewer was deadly quiet—except for the sounds of distant battle that filtered down to them from above.

They waited.

Eva felt herself tense. Could thirty seconds seem like a lifetime? Why was it taking so long? Had something gone wrong? Had the fuse gone out? Or was the explosive wet? She didn't even know if that made a difference. But sweet Joseph, Maria, why didn't the charge go off? Fearfully she turned to Willi. She started to speak . . .

Suddenly the explosion rocked the sewer, ripping the silence asunder. The roar rolled down the conduit in disappearing thunder—and once again the sewer was quiet.

They ran to the exit point. Dust was heavy in the air, settling slowly. They all held their lanterns aloft and peered into the huge, black hole that gaped open in the sewer wall. Bormann flicked on his flashlight. They crowded up to the opening, and Bormann aimed the beam of his torch into the blackness beyond.

Eva's hand flew to her mouth. Involuntarily she gave a little cry.

[83]

About ten meters into the branch sewer a solid wall of stone, brick, and rubble totally blocked the conduit.

It would be impossible for them to dig out.

They stood in stupefied silence. Suddenly stripped of hope they stared at the massive blockage.

Their plight was clear to them all. Before them a solid wall of building-stone rubble, behind them the fiery barrier caused by the Russian barrage.

They were trapped.

7

WILLI RAN UP to the massive obstruction. He pulled and tugged and pushed at the chunks of masonry; he climbed up the jagged embankment and probed at broken cement slabs and bulky sections of brickwork. He returned to Eva and Bormann.

"Herr Reichsleiter," he said soberly, "we will not be able to get out this way. What is your alternate plan?"

Bormann stared at him. "Alternate—plan?" he repeated.

"Yes, *Herr Reichsleiter.* What is the secondary plan in case the primary plan had to be aborted?" He looked at Bormann who stood staring awkwardly at him. *Unbelievable,* he thought. Every first-week commando recruit knew that a mission *always* had to have an alternate plan. It was the A of ABC.

"There is no alternate plan," Bormann said shortly. He was annoyed. The whole damned sewer escape *was* his alternate plan. He had, of course, thought that Hitler would go to Berchtesgaden. And he would go with him. Right up until the last possible moment he had thought that. Any sensible man would have gone. All had been placed in readiness for the Führer. He had seen to it himself. But no. The Führer had delayed, and delayed until it was too late and he, Bormann, now had to use his "secondary plan" in order to escape from Berlin. He had never really expected to have to use it. But that was none of that insufferable young SS officer's affair. "We will *have* to get out this way," he finished curtly.

Willi shook his head. "Impossible, *Herr Reichsleiter.* We must find another way out. This one is sealed without any possibility of breaking through." He frowned in thought. "A hundred meters or so back we passed a junction with a branch sewer. We will have to try there."

"How?" Bormann protested. "It is walled up, too. Solidly. There is no way we can get through there."

"We will have to try."

"It would take days. Weeks. If we can dig through it at all," Bormann objected. "We do not have that kind of time."

Willi looked him squarely in the eyes. "Yes, *Herr Reichsleiter*," he said smartly. *"Zu Befehl, Herr Reichsleiter*—at your orders. What do you wish me to do?"

Bormann glared at the young officer. Without a word Willi turned on his heel and stalked back down the conduit toward the walled-up junction behind them.

The diameter of the branch sewer was about two-thirds that of the main. The opening was sealed with a solid brick wall.

Willi used his mountaineering hammer to tap on the wall, probing different spots.

The barrier was forbiddingly solid.

"We will have to blast," Willi said. "It is our only chance."

"What with?" Bormann snapped impatiently. "We have no explosives. The only place a charge was set was at the prepared exit point."

"Yes, *Herr Reichleiter*," Willi said. He did not bother to explain to Bormann what he had in mind. "If the *Herr Reichsleiter* will permit, I think I have a way to get us through."

He looked questioningly at Bormann. He received only a disapproving scowl in return. He went up to the wall. He selected a spot in the middle of the barrier where two bricks abutted one another with a third overlaid. He began to chip away at the hardened mortar in the cracks. He turned to Bormann.

"Herr Reichsleiter," he said, "I need a hole chipped out in the wall right here. About four centimeters in diameter, and as deep as you can make it."

He handed the hammer to Bormann. Without waiting for any acknowledgment he turned to Eva.

"Frau Hitler," he said, "I need your help too, if you please."

"Of course."

"Take one of the woolen socks from my rucksack. Try to unravel the yarn as best you can. Then take three strands and braid them tightly. Make a length of braid about one meter long."

Puzzled she look at him. "I will do it," she said.

Willi collected the three rucksacks. He was aware of Bormann hacking and chipping at the wall. At least the man would make a start.

Each pack contained the same set of items. There was a Walther 7.65 and a box of ammunition. A first-aid kit. The matches in their waterproof cylinder. Wire clippers. The woolen socks. Army rations. A change of underwear. There was also a compass. Willi had taken his out and put it in his pocket.

Quickly he selected several key items from the rucksacks and placed them on an undershirt on the ground. The wire clippers. All three boxes of ammo. A roll of adhesive tape from the first-aid kit. And one of the match containers. He removed the screw top and emptied the container of matches.

Using his wire clippers as awkward pliers he pried off the lead bullets from the cartridges of all the extra rounds and poured the powder into the metal cylinder that had contained the matches. He was halfway through the third box when Eva came up to him. She held out a braided string.

"Will this do?" she asked.

"*Prima!*" he said. "First class!" He pointed to Bormann, chipping away at the brick wall. "Now. Please collect a couple of handfuls of the mortar the *Herr Reichsleiter* is chipping loose. Knead it with water until you have a thick dough."

Eva nodded. With only a glance at her manicured hands, she quickly walked over to Bormann.

Willi finished the last box of ammo and poured the powder into the metal match cylinder. It was not quite full. He wanted it full. As powerful a charge as he could get. He would have only one chance. He removed the clip from the Walther 7.65 in his own rucksack. He would not need the gun. He had his P-38 in its holster on his belt. He did not touch the full clips in the guns in the packs of Eva and Bormann.

He looked up as the sound of distant explosions rumbled through the sewer. Enemy artillery, he thought, laying down a barrage. We are still under German-held territory. He returned to his task.

He quickly removed the bullets from the additional rounds and poured the powder into his container. It was now full.

With the wire clippers he cut a pie-shaped piece out of the match container lid and screwed it back onto the cylinder. He walked over to Bormann who was still chipping away at the wall. Already he had a good-sized hole chiseled out.

Willi tried the powder-filled cylinder in the hole. A ridge on one side prevented it from slipping all the way in.

[87]

"Chip that obstacle away," he told Bormann. As the *Reichsleiter* set to work, Willi took the braided string from Eva. He soaked it in kerosene from one of the lamps and inserted one end of it through the clipped lid into the powder in the match container, fastening it with adhesive tape from the first-aid kit.

Bormann stood away from the wall, and Willi placed the makeshift explosive charge in the hole. It went all the way in. He turned to Eva.

"May I have the mud, please?"

Eva held out her cupped hands. A thick, paste-like mixture of mortar, dirt, and water lay in them. Willi used it to tamp the charge firmly into the hole, leaving only a small opening from which the braided fuse hung down the wall. He lit a match.

"Better take cover," he said. "I don't know how long this fuse will burn."

He waited until they had run down the tunnel a short distance. Then he lit the kerosene-soaked braid.

It flared up. At once Willy raced away. He had taken only a few steps when the explosion blasted the quiet in the conduit. The shock force caught him in the back; he lost his balance and fell sprawling to the bottom of the sewer.

As the thundering sound of the detonation rumbled down the tunnel he sat up. Eva came running.

"Are you all right?" she cried solicitously.

He smiled up at her. "I am," he said. "Thank you."

He stood up. The dust was settling as they walked back to the wall.

A jagged hole about two feet in diameter had been blasted in the brickwork. Bormann shone his flashlight into it. The hole was about twelve inches deep before it was blocked by a wall of chipped and scarred bricks!

Stunned, they stood staring at it. Willi thought quickly. If a second blast had to be set off to break all the way through, they would have to use all their ammunition from all their guns to succeed. If. If they could blast through at all. And they would be left without any protection once they got out.

He reached into the hole. He pushed with all his might at the piece of wall still blocking the hole. It did not budge. He turned to Bormann.

"Give me the hammer," he said.

Bormann handed it to him.

Using it as a little battering ram Willi pounded on the bricks, to no avail. He glared at it as if to look through it. How thick *was* it? Was there a cave-in behind it? he wondered bleakly. Is the damned conduit filled up with rubble? As the other one was? If only he could give it a few good whacks with a little power behind them. Find out. But how? What he needed was a real battering ram. A piece of wood. An iron bar, like the one he found before. He looked around. As far as he could see in the dim light the tunnel was empty of anything useful. He tried to recall. Had he seen anything as they walked by before? He remembered nothing. But there was another way. He turned to Bormann. He contemplated the stocky man.

"*Herr Reichsleiter*," he said, "with your permission, I will need your help. We must try to knock down the remaining obstacle. And we have to use a—a battering ram."

"There is nothing like that here," Bormann said.

"I know."

"Then what can we use?"

"Me," Willi said.

They both stared at him.

"I will try to kick it in," Willi explained.

"The hole is four feet up from the ground," Eva said.

"That is why I need the *Herr Reichsleiter's* help," Willi said. "Will the *Herr Reichsleiter* follow my instructions?"

Grimly Bormann nodded.

"We will stand back to back," Willi said. "Here. Before the wall. With me facing the hole. Like this."

He placed himself and Bormann in front of the hole.

"Link arms with me," Willi said. "And hold on." They did. "Now, *Herr Reichsleiter*, bend forward. Lift me up on your back. *Frau* Hitler, you steady us."

Legs spread apart, feet firmly planted on the floor, Bormann positioned himself. Grunting, he leaned forward, swinging Willi up off the ground with his feet in line with the hole.

"Back up just a little toward the wall," Willi directed. Bormann did, as Eva held on to him.

Willi lifted his right foot. He bent his knee and kicked. Hard. Into the hole. The heavy boot hit the brick forcefully at the end of the hole. Bormann swayed, but he held his position.

Again Willi kicked. And again . . .

And suddenly the brick obstruction broke loose and fell away.

Willi rolled off Bormann's back. The *Reichsleiter* shone his flashlight through the hole. On the other side the branch sewer looked clear.

Twenty minutes later they had enlarged the opening enough to be able to crawl through. Crouched in the tightness of the small conduit, they moved into it.

They had proceeded only about twenty feet when the drain widened into a large space ringed with a sewer bench. A narrow manhole shaft led to the surface—a ladder of step irons imbedded in the wall.

Bormann shone his flashlight up the shaft. At the top was the unmistakable form of a cast-iron manhole cover.

Willi climbed up the rungs. Holding on to the top rung with one hand he placed the other on the cover and tried to push it up. It moved, but it was too heavy for him. He mounted the step-iron ladder one more rung and put his shoulders to the massive manhole cover. He strained against it. It moved, lifted, and with a clatter slid off his shoulders onto the street above. He straightened up, stuck his head out of the hole—and froze.

Directly in front of him two pairs of black boots were planted firmly on the cobblestones. He looked up, and stared into the muzzles of two Schmeisser submachine pistols held by two SS men, their coarse, mocking faces leering down at him.

But it was the sight on the sidewalk immediately before him that shocked him.

From a lamppost hung a figure. A boy, clad in the uniform of the Hitler Youth. He could be no more than fifteen, although it was impossible to tell from his misshapen face. The rope around his neck had forced his bloated tongue out between the clean, white teeth of youth, and his sky-blue eyes bulged from their sockets in dead terror. Below the lamppost stood an elderly man, hands and feet tied, his eyes riveteted on the dead boy, the blood-red *Volkssturm* armband loose on a scrawny arm. Around his neck was a noose, the rope running up across the lamppost arm above. Several SS men were standing around him. On a large sign pinned to his jacket was scrawled: *VATER UND SOHN! VERRÄTER UND AUSREISSER!*—Father and Son! Traitor and Deserter! And beneath: *Hiding* Instead of *Fighting!*

Even as Willi watched, the SS men hauled on the rope, hoisting the man into the air by the noose around his neck. A cheer went up from the executioners as the man convulsed and jerked like a macabre jumping jack as his life was slowly being squeezed from him. He died with a final spasm which violently voided his bladder and bowels. The stench immediately expanded around him. It struck Willi and made him gag.

One of the SS men prodded him with his Schmeisser.

"Get out, you sewer rat," he snarled. He turned to the SS men at the lamppost. "Get another rope ready," he called. "We have found some more lamppost fodder."

8

EVA WAS CLOSE TO PANIC. There was a hard lump in her chest, ready to explode. Numbed with terror, she stood rigidly between Willi and Bormann staring fixedly at the half dozen SS men confronting them. The men were looking at them with vindictive eyes and cruel smiles of anticipation on their lips. She did not understand. These men were not the enemy. They were SS. Germans. Why, then, did they act so menacingly? It had something to do with the horrible sight on the lamppost. But she studiously kept her eyes averted from it. And her mind closed to its ramifications. She shivered. Instinctively she moved closer to Willi.

White-faced Bormann glared at the SS men. He knew what they were. An SS flying court-martial. One of the bands of homicidal ruffians that roamed the streets of Berlin in search of deserters, meting out their own brand of justice—whenever a likely candidate was run to ground. He had seen the reports. "The mad hangmen," one field commander had called them. He had read the reports, and he had sanctioned them. The idea was to make the cowards and deserters think twice before they abandoned their posts. It had been imperative to keep the Russians from closing the ring. *Every* man counted. A few lamppost warriors, he had reasoned, would keep the rest of them fighting. Buy time. And he had needed that time. Fear, he had thought. A fear greater than the fear of fighting the enemy. Such a fear would keep the cowards and the would-be deserters from laying down their arms and hiding. Such a fear would be provided by a flying court-martial, a pack of ruthless avengers. A pack he, himself, was now facing.

He searched the brutish faces of the men. He knew what he would find. They gave no quarter. He was suddenly painfully conscious of his shabby disguise. A *Wehrmacht* corporal. With the papers to match. How could he ever make those half-wit brutes believe who he *really* was?

He drew himself up. "I demand to see the officer in charge of your detail," he said brusquely. "I am *Reichsleiter* Martin Bormann. On a special mission for the Führer!"

The SS men roared with laughter.

"Scheissdreck nochmal! That's the best one yet," one of them guffawed coarsely. "We have had *Generals* and *Gauleiters*—all on special missions, of course. But never a *Reichsleiter!*" He laughed uproariously, joined by his comrades. It was not a reassuring sound.

"Let me speak with your commanding officer," Bormann snapped. "At once!"

One of the SS men jammed his Schmeisser into Bormann's stomach. *"Reichsleiter* Martin Bormann," he taunted. He tossed his head at Willi. "I suppose that one is *Reichsminister* Josef Goebbels!"

The men roared.

Bormann ignored the gun in his stomach. "Don't be an idiot," he said curtly. "The man is a nobody. Do with him what you wish." He glared at the SS man before him, authority glinting in his beady little pig's eyes. "But the woman goes with me. She is under *my* protection. And that of the Führer. Is that understood?" His eyes bored into the man. "Now. Where is your commanding officer?"

"Shut your trap, you swine!" the SS man growled malevolently. "You won't be so damned talkative once you swing from a lamppost."

Bormann's eyes never left the man.

"I strongly suggest, soldier," he said, his voice ominously low, "I strongly suggest that you do as I order. Now! It would not be too difficult for the Gestapo to find out who you are should you decide to sabotage the Führer's vital mission."

Uncertainly the man looked away. "Arrgh, shit!" he mumbled. He turned to two of his comrades. "Take the bastard over to *Rottenführer* Heiliger. Let him string him up."

Bormann turned to Eva. "Come," he ordered. Viciously the SS man stuck his Schmeisser between them. "The bitch stays here," he snarled. "We shall wait to see what the corporal wants to do with you." He grinned unpleasantly. "I would not set my hopes too high." He spat on the ground. *"Herr Reichsleiter* Martin Bormann!"

Willi watched the SS men march Bormann over to the group of men standing around the lamppost with its grisly burden. He was not surprised at Bormann's actions. He, Willi, was—of course—expendable. If the *Reichsleiter* could pull off his bluster, more power to him. But he doubted it. He, too, had heard of the flying court-martials. The SS thugs engaged in those vicious manhunts were of a vastly different breed from his own comrades in Skorzeny's units. Small, unimportant men suddenly finding themselves with enormous powers. Powers they could not handle—only mishandle. The most dangerous adversaries of all. Reason would be wasted on them, he thought. But perhaps intimidation? In any case he would keep himself fully alert for any developments. His primary duty was to safeguard *Frau* Hitler.

And the son of the Führer.

If all else failed, should he reveal his mission to the *Rottenführer*? That the woman with him was the wife of the Führer? That she carried his child? It was only a fleeting thought. He, himself, would not have believed it.

He watched Bormann angrily argue with the SS noncom. It was obviously going badly for him. The *Rottenführer* looked at his only identification—his corporal's *Soldbuch*. He laughed. He gestured suggestively at the two lifeless bodies dangling above him on the lamppost. He threw the *Soldbuch* in Bormann's face. With his Schmeisser submachine gun he gestured to two of his men to seize the raging Bormann.

At that exact instant a sharp, ear-splitting explosion rent the air. An artillery shell hit the wall of a gutted building, toppling it into the street. Instantly the SS men hit the ground.

Willi pulled Eva down with him. He tried to shield her from the flying debris with his body. In the eternity of a few seconds a thousand thoughts and impressions crowded in on his mind, eerily etching themselves on it in the flickering light from the burning buildings which brightened the night with a fiery glow.

A second shell hit. He saw the SS men at the lamppost scatter to seek cover. He saw the *Rottenführer* turn to race for the protection of an overturned truck, and he saw the bullets from Bormann's gun rip into his back, instantly cutting him down.

Another explosion rocked the street. Russian artillery, he thought automatically. From the sound of it, fourteen-pound 76.2 field guns. The shelling came from the south. Where was the battery? In the Grunewald somewhere? The 76.2 had a range of almost fourteen kilometers. Was it the same battery that had caved in the sewer?

Explosions blasted the already ruined buildings around them. He saw Bormann start to run toward them. He saw his mouth stretched open in a shout—"Eva!"—but the sound was drowned out.

He saw the SS men hugging the ground near him, awkwardly lifting their Schmeissers to fire at the running Bormann.

He saw the *Reichsleiter* falter, grab his left shoulder, whirl around and race for the nearest ruins in a broken field run, the bullets—spitting in a staccato stream from the erratic SS Schmeissers—pursuing him. And he saw him disappear into the building wreckage.

Another shell hit. Walls came crashing down. The SS men cowered on the ground.

It was now!

Willi sprang to his feet. Roughly he pulled Eva with him, and clutching her arm in an iron grip he ran down the street, away from the SS manhunters, away from the grisly lamppost—and away from *Reichsleiter* Martin Bormann.

The streets were almost deserted. Only emergency personnel was abroad. The citizens of Wilhelmstadt were crowded into their basements and cellars in refuge. Occasional fires lit their way as Willi and Eva ran on. They crossed a broad thoroughfare littered with burned-out vehicles pockmarked with shell craters. Willi quickly oriented himself on his map. Heerstrasse. Ahead lay the Havel Lake.

The houses were increasingly suburban as they neared the lake, but none of them had escaped extensive damage.

At the water's edge they came upon a gaily painted wooden shed. A little private boathouse. Miraculously the only damage to it was a peppering of shrapnel. A crater gouged out the road close by and a motorcycle had crashed against the door to the shed. The dead courier driver lay entangled with his demolished machine, one arm sticking up stiffly into the air as in a grotesque *Heil* Hitler! salute.

Willi pushed the wrecked motorbike and its rider aside, and, seeking refuge and rest, he and Eva entered the boathouse.

Several blocks to the north Martin Bormann sought refuge in the cellar of a bombed-out house. His breath came in shallow gasps, his heart pounded in his chest. He sank down against a wall and wearily leaned against it, swallowed by the darkness. He wrapped his arms around his knees and rested his head on them.

He had looked into the face of death, and he had not liked what he saw.

Nothing was as important as his life. He had already written Eva off. There was no way he would ever find her again. It was doubtful if she and that presumptuous *Obersturmführer* would survive the enemy artillery barrage or the wrath of the SS hangmen, when they found their leader shot. So be it. He would have to do without the Hitler treasure.

He stood up. Flensburg, and the waiting submarine, lay four hundred kilometers to the north. He would have to find transportation. Once out of Berlin he could commandeer a vehicle. The enemy was closing in on both sides of the salient. He had little time to spare.

Cautiously he emerged from the cellar.

Eva Braun Hitler had already been erased from his mind.

Willi stood inside the boathouse waiting for his eyes to accept the darkness. Eva stood close behind him. He could feel her tremble. Fear? Or exhaustion? Gradually his eyes adjusted and in the faint reddish light from the fires in the street he could make out his surroundings. To his right stood a table. A small lantern with a candle stump had been placed on it, and next to it a stack of deck-furniture cushions had been piled on the floor. With a match from his spare waterproof container he lit the candle.

He walked back to the door and closed it. The lock had splintered away from the doorjamb when the motorcycle had rammed into it, but there was a heavy dead bolt on the door. He pushed it home.

Holding up the lantern, he inspected the shed. Two windows were boarded up with heavy wooden shutters bolted from the inside. There was another door opposite the door to the street. It was closed, its dead bolt in place. Three or four wooden folding deck chairs were stacked along the wall in one corner along with a folded lounge. On one wall were some framed photographs of a small boat and several smiling people enjoying themselves; on another a bad oil painting of a schooner in a storm. A ceiling fixture in the shape of a ship's lantern suspended beneath a ship's wheel hung in the center of the room. Willi did not try to turn it on. There would be no electricity. In one corner a few pieces of clothing had been thrown across a pair of rubber boots. He put the lantern on the table. He unfolded the deck lounge and placed the cushions on it.

"*Frau* Hitler," he said, "we will be safe here for a little while. Why don't you get some rest?"

She looked at him, suddenly looking bone-weary. "What about you?" she asked.

"I will rest, too," he said.

She nodded. She lay down on the lounge. Willi searched through the old clothing. He came up with a heavy jacket. He put it over her. "Try to sleep," he said.

She nodded.

In less than a minute she was breathing the deep, measured breaths of sleep.

Willi unfolded one of the deck chairs. He sat down. He looked at the sleeping woman.

She was his responsibility now. And his alone. And so was the heir of Adolf Hitler. The future of the German Reich, the Führer had said. A new generation in his image, with his ideals.

He thought of Bormann. The *Reichsleiter* was lost to them now. They would never find him nor he, them. He wondered if he was still alive. He did not know what Bormann's plan had been for them to reach Flensburg under his leadership, nor what to do if they succeeded in doing so on their own. No need for him to know, the *Reichsleiter* had said. That had been his decision. At least the man had been consistent, Willi thought wryly. *All* his decisions had been wrong!

He was suddenly grateful for the Führer's foresight in giving him his personal instructions. Included among them was an address. An address in Potsdam. "Should a real emergency arise, Lüttjohann, use it," the Führer had said. "The people there will give you aid—and further instructions."

He clenched his teeth in determination. A real emergency *had* arisen.

He spread out his map on the table next to the lantern. Potsdam was fifteen kilometers to the south. At the southern tip of the lake. If they stayed on the *Ostufer*—the eastern shore—they would have to go through Grunewald. The Russians were there. The road on the *Westufer* ran past Flughafen Gatow. His map did not indicate if the Russians had taken the area as yet but there was bound to be heavy fighting around an airstrip. Both routes were undesirable.

The lake.

If he could use the lake itself he could reach Wannsee Forest at the southern end and, from there, Potsdam.

He looked at his watch. It was just past 0400 hours. If they were to travel on the lake it would have to be under cover of darkness. That gave them barely three hours. He looked at the sleeping woman. He was about to wake her up. He thought better of it. Let her sleep as long as possible. She would need all the strength she could muster later.

He looked at the bolted door on the lake side of the cabin. Perhaps. He opened it.

Below, moored to a short pier, a small motorboat lay bobbing gently in the wavelets lapping at the shore.

His first impulse was to get the woman and set off at once. He stopped himself. Preparation. Planning. Performance. The creed of the Skorzeny commandos.

The Bormann escape route had been mapped out to take them through German-held territory. He did not know if Potsdam had fallen to the enemy or not, but it was likely that they would run into enemy patrols. They would have to appear exactly like the thousands of other refugees who always eddied in the wake of war.

He took his SS identification papers from his tunic pocket. They would do him no good. Neither would the identity disc he wore around his neck. He tore it off and discarded it along with his I.D. papers. Better no identification than identification that would harm him. His uniform. He would have to get rid of it. He rummaged through the old clothing in the corner. There was a shirt. A colorful sports shirt and a pair of dark blue pants. He changed into them. The fit was acceptable. And he could use the jacket he had spread over Eva Hitler.

What else? He would keep his gun. That would not be out of keeping. But the army issue rucksacks and most of their contents would have to be left behind. He took out the rations and broke them open.

He went over to Eva. He shook her gently. *"Frau* Hitler," he called. "Wake up! We will have to leave here in a few minutes."

Eva sat up groggily. Startled, she stared at Willi. "Your clothes . . . " she exclaimed.

He smiled at her. "A little disguise, *Frau* Hitler," he explained. "Simply as a precaution." He gave her a ration. "Please eat something," he said. "We will have to leave here soon. For Potsdam."

"Potsdam!" Eva exclaimed, startled.

"The Führer instructed me," Willi told her. "Personally. I am following his orders."

Eva nodded. She began to eat some crackers from the ration box.

"There is a small boat below," Willi said. "We will use it to make our way down the Havel. To Wannsee. And Potsdam." He walked to the door. "I will check to see what condition it is in."

Eva stood up. "I will go with you," she said.

The boat was seaworthy. Its name, *FREUDENREICH,* was painted in ornate letters on the side near the bow. The word was a double-entendre. It could mean either "Joyful" or "Reich of Joy." It was immaterial, Willi thought. Neither meaning held true any more.

A permanently built-in outboard motor provided the power. Willi examined it. It had a simple pull-string starter. He pulled it. The motor fired, sputtered, and died. It was cold. He tried again. And again.

The motor would not start.

He looked at the fuel tank. It had no gauge. In a little tool box under a seat he found a dip stick. He used it. The fuel tank was dry.

He turned to Eva. "No gasoline," he said.

He looked around. Oars. He saw none. Even if he had, he realized, he would not have been able to use them. The build of the boat made it impossible even if that had not already been the case because of their strict time limitation. Rowing, they could never make it to Wannsee before dawn.

"Herr Obersturmführer Lüttjohann," Eva said hesitantly. "Willi. Would—would the fuel in a motorcycle work in that?" She pointed at the outboard motor.

Willi stood up. Of course! "Yes," he said, "it would. A capital idea, *Frau* Hitler!"

"Eva."

He smiled at her. *"Gnädige Frau,"* he said. "With your permission—Eva." He leaped back up onto the little pier. "Come on!"

At the door to the street he handed the candle lantern to Eva. "Hold this," he said. He pulled the dead bolt open.

All of a sudden a deep, angry growl reached them from outside the door.

Willi frowned. Cautiously he opened the door a few inches.

Instantly the head of a huge, black dog catapulted itself at the opening. One ear torn to bloody shreds, lips drawn back over long, yellow fangs and wild eyes shining with malevolent fury in the candlelight, it snarled and snapped at Willi, as it thudded against the door. At once, behind the attacking beast, a roar of maddened barking and savage growls rent the air.

Eva screamed. She dropped the lantern and the cabin was plunged into utter blackness as Willi quickly slammed the door and bolted it. The furious scratching on it by the frenzied dog outside mingled with the growling and yelping in spine-chilling pandemonium.

Willi fumbled his way to one of the windows next to the door. He unlatched the bolt on the wooden shutter and swung it aside.

He looked out.

A gruesome sight met his eyes.

A pack of six or seven large dogs, all of them filthy and unkempt, their hides matted with dirt and dry blood from wounds and cuts, were fiercely worrying and tearing at the body of the dead motorcycle courier lying entangled in his demolished machine outside the door. Growling and snarling, they tore at the dead man's clothing trying to yank him free. His one hand that had been raised in a mocking salute to death, its glove ripped off, was now a bloody, misshapen claw stripped of flesh.

Willi turned away.

"What—what is it?" Eva whispered.

"Dogs," he said, shaken despite himself. "Killer dogs."

"Dogs?" she whispered. Her mind struggled with the concept of dogs as killers. How was it possible? Fleetingly she thought of her own two sweet and loving Scottish terriers, Stasi and Negus, a birthday present from Adolf. Years ago. Gentle and fun they had been. A joy. And Adolf's own beautiful German shepherd, Blondi, who had given her life for her master. The Führer had wanted to be sure the poison in the phials really worked, and Dr. Haase had tried it out on Blondi. She had died at once. It had been so sad. And inspiring, of course. A faithful dog sacrificing its life for its master. She had cried a little. Blondi had given birth to a litter of darling little puppies only a few days before; they had still been clinging to the cold teats of their dead mother when Günsche had shot them to death, one by one, in the garden. So they shouldn't suffer. She wondered what would become of Stasi and Negus. Stasi was still at the Berghof in Bavaria. Negus was in the Bunker. She had loved them so. Such loyal and devoted companions. She looked toward the door. How? How could dogs turn into such terrible creatures?

"Dogs?" she whispered again.

"A pack of wild dogs," he said. He groped around for the fallen lantern as he spoke, his voice leaden. "Forced from their demolished and burned-out homes. Separated from their dead masters. Driven mad by the bombardment, the fires, the chaos of the fighting, they roam the city in packs. Searching for food. For survival."

He found the lantern. He relit the candle.

Eva was sitting on the floor, huddled against the wall. Even in the warm glow from the candle her face looked ashen. From the moment they had started out from the Bunker she had felt her nerves shrivel and die and disintegrate into tiny dead fragments. She had been forced to see a world she had not ever dreamed existed, to step into it and become part of it. A world where a father and son hung lifeless on a lamppost, a world where dogs became vicious killers. She shivered. She tried to crawl into herself, the only place of refuge left to her.

Willi shot her a quick glance. He recognized at once that she was about to go into shock. He had to get her mind off the horror outside.

"Eva," he said sharply, "I need your help." Dully she looked at him. "Find anything that will burn easily. Paper. Cardboard. That sort of thing. Put it on the table." She stared at him, impassively. "Move!" he snapped. "Now!"

She started. She got up. She began to look around. A shelf running above the door to the boat pier had a cut-out paper border of red hearts tacked to the edge of it. She tore it off. She collected the wrappings from the rations; even Willi's discarded I.D.

Willi had broken off a leg from one of the wooden folding deck chairs. He began to wrap the flammable material collected by Eva around one end.

"Those photos on the wall," he said. "Take them out of the frames. They will burn."

She plucked the framed photographs from the wall and tore the photographs out.

"And that oil painting," Willi said.

She ripped the painting from the frame. Willi cut it into strips with his knife. He wound the strips of canvas around the paper and photos, securing it all to the chair leg with a few strips knotted around it.

He inspected his handiwork.

The chair leg made a credible torch.

He turned to Eva. "This is what we have to do," he said earnestly. "We *must* get that motorcycle in here. We need the gasoline." His eyes locked onto hers. "Listen carefully. I will light the torch. When I say, you will open the door, just enough for me to reach through. When I am ready, I will tell you to open the door all the way—and then, slam it shut. Do you understand? I am counting on you."

Eva nodded.

"Good," he said. He smiled encouragingly at her. "You will do well."

He set fire to the makeshift torch. It took time before it was ablaze.

"Now!" he called.

Eva pulled the bolt away and opened the door halfway. Willi stepped into the narrow opening.

Instantly the dogs outside looked up at him. Growling and snarling, they fixed their crazed eyes on him. The big black leader of the pack, fangs bared, leaped for his throat. He thrust the flaming torch straight at the beast. The firebrand hit the dog in the open maw, and with a startled yelp it twisted in mid-air and crashed against the side of the cabin. Howling with fury and pain it scrambled to get away. Willi waved the torch before him. Stabbing the fire at the savage pack, screaming at them, he slowly drove them back from the motorcycle and its grisly rider.

The maddened eyes of the beasts—red pits of hate and ferocity in the glow from the blazing torch—never left him. But the flames made them keep their distance.

Not taking his eyes from the dogs, Willi bent down and tugged at the wrecked motorcycle. The dogs—seeing their prize being wrested from them—moved in. Willi jabbed the torch at them, driving them back.

He pulled on the bike. Slowly it moved. He realized he could not free it from the body entangled in it; he would have to drag both bike and body into the cabin. He yanked at the motorcycle. Hackles raised along their backs, tails between their legs, burning eyes riveted on Willi, the dogs slowly moved in. Willi glanced at the torch. The flames were getting weaker. It would not last much longer.

"Open the door!" he bellowed. He strained to pull the motorbike and its gory burden into the cabin. The sweat dripped into his eyes, blurring them. He blinked it away, keeping his gaze locked on the furious beasts.

With a sudden mighty heave he hauled the motorbike halfway through the door opening. It caught on the jamb, making it impossible to close the door. With the courage of desperation the dogs lunged for him. He flailed the burning torch at them, close enough to singe the hair on their muzzles. They howled with fear and rage. He felt the bike jar and move under his hand, slowly being drawn into the cabin. Eva.

With a final roar of defiance he hurled the torch at the frenzied beasts. He leaped over the bike in the doorway into the cabin, and yanked the machine all the way in—as Eva slammed the door on the charging pack of dogs.

The shelf above the door looked sadly naked with only one or two torn red paper hearts remaining where thumbtacks had fastened the decorative border to the wood, but on the shelf itself stood two steins. Gray, without the elaborate lids that adorn most steins, they bore an inscription instead of fancy ornamentation: *Gruss aus dem ZILLERTAL Hamburg–St. Pauli*—souvenirs from the famous Hamburg beer hall. Willi and Eva used them to transfer the gasoline from the wrecked motorcycle to the tank of the motorboat. As if by tacit agreement they averted their eyes from the mangled corpse trapped in the twisted bike. Nor did they speak of it.

The boat motor caught and roared into a steady purr on Willi's first try to start it. Within minutes they were well away from the little pier, cruising down the river.

Fires burning on shore on either side cast red ribbons of rippling light across the wavelets in a spectacular display of watery fireworks.

Willi was at the wheel. Eva sat close beside him. She turned to him.

"Willi," she said, "do you have a cigarette? I forgot. I left mine with the rucksack."

He shook his head. "Sorry."

She sighed. She ached for a smoke.

Willi turned to her. "We will not get to Wannsee for a couple of hours," he said kindly. "Get some sleep."

"I will," she said. "Soon." She shifted in her seat. She felt a compelling need to be close to someone.

Willi peered into the darkness. Ahead lay the Wannsee Forest. And the safe house in Potsdam.

SS Obersturmbannführer Oskar Strelitz cursed himself. He had let the Führer down. He had allowed himself to lose his charges—*Frau* Eva and her escorts.

When he had been trapped by the fiery cave-in in the sewer and been prevented from following Bormann and the others, he had had to run all the way back to the Tiergarten entry hole to get out. At gun point he had commandeered a dispatch rider's motorcycle and raced through the zoo, emerging on Bismarckstrasse, and he had tried to follow on the streets above the course of the old sewer all the way to the exit point in Wilhelmstadt that he had been told about.

He had been well into Wilhelmstadt when he had been caught in a Russian artillery barrage coming from the direction of Grunewald. A shell had landed a few meters in front of him. The explosion had knocked him from his bike and spun him against the curb. He had been dazed, but recovered quickly. The bike was wrecked. He had continued on foot and had come upon an SS flying court-martial in the process of hanging a Hitler youth from a lamppost. He had just begun to skirt the gang of SS thugs when he had seen Lüttjohann, Eva, and Bormann emerge from the manhole. He had lain in wait, trying to decide how best to rescue his charges from the SS hangmen, if need be, when a second Russian artillery barrage had hit.

He had seen Bormann shoot the *Rottenführer* and take off into the ruins. And he had seen Lüttjohann and Eva flee in the direction of Havel Lake.

As soon as possible he had followed them.

But *verflucht nochmal*—dammit all—he had lost them again.

He ran across Heerstrasse. Before him lay a suburban community on the shore of the lake.

Suddenly, ahead, he heard the furious barking of a pack of dogs. He ran to investigate.

At a small boathouse a pack of wild-looking dogs were howling, barking, and scratching on the door.

He took out his gun and fired into the air to frighten off the beasts.

They turned on him.

He had to kill two of them—one a big, black brute—before the rest turned tail and ran.

The door to the boathouse was locked. He kicked it in.

The room beyond was empty. Another door on the lake side stood open.

He played the light from his flashlight around the room. A piece of shiny metal glinted in the beam. He picked it up.

It was the I.D. disc of one *Obersturmführer* Lüttjohann, Willibald.

He ran to the open door facing the lake. Down a few wooden steps was a small pier, and on it—incongruously—stood two beer steins.

He leaped down the stairs, two steps at a time. He picked up one of the steins. He smelled it. Gasoline. Hardly the remains of a drinking party.

He looked out over the night-dark lake.

He had found his charges. And he knew where they were headed.

He, too, had heard the Führer's instructions.

Dawn was valiantly trying to penetrate the oppressive mixture of mist and smoke that hung in an acrid haze over the lake as the little motorboat neared shore.

It had still been dark half an hour before when they passed Schwanenwerder peninsula, protruding into the river from south Grunewald. All the luxury villas on shore were lit up brightly and they had plainly heard the loud talk, raucous laughter, and drunken bellows of the Russian troops, punctuated by an occasional shot. Willi—who had stayed in midstream on the broad river—had ducked into the protective darkness of the Kladow suburb on the west bank. They were therefore approaching the east shore of Wannsee above Pfaueninsel rather than coming in from the north.

The trees of Wannsee Forest loomed tall on the horizon. Willi headed toward a stretch of wooded lakeside rather than the open beach. Wannsee and Potsdam were supposed to be in German hands. He prayed his information was still correct.

Soon a small pier, a modest motor yacht sunk beside it, presented itself out of the mist. Willi headed for it.

There was only a narrow strip of beach between the water and the woods. A couple of small sailboats had been hauled up on land and lay on their sides, their masts at oddly disturbing angles.

Willi throttled down. They were only a few meters from the pier.

Suddenly a man stood up from behind the boats. He leveled a rifle at Willi. On his arm he wore the red brassard of the *Volksturm*. Three more men joined him. Three more rifles were aimed at Willi.

And the boat hit the pier with a soft bump, as Willi killed the motor.

A sudden alarming thought struck him.

He was without any identification.

9

THE SHRILL BELL on the field telephone rang insistently. Woody put down his coffee mug and picked up the receiver.

"World War Two, Agent Ward," he said cheerfully.

"How the hell can you be so damned chipper," Major Hall growled on the phone. "It's barely dawn."

"You bet." CIC Agent Woodrow Wilson Ward grinned at the receiver. "The dawn of a new day, and a new month. Mark my word, Mort. Major. Sir. The month of May will go down in history as the month the Nazi pricks finally got their ass kicked in. Or is that too much of an anatomically mixed metaphor?"

"Simmer down," Hall said sourly. "It's too damned early for that kind of crap."

"What's up?"

"You still interested in that five-point case?"

Woody sat up. "You bet! What've you got?"

"Don't know. Just got a call. Woke me up, dammit." He snorted in disgust. "Could be something. Could be nothing."

"Everything is something," Woody philosophized. "Give me the poop."

"MP unit in Weiden is holding an SS officer."

"Big deal."

"They seem to think he's more than just another SS mandatory."

"Why?"

"*You* get the details, dammit!" Hall exploded. He was never at his best early in the morning. "Get your ass down there and find out! Five-point case or not."

"Sure thing, Mort, sweetheart." Woody grinned. "Did they give you *any* clues?"

"They think the guy may be a left-over guard officer from that Flossenburg thing," Hall said. "Or he may have something to do with that much-touted Alpine Fort. Or Fortress. Or whatever. Never could figure out what the hell the difference is between a fort and a fortress."

"That's easy, Mort," Woody quipped. "A fortress has breast-works."

Hall groaned. "Your contact in Weiden is a Lieutenant Arin. Dirk Arin. MPs. And Woody," he said sarcastically, "don't try to crack the case with wisecracks."

He hung up.

Ten minutes later Woody was tooling toward Weiden in his jeep. His cheerful mood had vanished as he had thought over what Hall had told him.

An SS officer. Possibly one of the officers who had been in command of the Flossenburg March of Death. Unconsciously he gripped the steering wheel so tightly his knuckles showed white. If the bastard was one of those inhuman fiends, he'd *give up* five points to bring him to justice!

It had been less than a week ago. He had tried to forget it. He knew he never would.

Flossenburg was a *Konzentrationslager*—a concentration camp— ten miles northwest of Weiden. When the Nazis realized that it was in danger of being overrun by elements of the 11th Armored Division, the commandant of the camp had been ordered to march those inmates who could still walk to safer ground near the Czechoslovakian border. Fifteen thousand of them had started out on what was to be truly a march of death. More than half of them fell dead on the way. Most of the rest perished soon after.

For three days and three nights, without food, without water, without rest, they had been driven on by the brutishly ruthless SS guards and their officers, clad only in their thin, ragged, striped uniforms of the camp—walking, fleshless bags of bones. Those who were too weak and fell by the wayside were either shot or bayoneted to death by the guards. So emaciated were they that they hardly bled when gutted. The road shoulders for miles were littered with their corpses. Involuntarily he shuddered. He had seen them. And he had seen—and smelled—the hellish camp from which they came.

It was the smell of death. The stink of the starving, the suffering, the dying, and the dead. A cloyingly putrescent smell that burned itself into his nostrils and his mind to stay forever. He had seen the barracks holding hundreds of living skeletons ridden with disease and dysentery, lying in rows of wooden bunks four tiers high—the dying and the dead together, for no one had the strength to remove the cadavers, their body wastes seeping and dripping from bunk to bunk to collect on the floor in a fecal, slimy mass. And the stench.

Those had been the ones too weak to walk. Theirs had been a death in filth and stink rather than in the fresh air of the death march route. Theirs had been a death even worse.

He had seen the crematorium ovens, the torture instruments, the gas chambers. He had looked upon the shriveled bodies stacked along the barracks like cordwood, and he had gazed into the sunken, imploring eyes of the still living.

And he would never forget.

It had all been brought back to him when only the day before *Stars and Stripes* had headlined: *Real Horror of Nazi Camps* "UNPRINTABLE." He hoped some day someone would print it. But he had not read the report.

Then there had been the soul-shattering mass burial near the village of Neunberg, where the SS guards had indulged in a final orgy of butchery. The villagers, who had tacitly condoned the SS atrocities and ignored the pleas for help by the few survivors, had been forced by the American unit that occupied the burg to dig the graves and bury the hundreds of concentration camp victims slaughtered within the village boundaries, with the entire village—every man, woman, and child—in attendance at the ceremony.

The shaken US army officer in charge had given the assembled villagers a grim, unforgettable message. "Only God Himself," he had said, "has the terrible might and the infinite wisdom to visit upon you, your cohorts, and your leaders the dreadful punishment you deserve. May the memory of this day and of these dead rest heavily upon your conscience and the conscience of every German so long as you each shall live!"

Was the SS prisoner he was about to interrogate one of those leaders?

Some of the white sheets of surrender, which had saved the little town of Weiden from destruction when it was seized on April 22, still fluttered pitifully from windows and gables, as Woody drove into town.

He found Lieutenant Arin—a lantern-jawed young man with a shock of light brown hair and eyes that seemed used to laughing and found it difficult to accept their current, grim duty—in his office in a small inn, taken over by his Military Police unit.

"Couple of GIs hunting for eggs found him hiding in a barn," Lieutenant Arin told him. "They brought him to us, slightly the worse for wear. Pretty bedraggled."

"What have you gotten out of him?" Woody asked. "So far?"

Arin shrugged. "Not a hell of a lot," he said. "In fact—nothing. Name, rank, and serial number, that sort of crap. The local *Bürgermeister*—the man had just recently been put in office when his Nazi predecessor was arrested by you guys—thinks the man may have had a hand in that death march that broke up a few miles from here."

"What do you think?"

Again Arin shrugged. "Possible. Although he doesn't strike me as the concentration camp guard type. Who the hell can tell?"

"Okay," Woody said. "Trot him out."

"One thing," Arin added. "The guy speaks English. Pretty good at that."

Woody raised an eyebrow. "Did he say how come?"

Arin shook his head. "I think he kind of regretted having let on. Said a lot of Germans with a higher education speak English."

"True enough," Woody agreed. He filed the bit of information away in his mind. "Okay. Let's put him through the wringer." He glanced at the MP lieutenant. "How'd you like to be the good guy?"

"Good guy?"

"Yeah. The good-guy/bad-guy interrogation routine. I'll be the heavy."

Arin grinned. "Sure," he said. "But I don't speak the Kraut language."

"No need to. The guy will understand you if you speak English. You said so, yourself. And I'm counting on it." He bit his lip in concentration. "Now here's what I want you to do. . . ."

The SS officer stood up when Woody and Lieutenant Arin entered the room in which he was being held, but he did not quite come to attention.

Woody quickly sized him up. Around forty. Good build. Clad in an SS officer's uniform with all insignia removed. Dirty and surely bedraggled but apparently well groomed underneath, if such a thing was possible. Apprehensive without being scared stiff. Well, that could be changed, he thought grimly.

Woody glowered at the German. He had borrowed a pair of major's leaves and put them on his uniform. No need to seem too badly outranked.

"I am Major Isidor Cohen," he said, addressing the prisoner in German, his voice harsh with contempt and animosity. He saw the tiny, expected flicker of alarm dart through the Nazi's eyes. Good! "I am here to ask you a few questions. And—more important—to get them answered. Is that clear?"

The German officer drew himself up. "I am *Obersturmbann-führer* Leopold Krauss," he said. "My service number is . . ."

Woody interrupted him sharply. "I don't give a shit whether you are a Lieutenant Colonel or not, nor what your damned service number is, you Kraut bastard," he snarled. "I want to know your unit, its mission, and what the hell *you* were doing holed up in the hay!" He took a menacing step toward the startled German. "I've already got a damned good idea and I'd like to . . ."

Lieutenant Arin put out a restraining hand. "Major," he said, concerned, "please . . ." He spoke in English.

"Shut up, Lieutenant!" Woody snapped. "I'll handle this." He glared at the SS officer. "Well?"

"Obersturmbannführer Leop . . ."

Woody suddenly grabbed the front of the German's jacket and pushed him up against the wall.

"Listen you Kraut shithead," he shouted, reverting to German. "You don't give me that name, rank, and serial number crap! You answer my questions or I'll ram your name, rank, and serial number up your ass!"

Lieutenant Arin, obviously disturbed by Woody's rage, stepped up to him. "Major," he said firmly, "I must insist. The Geneva Convention . . ."

Woody whirled on him. He spoke English in the taut, low voice of fury, just loud enough for the German to overhear. "Insist! You listen to me, Lieutenant. I have a damned good idea what this bastard is. One of the officers from that death march from Flossenburg. Thousands of people died. You hear? Died horribly. At the hands of such as he. *He* is one of those responsible. I say, to hell with your Geneva Convention!"

"I know that, Sir," Arin said urgently. "We are pretty convinced he *is* one of the Flossenburg camp officers. What else would he be doing here? We are about to send an exchange shipment of

PWs to the Russians. Some of the prisoners who died on that death march were Russian PWs, and the Russkies really want to get their hands on those responsible." He nodded toward the German who stood rigidly listening, his pinched face growing ashen. "I am including him," Arin finished.

"The hell you are," Woody shouted. "I want him. I'll take him. I know just how to handle a bastard like that—or my name isn't Isidor Cohen!"

"He is my prisoner, Major," Arin said coolly. "As long as he is in my charge he will be treated according to the Geneva Convention. And I have decided he goes to the Russians."

"Listen," Woody started to interrupt. "What the . . ."

"Of course," Arin went on, "I can't be responsible for what happens to him on the way over. In the last group there was another suspicious SS bastard. My men knew about it. He arrived at the Russian exchange point with both his arms and both his legs broken. In several places. He—eh, slipped getting out of the truck, they said."

"I don't care if his damned neck is broken," Woody said. "In sixteen places. But *I* want to be in on it. Personally. I . . ."

"Please, *Herr Major*," the SS officer suddenly said. He spoke English with a pronounced British accent, his voice tight and strained. "May I speak?"

The two Americans turned to him.

"You speak English, do you?" Woody asked coldly.

"Yes, Sir."

"So what have you got to say?"

"I was *not* connected with—with the Flossenburg camp, *Herr Major*," the German said anxiously. "In any way."

"Of course not," Woody said, his voice dripping with sarcasm. He turned to Lieutenant Arin in disgust. "I've had enough of that bastard," he said icily. "Send him to the damned Russians!" He strode toward the door.

"Wait! Please wait!" the German called.

Woody turned. "Well?"

"I come from the Führer Bunker in Berlin, *Herr Major*. I left there yesterday."

Woody returned. He sat down.

"Talk!" he snapped.

"I was a foreign affairs analyst in the Ministry of Propaganda," the German said. "Attached to the Führer Bunker. I worked with Dr. Goebbels. That is the reason for my English."

"What are you doing here?"

"I got out of Berlin late last night," the German went on. "I was on my way to the Alpenfestung—the Alpine Fortress. To Berchtesgaden. I knew there were German troop concentrations there. I thought—I thought I would be safe there. But there is only a narrow strip of territory between your forces and the Russians that is still held by us, and my map—my information—was not up-to-date, so I—I got lost. I found myself in American-held territory. I was hiding. Waiting until dark. So I could get back." He looked imploringly at the two Americans. "Please believe me."

Woody looked at the frightened man. He did believe him. He was convinced he was speaking the truth. The man was a mandatory arrestee because of his rank, but he was no five-pointer, for sure. He'd send him back to the Army Interrogation Center. They'd have a ball with him.

"Berlin is in chaos," the German continued. "The Russians are everywhere. Conditions in the Bunker are on the verge of total collapse—after the Führer's death."

Woody started. He sat up. He gave the SS officer a quick look. "Hitler is *dead?*" he exclaimed.

The German nodded. "The Führer committed suicide. Yesterday afternoon."

"You are certain of that?"

"I am. I saw the bodies. Before they were burned. In the Chancellery garden."

"Bodies?"

"The Führer's. And Frau Hitler's."

"Hitler had a *wife?*" Woody stared at the man.

"Yes. He got married the day before yesterday. The day before he took his own life."

"To whom?" Woody asked. He suddenly remembered. That Nazi dentist had mentioned a woman. "That mistress of his? Eva—Eva what's-her-name?"

The German officer looked at him with some surprise. "Yes," he said. "Eva Braun."

"I'll be damned."

Woody contemplated the German. He might be of more interest than he had first thought. If. If his story held water. He believed it would. But it was all strategic information. The province of Army Interrogation Center. Not tactical. Not his. He turned to Lieutenant Arin.

"He's all yours, Dirk," he said. "You did damned well. You

lie with the best of them. That Russian bullshit was a lulu. The bastard sure bought it." He nodded toward the German. "Send him back to AIC. Include what we learned in your report."

"Will do."

Without a further look at the Nazi officer, Woody left.

It was late in the day when Woody strode into the Iceberg Forward office of Major Hall.

"Hey," Hall greeted him. "Have you heard the news? Hitler is dead!"

"I know."

"The Führer, Adolf Hitler, fighting to the last breath against Bolshevism, fell for Germany this afternoon in his operational command post in the Reich Chancellery, quote—unquote. Doenitz has taken over."

"I know," Woody said. "It's a lot of bullshit."

"What do you mean?"

"Hitler killed himself. He took poison," Woody said. "He didn't die a hero's death. He crapped out."

"How the hell do you know that?" Hall asked.

Woody told him. He gave him a full report on his interrogation of *Obersturmbannführer* Leopold Krauss, late of the Führer Bunker.

"I feel kind of sorry for that broad, Eva Braun," he finished. "She sure made a piss poor choice of lovers. Some honeymoon. Bride one day—the next, *kaput!*"

10

———◦•◦———

FEARFULLY EVA WATCHED the four scowling men with their *Volkssturm* armbands. They were all up in age, even as much as fifty, she thought. How could they be like this? She was bitterly afraid—mostly because she did not understand what was happening. First the SS—now the *Volkssturm*. Their own people! Why were they being held prisoners? They were not the enemy. Just before Willi calmly had surrendered to the *Volksstürmers,* he had whispered to her out of the corner of his mouth: "Careful. Don't say anything. Let me handle it." But he had done nothing at all, except to tell the men that they were refugees from Berlin trying to get to some relatives in Potsdam. He had admitted that he had no identification—it had been lost in a shelling, he'd said, and he had meekly handed over his gun to them. The men had seemed uncertain. They had tied them up and the four of them had been arguing almost an hour about what to do with their two prisoners who sat, hands tied behind their backs, leaning against one of the beached sailboats.

One of them wanted to march them back to their headquarters and let their superiors decide. Another argued that Willi and his woman were probably deserters—or worse—and deserved to be done away with on the spot. The two others maintained that inasmuch as they were supposed to be relieved at noon—only six hours or so away—they should wait and all of them take the prisoners back.

Their sour-faced leader, who appeared to be self-appointed, was a wizened little man whose arms were so thin he'd had to pin the regulation size *Volkssturm* armband together so it wouldn't slip off his sleeve. His gray hair was cropped so short that it looked as if his beard stubble reached all the way to the crown of his head. He wore steel-rimmed glasses and had a slit for a mouth which was so tight-lipped it hardly seemed to move when he spoke. A vindictive little *Beamte*—civil service type used to riding rough-shod over others. Eva looked at him. He gave her a disquieting feeling.

The man was, of course, a stickler for rules and regulations, and his opinion prevailed: No one was supposed to leave his post until relieved. They would all wait. Rules also prescribed that all men must have identification papers. Willi had none, and conse-quently had to be considered an enemy of the people and must be treated as such. At least until his fate, and that of his woman, were decided by higher ups.

Willi seemed to be half dozing as he slouched against the boat. But his thoughts were racing—observing, assessing, and forming a plan of action.

It would be impossible to wait six hours—and then take the chance of being detained even further by some half-baked *Volkssturm* outfit. Potsdam could fall any time, and he preferred to get there while the town was still in German hands.

When he informed his *Volkssturm* captors of his true identity, he realized that he hardly looked the part of an SS officer in his gaudy sports shirt and mufti pants. He did not blame them for not taking him at his word. In their place he would have done the same. He cursed himself for having discarded his I.D. too soon. On the other hand, had he held on to it and been intercepted by a Russian patrol, which could easily have happened, his cover as a refugee who had lost everything would most certainly have been shattered.

Out of half-closed eyes he studied the four men who were guarding them. They seemed competent enough. They were more than adequately armed. Each had a Mauser Gewehr 98, the stan-dard army rifle, and two or three Stielhandgranaten 24, the com-mon stick hand grenade, clipped to his belt along with his ammo pouch. The pedantic little leader had appropriated his, Willi's, P-38 for himself, and a couple of Panzerfäuste lay ready nearby.

He considered the men. He regretted having to kill them. They probably had wives waiting for them. And children. Grown chil-dren. But there was no other way.

Eva—and the child of Adolf Hitler—came first.

"*Holla! Mensch!*"he called to one of them. "Hey! Fellow! If I don't get to a tree in a hurry my damned bladder will burst!"

Uncertainly the *Volksstürmer* looked at one another.

"How about it?" Willi asked plaintively.

The leader turned testily to one of the others. He nodded toward a nearby thicket around a few tall evergreens. "Take him over there," he growled unpleasantly. "He gave the man the P-38. "Take this. And keep him covered."

The *Volksstürmer* took the proffered gun. He checked it. It was loaded. He gestured to Willi. *"Los!"* he said. "Get up!"

Willi, his hands bound behind his back, struggled to get to his feet. In so doing he leaned toward Eva. Urgently he whispered: "Eva, *whatever happens,* trust me!"

He stood up and started to walk toward the thicket. The *Volkssturm* man followed him, covering him with the gun.

They reached the undergrowth.

"Far enough," the guard said.

Willi turned. He looked back toward the boats. They were still in plain sight. He grinned suggestively at the *Volksstürmer.*

"Du sollst dich schämen, Opapa!" he scolded. "Shame on you, Grandpa! You want to give the young lady a free look at me? Perhaps you would like to join me? We could give her a great show, you and me!"

The man reddened. "Go on with you," he snapped. "Behind the bushes."

Willi shrugged. He walked into the thicket, out of sight. He stopped. Looking over his shoulder at his guard, he nodded at his bound hands.

"How about it?" he asked. "Do I get to use my hands—or will you pull it out for me and hold it while I piss?"

Angrily the man gun-gestured. "Turn around," he said. "And no tricks. Your own gun will be right in your back."

Willi turned. He felt the gun press into the small of his back. From now on, he thought, from now on, old man, it will be exactly as a training exercise: First, get your enemy as close as possible behind you. He had. He waited. He felt the man tug at the ropes around his hands. He felt them loosen.

Now!

With all his might he stomped his heavy boot heel down on the man's instep. In the same split instant he twisted away to his left and delivered a sharp, two-handed blow to the man's wrist, numbing the hand holding a gun suddenly pointing at nothing. The man had time only to grunt in surprise and pain as the gun flew from his grip, before Willi crashed a knee into his groin. Gasping, gagging, the old man collapsed.

Willi never stopped moving. He tore his hands from the loose rope. He ripped the *Volksstürmer's* belt from his trousers and tied his feet. He used the rope to tie the man's hands and stuffed his handkerchief into his mouth, tying it there with his own.

He picked up his gun and returned it to its holster. For a brief moment he stood listening. He heard nothing.

He bent over the old man lying twitching in agony on the ground. It had been almost too easy. The *Volksstürmer's* reactions had been more than twice as slow as the slowest commando recruit in training.

One down—three to go, he thought.

He unclipped one of the stick hand grenades from the man's belt and silently, stealthily he ran into the forest, circling back toward the boats.

Eva sat propped against the boat. She did not like to be alone. She was increasingly frightened. Willi seemed to have been gone a long time. She knew he had some sort of plan in mind. She thought that was what he had meant when he whispered his warning to her. But what? Had he escaped? Was he running away? Leaving her? She suddenly felt cold. She glanced at the three remaining *Volkssturm* men. They, too, were getting apprehensive, she thought. They were glancing at one another. The leader turned toward the thicket.

"Werner," he called, "is everything in order?"

There was no reply.

The men looked worried.

Suddenly a wild cry rent the silence.

"Grenade!"

And a hand grenade came flying over the sailboat to land in the middle of the little campsite.

Instinctively the three men hit the ground, covering their heads with their arms.

In the same split moment Willi came sprinting around the boats. He ripped the rifle from the first man he came to and kicked him in his throat with his boot as he turned. Even as the man rolled over, rattling through his crushed larynx, trying desperately to suck air into his lungs through his mangled throat, his fingers digging convulsively into the earth, his eyes rolling back in agony, Willi was by the side of the second *Volksstürmer*. He smashed his rifle butt into the man's back, instantly breaking his neck. Dazed, the leader was just sitting up, fumbling for his gun, when Willi swung his rifle and caught him with the butt under his chin in a crushing blow that shattered his jaw and drove the splintered bone up into the roof of his mouth.

Willi ran to Eva. Quickly he untied her. Wild-eyed she looked at the carnage created in the span of a few seconds.

And at the grenade lying on the ground.

"I did not arm it," Willi said. "I was quite certain they would be too scared to notice."

She stared at him. It had all happened so fast her mind had scarcely had time to absorb it.

Willi picked up the grenade. He had not even unscrewed the *Sicherungskappe*—the closing cap at the end of the wooden handle, so the pull cord could be yanked to ignite the five-second fuse.

The *Volksstürmers*—as he had anticipated—had been too shocked to take notice.

He tossed the grenade at the body of the leader.

"Come, Eva," he said, "we have been here long enough."

Using his compass to orient himself, Willi picked out a landmark and started into the forest, Eva at his side. He estimated they had about two kilometers to walk before they hit the main thoroughfare of Königstrasse which bisected the area from east to west, and another two kilometers to the narrow body of water that separated Wannsee from the Babelsberg district of Potsdam where the safe house was located. Alone he could have made it in forty-five minutes, with Eva he estimated twice that.

If there were no further delays.

They stayed off the roads and paths, making their way through the forest itself. They skirted any signs of people. Many escapees from Berlin, their homes totally destroyed, had sought refuge in the Wannsee woods, living in makeshift shelters, some even with timber-shored dugouts. The refugees were not above preying on passersby—or on each other—for survival.

When they reached Königstrasse it was clogged with traffic going west, military and civilian. Trucks, armored vehicles, and army wagons competed for the roadway with hand-pulled carts, baby carriages piled high with belongings, and an endless stream of people on foot, carrying bundles and children in their arms.

They managed to get across the road, and soon they reached the bank of the channel that separated Wannsee from the Babelsberg district of Potsdam. The Böttcherberg bridge—although damaged—was still standing. It took them the better part of an hour to get across, but they were finally in Babelsberg on the outskirts of Potsdam.

Babelsberg was the industrial section of the town, which was chartered in the year 1400 after having existed as a fishing village since before 1000. The town had been enriched by Frederick the

Great, Eva knew. The Führer had told her. The warrior king had his palace retreat, *Sans Souci,* there, where he held his famous, philosophical suppers with his friend Voltaire. Adolf had told her all about it. *Sans Souci,* she thought ruefully. She knew it meant *Carefree.* Not today.

It wasn't the first time she had been to Babelsberg. The Potsdam suburb was also the center of Germany's motion picture industry. The great UFA Studios were located there. In Neubabelsberg. As so many others, Eva had been movie star struck in her earlier years; she had always enjoyed the films Adolf showed almost every night at Berchtesgaden. And five years before she had visited the glamorous UFA Studios. She had seen there the great but arrogant German film star and director, Luis Trenker. He had written, was producing, and directing, and starring in a film about Giovanni di Medici and was at UFA on some sort of business. She had, of course, met him before. Years earlier. In Munich. She never did care for the man. She really thought him a disgusting fellow, and she had said so. She once had danced with him, and he had become embarrassingly familiar and suggestive. She looked at the battle-scarred buildings. She sighed. How different it all was from then.

They were crossing a railroad marshaling yard. Though crater-pitted and rubble-strewn it was apparently still partly operative. Rolling stock, much of it disabled, filled long stretches of track. On some of the cars a singularly nonprophetic propaganda slogan had been painted: *RÄDER ROLLEN FÜR DEN SIEG*—Wheels Roll For Victory.

They were suddenly aware of a great commotion around two freight cars that stood off on a siding. A mob of about fifty or sixty people, men and woman, were breaking into one of the cars, which apparently was loaded with rations for the armed forces. Shouting, pushing, and clawing they were pulling boxes and crates from the door they had forced open, spilling cans, loaves of bread, slabs of bacon, sacks of potatoes, and other foodstuff on the ground, shoving and fighting each other for it.

Willi and Eva hurried by.

All of a sudden several trucks came roaring into the yard. Bouncing and lurching over the rough ground and the tracks, they split into two columns and quickly surrounded the area. From them poured a detachment of *Waffen* SS soldiers, rifles on the ready. The looters were trapped inside the ring.

And so were Willi and Eva.

Willi looked around quickly. Just ahead of them stood a little switch yard tool shed. Pulling Eva along, he raced for it. The door to it was locked with an old padlock. Quickly Willi searched about. A length of twisted metal from a piece of machinery demolished by the shelling and hurled out into the yard lay nearby. He snatched it up. He jammed it into the loop of the lock and brought his entire weight to bear on it. The lock broke. He tore it from the hasps and threw the door open. He pulled Eva inside.

He looked around. Tools. Shovels. A couple of railroad lanterns. An old greasy leather cap hanging on a nail. A large bin, lid open, the bottom covered with brake sand. Three sacks of sand, and a barrel of iron spikes.

"Get into the bin," he said urgently. "Scrunch down as far as you can." He grabbed one of the sacks of brake sand and tore it open.

"The—bin?" Eva exclaimed, startled.

"There is no time for questions," Willi snapped. "Just do what I say. Now! Into the bin!"

Eva climbed into the large bin. It took two sacks of sand to cover her up to her neck. She sat staring up at Willi—a detached head with huge, frightened eyes.

"Don't move," Willi said hurriedly. "Don't make a sound. Stay there until I come for you."

He placed one of the empty sacks over her head, hiding it, and stuck a shovel in the sand that covered her. He picked up a small sledgehammer and a crowbar and put on the soiled cap. He left the shed.

Outside he quickly looked around. The soldiers were closing in around the railroad cars, the looters were being herded together, gun-butted into submission. There were occasional shots as some of them tried to get away, paying for their hunger with their lives. They were the lucky ones, Willi thought.

He walked over to a double turnout switch on the tracks. He swung his sledge and gave the rail a few good whacks. Two grim soldiers came up to him, their rifles pointed at him.

"You," one of them ordered gruffly, "get over there!" He gestured menacingly with his gun. "With the others. Move!"

Willi looked up. He blew his nose with his fingers and wiped them on his oily cap.

"Sure," he drawled. "And when the supply special due to come through derails—who shall I say ordered me away from my work?" He looked, eyebrows raised, at the soldier.

"What do you mean—derails," the soldier demanded to know, glowering at him.

"See for yourself." Willi pointed to one of the intersections of the inner rails. "The wing rails at that frog have been knocked out of alignment. By the shelling." He nodded up the tracks. "And that tongue over there on number two split is bent. How the devil do you think the train will pass over this turnout without derailing?"

He gave the rail a mighty blow with his sledge, leaned forward and inspected it critically. The two soldiers looked at one another uncertainly.

"If you got nothing better to do," Willi said, "I sure could use an extra hand. There's too damned much for me to do alone." He nodded toward the shed. "Tools are in there."

"You do your job—we will do ours," the soldier growled sourly. They turned and walked away. They stopped at the shed. One of them stepped inside. He quickly reappeared, and the two soldiers walked toward the prisoners and soldiers crowded around the freight cars as Willi kept banging away on the rails.

Half an hour later the marshaling yard was empty. Willi hurried to the shed. He helped Eva from the bin. Her legs were cramped and her clothes full of sand. It was everywhere. It had penetrated through every opening in her clothing and stuck to her skin. When she moved it felt as if her underthings were lined with sandpaper. She had never been more uncomfortable. She realized it would be some time before she would be able to get it all cleaned out.

But she was safe.

The safe house Willi knew from his instruction was a small shop which sold musical instruments. The owner-operator lived upstairs. The address was Geigestrasse 77.

It was still early in the day when Willi and Eva stood staring at a huge pile of rubble and broken bricks that had once been a building.

They were looking at Geigestrasse 77.

11

—•◆•—

Eva sank down on a chunk of brickwork tumbled from a ruined wall. She was exhausted, and her exhaustion seemed to double with the shock of seeing the house she had thought of as a place of refuge blasted into ruins. Willi joined her. She looked at him.

"What do we do now?" she asked, her lifeless voice betraying her discouragement.

"We try to find out if the people who lived here are still alive," Willi said. "We try to find them."

"Even if we do," Eva said disconsolately, "how can they help us now?"

"I do not know how," Willi said firmly. "But I do know they can—and will. I am certain that the possibility of this house being destroyed in an air raid or artillery bombardment was taken into account when the center was set up. All we have to do is find the people who ran it." He frowned. "The only question is—how?"

Eva bit her lip. She looked pensive. "Willi," she asked, "have you ever read any of the books by Karl May?"

He eyed her, puzzled. He shook his head. "No," he said. "Who is Karl May?"

"He was a German author," Eva told him. "But he wrote a lot of books about the American Wild West. Indians, and cowboys, and gold prospectors. He was one of the Führer's favorite authors. Adolf read the Karl May books when he was a boy—and when he reread them a couple of years ago he gave them to me to read. He told me that those books really had opened his eyes

[121]

to the world. They had given him a lot of—of insight, he said."

Willi looked at her curiously. What was she getting at? They were not playing cowboys and Indians. "How can that help us now?" he asked.

"Well," Eva said, "the hero in the books was a man called Old Shatterhand who fought the wicked Ogellallah Indian tribe, and I remember something he once said, when in a fight with the Indians all his pack animals had run away, and he had to find them. He said: 'If you want to find a mule—think like a mule.'"

Willi sat up. "Eva," he said brightly, "the Führer—and you—are definitely right! Karl May *is* worth listening to." He grew thoughtful. "If you want to find a mule—think like a mule. Or, if you want to find the people who ran this station—think like they would."

He turned to her. "Very well, let us do just that. This place was set up to take in certain—travelers in need."

"So they would expect strangers to show up," Eva said.

"And therefore, when the building was destroyed they would have to keep an eye on it, or what was left of it."

"So they could not go too far away." Eva was growing animated. It was like a game.

"But they cannot just hang around the ruins. That would be too suspicious."

"But still, they would have to keep a constant lookout, would they not? Or they might miss somebody."

"Right. They would have to find a way to stay in the neighborhood—close enough to be able to watch the old house—and with a legitimate reason for being there."

"With friends?"

"Perhaps."

He looked around. There were many people on the street, all hurrying along on grim purposes of their own. Only one person was not on the move. A middle-aged woman. At a two-story house almost directly across from the demolished safe house she was busily tending a minute vegetable garden in a wooden box hanging from a ground-floor window.

Out of the corner of his eyes Willi watched her. He saw her cast an occasional quick glance in their direction. He stood up.

"Come on, Eva," he said, stretching, "I think I have found someone who may be able to help us."

They made their way across the street and walked up to the woman. "Excuse me," Willi said. "Could you please tell me. That ruined house across the street. Was that Geigestrasse 77?"

The woman nodded. She looked at Willi noncommittally. "Were you looking for the music shop?"

"Yes."

"It was bombed out," she said unnecessarily. "Only two days ago. It was such a terrible thing. Luckily the Bocks were in the cellar and escaped with their lives."

Willi gazed at her. "My father had a violin for repair," he said. "I was trying to find out if it was ready. Do you know where the Bocks have gone?"

The woman regarded him placidly. "They had nowhere else to go," she said. "They are staying in the attic—right here. The poor man lost everything. Except the few instruments he had in the cellar. I shall see if he has any information about your father's violin. You wait here." And she disappeared into the building.

They waited. Willi was fully aware that he had delivered himself and Eva into the hands of an unknown woman. There had been no choice. They would have to play out their hand.

Presently the woman reappeared. *"Herr* Bock would like to see you," she said. "Please come with me."

Konrad Bock, the owner of the bombed-out music shop, looked to be about fifty-five. His left arm was in a sling and he limped slightly. He greeted them politely, if, Willi thought, a bit warily.

"You have something to ask me?" the man said.

"Yes." Willi looked straight at him. "My father had a violin for repair with you. I was wondering if it was ready."

Bock nodded. "What is your father's name?"

"Wolfram Amadeus Schneeberger," Willi said.

Again Bock nodded. "The charge is forty-seven Marks and fifty-nine Pfennige," he said.

Willi sighed audibly. He had given the password. And he had received the correct countersign.

"Who are you?" Bock asked.

"Obersturmführer Lüttjohann," Willi answered, drawing himself erect. "We come directly from the Führer Bunker."

Bock nodded toward the woman. "My wife," he said, "Helga."

"You both look tired out," Helga Bock said solicitously. "I will make you a nice cup of hot coffee. *Ersatz* of course."

She busied herself at a little potbellied stove.

"Did you ask around to find me?" Bock asked, obviously concerned.

"No," Willi said, *"Frau* Bock was the first person we spoke to. We showed no curiosity."

Bock nodded. *"Ist gut,"* he said. "Curiosity kills more than cats these days." He glanced at Eva. "That is why I do not want to know who the woman with you is."

It was just as well, Willi thought. The Führer's stern words echoed in his mind: You will reveal her identity to no one, he had charged him. Absolutely no one must know who she is—until the proper time.

"As you wish," he said.

"We were told that you might come to us," Bock said. "We were told that it was only a remote possibility." He studied Willi. "I assumed that meant only if other plans went awry."

Willi nodded. "They did," he acknowledged.

Bock held up his hand. "I want to know no details," he said. "I will tell you what my orders are to assist you and what will now happen to you."

As Willi and Eva gratefully sipped the bitter but hot *Ersatz* coffee, Konrad Bock filled them in.

"Have you heard of the *B-B Achse?*" he asked Willi. "The B-B Axis?"

"No."

"Do you know of the SS escape route called *Die Spinne*—the Spider?"

"Yes. We were told of its existence at Neustrelitz. It is supposed to be a clandestine, highly organized escape route for the use of high-ranking members of the SS and the government. It will enable them to escape enemy capture and aid them to travel to foreign countries where new identities have been prepared for them. And from there they can work for the resurrection of the German Reich and the ideals of the Führer, Adolf Hitler." He knew it by heart. That was exactly what he had been told.

"That is correct," Bock nodded. "The *B-B Achse* is the elite arm of the organization. It is an escape route that starts in northern Germany—in Bremen—and ends in southern Italy—in Bari. Therefore the name, B-B Axis. From Bari transportation is arranged to the Middle East—or to South America."

Spellbound, Willi and Eva listened.

"The route goes south from Bremen through Germany and Austria," Bock continued. "Across the Alps and into Italy. Then down the coast of the Adriatic Sea to Bari."

"Are we to travel that route?" Eva asked, obviously disturbed.

Willi glanced at her. He knew what she was thinking. Such a journey, under the circumstances in which it would have to be undertaken, might take months. Would the rigors—and the time—

permit her to complete it? Even though she did not show it now, she would soon become visibly pregnant.

Bock ignored the girl. He kept talking to Willi. "The route itself consists of a series of *Anlaufstellen*—stops, or safe houses," he explained. "Every forty or fifty kilometers. These *Anlaufstellen* are staffed by loyal party members. You may trust them. Strict secrecy is enforced. The staff of each stop knows only the next stop on the route."

He stopped to accept a cup of *Ersatz* coffee brought to him by his wife. He sipped the hot, bitter brew. He continued.

"Each stop will provide you with needed funds, with means of transportation, protection, and suitable identity papers. You will be sent from stop to stop until you reach Bari."

He regarded the two young people solemnly.

"The Russians are already in Potsdam," he said. "In the southern part of town. It is literally a matter of hours before they will be here. You must leave as quickly as you are able." He looked at his wife. "Helga and I will be leaving, too. Today. We cannot afford to be captured by the Russians."

"Will you travel via the *B-B Achse* too?" Willi asked.

"No. We will not. And neither will you. Yet. The final links in the route are still being forged. Cooperation by certain organizations that enjoy acceptance by the world is still in the process of being arranged. You will go to a safe house to which I will direct you. There you will wait until it is safe for you to begin your exfiltration journey."

"How long a wait?" Willi asked. He glanced at Eva.

"Two—three weeks."

"Will you go with us?"

"No. We will travel separately. With different covers. Helga and I will only try to reach territory occupied by the Americans. We do not want to leave Germany. We will be refugees, but we will manage. You must continue to your destination. When you leave Potsdam you will join the stream of foreign laborers that even now are straggling west. Many of them are leaving the breweries here." He shrugged wryly. "All through the war they did not close down the breweries for a single day. They were, of course, declared essential, by government decree. But now . . ."

He sighed.

"I will provide you with papers that will identify you as brewery employees, natives of Luxembourg," he continued. "I was informed you speak French. Enough to convince Russian or American patrols. And both French and German are spoken in Luxembourg, so you should have no problem using either."

Willi nodded.

"I will give you exact information about your destination, how to get there, and how to identify yourselves when you arrive. You will be told there what to do next."

"Where are we headed?" Willi asked.

"You will travel—by bicycle—to the village of Rübeland. In the Harz Mountains."

Willi looked up, startled. "But—that's—that's . . ."

"One hundred and sixty-two kilometers from here," Bock said soberly. "And it will all be through enemy-held territory."

12

———•◦•———

THE EXODUS FROM Potsdam had been a nightmare. Thousands of people—refugees, slave laborers, fleeing troops—all of them terrified and quick to kill, had clogged the roads in a morass of savagery and panic. Wrecked and burned-out vehicles, military and civilian alike, littered the sides of the highways, many abandoned because of lack of fuel. And among them a pitiful jumble of broken carriages and bicycles and carts with dead horses collapsed in their harnesses. The going had been tortuous and by nightfall they had barely gotten out of town.

That first night Eva and Willi had simply collapsed in the grass of a little glade off the road near the village of Klaistow along with hundreds of other exhausted fugitives. It had been cold, and they had slept fitfully and uncomfortably, entwined with their bicycles to keep them from being stolen.

They had not been challenged once. But even if they had been, Willi was confident. Their false papers were excellent—and actually not false at all, except for the information in them. They had, in fact, been made by *Aktion Birkenbaum*—Operation Birch Tree—an SS branch that had been created especially to manufacture forged documents and foreign currency such as dollar and pound notes for the express purpose of supplying escape route travelers with foolproof identification papers and readily accepted funds.

And Konrad Bock had thought of every detail. He had even given Willi a small Luxembourg flag to fly from his bicycle. Crude, obviously homemade, its three bright, horizontal stripes of red,

[127]

white, and blue fluttered gaily from his bike, clearly marking him as a liberated slave worker—homeward bound. Submerging themselves in the tumultuous scramble they had escaped scrutiny by enemy patrols.

At first Willi had been worried that Eva might be recognized. But he had soon realized that very few people even knew of her existence, let alone what she looked like. The realization that such recognition would not be a problem had been a relief.

The roads finally became less clogged, and they only ran into occasional groups of refugees or foreign workers trudging west past the scattered debris of battle—a disabled tank, an overturned cannon, a smashed-up troop carrier.

They had stayed off the main highways and kept to the backcountry roads—some hardly more than dirt paths—traveling from one small village to another, encountering the same sullen, hostile faces in all of them, and the same disinterest from the occasional Russian patrol.

The second night they had spent in the remains of a partly burned barn at an abandoned farm near the village of Wiesenburg, and the third night—the most comfortable—in a forest outside Güterglück, perched high in a *Hochsitz*—a sort of sheltered crow's nest built up in a tree and meant for a hunter to sit in comfort and await an easy shot at an unsuspecting deer grazing below. They had hidden their bikes under branches and leaves and hauled the *Hochsitz* ladder up after them. It had been the only night they had felt safe. Eva had gone to sleep in Willi's arms. It had seemed natural.

It was Friday, May 4, a few minutes past 1400 hours. Willi and Eva had just passed through a village called Förderstedt, according to Willi's map, about twenty-five kilometers south of the town of Magdeburg. They were both fatigued. Eva was at the end of her strength. Every muscle in her body ached, her shoulders were cramped, her thighs were chafed raw by the bicycle seat and her legs sent waves of pain through her with every pump of the pedals.

Willi, hungry for news, had found part of a current newspaper crumbled up on the street as they rode through the village. A crudely printed, makeshift local tabloid. Hamburg had fallen to the British. The occupation troops in Holland and Denmark were surrendering. It would soon be all over.

They had stopped at a farm just outside the village and had asked to be allowed to wash themselves at the farmyard pump.

The farmer had taken a resentful look at the little Luxembourg flag and had gruffly ordered them off his property.

Willi looked at Eva, valiantly pedaling along the road beside him. He admired her stamina and her determination. She had not complained. But he was gravely concerned. He knew she could not last much longer and he was worried that they might not reach their destination before she was forced to give up.

They gave way and rode out onto the road shoulder as a truck approached them from behind. It was an American weapons carrier. In the back sat a handful of soldiers peering out over the tailgate. They waved and yelled at Eva.

Willi was suddenly struck by an idea.

"Fall!" he called to Eva. "Fall off your bicycle!"

She turned to him uncomprehendingly.

The truck was rapidly drawing away.

Willi quickly brought his bike up next to Eva. He swerved toward her. He gave a quick kick to her front wheel.

Eva lost control. The bike went out from under her and she took a headlong spill.

Willi stopped at once. He threw his bicycle to the ground and ran back to Eva. He bent over her. He was aware that the truck had stopped. He did not look back.

Eva was crying. She was exhausted to the point of collapse. She hurt all over. She felt absolutely terrible—and . . . Why had Willi made her fall? She lifted her tear-streaked face to him. "Why?" she sobbed. "Why did you do that? I—I hurt my knee." She tried to get up.

"Don't!" Willi said tightly. "Stay down! And let me do the talking." The urgency in his tone of voice sobered her. She obeyed.

Willi did not look up as the truck came backing up. One of the soldiers called to him.

"*Frau—kaput?*"

Willi looked up at him. Carefully he helped Eva sit up. "*Ja,*" Willi said in German. "She has been hurt. Her knee is bruised."

The GI threw up his hands. "*Nix sprechen sie Deutsch,*" he said.

"*Parlez-vous Français?*" Willi tried. "Do you speak French?"

The GI shook his head and shrugged. "*Voulez-vous couchez avec moi?*" he grinned. "That's all I know, Buddy."

Willi helped Eva to her feet. "Limp," he whispered to her. She leaned on him as he helped her over to her bicycle. The GI—obviously the linguist among them, Willi thought contemptuously—

[129]

jumped down from the truck. "Smile at him," Willi whispered. Eva gave the man a wan smile. The GI pointed to the flag on Willi's bike.

"*Luxembourg—nach Hause?*" he asked. "Home?"

Willi nodded vigorously. "*Ja*," he said, still speaking German. "We are from Luxembourg. We are trying to get home." He picked up Eva's bike. He examined it. It was undamaged. He looked at her knee. It was slightly skinned.

The GI watched. He pointed to Willi, to Eva, and to the truck. "*Du*," he said. "You. *Frau. Mitkommen.* Blankenburg?"

Willi gloated inside. They were being offered a ride. It was exactly what he had hoped for. The *Amis* were following his scenario perfectly. It was a good fifty kilometers to the town of Blankenburg in the Harz, and from there only seven kilometers to their destination. He grinned hugely and nodded vigorously.

"*Ja, Ja!*" he said. "*Bitteschön!*"

The GI helped Willi load the bikes on the truck—and several eager and willing hands reached out to help Eva climb over the tailgate.

The hour-and fifteen-minute ride was full of laughter and pleasantries as the GIs tried to make conversation and solicitously administered to Eva's knee with materials from their first-aid kits.

Eva seemed to regain her strength and spirit, Willi thought. She had winked at him, and he knew she understood why he had made her fall off the bike. Somehow it made him feel better.

She waved enthusiastically to the *Ami* soldiers as the truck pulled away after having deposited them and their bikes in Blankenburg—Harz.

Willi looked after the departing truck. They were either fools, those *Amis*, he thought, or monumentally naïve.

The road to Rübeland was winding and mountainous, and they walked a good deal of the way, pushing their bikes. It was 1627 hours—an hour and five minutes later—when they rode into the sleepy village of Rübeland.

They had reached their destination.

The address in Rübeland Willi had been given by Konrad Bock turned out to be a tiny novelty shop that in the days of flourishing tourism had sold souvenirs of the *Baumannshöhle*—the ancient, spectacular cave that was one of the tourist attractions of the Harz Mountains. The shop was closed, but in the little display window some of the uninspired *Andenken*—mementos—were still exhibited. Faded, once-gaudy pillows with the embroidered message *Grüsse aus dem Harz*—Greetings from Harz; postcards and bits of rock from stalactites; dusty little glass balls filled with water around a fake cave scene and tiny white particles that would swirl around the miniature rock pillars when shaken; and a framed, amateurish oil painting of a scene from the caverns entitled *Saülenhalle*—Hall of Columns—with the legend, *Von Inhaber Herbert Kotsch Gemahlt*—painted by the owner, Herbert Kotsch. On the green window backing next to it was a rectangular area where the paint had faded in telltale manner.

Herbert Kotsch, a stodgy, taciturn man in his fifties, and his wife, Gertrud, lived in cramped quarters behind the souvenir shop. They had placed Willi's and Eva's bicycles in a ramshackle lean-to in back of the house, and taken them into their little *Stube*.

Willi had been surprised—and not a little apprehensive—at seeing *Ami* jeeps and trucks moving through the village. There seemed to be more enemy activity than would be expected for such a remote area. It disturbed him. He asked about it.

"They will not bother you," Kotsch said.

"It is because of the factories," his wife said. Kotsch glowered at her, but she went blithely on. "Down near Nordhausen. Only forty kilometers south of here."

"What factories?" Willi asked.

"The ones that make the *Vergeltungswaffen*—the Weapons of Reprisal—the V-1 and the V-2. For Pennemünde. The factories are hidden in the underground caverns there. Huge they are. Thousands of foreign laborers worked there. That is why the SS troops defended it so stubbornly and courageously—and for so long. Only two weeks ago were the *Amis* able to overrun the Harz," she said proudly.

Willi frowned at her. "With all the enemy activity will it be safe for us to hide out here?"

The woman laughed. "But of course! With them being so busy with the factories will they have time to look for anything else? And who would expect anyone to hide in the midst of the enemy? Besides," she said mysteriously, "we will take you to a place no one could ever find you."

"Tonight," Kotsch said. "After dark. It is a place only I and *Mutti* know about. It is ready for you."

It was shortly after 2100 hours when Herbert and Gertrud Kotsch led Willi and Eva to the entrance to the *Baumannshöhle*.

Everything was boarded up except the heavy wooden door to the anteroom, which was locked. Kotsch unlocked it. Inside they each picked up a large reflector carbide lamp that had seen years of service and in single file, with Kotsch leading the way, they started down into the caves below.

It was an eerie, shadow-filled fairyland that unfolded itself before them as they made their way deeper and deeper down into the fantastic caverns. They walked along a narrow pathway through great halls with multicolored stalactites hanging like giant stone icicles from the vaulted ceilings, glistening and glittering in the light from their lamps. They wound their way through witching, unearthly galleries of tall, gnarled columns and misshapen toadstool stalagmites, past grottos of fluted, translucent sheets of rock, petrified waterfalls, and shimmering flowstones. It was grotesque and beautiful—forboding and sheltering.

They came to the last chamber of the caves open to the public.

Kotsch squeezed through a narrow opening. The others followed. Behind was a tight crawlway.

"This part of the caves is largely unexplored," Kotsch said. "It is a dangerous place for one who does not know his way. There are pitfalls and other hazards, and it is easy to get lost in the labyrinth of passages."

The crawlway widened and they were able to stand up. They walked on. Suddenly Eva stumbled. She put out a hand to keep herself from falling and scraped it along the rocky wall. She gave a little cry. Willi shone his lamp on her hand.

"It is nothing," Eva said. "Just a little scratch." She took a small handkerchief from a little pocket in her skirt. She cleaned the abrasion and wound the cloth around her hand. "It will be fine," she said. Carefully they moved on. A short distance farther on Kotsch turned into a narrow side passage and they entered a chamber of softly rounded rock, craggy walls, and striated rock curtains.

In the light from their lamps they saw two cots standing at one end of the chamber, heaped with army blankets. It was evident that the place was well stocked with all provisions necessary for comfortable survival.

Kotsch turned to them. "This is where you will stay," he said. "And wait."

"You will find everything you need," his wife said. "I have seen to that. You will not be cold. It is always comfortable down here. A little damp, perhaps, but the temperature is always the same. I have left you a deck of cards. You can play *Skat,* perhaps. You will find food and drinking water over there." She pointed. "And several two-pound cans of carbide for your lamps. And there are books for you to read."

"Any Karl May?" Eva asked, in a pathetic attempt at gallows humor.

"Karl—May?" *Frau* Kotsch asked, puzzled.

"It is all right," Eva said. "I—I was only . . ." She let the sentence die.

"I have also left you a calendar," the woman continued. She walked over to a crate and picked up a large, wind-up alarm clock. She began to wind it.

"And this," she said. "Down here time can be distorted. You must keep the clock going, and cross out the days on the calendar. That way you will not lose track of time."

"How long will we be here?" Willi asked.

"We do not know," Kotsch said. "They will inform us."

"If it is more than three weeks," *Frau* Kotsch added, "we will come to you. We will bring news and provisions. But, until then, it is best we leave you alone. We will not go near the caves. *Gott sei mit euch*—God be with you."

They left; their spectral shadows malformed on the gnarly walls until they disappeared.

Willi and Eva stood staring at the cave which would be their home for the next few weeks. With all the comforts, with all the provisions, and with the safety it afforded it was still a dark, dank, and depressing place.

Eva shivered. She had felt claustrophobic in the confines of the terrible sewer. Here—with the weight of the earth above her—the crushing feeling was ten times worse. She felt threatened. Imprisoned.

The next three weeks would be a harrowing ordeal, she thought dismally.

But she and Willi both knew that their real ordeal lay ahead.

At the same hour, 350 miles to the north, a German staff car threaded its way through the dark, narrow streets of the old harbor town of Flensburg on the Danish border, bound for the submarine pens of the *Kriegsmarine* at the heavily damaged naval base. The streets in this, the last bastion of the dying Nazi Reich, teemed with soldiers and were jammed with military traffic.

After passing through checkpoints and barriers, the vehicle came to a stop at an undamaged berth. In the black waters under the leaden night sky rode a Type XXI, ocean-going, *Schnorckel*-equipped U-Boat.

A short, stocky man dismounted from the staff car. Hunched in a large SS leather greatcoat, the collar turned up, effectively concealing his face, he walked rapidly to the gangplank and boarded the submarine, disappearing into its bloated metal womb.

Below, in his cramped quarters, *Reichsleiter* Martin Bormann at once felt the crushing feeling of claustrophobia crowd in on him. Grimly he clenched his teeth against it. He forced himself to ignore it. How else would he cope, once underway, with the weight of an ocean above him? It would be a long voyage to Argentina.

As he felt the powerful engines throb to life with a deep, trembling rumble he gave a fleeting thought to Eva Braun Hitler and the insufferable young SS officer with her. He regretted having lost the Hitler fortune to which the girl had been the key, but he did not have to rely on it. He had seen to it that he would never want for anything. That, after all, was the only matter of importance. Not the resurrection of the Third Reich.

He had no doubt that Eva and the young man were lying dead in the streets of Wilhelmstadt—or swinging from a lamppost.

If not, they soon would.

There was no way they could survive.

PART II

———◆———

May 31 – June 14, 1945

13

———•••———

CIC AGENT WOODROW WILSON WARD watched the long-legged, statuesque woman walk toward him, a cup of steaming coffee in her hand. What a looker, he thought. She moves with the elegance of one of the three Graces. Thalia, of course. Who the hell but she could look like a goddess at 0700 hours in the morning—without makeup? He remembered being totally smitten when he saw her in the film *Destry Rides Again*. A couple of years before the war. Marlene Dietrich. Would anyone ever believe that *she* was serving him coffee at 0700 hours in the dingy dining room of a small hotel in Regensburg? Hell, no. But that didn't matter. *He* knew.

Marlene handed him the coffee cup. "Good morning," she said, smiling at him. Her husky voice caressed his ears. "Here is your coffee. I know you take it black."

"Good morning," he said. "Thank you."

He watched her return to the coffee urn. Some woman, dammit!

When Corps had moved to Regensburg, CIC had set up shop in a small *Gastwirtschaft* next to a theater on Maximilianstrasse, and one day Marlene Dietrich had shown up. She was in the ETO, and had been for months, entertaining the troops. He remembered, back last October, somewhere in France—at Pont-à-Mousson just north of Nancy it had been—he'd attended a USO show starring Marlene Dietrich. In the middle of a song—from *Destry*—German artillery had opened up. It came in pretty heavy. And he remembered La Dietrich calmly saying: "We had

[137]

better cut this show short, boys. The Germans know I am here. They don't like me much, and I'm sure they're firing at me! I don't want anyone to get hurt." So the show was cut short and the piano and sound equipment loaded on the truck, and it wasn't more than five minutes later that the Krauts laid a shell right on top of the damned building, blowing it to smithereens! Marlene had been calm as a cucumber. Now that's elegance!

Apparently she preferred staying with the CIC rather than in the Officers' Guest Quarters up the street. And every morning, first thing, she was there to serve the agents coffee. She was obviously fascinated with investigation and interrogation work. And, of course, she spoke German fluently. So they'd let her question a few suspects, and he'd been impressed with her perception and astuteness. She was one bright lady—besides being the best-looking dame in the ETO—who made one helluva cup of coffee.

She was probably the closest he'd get to glamour—as in "five-pointer-glamour case," he thought gloomily. As he'd feared, occupation duty had quickly settled down to a routine of chasing after garden variety Mandatory Arrestees and minor War Criminals. It was now over three weeks after V-E Day, and it was still the same. He sometimes had the feeling he'd have to go through the entire two-inch thick Mandatory Arrestee & War Criminals Wanted List all by himself before they'd let him go home.

His despondent thoughts were broken off when the field telephone rang. He picked it up.

"Ward," he said. "CIC."

"Hope I didn't disturb your beauty sleep, Woody, my boy." It was Major Hall, being disgustingly cheerful.

"Who needs sleep," Woody grumbled. "I get enough of that on the damned job."

"Well, get your ass over here," Hall said. "I've got something I want to show you. I think it'll give you a kick. And Woody, make it *now*. I've got to get this thing back where I got it."

"Coming, Mother!" Woody wailed, imitating the inimitable Henry. He hung up.

Woody threaded his jeep across the railroad tracks near the demolished Albertstrasse *Bahnhof*. He bounced along a narrow path that snaked between deep bomb craters and corkscrew twisted rails, the result of plaster bombing attacks on the switching yards by the AAF. Actually, most of the picturesque old town of Regensburg had escaped damage by the Allied air raids which had been directed mainly against the Messerschmidt factories on the outskirts of town, against the shipping basins on the river and, of course, against the railroad marshaling yards, all of which targets had been almost totally destroyed. The only real damage to the inner city had been inflicted by the Germans themselves when they blew up the famous twelfth-century stone bridge, the *Steinerne Brücke,* in a futile attempt to stop the American advance.

Tooling down Landshuterstrasse toward Iceberg CP near the airstrip, Woody reflected on the leaflet guide to Regensburg put out by HQ. "From the dawn of history," it had stated poetically, "man has found important reasons for a settlement at this spot where the Regen River joins the Danube, Europe's longest waterway. Numerous traces of prehistoric Stone Age villages have been found and identified, some dating back about 5,000 years."

Fifty centuries, he mused. No fly-by-night dump, this Regensburg. A history of richness and renown, according to the pamphlet, and certainly one of violence and war, carnage and destruction. From the savage raids against the early Celtic settlements and the pre-Roman community of Radespona; through the bloody Roman conquest and the fortification by Marcus Aurelius, who renamed this center of Roman power on the Danube, Castra Regina, and in A.D. 179 built the Porta Praetorius—parts of which he had seen, still standing; through the besiegement and capture by Charlemagne; the ravages and massacres of the Thirty Years War and the devastating defeat before Napoleon's invincible troops; to the havoc wreaked by World War II, which once again had reduced large parts of the city to rubble and ashes.

He had read the pamphlet from cover to cover. He always got a wry kick out of those War Department publications with their neat TM numbers and official Distribution Instructions. It was as if the army were catering to a group of tourists rather than a bunch of foot-slugging GI Joes. Sightseeing information and historical commentary; cultural tips and language lessons in polite conversation: "Pardon me, gracious lady, while I arrest your husband."

Iceberg CP, which once again reunited Iceberg Forward and Rear Echelons, was located in a group of large *Kasernen*—barracks—only two miles southeast of the CIC quarters in the city proper. Once occupied by the German 10th Mounted Artillery Regiment, the complex of gray stucco buildings was virtually undamaged. The office of Major Mortimer L. Hall, CO of CIC Det. 212 was on the second floor of CP Building No. 1.

Woody's teammate, CIC Agent Jim Mahoney, was sitting in Major Hall's office when Woody entered. He waved a bunch of papers at him.

"One ball!" he guffawed. "One helluva ball! Ain't that a pisser?" He shook his head in hilarity.

"What the hell are you talking about?" Woody asked drily. "Your fraternization equipment?"

"The Führer," Jim grinned. "The great Nazi superman. One ball!"

"What he is trying so eloquently to express," Hall explained, "is that according to the Russian report of the autopsy performed on Hitler, the bastard had only one testicle."

"Looked all over for the missing one, they did; couldn't find the damned thing," Jim choked. "I knew all the time the prick was half nuts!"

Woody took the report from him. "How the hell did you get that, Mort?" he asked.

"I saw it in the office of the AC of S, G-2," Hall said. "Somehow they got hold of a copy. Unofficially. Maybe they pinched it from Krasnov's files. Copied it. It's strictly confidential. I've got to get it back, pronto. Before Streeter comes in. But I thought you'd like to see it before I do." He glared at Mahoney. "I hadn't counted on laughing boy, here, horning in." He eyed Woody. "Didn't you come up with some joker the other day who told you about the suicides? And the burnings?"

"Yeah. That SS refugee from the Führer Bunker." Woody nodded. He began to look through the report.

"I can only let you have it a few minutes," Hall said. "I don't want to get my ass in a sling."

Woody stared at the report. He was appalled. It made sickening reading. Children—six of them—the Goebbels kids, ranging in age from four to twelve, dead by cyanide poisoning, their mouths and tongues lacerated by the glass splinters from the ampules crushed between their teeth, their little bodies twisted in the convulsions of violent death . . . The roasted bodies of Joseph Goebbels and his wife, burned, charred almost beyond recognition . . . The bloated, uniformed corpse of a general, dead by poison, his face and shaven head splotched and discolored with the spots of *livor mortis* and gashed in the violence of his death throes . . . The incinerated bodies of Adolf Hitler and Eva Braun— or rather what remained of them after the conflagration had consumed them; Hitler, his fire-seared brain and dura matter visible in his skull, which was partly eaten away by the flames and with his scorched and crumbling scrotum encasing the single charcoal testicle . . . Eva, with almost the entire top of her cranium and her facial bones seared away, her mammary glands deformed and charred—she and the Führer both identified in the only way possible, through the remaining teeth and the dental work performed on them. Eva, through a special bridge with artificial teeth and Adolf, through the extensive work on the teeth in both his upper and lower jaw . . .

Woody handed the report to Major Hall. "Man," he whispered. "What a mess. What a God-forsaken mess."

On his way back to town the harrowing images conjured up by the report would not leave his mind. But there was something else. Something that nagged at the edges of his memory. Something he had read in that gruesome Russian autopsy report. Something he had been too shaken to recognize.

What?

He willed himself not to dwell on it. He knew that if he tried to force the memory to the surface it would resist and remain submerged. He had to let his conscious mind ignore it, and it might suddenly pop up.

He was nearing the railroad tracks. He wondered how long it would take to make repairs.

He stomped on the brakes.

The jeep skidded to a halt.

Repairs! That was it!

He knew what had been bothering him.

Quickly he turned the jeep around and barreled down the road—back to Corps CP.

He ran up the stairs to the CIC office, two steps at a time. He knew he had a case. A real case. A damned glamor case.

A five-pointer for sure!

The adrenalin that shot through his body and the familiar surge of exhilaration told him that.

He burst into Hall's office. "Mort," he cried, "let me see that autopsy report again."

Major Hall looked at him in startled surprise. No can do, Woody," he said. "Streeter has it already."

"Never mind," Woody snapped. He strode up to Hall's desk, obviously agitated. "I remember it." He stared at his CO. "Mort," he said emphatically, "that damned report has a hole in it big enough to drive a 2½-ton truck through!"

"What the hell are you talking about?" Hall asked.

"Document No. 13," Woody said. "The autopsy report on Eva Braun. Or rather Eva Braun Hitler. The Russians claim they identified her positively through a special dental bridge. Right?"

He looked searchingly at Hall.

Hall nodded. "So?"

"So, that damned bridge they're talking about wasn't in Eva's mouth when she died and when she was burned! It was never fitted! It was lying in some dental lab somewhere else in Berlin. That dentist I caught. In Albersdorf. Remember? He was running off at the mouth about Eva Braun and he definitely said so. So how the hell could the Russians use that damned bridge as positive identification?"

"Go on."

"Don't you see, Mort? It wasn't Eva Braun who was burned with Hitler. It couldn't have been. It was someone else. A—a substitute. Anyone."

"It could have been Eva—without her teeth."

"Okay. Sure. But that is not *certain*. There *is* no positive identification of her body, as the Russians say. The only thing that's positive is that the Russians are monkeying around with the identification of Eva. *That's* certain, dammit! Based on the forensic evidence in their autopsy report there is absolutely no basis to claim they found Eva Braun's body. Nothing. Except that damned bridge. And that's turned out to be a crock."

"So?"

"The Russians are lying, Mort. They want us to believe it *was* Eva Braun. Hitler's wife. But that damned dental bridge they used to identify her wasn't anywhere near the body when it burned. They must have planted it there *after* they found the body. If they found it at all! They're pulling something, Mort. What? Why? Ask yourself why? What the hell gives? And if the Russians aren't trying to pull a fast one the damned Nazis are! And I sure as hell would like to know *their* reason!"

Hall frowned. "It's possible your dentist informant gave you a bum steer," he suggested.

"Possible, but I do not buy it," Woody countered firmly. "Not by a long shot. I am convinced—totally convinced—that dentist gave me the straight poop."

He looked earnestly at Hall.

"I'm right, Mort," he said with quiet conviction. "I feel it in my guts. Eva Braun did *not* die in the Bunker. It was not *her* body that was burned with Hitler's."

"So, what if it wasn't Eva's body?"

"Okay," Woody said. "What if it wasn't Hitler's either?"

Hall stared at him.

"Look, Mort," Woody said earnestly, "if the Russians lied about

[142]

Eva, Hitler's wife, being dead, they might also lie about Hitler himself. Suppose she *is* alive. Suppose *he* is too. Shouldn't we know? And why the hell the masquerade, anyway?"

Hall contemplated the young agent. It was some can of worms he'd just opened. "I think you'd better have another talk with that dentist of yours," he said grimly. "I'll arrange it. Right now. AIC is still in Erlangen. "I'll give them a call. Tell them you'll be there in . . ." He looked up at Woody. "What is it? Seventy-five miles?" Woody nodded. "I'll tell them you'll be there within two hours."

He quickly consulted a directory. He made the call and was connected.

"This is Major Hall, Commanding Officer of CIC Detachment 212," he said on the phone. "We sent AIC a PW, one . . ." He looked at Woody.

"*SS Sturmbannführer* Franz Gotthelf," Woody prompted.

"*SS Sturmbannführer* Franz Gotthelf. That's correct, a major. We need to know to which detention camp he was shipped. That's correct, we want a follow-up interrogation. Okay, I'll hold."

He looked at Woody. "They're looking up their records." He listened. "Just a minute."

He turned to Woody. "When did we forward him?"

Woody frowned. "Shit!" he said. He thought. "Late April," he said. "Just about a month ago."

"Somewhere around April 30," Hall said. "I'll hold." He waited. Again he listened. He frowned. He looked up at Woody. "Who?" he asked. He looked startled. "Thank you." He hung up.

"They don't have him," he said slowly. "He was turned over to the Russians shortly after we sent him down. Proper requisition orders and all that crap." He looked soberly at Woody. "And here's the kicker. The transfer was requested by Krasnov!"

Woody gaped at him. "Major Krasnov? Vasily Krasnov? Our resident Ivan? The Russian Liaison Officer to Corps? What the hell for?"

"Beats me."

"Where's his office? I want to see him. Right now."

"Building II, third floor."

Woody was halfway out of the door.

Major Vasily Stepanovich Krasnov, 2nd Ukranian Front, Special Occupation Liaison Officer to US Army, XII Corps, smiled at Woody, a speculative smile without warmth that didn't reach his water-blue eyes above his high, rosy cheekbones.

"Yes," he said. "Your CIC Major Hall just called to tell me

you would be over, Comrade Ward. What do you wish with me?"

"I need some information, Major," Woody said. "I need to know the disposition and the whereabouts of a certain subject, a German, one *SS Sturmbannführer* Franz Gotthelf, whom you requested be turned over to your people by AIC about a month ago. A dentist."

Krasnov frowned in puzzlement. He gazed at Woody, his eyes guileless.

"What—dentist?" he asked.

14

It was three days later when Woody left his jeep at the Dismount Point near Building No. 1 at XII Corps CP. He was still seething, and visiting Corps CP again brought up his rancor, bitter in his craw. That red bastard Krasnov had brazenly lied in his teeth, and had obviously enjoyed doing so. He had categorically denied ever having heard of a German dentist named Gotthelf—or anything else for that matter—or ever having requested his transfer to Russian authorities. In fact, he doubted the man even existed. And this despite the records at Army Interrogation Center and CIC Detachment 212's own reports which clearly showed the Russian liaison officer to be a damned liar! So much for "liaison" with the Soviets. Woody had been unable to get anywhere in his quest.

It had convinced him that something—whatever the hell it was—something was being covered up, and his own familiar feeling of taut alertness in turn convinced him that he was on to something big. He had refused to quit. Despite—or more likely because of—Krasnov's duplicity, Woody was determined to pursue the matter of Eva Braun. It was on her he had concrete evidence. It was on her he might be able to build a case. And it was on the outcome of that case the question of Hitler, himself, would hinge.

He had sent out queries to all the CIC units covering the area west of Berlin—especially to units of the Ninth Army directly to the north. If Eva was still alive she would have fled Berlin, he reasoned. Of course, there was no guarantee that she had gone west, but it was odds on she had. No Kraut voluntarily fled into Russian-occupied territory.

He'd had a helluva time wording his query so it didn't come out pure gobbledygook. He didn't have the foggiest idea what Eva looked like—and no one else seemed to know—so he could give no description of her. Anyway, he hadn't wanted to be that specific. Not yet. So he had requested information about a young woman, using any name, exact age unknown, who had fled Berlin on or immediately after April 30, whose papers were either flawless or nonexistent—depending upon the circumstances of her flight, he thought—and who was in need of major dental work. A bridge. He had debated with himself whether or not to include that last bit. He anticipated the hubba-hubba ribbing he'd get. It would be of value only with regard to subjects interrogated *after* the query had been received. Who the hell would have said, "Open wide, please," during the course of a normal interrogation? In the end he had decided to leave it in. It was, after all, the only real clue he had. But he had also realized that there would be thousands of young women fitting his description.

Already he'd had several responses—some more or less tongue-in-cheek, most of them easily dismissed. He had spent most of his waking hours for three days poring over the others without finding anything that seemed worthwhile pursuing. He had actually questioned half a dozen young women—one of whom turned out to be an *SS Feldmatratze* (an SS Field Mattress), a whore who'd had her teeth knocked out by a drunken client. She'd offered her favors free to anyone who'd get them fixed.

He hadn't expected to jump into the crapper and come up smelling like a daffodil, but he was beginning to think the inquiry had been a futile effort, the whole damned search a lost cause—even with the hundreds of investigators he must have reached, and the thousands of subjects examined by them.

And now this latest one. Not really what he'd expected. Not a direct lead. But he knew the agent who'd called him about it and he knew the guy was on the level. So, next stop—Corps CP.

Major Hall looked up when Woody entered his office. "What's so all-fired important that you have to see me at once?" he asked. "You don't usually ask anyone anything."

Woody plunked himself down in a chair. He looked straight at his commanding officer. "I want a three-day R&R pass, Mort. Starting right now."

Hall snorted. "I could use a few months in Miami myself," he said drily. "Nothing doing."

"At least listen to my reason."

"Shoot." Hall leaned back in his chair with exaggerated patience.

"It's about the Eva Braun thing," Woody began.

"I thought it might be," Hall commented caustically. Woody ignored his sarcasm.

"I think I may have a pretty damned good lead," he said. "This guy at VII Corps CIC, in Halle, up north, Ninth Army territory, he called me about an elderly couple picked up on a curfew violation. Turned out they had no place to stay. They said they were refugees from Potsdam. They said they left there on May 1."

"Adolf and Eva, I presume," Hall remarked, straight-faced.

"Oh, shit, Mort, I'm serious," Woody snapped. He realized he was being too testy. The damned case was apparently becoming too much of an obsession with him. He'd have to watch it. He grinned disarmingly.

"Actually they said their names were Konrad and Helga Bock," he said. "This guy I know at VII Corps CIC—we went through basic together—well, he kind of put them through the wringer. That old hunch, you know. It turned out they'd been involved in a scheme to exfiltrate big-shot Nazis before we could nab them." He looked at Hall. "You've heard the rumors about those escape routes."

Hall nodded.

"Well, the last couple of escapees who came to them were sent on their way just before the Russians overran the place. And, get this, Mort, those two escapees were a young man—an SS officer—and a young woman. The *only* woman they processed. A woman they'd had orders to give priority, triple A, super-duper treatment to!" He looked earnestly at his CO. "Mort, I've *got* to talk to that Potsdam couple. How about it?"

Hall shook his head. "How the hell can I justify an R&R pass for you?"

"How the hell can you not?" Woody countered. "You wouldn't want to go down in history as 'For-want-of-a-nail-Hall'—or rather 'For-want-of-a-three-day-pass-Hall,' would you? The man who bungled the biggest damned case CIC Detachment 212 ever had?"

Hall looked at him skeptically. "Why do I get the feeling I'm being conned?" he asked.

"Perhaps because you are," Woody grinned. "But no kidding, I really think it's something we should investigate."

"Why not send VII Corps the information you have? Let them get on the case."

Woody looked aghast. "Mort!" he exclaimed, horror-struck. "You wouldn't!"

Hall threw up his hands. He gave a little laugh. "No, I wouldn't." He grew sober. "However—no pass," he stated firmly.

"Shit!"

"But . . ."

Woody's ears pricked up. "But?" he repeated.

"But . . . I'll arrange a twenty-four-hour TDY with VII Corps CIC for you. That's the best I can do."

"Mort, you're a fucking sweetheart," Woody exclaimed enthusiastically. "I'm practically in Halle already!"

"Just be back here on time," Hall said drily. "I don't want my agents spending their energy in another detachment's territory."

Woody made the two-hundred-mile drive to the town of Halle in just under six hours. He thought it pretty good time considering the condition of the roads. With no surprise he saw that Halle had suffered the expected wartime consequences of being an important rail hub at the junction of main railroad lines from Berlin, Leipzig, Hanover, and Frankfurt. The town's only real claim to fame was the fact that the composer, Friedrich Handel, was born there; a bronze statue of him dominated the market square in the center of town. Woody felt oddly exhilarated as he came to a stop at the building taken over by the CIC. He had a hunch— a damned strong hunch—that his trip would pay off.

He was right.

Helga and Konrad Bock, frightened and exhausted from their flight from Potsdam, seemed downright relieved to talk.

They freely told Wood of their activities as a preliminary link in the escape route called the *B-B Achse*. They told him what they knew about the organization and its supposed operation, although their knowledge was only sketchy. They told him about the young SS officer and the young woman who had been the last "travelers" they had processed in Potsdam, in the eleventh hour of their escape from the Russians, and how they had wandered aimlessly, west and south, with other displaced persons seeking refuge in American-occupied territory, until they were picked up by the Military Police for curfew violation in Neumarkt on the northern outskirts of Halle. Woody watched them closely as they talked. They displayed no more than the normal nervousness at being interrogated by an enemy officer. He believed them.

"The two young people," he asked. "The young man and the woman. Where did you send them?"

[148]

He was suddenly alerted. Had the two people tensed at his question? If so, why? It had been almost imperceptible, but it had been there. And he recognized it. Fear.

"We had instructions to send them to the Harz," Konrad Bock answered. "To the Harz Mountains. As I told you, the escape route had not as yet been completed. They had to wait. Somewhere. In hiding."

"Where in Harz did you send them?"

The Bocks glanced at each other before Konrad answered. There was an obvious closeness between them, Woody thought.

"To the village of Rübeland", Konrad said. "To a man called Herbert Kotsch. He has a souvenir shop there. At the *Baumann-shöhle.*"

"Is that where they went into hiding?"

"I do not know. We only had the name."

"Are they still there?"

"I do not know."

Woody looked straight at them. "Did you know who they were?" he asked.

This time there was no mistake—even though the tiny flicker of fear that darted through the woman's eyes was quickly gone.

"No," Konrad said. "Only the name of the SS officer. He told us. Lüttjohann, it was. We did not know the woman. I—I told the officer I did not want to know." He looked away.

Woody turned to the woman. "And you, *Frau* Bock, can you describe the young woman to me?"

Helga Bock's eyes flitted toward her husband. He sat stoically silent, staring straight ahead, as if he were afraid their eyes would meet. The woman was obviously disturbed. Frightened.

"She was in her thirties, I think," she said haltingly. "Blond. Nice-looking. She . . . she . . ." She swallowed. "I—I do not really remember . . ."

"And yet you told me she was the *only* woman you processed," Woody said, his voice arctic, his face stiff with anger. "Did that not make you curious enough to take a good look at her. To wonder?"

The woman nodded. "Yes," she said quickly. "Oh, yes! And I did. But—but I . . ." Again she sought help from her silent husband. Woody broke in, frowning at her. "And you also said you'd had special orders about her and the man with her. Yet you can't describe her?" He made himself sound as outrageously incredulous as possible. Konrad Bock spoke up.

"There was nothing unusual about the woman," he said flatly.

"We did not know her. We do not know who she was. We have told you all we know."

"Very well," Wood said. He made his tone of voice tell them he did not believe them. He stood up. He picked up his helmet—a gesture of finality. He looked from one to the other of the two Germans. "You understand, of course, that your story will be checked out. Thoroughly. There are many people in our hands who were involved with activities such as yours. Perhaps even with you. It will take a little time, of course, but we will find out. You will be held in custody until we do." He paused. He looked at the woman. "Unfortunately," he said, "we have no facilities to keep male and female prisoners together. You will therefore be separated. I can't tell you for how long. But—since you have told me all you know—we should be able to verify it in due time."

He turned to leave the room. "Unless," he added, looking back at the stricken woman, "unless, of course, you have something more to say. Now. Something you may have remembered. Something that will *convince* me that you are telling me everything you know." He gazed directly into the frightened eyes of Helga Bock. "In that case, I will see to it that you are issued proper papers so you can be on your way to wherever it is you want to go." He shrugged. "However, as it is, I will instruct the Military Police to take you to your separate detention camps."

Helga, distraught, turned to her husband. *"Konrad.* Please! Please!" she whispered hoarsely. She grabbed his arm. "I—I cannot bear to be alone."

Konrad Bock stood ramrod stiff. He said not a word.

Helga looked back at Woody. The tears were running down her cheeks. She was oblivious to them.

"There is—one thing, *Herr Offizier,"* she sobbed. "Just one thing I—I have not told you. I swear it!" She tried to compose herself. "Some while ago," she said, her voice broken, "five years, it was, I worked at the UFA film studios. At Neubabelsberg. In the wardrobe department. And—and one day there was a visitor. She was with Luis Trenker. The film actor. We—were told she was the Führer's woman." She looked at Woody, her eyes beseeching him to believe her. "The young woman who came to us later, I thought—I thought . . ." Her eyes pleaded desperately with her inquisitor. "I cannot be sure, but I thought I recognized her. I thought it was the same girl." She looked down, spent. She removed her hand from her husband's arm.

"You know her name?" Woody shot at her.

"Braun," Helga whispered. "Eva Braun."

[150]

"Why did you try to hide this from me?" Woody snapped at her. She shrank from him. Konrad suddenly spoke up.

"Leave her alone," he said. "It was *I* who told her to say nothing." He looked at Woody, eyes blazing. "We did not want *anyone* to know that we recognized the woman. It was dangerous knowledge to possess. You must realize that. And now? We have all heard that the Führer married *Fräulein* Braun. And that they died together in Berlin. The Russians have said so. Would you have us shout to the world that we, Helga and Konrad Bock, refute what the conquerors claim?"

For a while Woody stared at him.

"I will see that you get your Military Government travel papers," he said curtly. "I will expect you to cooperate fully with the officer who will be questioning you before you are let go. Is that understood?"

Bock nodded. For an instant he debated with himself if he should tell the American about the SS officer who had come to them just before they fled Potsdam. The officer who had had papers signed by the Führer himself. The officer who had also wanted to know where the young couple was going. Strelitz had been his name. *Sturmbannführer* Oskar Strelitz. He decided against it. He had not been asked. Volunteering information would only mean more interrogation, more trouble. "It is understoood," he said.

Woody turned on his heel and left the room.

It had been like swatting gnats with a sledgehammer, he thought, but he had gotten the information he was after.

Or—had he?

Was a maybe-I-think identification enough to convince the brass? Would *he* accept it if he were in Hall's shoes? He realized he would not. He needed more proof—definite proof—that Eva Braun was alive.

Perhaps the answer was to be found in the Harz. It was only about a hundred miles away.

He could be there in a few hours.

He looked at his watch. It was already past 1800 hours. And he still had to get some chow. Even if he left for Rübeland at once he wouldn't get there until well after dark—the middle of the night for the Kraut yokels. He might as well stay on in Halle and get in some sack time; go to Rübeland first thing in the morning.

The tiny village of Rübeland was a mere pinprick on the map— and not much more in the flesh, or in the half-timber, as it were—

and Woody had no trouble finding the little souvenir shop owned by Herbert Kotsch.

He stopped his jeep in front of the little building, dismounted and stood staring at it.

Across the narrow display window two rough, wooden planks had been nailed in a cross from corner to corner, and on the door a crudely hand-letter sign read: *GESCHLOSSEN*. CLOSED.

15

—•••—

WOODY WALKED UP to the display window and peered in. The space behind was empty, the faded, dusty, green felt that covered the display tiers showed clean and darker spots where the various souvenir items had stood. He tried the door. It was locked. He had expected it.

He had come to a dead end in his search for Eva.

Dammit!

Across the street, swinging on a squeaky wooden gate in a fence around a small garden, a boy—four, at the most five—was watching him with open curiosity. He jumped off the gate and came over. He stared at the jeep with obvious awe. He looked inside at the dash. He turned to Woody.

"Are you looking for *Herr* Kotsch?" he asked.

"Yes," Woody answered, "I am. Do you know where he is?"

The boy shook his tousled towhead solemnly. "He skipped out," he said. He looked wide-eyed at Woody. "Are you going to arrest him?" he asked. "And shoot him?"

"No," Woody grinned. "I just want to talk to him."

"You cannot," the boy stated with irrefutable logic. "He and *Frau* Kotsch they both left." He ran a small grimy hand over the hood of the jeep in obvious adulation. "They got themselves two new bikes," he said. "They put a lot of bundles on them."

"When did they leave?" Woody asked. "I bet you know."

The boy nodded. He squinted toward the tower of the small village church visible down the street. It had a clock with an ornate ironwork face. It showed just past ten. The boy counted on his grubby fingers. He held up three of them.

"Three," he said. "Three hours ago."

Woody cursed himself. If only he'd gotten here last night, dammit! Instead of feeding his face and drawing bunk fatigue.

"Do you know where they went?" he asked, knowing it was a futile question.

The boy shook his head. "Away," he said.

Woody squatted down beside him and looked him in the eyes. "Which way?" he asked. "Did you see which way they went?"

The boy nodded solemnly.

"Will you tell me?"

Again the boy nodded.

"Which way was it?"

The boy pointed down the street. "That way," he said. "It is the road to Hasselfelde. My aunt Ingeborg lives there." He looked at Woody. "My name is Kurt," he said. "Are you going to shoot *Herr* Kotsch?"

Woody laughed. "No way," he said. "Say, Kurt," he exclaimed, "how would you like to go for a ride in my jeep?"

The little face lit up as brightly and as suddenly as a streetlight at dusk.

"Hop in then," Woody said. Kurt scampered into the front seat. Woody slid in behind the wheel. "Tell you what," he said. "We'll drive on down toward Hasselfelde. Perhaps we'll meet *Herr* Kotsch and his wife." He looked at the boy. "You know them don't you, Kurt? You can tell me when we see them, right?"

Kurt nodded. "We can wave to them," he said.

"You bet."

Woody took out his map and spread it on his knees. Hurriedly he consulted it. Hasselfelde was twenty-three kilometers south of Rübeland. It was worth the chance. Kotsch had a three-hour head start. The roads were hilly. He and his wife could have made four or five kilometers an hour. Say they'd covered fifteen kilometers. From the town of Hasselfelde three main roads branched off to the towns of Braunlage, Nordhausen, and Harzgerode. There was no telling which one the Kotsches would take. If he were to catch up with them it would have to be before they reached Hasselfelde. It would be tight.

He put away the map. "Here we go, Kurt," he said cheerfully. "Push that button in the middle of the steering wheel. Hard."

Kurt did. He squealed with delight at the blast from the strident horn. He pushed it again and again as the jeep careened out of the village of Rübeland on the wooded road to Hasselfelde.

"Can I steer?" Kurt shouted gleefully.

"Sure," Woody said. "Put your hands on mine."

They drove on. Half an hour later they passed a black-and-white signpost which read: HASSELFELDE 4 Km. The kilometers—and time—were running out.

Woody was beginning to wonder. It might not have been such a bright idea after all. The whole thing might turn out to be nothing but a joyride. He didn't even know if the boy knew how to tell time. Or count. Some situation, he thought wryly. His whole damned five-pointer case depended on the reliability of a five-year-old kid.

They slowed down to negotiate a sharp curve in the forest-lined road. As they came out of it they saw two figures on the road ahead—a man and a woman, pushing two bicycles loaded with bundles and suitcases.

Kurt whooped. He began to wave and shout. *"Herr Kotsch! Herr Kotsch! Ich bin es!* It is me! It is me!"

The two people stopped and stood staring in shocked apprehension as Woody brought his jeep to a halt just ahead of them. He dismounted. Automatically he checked his gun in its shoulder holster. He walked up to the couple. He addressed the man.

"Gutentag, Herr Kotsch," he said pleasantly.

The man and the woman stared back at him, their eyes wide in fearful astonishment.

Kurt came running up. "It is me, *Herr* Kotsch," he cried in delight. "I was riding in an American jeep. A real American jeep! And I was steering!" He was suddenly aware of the man's ashen, apprehensive look. His little face grew sober. "Do not worry, *Herr* Kotsch," he said solicitously. "The American soldier will not shoot you. He said so."

At gun point—a wide-eyed Kurt watching—Woody patted down both Kotsch and his wife. They were carrying no weapons. He had them take their seats in the back of the jeep and placed their heavily loaded bicycles across their laps. It was uncomfortable, but it would serve to keep them from doing anything unexpected. And with the excited Kurt at his side, he took off back toward Rübeland.

They were about halfway there when a small convoy came rolling down the road toward them, apparently a supply column consisting of one jeep and three weapons carriers. Woody stopped his jeep in the middle of the road. He dismounted and stood waiting until the convoy came to a stop a short distance ahead.

A second lieutenant jumped from the lead jeep and purposefully strode up to Woody.

"What the hell do you think you're doing, soldier?" he barked angrily. "Get that damned jeep out of the way!"

Woody pulled his ID from his pocket. "W. W. Ward," he said. "CIC. In need your help." He showed his ID to the lieutenant. The officer scowled at it. "What do you want?" he asked curtly.

"I need a jeep and two men."

"We only have one jeep," the lieutenant said. "Mine."

"So I notice."

"You—you can't just—just commandeer *my* jeep," the lieutenant sputtered.

"I not only can," Woody said calmly, "but I am."

"Listen—eh—eh . . ." In vain the lieutenant looked for Woody's rank insignia. "What the hell *is* your rank?"

"My rank is confidential," Woody said, giving the officer the familiar spiel. "But at this moment I am not outranked! So, please carry out my orders, Lieutenant, right now!"

The lieutenant glared at him. "Kowalski," he called over his shoulder, "over here. On the double!"

The driver of the jeep, a corporal, came running up. The lieutenant turned to him. "This CIC agent needs the jeep," he said sourly. "You and Henderson go with him. When he's through with you, report back to the CP."

Without another word he turned on his heel and stalked back to the lead weapons carrier.

Woody and Kurt, the Kotsch bicycles in the back of their jeep, led the way into the village of Rübeland, followed by the second jeep, driven by Kowalski and with Herbert and Gertrude Kotsch, guarded by the second GI.

Woody deposited Kurt on his swinging gate, the boy aglow with adventure, and brought the Kotsches into the souvenir shop. He had the GIs bring in the loaded bicycles.

Stiffly the Germans sat watching as he searched their bundles and suitcases. He found nothing out of the ordinary.

He glared at Kotsch and his wife in silence, letting only his cold eyes move from one to the other, until he could practically feel their tense discomfort exude from them. For the subject of an interrogation the waiting, the not knowing what the interrogator knows nor what he will ask is always the worst. A man's own doubt-filled mind is his worst intimidator. He tried to think the way *they* would. That was all-important. Not how he thought they *ought* to think, but how they really did think. It was a trick of the trade and it was not easy. But it was the difference between a green interrogator—who often gave away more than he got from a clever, trained subject and likely as not was told only what he wanted to hear—and an experienced investigator. A good interrogator as a rule did not reveal how much he knew. Of course, he thought, there were occasions where violating the rules paid off. This might well be one of them. He had a hunch that Herbert Kotsch was not the simple, taciturn nonentity he made out to be. He had not told the man how he came to know his name. He would not do so. He knew it worried him.

"Why," he finally asked, "why did you leave Rübeland?" His tone of voice was low and distant, yet murderously dangerous. It contained the disquieting hint that he already knew the answer.

"We had to," Kotsch answered. "We no longer could make a living here."

"We had a good business," Gertrud broke in. "When the tourists came to visit *Baumannshöhle*. But now no one comes. No one buys souvenirs. We had to try to find something to do. Somewhere else. In Göttingen, perhaps. That is where we were going."

"Leaving your entire stock of merchandise behind?" Woody asked incredulously. He nodded toward several large cartons stacked in the room.

Gertrud shrugged helplessly. "What else could we do?" she asked. We could not take it all with us. We—we would have tried to find a buyer for it. In Göttingen. Perhaps someone to take over the shop."

It sounded plausible. Totally plausible. Why, then, did he have a feeling it wasn't? That there was something else? Something the Kotsches were hiding. And not just their true identities and activities. Or was he reading something into their fears that was not there?

He examined the identity papers taken from the two Germans. They were excellent—completely in order. Including the MG travel permit signed by a U.S. army officer named Johnson. All of them forged, he was sure. Bock had been right. The SS boys in Operation Birch Tree were top drawer.

"Your papers seem to be in order," he said. He held up the travel permit. "When did you get that?"

"The day before yesterday," Gertrud said. "It is dated. See? June

2. We got it in Blankenburg. There is an American command there. Captain Johnson gave it to us when we explained to him our troubles."

"So I see," Woody said. "Then Captain Johnson would still be in Blankenburg." He looked straight at Kotsch.

The man returned his gaze.

"Soldiers come, soldiers go," he said.

Woody kept his eyes fixed on the German. It was time to hit him—hit him hard with the jackpot question. He watched them both closely. "And did Captain Johnson know of your work for the *B-B Achse?*" He bit the words out.

They were good. Both of them. The woman drew in her breath—sharply, but almost imperceptibly. The man's eyes widened slightly, then grew hooded. But the air in the room was suddenly rife with the odor of sweat and fear, mingled with the dry smell of sun-baked dust.

It was enough. Konrad Bock had told him the truth about the couple in Rübeland.

"What—what is a *B-B Achse?*" Gertrude whispered uncertainly. "I—we . . ."

"Be quiet, *Mutti*," Kotsch stopped her. He turned to Woody. "We do not know of any *B-B Achse,*" he said. "We do not know what you talk about."

Well, well, Woody thought. Taking over are you, Herbie. "Don't you?" he mocked. "Then you have an exceedingly short memory, *Herr* Kotsch. Within the last few weeks you concealed two travelers who were to use the *B-B Achse* escape route. A young SS officer. And a young woman. We know all about that already, *Herr* Kotsch. And we know all about your SS-manufactured identity papers and your forged travel permits!" He threw the papers at the German. Kotsch did not move.

"All you will do now," Woody said, "is to corroborate certain facts for me. One: When exactly did you send the two young people on their way? Two: The exact address you sent them to."

Kotsch looked him straight in the eye. "I know nothing of what you say," he said firmly. "Nothing."

Woody stared at the man. A gust of foreboding whipped through him. Had he overplayed his hand. No, dammit! He *knew* they were involved with the escape route. But how the hell get them to admit it? And, more important, tell him what he had to know?

He had only one thing going for him. A nebulous feeling. A hunch. A hunch that had no logical explanation, but which was familiar to every seasoned CIC investigator. Something was wrong.

There was something he had overlooked. He let his eyes roam the little room. He dismissed the cartons of souvenirs. There would be nothing of interest there. The Kotsches had been content to leave it all behind. The bundles and suitcases? He'd gone through them—perhaps not thoroughly enough. And, of course, a complete body search. He'd wait to the last with that. He hated it. It seemed degrading to both the searcher and the searched. The human body has seven orifices and every one of them had to be thoroughly probed. He looked at Gertrud and Herbert Kotsch. It might have to come to that. He hoped not, but he could leave nothing undone.

He fixed his eyes on the two bikes. Each had had a bundle tied to the handlebars, another to the luggage rack over the rear wheel, and a suitcase hanging from the rack on each side of the wheel. It had all been piled back on the bikes after having been searched.

He turned to Corporal Kowalski. He pointed to one of the bikes. "Bring that bicycle over here," he said. Out of the corner of his eye—on the face of the woman—he saw what he was looking for: The slight, sudden muscle tenseness; the subtle change in breathing rhythm; the minute glint of alarm in the eyes. Was there something hidden in the bags after all? He looked at the two Germans. He wondered if they actually were who their papers said they were.

Suddenly it was clear to him. If course! That was it. Had to be. The ID papers and travel permit had been forged for the Kotsches by the SS; that he knew. But that was not all. Operation Birch Tree had had further duties.

"Grab the bags," he ordered Kowalski and the other GI. "And the suitcases. Go over everything with a fine-tooth comb. The linings. The seams. Every inch."

He watched the woman; she was the one who had the least control over her micro-momentary reflexes. Kotsch himself was like a damned cigar-store Indian. He expected to see apprehension and alarm on the woman's face. Instead, she seemed to relax.

What the hell was going on?

"*Herr Offizier,*" Kotsch said suddenly, "before you destroy our few remaining belongings, I have a statement to make."

Woody held up a hand, stopping the GIs in their search. "Go ahead," he said.

Kotsch drew himself erect. "I am *Oberst* Herbert Kotsch," he stated. "Colonel in the German Army, Retired." He suddenly spoke in a firm, authoritative voice. "You are correct. My wife and I did work for an organization that attempted to aid our country's leaders escape the vengeance of the conquerors. I was gassed in the First World War. At Marne. I could not serve my Fatherland, the Third Reich, on the field of honor. Only in this way."

"What about the young couple I asked about?" Woody pressed at once.

Kotsch nodded. "They were here. We afforded them a place to hide. That was all."

"Who were they?"

"We asked for no names."

"Where are they now?"

"They left here two days ago," the colonel said. "I do not know where they are now."

"The hell you don't!" Woody shot at the German officer. "I *know* how the escape route works. You would have sent them on to the next stop."

"You are mistaken," Kotsch said evenly. "We were not part of the route itself. Only a temporary waiting station. The couple you ask about would have been instructed where to go by others. Not by us."

Woody glared at him. Dammit!—it could be true. It did fit with what Konrad Bock had told him. Then, who? Who had given the young SS officer his instructions? The Bocks? No. His instinct—his hunch—told him that the Bocks had told the truth.

Not so Colonel Herbert Kotsch, Retired, and his wife.

Not the full truth.

He glanced at the woman. Suddenly silent, having abandoned her usual garrulous ways, she was content to let her husband do the talking.

Woody turned to Kowalski. "Go ahead, Corporal," he said. "Let 'er rip! The Colonel here has lost his memory. Let's see what *we* can find."

Surreptitiously he watched the woman. The expected reaction did not occur. No tension. No apprehension. Nothing! It did not make sense. A moment ago when he had . . .

Dammit! It did make sense!

Abruptly he nodded to the GI. "You," he said. "Soldier. Wheel that bike over here."

This time the reaction, the sudden tenseness, was there. Visibly so. The woman stared at the bike being pushed over to him as if it were made of solid gold—and about to explode.

He looked at it, curiously. It appeared quite ordinary. It had obviously seen quite a lot of use. The seat was padded; it was large and thick, made for comfort.

The seat!

Quickly he took out his knife and with a single cut slashed open the saddle. He pried the leather apart. Inside was a compact stuffing of spongy rubber. Nothing else.

The woman was staring at him, her mouth half open, her eyes wide. Unconsciously she tried to moisten her dry lips with her tongue.

Woody gave the saddle a forceful wrench and twisted it off the seat tube. He peered into the hollow frame. A couple of inches below the rim—leaving only enough space to give the saddle pin a purchase—a string was taped to the inside of the steel tube. With a finger he fished it up. He hauled it out. Attached to it was roll after roll of tightly wound new $100 bills!

He had found the further product of Operation Birch Tree!

He looked at the two bikes. He had no doubt the hollow frames of both of them were stuffed with U.S. currency. Forged, of course. But so masterly executed that only an expert might detect it.

The damned bikes *were* worth their weight in gold, he thought wryly. And they *had* just exploded in the faces of Herbert and Gertrud Kotsch.

He glanced at them. They stood frozen, chalk-faced, staring at the bikes.

It suddenly all made sense.

Gertrud and Herbert Kotsch were skipping out. Absconding with the funds given to them by their organization for dispersement to escape route travelers, hoping to be able to disappear with their loot in the chaotic aftermath of the war. Sterling characters. No wonder they had been willing to sacrifice their paltry souvenirs.

They had their own little personal fortune. It was their anxiety over that which he had detected. That was what had been nagging him all along.

He smiled sardonically at Kotsch. "Well, *Herr Oberst,*" he said. "It looks as if this leg of the *B-B Achse* will be without funds for awhile."

Kotsch remained silent.

"Consider yourself lucky," Woody went on. "The forgeries are good. Damned good. But sooner or later you would have been caught. And would have had to pay the price." He regarded the man speculatively. "You will, of course, have to be tried by the Military Government courts—you and your wife. You will, of course, be placed in a Detention Camp. Probably near Halle." He looked at the bikes. He sighed. "I will do my best to ensure your safety there," he said. "But—I can promise nothing."

Kotsch looked up. "Safety," he frowned. "Promise? I do not know what you mean."

"Oh, it's quite simple, *Herr Oberst*," Woody explained guilelessly. "The Halle Detection Camp is like the other camps. Internal security is provided by the internees themselves." He looked pityingly at the Kotsches. "Once they learn that you tried to defraud your organization—betrayed the Reich, as it were—running off with their money given you in trust, your safety may be endangered. I . . . ."

"We did not!" Kotch burst out. "Our orders . . . ."

"But will your fellow internees know that?" Woody asked. "Will they believe you—or the evidence?" He glanced at the bikes.

Kotsch clamped his mouth shut. He knew the answer.

"Unfortunately," Woody went on, "unfortunately we have had a few rather messy cases like this before. And there *are* other internees at the Halle camp who worked in organizations such as yours." He shrugged. "They may take actions that—I'm sure you understand, *Herr Oberst*—that are difficult if not impossible for us to control."

The Kotsches looked soberly at one another, fear pinching their faces. Gertrud instinctively moved closer to her husband.

"Of course," Woody said tentatively, "no one at the camp need know of your—eh—temporary lapse of discretion. I could keep that between us."

Kotsch looked at him. "For a price, I take it," he said bitterly.

Woody could almost see the wheels spin in the German's head. He would rather take his chances with his enemies than with his own kind.

"For a price," he nodded.

Kotsch sighed. He clutched his wife's arm.

"The address is Bebelgasse 49," he said tonelessly. "In Eisenach."

"And the password?"

"*Baumannshöhle.*"

"Countersign?"

"*Hermannshöhle.*"

Woody turned to Kowalski. "Corporal," he said, "you will take the prisoners—and their bikes—with you when you return to your unit."

"Yes, Sir."

"I will write a report and forward it to your CO." He turned to Kotsch. "Just one more thing, *Herr Oberst,*" he said. "I want to see where that young couple was hidden."

Kotsch shrugged. "I no longer have the key," he said.

"Don't worry," Woody assured him. "We'll manage." He motioned to Kowalski. "Corporal, you come with us."

The lock on the door to *Baumannshöhle* yielded to the second blow of Kowalski's gun butt. By the light of the carbide lamps the three men descended into the caverns below. They made their way through the halls and chambers, past contorted pillars of stone and glistening stalactites and stalagmites, marveling at the spectacularly gnarled and craggy rock formations. They squeezed through the narrow opening at the end of the public caves, negotiated the tight corridor, and finally stood in the chamber that had been the hiding place for the *B-B Achse* travelers.

Woody looked around. Two cots, folded, stood leaning against the wall. A pile of German army blankets lay next to them, as well as several books. At the opposite end of the cave stood a few still-sealed crates and cardboard boxes, and several more open ones, some filled with debris, torn rations wrappings, and empty food and carbide cans. Woody walked over to the trash boxes. He tipped one of them over. The trash spilled out onto the rocky floor: the crumpled paper, empty cans, and a deck of well-worn playing cards as well as other refuse. He overturned another with more debris and rubbish, and another. In the trash was a small piece of dirty, white cloth. He picked it up. It was a small handkerchief spotted with what looked like dried blood.

He looked closely at it.

In one corner were embroidered the initials *EB.*

He had found his proof.

Eva Braun *was* alive.

16

———•◦•———

Y OU'RE AWOL!" Major Hall growled at Woody as he walked into the CIC office. It was just after 0800 hours, Tuesday, June 5. "You were supposed to report back here yesterday, dammit!"

"I know, I know, Mort." Woody put up a defensive hand. "But . . ."

"I could throw the damned book at you."

"But you won't," Woody said. "Not after you've heard what I have to report."

Hall looked speculatively at the young agent. Something was obviously up. Something important. He'd only given lip service to his annoyance when he made his AWOL threat. Hell, CIC work was too damned flexible to bother with that kind of crap. But, dammit, Woody should have at least reported in. He'd actually worried about him gallivanting about outside his jurisdiction on some wild goose-step chase. He did not like to worry about his boys.

"It had better be good," he grunted.

"It is," Woody quietly assured him.

Quickly, concisely he told his CO of his interrogation of the Bocks in Halle; his tracking down of the Kotsches in Rübeland; their admissions; and his finding of the *EB* handkerchief. Hall listened to it all without interrupting him.

"Eva *is* alive, Mort," Woody finished. "I know it in my guts."

Hall nodded. "I tend to agree with you."

"So—the question is why? Why the elaborate hoax to make

her appear to be dead? Why the charade carried out by both the Nazis and the Russians, including our lovable Major Krasnov? Why?"

"I'll be damned if I know," Hall said. "What the hell is so all-fired important about her anyway?"

"I don't know," Woody said soberly. "I honestly don't know. I only know that we'd better find out."

"And I suppose you already have a plan for doing just that," Hall commented caustically.

"I do."

"Let's hear it," Hall said.

Woody told him.

Hall sat staring at him. "You're out of your gourd," he said. "No way."

"Okay, Mort," Woody conceded, "I realize you can't okay an operation as unorthodox as that." He looked straight at his CO. "I want your permission to go over your head."

Hall contemplated him. "Streeter?" he asked.

"I was thinking of Buter."

Hall pursed his lips. "It'll have to go through channels."

"As long as it gets all the way to Buter."

"What you propose is without precedent," Hall said. "You realize that?"

"I do."

"You won't get to first base."

"I can try."

For a moment Hall sat in silence. It *was* a totally unique situation. It could be an important case. A helluva case. Perhaps it did warrant unique procedures. He sighed.

"I suggest you write up a report," he said. "One hell of a good one. Buter will want to know details before he goes out on a limb with this one. Write it through channels. To me. I'll walk it through. In person." He looked at Woody. "And, Woody, if you *are* going ahead with this crazy scheme, write the damned report yesterday. You don't have much time to screw around."

S E C R E T

5 June 1945

SUBJECT: EVA BRAUN HITLER, the death of
TO   : OIC, CIC Detachment 212

SECRET

class. by auth.
Richard H. Streeter, Col.GSC
AC of S, G-2, XII Corps
APO 312
5 June 1945

Richard H. Streeter

Col. GSC

I. *CASE CHRONOLOGY*

1. On 28 April 1945 the capture of SS Sturmbannführer Franz Gotthelf was effected in Albersdorf, O-979623. During interrogation subject disclosed he was a dentist having worked with Brigadeführer Hugo Blaschke, personal dentist to Adolf Hitler. Among high-ranking Nazi patients of subject was *Eva Braun,* described by subject as Hitler's mistress. Subject had worked on a dental bridge for said *Eva Braun.* Subject stated this bridge was never fitted, but remained in dental laboratory in Berlin when city fell to Russian forces.

2. On 1 May 1945 SS Obersturmbannführer Leopold Krauss was interrogated in Weiden, O-869427. Subject stated he had been a Foreign Affairs Analyst in the Ministry of Propaganda attached to the Führer Bunker in Berlin. He stated he had fled Berlin 30 April 1945. He further stated that Adolf Hitler had married *Eva Braun,* 29 April 1945, that both Adolf Hitler and *Eva Braun Hitler* had committed suicide, 30 April 1945 and their bodies burned in the garden of the Reich Chancellery. SS Obersturmbannführer Leopold Krauss was evacuated to AIC, 1 May 1945.

3. On 2 May 1945 the Reich Chancellery and the Führer Bunker fell to Russian forces. The remains of Adolf Hitler and *Eva Braun Hitler* were found.

4. On 6 May 1945, according to AIC records, SS Sturmbannführer Franz Gotthelf was turned over to Russian military authorities by AIC at request of Major Vasily Stepanovich Krasnov, Liaison Officer, XII Corps, to assist in identification of remains of Adolf Hitler.

5. On 8 May 1945 the Forensic-Medical Commission of the Soviet Army issued and disseminated internally an autopsy report covering the bodies found burned in the Reich Chancellery garden, 2 May 1945, by members of the Soviet Army Counter Intelligence SMERSH. A copy of this report was obtained by AC of S, G-2, XII Corps. The report contained 13 (thirteen) autopsy documents; 5 (five) adults; 6 (six) children and 2 (two) dogs. Document No. 12 covers the identification and autopsy report of Adolf

Hitler. Document No. 13 covers the identification and autopsy report of *Eva Braun*.

6. According to Russian autopsy report positive identification of the bodies of Adolf Hitler and *Eva Braun* was made by use of dental records and interrogation of dental workers familiar with these records. The decisive item of identification in the case of *Eva Braun* was a dental bridge "of yellow metal" (gold) with artificial teeth attached. In part the autopsy report states: "Almost the entire top of the cranium and upper part of the frontal cranium are missing; they are burned. Only fragments of the burned and broken occipital and temporal bones are preserved as is the lower part of the left facial bones." The bridge used to identify the body is reported to have connected the second right bicuspid and the third right molar. It is described as follows: "On the metal plate of the bridge the first and second artificial white molars are attached in front; their appearance is almost indistinguishable from natural teeth." The report also states that: "On the right side no teeth were found, probably because of the burning."

7. This investigator, in an attempt to conduct a follow-up interrogation of dental assistant SS Sturmbannführer Franz Gotthelf (see: I-1) regarding his work on the crucial *Eva Braun* dental bridge, and unable to locate this subject at AIC, contacted Major Vasily Stepanovich Krasnov, Russian Liaison Officer, XII Corps. Major Krasnov, who had originally requested subject Gotthelf be turned over to Russian authorities, denied any knowledge of the matter and that he had made the initial request. It was the official Russian position that no such individual as SS Sturmbannführer Franz Gotthelf existed.

8. On 3 June 1945 this investigator, on TDY with CIC, VII Corps, interrogated subjects Konrad Bock and his wife, Helga, in Halle P-822839. The Bocks stated that they had been active in travel expediting of high-ranking Nazi fugitives seeking to exfiltrate Germany via an escape route called the B-B Axis because it runs between the towns of Bremen in Germany and Bari in Italy. They further stated that two young people were provided with forged documents and travel orders on 1 May 1945, an SS officer named Lüttjohann and a young women who gave no name—the only woman processed by the Bocks. Subject Helga Bock stated that she believed this woman to be *Eva Braun*.

9. On 4 June 1945 this investigator interrogated Herbert Kotsch, a colonel in the German army, retired, and his

wife Gertrud at Rübeland, P-843620. This couple had also worked for the B-B Axis escape route. They stated that Lüttjohann and the woman had been in hiding in Rübeland for about three weeks and had embarked on their exfiltration on 2 June 1945, proceeding to a route stop at Bebelgasse 49 in Eisenach, O-933924.

10. During a search of the place of concealment used by Lüttjohann and the woman by this investigator, a woman's handkerchief, with the initials *EB*, was found.

II. *ANALYSIS*

Upon analysis of the above intelligence the following facts emerge:

1. The body of *Eva Braun* was positively identified by means of a crucial dental bridge.
2. According to SS Sturmbannführer Franz Gotthelf this same bridge was never fitted on subject and remained in a Berlin dental laboratory at the time of the alleged death and cremation of *Eva Braun*.
3. Had this bridge been on the body during the reported cremation, which was so severe it burned away most of the facial and cranial bones, the gold would have melted and the artificial teeth would have exploded or disintegrated. (Source: Bernard T. Haskins, Major (DC) 0562347, Unit Dental O. (AUS), Medical Detachment Headquarters Company, XII Corps.)
4. Subject Helga Bock saw *Eva Braun* alive on 1 May 1945, the day after the alleged suicide. Subject is considered reliable.
5. A handkerchief found in the place of hiding used by the woman believed to be *Eva Braun* bore the initials *EB*, indicating it did belong to said *Eva Braun*.
6. The Russians, for unknown reasons, are misleading the Allies in regard to the death of *Eva Braun* and—by inference—that of Adolf Hitler.

III. *CONCLUSIONS*

Based on the above the conclusions reached by this investigator are:

1. The crucial dental bridge was *not* on the body of the woman identified as *Eva Braun* when said body was burned.
2. The bridge was added to the remains at a later date, reasons unknown.
3. The cremated body therefore could not have been identified as that of *Eva Braun*, but that of someone else, since

Eva Braun was seen alive after the cremation took place.

4. For reasons unknown the Nazis wanted the world to believe that *Eva Braun* was dead; and the Russians for their own purposes are perpetuating the deception.

5. *Eva Braun,* accompanied by an SS officer, is at this moment attempting to exfiltrate Germany via the B-B Axis escape route.

IV. *RECOMMENDATIONS*

The questions arise *why* the elaborate deception was carried out by the Nazis, and *why* the Russians are perpetuating it? It is believed imperative that these questions, which pertain to the vital facts regarding the reported deaths of both *Eva Braun* and Adolf Hitler, be investigated and concluded.

Since under the circumstances it is not possible to conduct a normal search and seize operation, it is recommended that this investigator be placed on special detached duty from CIC Det. 212 to operate undercover, and via the B-B Axis pursue the subjects until said subjects can be identified and apprehended.

Because time is of prime importance in this case it is requested that orders to this effect be cut, effective immediately.

Distribution: None

Woodrow Wilson Ward

Woodrow Wilson Ward
Special Agent, CIC Det. 212

Fwd to:
Richard H. Streeter, Col. GSC
AC of S, G-2, XII Corps
5 June 1945
by

Mortimer L. Hall

Mortimer L. Hall, Maj.
CO, CIC Det. 212

Fwd to:
Irwin Buter, Brig. Gen. AUS
Chief of Staff, XII Corps
5 June 1945
by

Richard H. Streeter

Richard H. Streeter, Col. GSC
AC of S, G-2 XII Corps

SECRET

[169]

Brigadier General Irwin Buter, Chief of Staff, XII Corps, put down the report. He looked at the three men seated before him. "That's quite a yarn," he said. "Disturbing—if the conclusions drawn are correct. Interesting—even if they aren't." He turned to his Assistant Chief of Staff, G-2, Colonel Richard H. Streeter. "Dick," he said, "how about it?"

"I recommend we find a way to carry out Sergeant Ward's recommendations," Streeter said. "I think it's important to find out why the Nazis and the Russians are playing games. That's why I brought it to you at once. It's a helluva unorthodox operation the sergeant proposes, but I think we can find a way to authorize it. And I think we should. No directives cover anything like it . . ."

"I'm not surprised," the general interjected.

". . . so we can write our own."

Buter nodded. He turned to Major Hall. "Major," he said, "what is your recommendation? The operation would be in your ball park."

"I am for it, Sir," Hall said. He frowned lightly. "There are—eh—some precedents for CIC agents to operate—eh—under-cover. Agents have been placed in PW enclosures, for instance."

Woody glanced at Hall in surprise. Good for old Mort, he thought. He's really boosting this thing.

Buter nodded. He hid a little smile. Not much of a precedent, he thought with amusement. But it shows that the boy's superiors are behind him. He turned to Woody.

"What makes you think you can carry it off, Sergeant?" he asked.

"Sir," Woody said, "I speak German fluently. I have a thorough knowledge of the German armed forces and the SS."

Buter tapped the report lying on the desk. "You state in your report that the escape route taken by Eva Braun ends in Bari, Italy. Why is it necessary for you to travel the entire route? Why not place a team in Bari and pick up this Eva Braun when she gets there?"

"Several reasons, Sir," Woody said. "First, we have no idea what she looks like, nor what name she travels under. Secondly, there is always the possibility that she may leave the regular escape route at any point along the way. We would have to know. Also, the Nazi B-B Axis operatives are certain to have Bari under close observation; it is an important port of embarkation for top fugitives. Anything out of the ordinary, any unusual activities or presences would be detected and the exfiltration operation changed. We might lose her entirely. Only by traveling the route itself can anyone catch up with the subject and be certain to apprehend her before she leaves Europe."

"What makes you think you *can* catch up with her? She and her companion already have several days' head start."

"I think I can travel faster, being alone," Woody said. "than the SS officer can with Eva Braun along."

"Why travel the whole route? Why not enter the stream of it at a later point?"

"That is not possible, Sir. I know only one route stop. In Eisenach. That stop in turn will know the next stop in line along the route—and so on. I will have to go from stop to stop."

Buter nodded. "I see. And how will you accomplish being accepted as a B-B Axis fugitive?"

"Sir, I will assume the identity of an SS Captain, an officer who was in charge of the guards at the Flossenburg Concentration Camp. A wanted war criminal. He is in our custody. We have his papers."

Buter leaned back in his chair. He studied Woody for a moment. "Why are you volunteering for this mission?" he asked. "I have seen your record. It is one you can be proud of. Why are you committing yourself to an operation which not only will take considerable time, but is also exceedingly risky and dangerous? You could be home in a week or two."

"Sir, I still need seven points."

Buter nodded. "As of today," he said. "Monday the point requirements for enlisted men will be lowered. You'll have more than enough to be sent home."

Woody stared at the General. "Be sent—home," he repeated. The thoughts tumbled in his mind. He didn't need the damned five points! He could chuck the whole stinking case. Right now. And be home free. In a couple of weeks. He suddenly realized he didn't care. To hell with the points. To hell with going home—before he'd cleared up the Eva case. No way was he going to let go now. Sheepishly he realized that secretly he'd felt that way all along, but the decision had been buried by the obligatory griping. "Sir," he said solemnly, "I consider the case of extreme importance. A lot of questions have been raised by developments that need to be answered. If Eva Braun Hitler is still alive—is Adolf Hitler alive, too? Why did the Nazis go to such lengths to hide the fact that she is, in fact, alive? And why have the Russians gone along with it? Those are just some of the points that need clarification." He paused. He looked earnestly at Buter.

"Right now, Sir, I know more details of the case than anyone

[171]

else. I conducted the investigation and all the interrogations. There is no time to train another agent or an OSS operative, no time to get them ready to take over the mission. Right now, Sir, I am the man best qualified for the job."

Buter carefully took the measure of the young agent sitting across from him. He nodded.

"I agree," he said. "Go to it!"

Woody was getting impatient. Now that the "go" decision had been made he was itching to be on his way. But what little remained of Tuesday and most of the night had been taken up with damned preparations. Hall, with the full concurrence of both Streeter and Buter, insisted that all possible safeguards be employed in the operation. They were right, of course, but damned precious time was being pissed down the latrine.

There'd been the ID papers to obtain; the permits to forge; the clothing; the visit to Doc Elliott; and now—well into the morning of Wednesday—there was the matter of equipment and weapons.

"I'm not going to carry *any* weapons," Woody stated emphatically. "Not even a penknife. I may feel naked, but that's it. It would be totally out of character for a bonafide refugee, and a dead giveaway if I were searched. No special tricks."

"I agree," Hall mollified him. They were walking across the north sports field toward the HQ CO Supply Building. "I still want you to talk to Forbes. He's quite a character. I think you'll find it worthwhile."

"What the hell is a Limey Sergeant Major doing at Corps anyway?" Woody grumbled.

"It's a long story," Hall said.

"I'll just bet," Woody snorted.

"Forbes was a member of the SOE. The Special Operations Executive. The British espionage and sabotage organization—the counterpart to our cloak-and-dagger boys. He was part of a so-called Jedburg team—a team of agents made up in England of men of two or three nationalities for operations on the Continent. He was dropped into Czechoslovakia. When his position was overrun by the Russians, he chose to make his way to American-held territory and showed up at Corps. He's going to be sent back home as soon as we can get around to it," he said. "Meanwhile he's having the time of his life showing our boys some of the tricks he developed for SOE."

"Sounds like a real Rover Boy," Woody muttered.

[172]

"Actually, he was a music hall performer," Hall told him. "A magician and escape artist. Played the provinces mostly, I'm told."

"And I bet his idol was Houdini," Woody snorted.

"No bet," Hall said, with a grin.

Sergeant Major Henry Asquith Forbes, formerly "Forbes the Fabulous," a bear of a man with a personality like a gust from a blast furnace, looked Woody up and down. From the pained expression on his craggy face it was evident he'd didn't like what he saw.

"You're the bloke what's going undercover," he stated rather than asked.

Woody gave Hall an irate glance. Why the hell not advertise his mission in the *Stars and Stripes,* for chrissake!, he thought angrily. Forbes seemed to read his mind. "I don't know what your bloody job is, mate, and I don't bloody well want to know," he barked. "*My* job is to fit square pegs into round holes." He squinted dubiously at Woody. "I'll do my best for you."

"Sergeant Major Forbes has developed some very useful—and ingenious—special equipment," Hall said, trying to calm the blossoming animosity.

Woody still bristled. "Listen, *Sergeant Major,*" he snapped. "I'm not about to run around loaded down with outlandish Buck Rogers contraptions stashed all over me. I don't care what brilliant gimmicks you've come up with. By now the Krauts, and everyone else, know all about them. I sure don't want some zealous SOB to do a job on me and come up with razor blades in my cap visor or a saw in my lapel, or whatever you special equipment experts can dream up. Not on this job. Nothing doing!"

Forbes looked at him with pitying disdain. "Making quite a to-do about it, aren't we, what?" he snorted. "And what would you do if you found yourself on a sticky wicket, old chap?"

"I'd manage—old chap," Woody countered bitingly.

Hall stood silent. He rather enjoyed the cockfight aspect of the confrontation. He'd let them work it out for themselves, he thought. He was confident they would. They were both tops in their fields, and top men sooner or later find that out about each other and get to appreciate one another. He also realized that Woody was keyed up. Needed to work off steam. It was good for him.

"Don't be a ruddy ass, chum," Forbes said. "*All* missions have bloody pitfalls. You can lump them into two principal situations:

getting the bloody hell out of somewhere, and finding your bleeding way around after you've gotten out." He cocked his head at Woody. "And what would you do, then, mate—in case?"

"In case—what?"

"In case things got a bit dicey and you bloody well had to get out of some bloody lock-up. And find your way around a strange countryside. What would be the tools most useful to you?"

"A sledgehammer and a Baedeker Tourist Guide," Woody said sourly. "Don't tell me you've sewn them into the lining of my clothes!"

"It is a regular music hall comedian we are, is it?" Forbes scoffed.

"I know all about your special tricks."

"Do you now?"

"Yes, I do now, *mate*."

Forbes made a show of ignoring Woody's attempt at parody. "How about a powerful saw? And an accurate compass? The two most valuable tools for an agent in the field?"

"Sure," Woody said. "And I—*and* the Krauts—know all about your saws hidden in pencils or jacket lapels. And your compasses in buttons, or heels, or toilet kits, or what-have-you. No thanks."

Forbes gave him a withering glance. "Well then, you should have no trouble with this."

He turned on his heel and stalked in stiff-legged affront to a table. He grabbed a jacket, a pair of pants, a cap, and a pair of boots. He carried the bundle over to Woody. He threw it at him."

"Here they are," he barked.

"What?"

"The saw. And the compass."

"Where?"

Forbes flicked a ham-sized fist at the bundle of clothes. "You can bloody well look for them, *mate!*" he snapped.

Woody did. With a vengeance.

He pried off the heels of the boots and examined every seam and sole minutely. He went over every inch of clothing and cut into lapels and seams and linings. He tried every button and almost ripped the cap apart.

He found nothing.

He looked at Forbes with grudging respect. "You mean there really are a saw and a compass in that mess?"

Forbes grinned broadly. "You bloody well better believe it," he boomed. "Put'm there myself."

"Okay. I give up. Show me."

Forbes pointed to one of the boots. "That boot," he said. "Give it to me."

Woody did. The boot was in bad shape. He'd wrenched off the heel, split the sole, and generally mutilated it trying to find something.

Forbes removed the shoe lace. He gave it to Woody. "Twist the aglet," he said. "Clockwise."

"The—what?"

"The aglet." Forbes took hold of the metal tip of the shoelace. "This."

"Oh *that's* what they call that thingamajig," Woody said. He took hold of it.

"Twist it," Forbes instructed him. "A full turn. Then pull."

Woody did. The aglet came loose in his fingers—and from the lace he pulled out a flexible length of saw-toothed wire hidden inside. He stared at it.

"It will cut through anything," Forbes said proudly. "Including padlocks and steel bars. Given time. It's made of very special steel wire so flexible it can be tied in knots. They use something like it in cranial surgery. Call it a Gigli saw." He took the shoelace. "The inside of the lace is coated with a slick substance so the saw teeth won't catch when you pull the wire out."

Woody looked at the wire saw. He at once recognized its value. He was impressed. "And the compass?" he asked.

"You've got it in your hand," Forbes beamed.

Woody stared at the aglet he'd pulled off the shoelace. "This?" he exclaimed incredulously.

"Right, mate. The aglet. The metal's been magnetized. You balance the thing on a pin—where that little indentation is at the seam—and it shows north."

"I'll be damned." Woody looked at the Sergeant Major. "You're okay, buddy," he said. "I'll take one of each. Gift-wrapped!"

Forbes grinned hugely. "You got it, mate." He grew sober. "And here's wishing you'll never have to make use of them."

Amen, Woody thought. He'd keep that good thought. He had a hunch he could use every one he could get.

Tomorrow—first thing—he was off for Eisenach.

And his first stop on the *B-B Achse*.

17

THE SPOT ON THE INSIDE of his upper left arm where Doc Elliott had made the little scar itched like hell. He had to exert all his willpower not to scratch it. Doc had warned him not to touch it—or he would destroy the effect. It had, of course, been necessary to create the little wound. There had been no time to do a tattoo that would look even halfway seasoned. And he couldn't be without the customary SS tattoo denoting his blood type if he were to masquerade as an *SS Hauptsturmführer* successfully. Somewhere along the line some bastard was sure to do a little checking. But it wasn't unusual to find a more or less fresh scar. Most SS attempted to remove the telltale tattoo.

Woody stood across from No. 49 on Bebelgasse in Eisenach staring at the house that was the *B-B Achse Anlaufstelle* given him by Herbert Kotsch. He hadn't quite gotten used to being a fugitive SS officer yet. Every stitch of clothing he wore—from the worn and mended socks on his feet to his *Wehrmacht* cap stripped of insignia on his head—had been procured from a PW camp, with slight alterations courtesy of Sergeant Major Henry Asquith Forbes. It had, of course, been counterindicated to clean the damned clothes before he put them on, so he'd shrugged into them, sweaty and smelly as they were. He felt thoroughly unclean, and his flesh still crawled when he thought of it. He wasn't even sure the damned delousing powder the original owner had been dosed with in the PW camp had really done its job.

In his pocket he had papers that showed he was a discharged *Wehrmacht Obergefreiter*, a corporal named Hans Bauhacker from the Schleswig-Holstein town of Flensburg: a few personal papers, dog-eared photographs, and the like—taken from the same prisoner of war who had "contributed" the ID and the clothing—as well as a US Military Government travel permit allowing him to proceed to his brother's farm near the village of Helmers some fifteen kilometers south of Eisenach, signed by the same fictitious captain in Blankenburg who had signed the pass for Herbert Kotsch. In keeping with the unwise practice of so many Nazis in hiding who couldn't bear to discard their real identification papers—just in case—he had the ID card of one *SS Haupsturmführer* Fritz Diehl, the Flossenburg officer, taped to the instep of his right foot.

He was as ready to knock on the door of the *B-B Achse* as he'd ever be.

He started across the street—one *SS Hauptsturmführer* Fritz Diehl, concentration camp guard, war criminal, in search of escape, carrying the false papers of one *Obergefreiter* Bauhacker. It suddenly struck him with chilling effect that were he to be picked up by US military police he had no papers to prove that he was an American.

He was totally committed.

Eisenach, a town of some sixty thousand souls swelled by the unwanted influx of occupation troops, was the birthplace of Johann Sebastian Bach and lay at the foot of Wartburg Castle which Richard Wagner made famous when he used it as his setting for the contest of minnesingers in his opera *Tannhäuser*. That was all Woody knew about the town. It was probably as much as could be expected from any SS concentration camp guard.

Bebelgasse was in a seedy part of town. Woody kept his eyes on the building as he walked across the street. The windows were boarded up and on the front door a large sign had been tacked up. OFF LIMITS TO ALL US PERSONNEL, it read.

He stared at the sign, puzzled.

Then, suddenly, he knew.

A whorehouse! The *B-B Achse Anlaufstelle* at Bebelgasse 49 was a cathouse!

He chuckled to himself. It was a natural for a stop in an escape route chain. Various more or less furtive individuals, most of them male, coming and going at all hours. Couldn't be more appropriate. And as a bonus—off limits to the enemy! He'd have to remember to tell Mort to put whorehouses high on the check list. He was sure no one would object.

He rang the bell. Presently he was aware of being scrutinized by an eye through a small peephole. The door opened. A plain-looking girl, her mousy hair drawn back in a tight bun, watched him with wary eyes.

"Yes?" she said.

"I would like to see the—person in charge," he said.

The girl openly appraised him, obviously displeased with his seedy look. She stood aside. She pointed to an open door leading from the foyer. "Wait in there," she said, adding "please" as an afterthought.

Woody walked through the door indicated by the girl. He found himself in a little waiting room maintained for the clients of the establishment. His eyes quickly took it in. Fake Louis XIV furniture covered in worn red plush. On the floor a threadbare imitation Oriental rug, the walk pattern from the door to the sofa that dominated the room plainly outlined. On the walls a reproduction of a painting of a voluptuous, reclining nude, framed in a badly chipped, ornate gold frame, and two framed pornographic Japanese prints drawn with amazing detail, one with its glass cracked. In one corner stood a large, carved chest and next to it a floor vase with dusty wax flowers; in another a lamp with a heavy pink shade—and over all hung the sweet, cloying scent of too much cheap perfume.

Gingerly he perched himself on the edge of the sofa. On a small table before it a few dog-eared magazines were spread out. He picked up one of them. It was a February German language issue of *Signal,* the biweekly Nazi propaganda magazine which in its heyday had been published in twenty languages. He wondered briefly if the whorehouse which now served as a stop on the *B-B Achse* had been one of the hundreds of brothels the Nazis had set up to serve their foreign workers so they wouldn't pollute the establishments patronized by the upstanding, pure Aryan Germans. From *Bordell* to *Anlaufstelle* in one far-from-easy lesson, he thought wryly.

He flipped through the magazine, stopping to look at an article entitled, "The Seed of the Third World War." He was just reading a quote by Henry Wallace, warning America against double-crossing the Russians, when a throaty female voice interrupted him.

"What can I do for you?"

He jumped up. In the doorway stood a woman. Her heavy makeup made it impossible to tell whether she was forty or sixty, although Woody thought nearer the latter. Large-bosomed, thick around the waist, she had long blond hair, obviously dyed and totally lackluster, which fell down over her shoulders. In contrast, her full lips and long, curved nails were shiny blood-red and made her look like a vampire with short teeth who had just come from a feast. She wore a soiled embroidered Japanese robe. Woody stared at her.

"I am Madame Zorina," the woman said. "What can I do for you?" She smiled, revealing tobacco-stained teeth.

"I—I was hoping for a little relaxation," Woody said. "I have just traveled a long way. All the way from the Harz."

"Really," Madame Zorina nodded, her expression unchanged. "I myself know the Harz well. A lovely place."

"Yes, it is," Woody agreed. "And so many interesting places to visit. I was so impressed with the caves. Especially the *Baumannshöhle*."

"It is impressive, isn't it?" Madame Zorina said. "But personally I prefer the *Hermannshöhle*."

"And I the *Baumannshöhle*, Madame," Woody said. He drew a sigh of relief. Kotsch had given him the right dope after all.

The woman turned and closed the door to the foyer. She inspected Woody.

"Who are you?" she asked.

Woody drew himself up. For a second he debated with himself if he should click his heels. He decided against it. No need to overdo it.

"I am *Hauptsturmführer* Fritz Diehl," he said. "I was sent here by *Herr Oberst* Herbert Kotsch."

Zorina nodded. She seemed suddenly interested. Pleased. Woody picked up on it. He wondered why.

"Your papers." She held out her hand. Woody gave her the papers purloined from the *Wehrmacht* corporal PW, Hans Bauhacker, and his travel permit. Zorina looked them over.

"Your papers are excellent," she said. "One would not know they are not genuine." She glanced at the AMG travel permit. "Kotsch is an idiot," she mumbled. "He is using that Johnson name too often. Only four days . . ." She stopped. It was all Woody could do not to urge her to go on. Four days ago. Eva?

"Your real papers, you still have them?" Zorina asked.

Woody nodded.

"Let me have them."

He sat down on the sofa. He took off his right boot and sock and removed the ID card from his instep. He gave it to the woman. She merely glanced at it.

"You are a fool, Diehl," she said matter-of-factly. "Like so many of you. We will get rid of this. Fritz Diehl must no longer exist."

She walked over to the large chest. She opened it. She took out a heavy blue bathrobe. "Take your clothes off," she said. "Everything. We will have them cleaned."

It was obvious Zorina was not going to leave. Woody hesitated only a moment. What the hell. It was doubtful it was the first time Zorina had seen a man undress. He stripped, watched closely by the woman. Not until he stood stark naked did she hand him the robe.

"I will give you a little alcohol," she said. "Use it on your arm. It will help the healing."

"Thank you," he said. She hadn't missed a thing. He blessed Doc Elliott.

Zorina opened the door. "Maria!" she called. The mousy girl appeared at the door. "Take these clothes," Zorina instructed her. "Have them cleaned."

Maria nodded. She began to gather up Woody's discarded clothing.

"You will have a bath," Zorina said to Woody, "and then I will give you your further instructions."

Woody nodded. "Fine."

Maria started out of the room with the dirty clothing. "Wait!" Zorina called to her. She pointed at Woody's boots. "The boots. Take them, too. Have them cleaned."

Woody hoped the woman didn't notice the flicker of alarm he knew must have flitted through his eyes.

She seemed not to.

He was lying on his back on the big brass bed, his arms behind his head, staring unseeingly at the ceiling. He was still in the blue bathrobe. The little room smelled of the same cheap perfume as the waiting room. Zorina must have gotten a good deal on the stuff, he thought. The room was exactly as he'd always pictured a cheap whorehouse room would be—to the point of being corny. Chintzy curtains, colored lights, loads of gaudy pillows, and a huge bed with one creaking spring. He could imagine the action it had endured.

Without knocking Madame Zorina opened the door and entered the room. She walked over and sat on the edge of the bed. She stared down on the supine Woody, a strange look in her eyes.

Oh, no, he thought. Duty goes only so far.

A small frown crept onto Zorina's brow. "Diehl," she said solemnly, "there is a problem."

His heart skipped a beat. What the hell now?

"I want to have a talk with you," the woman went on. She bit her lip, getting lipstick on her stained teeth. "I know it is breaking the rules, but I must ask you some questions."

"I will try to answer them, Madame," Woody said. He hoped to hell he could. His mind began to cast around for a way to get the hell out—if things should blow up in his face.

"Why are you seeking to escape from Germany?" Zorina asked.

Woody gaped at her. "Why?" he repeated. "I am wanted by the *Amis*. They have branded me a war criminal."

"Why?"

"Because I did my duty, Madame," he said stiffly. "As an officer in the SS in charge of the guards at Flossenburg."

Zorina let out a deep breath.

"You are the one," she said.

"Woody stared at her. "I—I do not understand, Madame," he mumbled. He tried to sit up on the bed. Zorina put a restraining hand on his shoulder.

"I told you I had a problem," she said. "You have just solved it for me."

"I? What—problem?"

She studied him. "There is someone else here waiting to travel the *Achse*," she said slowly. "The organization—someone high in the organization—sent this special refugee to me. Personally."

"But—what has that to do with me," Woody asked, puzzled. "Who is this—refugee?"

"A girl," Zorina said. "Her name is Ilse. Ilse Gessner. She cannot travel the route alone. She must have an escort. You. You will travel as brother and sister."

Woody's mind was suddenly awhirl. He fought to control his chaotic thoughts. Girl? Escort?

"But," he stammered, "I . . ."

"There is no but, *mein lieber Diehl*," Zorina said firmly. "You will accept my decision. When you travel the *Achse* it is the first commandment that you must do exactly as you are instructed by the operatives. Is that understood?" There was an edge of steel under the heavy makeup, the dyed hair, and the diaphanous robe.

"Of course," he said. A girl? Was it possible? Could it be Eva? Had she lost her officer companion? Was she stranded here in the damned whorehouse? Was it all going to be as easy as that? Hell, no, he thought. Only in the movies. He half-listened to Zorina's explanation.

"There is no choice," she said. "Ilse has been here too long already. Soon it will be suspicious—unless she starts to work like the other girls. And that is out of the question. So far there has been no one suited to take her along. The last young officer to come through here already had a woman with him. They left here only yesterday." She looked at him. "You and Ilse will leave tomorrow."

Woody's heart pounded. He hoped Zorina would think it was her touch that caused it. Eva. Eva and her companion. So she wasn't the one he'd have to play nursemaid to. He hadn't really believed it. But—she had been here! She and her escort officer were only one—two days ahead. He cursed under his breath. Zorina had robbed him of his edge. Saddled with a damned broad he'd be slowed down to the same pace of Eva and her companion. Shit! How the hell could he get out of that? He debated with himself if he should protest. Better not. Better not rock the damned boat lest the bilge wash off his camouflage. He looked at Zorina.

"Who is this Ilse Gessner?" he asked.

Zorina stood up. She looked pleased with herself. "I will send her to you," she said. "Tonight you will stay together. In this room. You will have to get used to that. So best you begin at once."

She left.

Woody stood up. He gathered the blue robe around him and tied the frayed belt. Dammit! That's all he needed. A damned broad in tow.

There was a timid knock on the door.

"Come in," he called brusquely.

The door opened. In the doorway stood a young woman.

Ilsa appeared to be in her early twenties. She looked at once sensuous, composed, and vulnerable. A full, hungry mouth was partly open; wide, innocent, disturbingly seductive eyes regarded him. A flimsy, cheap-looking negligee, in which she managed to look graceful, did little to hide her long-waisted, small but firm-busted body. With her short, soft-brushed hair—auburn in color rather than Nordic blond—she was enormously appealing.

"*Herr* Bauhacker," she said, her voice soft and melodious, "I am Ilse. Madame Zorina sent me to you."

For a split moment Woody was puzzled. Bauhacker? Then he remembered. It *was* a bit tricky, he thought. Here he was, CIC Agent Woodrow Wilson Ward, pretending to be *SS Hauptsturmführer* Fritz Diehl, using the cover identity of *Obergefreiter* Hans Bauhacker. He almost laughed out loud. Imagine what Abbott and Costello could do with that one!

He stared at the girl.

Suddenly the idea of being saddled with her seemed less of a handicap.

It was midmorning the following day when Woody stood in the perfume-scented foyer waiting for Ilse to join him. At the last minute she had wanted to say goodby to some of the girls who had befriended her during her stay at the brothel. Zorina had beneficently allowed it. He felt a little better. His clothes had been cleaned, but not pressed; his boots were still drab and scuffed. It would not do to appear in too much sartorial splendor as a refugee on the roads of a defeated Germany, Zorina had pointed out.

The night had been a singularly restless one. Too much was crowding in on him to allow him to relax. His mind kept trying to visualize what lay ahead, unable to do so, and therefore conjuring up lurid images in petulant self-defense.

Ilse had slept in the big brass bed. Alone. He had tried to sack out on a blanket on the floor, which hadn't made falling asleep any easier. Most of the night he'd only dozed, unable to fall asleep not only because of his restless thoughts, the hard floor and the suggestive noises that reached him from the rest of the house during an obviously busy night, but also because of the proximity of the lovely girl.

Although they had talked, they had said nothing of importance to each other. An *Achse Anlaufstelle* was not the place to ask questions or volunteer information, and he knew little more about the girl than Zorina had told him. She less about him. They had taken each other's measure, as far as they could. He had been reminded of a trip to the zoo. In San Francisco. When he was a boy. With his father he had watched as a female tiger had been introduced into the cage of a male for the first time. The big cats had watched each other warily. They had walked around the cage testing the air, keeping apart, maintaining their own privacy. But obviously interested.

It had been like that.

He let his mind run over the instructions they'd been given by Madame Zorina. One more time.

Ilse now had papers that showed she was Ilse Bauhacker, his sister. They had a US Military Government travel pass to go to Coburg where their parents lived. At least as far as they knew. They were supposed to be at the Wartburg turn-off signpost on the road south to Meiningen just outside Eisenach at noon. A truck, a wood-burner, carrying a load of rock salt, would pick them up. They were to wave their arms at the driver and, when he stopped, ask for a ride to Göttingen which was in the exact opposite direction. Only the *Achse* driver would agree, and take them to their destination. Once there, Woody would give him two hundred marks. The money was safe in his inside jacket pocket. They had been lucky, Zorina had said. It was only rarely that she could arrange motor transportation at such short notice. They'd be in Coburg at the next *Anlaufstelle* before the day was done.

It was possible, Woody thought. Just barely possible that Eva would still be there.

Madame Zorina came up to him. She looked tired after the night's activities. Her makeup could not entirely hide the black pouches under her eyes. She had obviously fortified herself with a nip or two. She still wore her Japanese robe. Woody wondered if she lived in it.

"Ilse will be here in a moment," she said. She looked at Woody. "Is everything clear?"

He nodded. "Yes."

"I know you are impatient, *mein Junge,* at having to take Ilse along." She smiled, exposing her tobacco-stained teeth. "But you will not regret it, I promise you. She is an extraordinary girl. She is well educated. Part of her schooling was at the Sorbonne. In Paris. And at an exclusive finishing school in Heidelberg run by the SS. She speaks French, of course, and she has some English, too. She is a strong girl. She can stand exertion. She will not let you down. You will have no trouble with her on that score. She is an excellent tennis player and a competition-class swimmer. She is in good shape."

You can say that again, Woody thought. In more ways than one.

"Anything else," Zorina finished, looking at him out of the corners of her eyes, "any personal matters, she will have to tell you herself. If she wishes. I can only assure you she is well qualified to travel the *Achse.*"

Ilse came into the foyer. She walked up to them as Zorina reached out and folded Woody in her arms. She gave him a moist kiss full on the mouth. She drew back and looked at him. His lips and chin were smeared with her lipstick. With a little laugh she used one of her ample sleeves to wipe it off.

"By the way, *mein lieber Junge,*" she said teasingly, "I checked out your story about being in charge of the guards at Flossenburg—as you knew I would." She shook her head in mock re-proval. "You were not a very nice boy, were you?"

She patted his cheek affectionately. "Off you go," she said. "I know all will go well."

Woody had suffered the leave-taking in silence, embarassed and ill at ease.

He missed the dark look Ilse gave him at the mention of the Flossenburg Concentration Camp.

18

It was 1417 hours, Friday, June 8, when the ramshackle wood-burner came to a wheezing halt at a black-and-white striped roadside signpost which read: COBURG.

The driver turned to Wood. "This is as far as I take you," he said. "You know where to go from here."

Woody nodded.

"Good luck," the man said. He held out his hand. Woody shook it.

"Thank you," he said.

The man pulled his hand away. He glowered at Woody, *"Nanu!"* he growled in annoyance. "Hey! Shall I have trouble with you?"

Sheepishly Woody remembered. He pulled out the two hundred Marks. He gave the money to the sullen driver. "Sorry," he said. "Thanks for the ride."

They got out, and stood at the roadside watching the wood-burner chug off.

The *Anlaufstelle* was near the Coburg Square in the middle of town. From the directions given him by Zorina, Woody estimated it would be a half hour's walk. He looked at the girl. They had said little to each other since they left Zorina's establishment. The cab of the truck had not seemed to lend itself to conversation. All three had sat quietly, Ilse between the two men. He had been acutely aware of her closeness on the cramped seat, and had allowed himself to fantasize. It had been a stupid thing to do.

He should be concentrating on more important matters. Like catching up with Eva.

And survival.

He looked around. On a hill overlooking the town stood Coburg Castle. At first it seemed undamaged, until he suddenly realized that he could see right through the tall, gabled roof of one of the main buildings. Only the steepled supporting timbers remained, scorched and black against the sky.

The safe house was a small *Gasthof*—a small hotel on a side street off Coburg Square. The streets on the outskirts of town were still cluttered with the piled-up remains of barricades erected in a futile attempt to stem the enemy tide; now dismantled and as useless as ever. They walked past the dismal reminders of defeat, ignoring them and their futility as studiously as the townspeople did. They crossed Coburg Square, passed by the gutted *Adolf Hitler Haus,* and presently they stood before a dingy little hotel ambitiously calling itself *Zum Stern*—At the Star.

They had arrived at the Coburg *Anlauffstelle.*

Ever since he and Eva had emerged from the caves in the Harz Mountains, blinking at the sun like hemeralopic troglodytes, Willi had been keyed up, on the lookout for trouble. Any trouble. Although everything along the *Achse* escape route had run as smoothly as the wheels in a well-oiled machine. He was impressed but not surprised at the capability and ingenuity of the SS organization.

Eva had been uncomfortable in Madame Zorina's establishment, but he had spent a delightful couple of hours—on the house. The stops in the *Zum Stern* hotel in Coburg and in Neustadt had been uneventful as they had been passed on with efficient dispatch.

The accommodations in the *Anlaufstelle* in the little Bavarian town of Nördlingen halfway between Nürnberg and Munich were cramped but adequate. *Achse* travelers were put up in the cellar or in the attic of a small tailor shop run by one Reinhold Hacker, who specialized in the repair and alteration of old clothes, a thriving business in postwar Germany. Hacker's living quarters were on the second floor of the little half-timbered building. Behind the shop was his cluttered workroom, curtained off by a heavy portiere of blue velvet, badly faded in the folds, that hung across the doorway. It was a good choice for a stop. All sorts of people came into the shop every day. Strangers would not be noticed.

[187]

Hacker was making arrangements for them to leave the next morning. For the town of Memmingen about 120 kilometers directly to the south. It was a long haul and he had promised them motor transport. Meanwhile he had cautioned them to stay in their attic quarters except for the necessary trips to the grimy little bathroom off the workshop. And that was exactly what they were doing.

Eva was sitting on the mattress that served as her bed, looking up at the tiny patch of blue sky visible through a skylight window in the roof. The whirring sound of Hacker's old treadle-operated sewing machine, occasionally interrupted by the thin tinkling of the shop doorbell announcing a customer, floated in the air along with the dust particles in the beam of light from the window.

She wondered if she would have a sewing machine of her own in the new world she was headed for. She looked forward to sewing little things for her son. Adolf. Little Adolf, she had decided to name him.

A pang of grief swept through her. His father would never see him. He would have loved him so, she thought. She just knew that Adolf would have been a good father. A wonderful father. He always loved the little children who came to him with their flowers and their awkward little curtsies. He would always pat their cheeks and have a kind word for them.

She remembered a speech Adolf had once made to the National Socialist Women's Auxiliary. "I should love nothing more dearly than to have a family," he had said. She had been in the audience and she remembered his words very clearly. "When I feel I have accomplished my historical mission, I intend to enjoy the private life which I so far have denied myself. I intend to have a family of my own." And he had looked right at her. She had been certain of it.

She sighed. The world had robbed Adolf of a family—and his son of a father.

For a moment she sat, lost in daydreams, listening to the distant whirr of Hacker's sewing machine.

Willi watched the girl. A bond of affection had sprung up between them. It had quickly become obvious to him that Eva was a young woman very much in need of affection, something she had done without through most of her life. At times he had wanted to take her in his arms and comfort her, but the thoughts of the Führer and his unborn child forbade any such action. It would

[188]

likely as not have led to a deeper involvement, which, of course, was out of the question.

But they had talked. The hours of waiting in the various *Anlaufstellen* had been longer than any other hours they had ever known. It was disquieting to be so completely dependent on others, on strangers, as they were, and their mutual uneasiness had brought them together.

Eva sighed. She hugged her knees. He knew she missed her cigarettes, but there was a strict rule of no smoking in all of the *Achse* hiding places. She looked troubled. It was a special look he had seen on her face before. He wondered where her thoughts were taking her. She had told him many little confidences during the long days in the *Baumannshöhle*. Her moments of delight. And of anguish.

The thrill when the Führer, on her twenty-seventh birthday, with obvious pride had presented her with one of the very first Volkswagens which he had just ordered mass-produced for the people . . . Her joy in sports, a joy he shared; skiing, swimming, and hiking, and her childlike excitement over the 1936 Olympics—until her jealousy of the beautiful and talented Leni Riefenstahl, the "priestess of the Nazi Olympics," who found such obvious favor with the Führer, had soured her on the event . . . Her genuine happiness in the memories of her times alone with "the Chief," a term of endearment she often used when she spoke of the Führer . . . Her pleasure in his small attentions . . . And the hurts, the aches. The humiliation she felt at being snubbed by the grand ladies of the Nazi regime, the wives of the high-ranking officials who surrounded her lover, affronts which often thinly disguised an icy animosity. Emmy Goering, Anneliese von Rippentrop, Elsa Himmler, and Magda Goebbels in the forefront. Only once had the Führer angrily stood up for her. Emmy Goering had given a party for all the lady secretaries, assistants, and servants of the Berghof—and on the list had been Eva Braun. Emmy Goering was never again allowed at the Berghof . . . And he knew of the disappointment, the lonely ache when she was being excluded from the glamorous affairs and the big balls attended by the Führer . . . He had felt the raw pain beneath her bantering confession, that after hearing Goebbels proclaiming in a speech that "the Führer is totally devoted to the nation and has no private life," she had referred to herself as *Fräulein Kein Privatleben*—Miss No-Private-Life . . .

And in a moment of emotional anguish she had even let slip in a wretched whisper the two times she had attempted to take her own life when the misery and agony of her relationship with the Führer became unbearable.

He watched her. Her eyes haunted, she was staring out through the window, seeing something other than the bright, blue sky. He frowned, concerned. Something was obviously tearing at her, he knew not what. But he could not afford to have her fall to pieces. Not now.

He touched her arm. "What is it, Eva?" he asked gently. "I am your friend. Perhaps I can help."

Eva turned to him. She looked at him as if seeing him for the first time. Suddenly she sobbed. She flung herself impulsively into his arms and buried her face in his shoulder. She wept. Uncontrollably. Great sobs shook her body as she clung to him.

He held her. He let her cry.

Presently she stopped. She lifted her tear-stained face to his and gazed at him, her eyes liquid in anguish. "I am sorry, Willi," she whispered. "I . . . I . . . ."

"It is all right," he said quietly. "Why not tell me what is troubling you?"

For a moment she sat silent. She looked down, her eyes not meeting his.

"It—it was so terrible," she whispered. "And I was there. I—helped. And—she looked so much like me. I—I killed her, Willi. She is dead because of me. *I* should be dead!"

"Who, Eva? Who did you kill?"

She told him. In a rush of anguished words she told him about the young woman who had taken her place in the bunker. Told him how she changed clothes with her and how she helped put her own dress on the unconscious girl. She told him about the death spasms that racked the young woman's body when the poison phial was crushed in her mouth, and how her own life had been saved by the deliberate sacrifice of another. And she told him of the guilt that had gnawed at her, eaten her—and grown into a monster in her mind, threatening to devour her sanity.

She looked at him, tears brimming in her eyes.

"But I did not do it for me," she sobbed. "I did it for Adolf. For the Führer. And for our child. You must understand that, Willi. Please . . ."

He nodded. "I do understand, Eva," he said quietly. "And you were right in doing what you did. You need feel no guilt. The life of the Führer's son is above all else." He looked solemnly at her. "Put away your guilt," he said. "Guilt is like any other pain.

Whether real or imagined, it hurts just as much. Don't be hurt by a guilt you need not feel."

She nodded. She wiped her eyes. She felt better. Perhaps she had just needed to confide her feelings to someone. Willi was right. What had been done was for the greater good; for the future.

"I will be fine," she said resolutely. "Thank you, Willi."

He smiled at her. He had suspected that something like what Eva had told him had taken place, but he had, of course, not known the details. It must have been an ordeal for a girl, unaccustomed to the necessity of violence. He looked into her face. The shadows in her eyes were still not completely driven out. She had escaped from the bunker, he thought, without a scratch.

Unless you look inside her head.

The air in the little hotel room was charged with tension. Grim-faced the man looked at Woody. "There is nothing I can do," he said flatly. "You and your woman will have to remain here at the *Zum Stern* for a few more days. Perhaps a week."

The dawn of Saturday, June 9, was cloudy, gray, and dismal. It matched Woody's mood perfectly as he listened to the dour *Anlaufstelle* agent destroy his mission with a few words.

He faced a real dilemma. If he was delayed a week, even a couple of days, he would never be able to catch up with Eva and her escort. On the other hand, if he made too much of a damned fuss, he might arouse suspicion and finish off his whole operation himself. There had to be a way.

"Even if the next stop on the route has been closed down," he argued, "for security reasons, as you say, you must have alternatives—other than just having us waiting it out."

The agent looked at him suspiciously. "Why?" he asked tersely. "Why are you so anxious to be on your way? You are quite safe here."

"Ah," Woody said, "that's just it."

The man glared at him, sharply. "Explain yourself," he snapped.

Woody looked straight at him. "I did not want to say this," he pointed out. "But—how safe are we here? Right now—yes. But when more and more travelers gather here to wait, the risks of discovery increase. Perhaps they become too big for me to accept."

The agent frowned at him.

"I am merely looking for a way to minimize any risk that grow out of the closing down of the next stop on the route," Woody explained. "Our risks—as well as yours. The fewer travelers you have to shelter here, the better the odds are for you. The less danger there is. For you."

The man looked thoughtful.

"When you were told of the *Anlaufstelle* shut-down," Woody continued, "you must have been given other instructions. Alternatives. Emergency measures." He let a hint of authority creep into his voice, the ring of a man used to giving orders, and having them obeyed, "I know no plans are made without a backup," he said sharply. "What is it?"

"It will not work," the man said.

"Let me judge for myself," Woody said brusquely. "What is it?"

"We were given the location of the stop next on the route after the one that had to be closed down," the agent said. "For emergency purposes." He looked at Woody. "But it will not work. It is too far. Over a hundred and twenty-five kilometers. Only with motor transportation could you make it. And we have none available."

What transportation do you have?" Woody asked.

"Only bicycles."

Where is the stop?"

For a brief moment the man contemplated him. "In Neustadt on the Aisch," he said. "Between Würzburg and Nürnberg."

"Are our papers ready?" Woody asked. "Up to date?"

The man nodded.

Woody made a fast calculation. A hundred miles. Give or take. They should be able to make it in ten hours on bicycles. They *should* be able to reach Neustadt before curfew. Anyway, they had to try. They had no choice. Resolutely he turned to the *Anlaufstelle* operative. He thought he caught a flash of animosity in the man's eyes. He dismissed it.

"I want to leave for Neustadt," he said firmly. "Within the hour!"

Woody was getting worried. There was a damned good chance they wouldn't reach the stop in Neustadt in time. They had been on the road over two hours and they were just pulling in to the little town of Lichtenfels, only fifteen miles south of Coburg. He cursed under his breath as he pumped the pedals on his bike. Dammit! He hadn't counted on the fucking baskets! Their travel permits stated that they were delivering a load of the famous Coburg baskets to Neustadt. Each of their bikes had a little cart—mounted on bicycle wheels hooked to the back—piled high with the damned things. Even though Ilse valiantly tried to keep up, it slowed them down. Especially on the upgrades, where they often had to dismount and push. No way would they make it, Woody thought gloomily.

He looked back at Ilse, fighting her bike behind him. Sweat stains darkened her blouse under her arms and between her breasts. And locks of auburn hair were caught in the perspiration on her forehead and neck. She looked flushed—and totally desirable.

He smiled at her. He pointed ahead. At the roadside stood a small inn. A sign, with its paint peeling, named it: *Zum Grünen Kranze*—At the Green Wreath.

"Well stop and rest there," he called to her. "Get something cold to drink."

Ilse smiled and nodded.

In the distance, behind them, Woody saw a small cloud of dust rising from the dry dirt road. Rapidly it came nearer and presently a man on a motorcycle roared past, enveloping them in dust.

Woody coughed. When the dust settled, he saw the motorcyclist, a civilian, come to a stop at the inn. He dismounted, wheeled his motorcycle into the shade at the side of the building, and entered the inn.

Woody began to pedal as fast as he could. Startled, Ilse tried to keep up. In a couple of minutes he came to a halt at the inn. He pushed his bike up next to the parked motorcycle. He inspected it. It was a Belgian make, late 1930s model.

Ilse joined him.

Woody stood staring at the motorbike. It was against all the rules laid down by the *Achse*—but what the hell. He had to take the chance, or he might as well kiss his whole damned mission goodby. He didn't want to come crawling back to Buter telling him he screwed up. The guy would nail his balls to the nearest wall.

"Quick!" he said. "Grab half a dozen of those damned baskets." He turned to the motorcycle. "This thing is going to get us to Neustadt in no time!"

At once, without questioning him, Ilse grabbed some of the wicker baskets. She hung a few of them over each arm. Woody kicked up the side stand and mounted the bike.

"Get behind me," he said. "And hold on."

She did—the baskets sticking out to the sides like wicker wings of a wheeled Pegasus.

Woody stomped on the kick starter. The motorcycle roared to life—and in a cloud of dust they careened down the road.

They were making excellent time. Less than an hour later and thirty miles closer to their destination, a few miles before the town of Bamber, the motorcycle engine sputtered, missed—and died.

Using a long straw Woody tested the fuel tank.

It came up bone dry.

They were still a good fifty miles from the *Anlaufstelle* in Neustadt. They had no transportation—and they were saddled with half a dozen baskets they could not discard because their travel permits specifically stated they were bringing them to Neustadt.

Woody kicked the motorcycle. Dammit all to hell!

He peered ahead up the road. In the far distance he could make out the skyline of the city of Bamberg. They had no choice. They'd have to push the damned bike with the damned baskets—and hope they'd be able to find some gasoline in town.

He knew the chances were as close to nil as they could get.

It was just before noon when they passed by a railroad yard on the northern outskirts of the city. Parked at a warehouse were three or four American 2½-ton trucks.

Woody stopped. While Ilse sat down on the grassy road shoulder to rest, he took the opportunity to inspect the contents of a small leather pouch attached to the rear of the seat. A short chain and a combination lock to secure the motorbike when unattended; it would do him no good, he did not know the combination of the lock; a few open-end and box-end wrenches wrapped in an oily rag. That was all. While he looked it over he watched the trucks. One GI was guarding them. He stood, smoking a cigarette, at the lead vehicle. No one else was in sight.

Woody motioned to Ilse. "Come on." He began to wheel the motorcycle along the road toward the railroad yard. And the trucks. "Look, Ilse," he said urgently, "when we get to the trucks we'll stop again. You go on up to the soldier. Talk to him. Understand?"

Ilse shot him a startled glance. "Talk?" she said. Then, quickly, she saw what he was after. "Yes," she said. "I will do it. I will keep him—occupied."

Woody watched the girl walk up to the GI. Apparently she asked for a cigarette. He saw the grinning GI give her one and light it for her, while he ogled her. Ilse was smiling and chattering. She'd keep the guy busy, Woody thought. Long enough.

He wheeled the bike to the far side of the trucks, out of sight of the sentry. There were three trucks. He ran to the nearest one. In the side rack were two Jerry cans. Gasoline.

[194]

He stopped in consternation. A steel chain ran through the handles of the cans. They were locked to the truck. His eyes flew down the road of trucks. All the cans had chains.

He stared at the can before him. It was all there. Every drop he'd need—and a helluva lot to spare. But how the hell was he going to get it?

Siphon it! He could siphon out enough of it. Even as he thought it he knew it was impossible. What with? He had no tube. Nothing. So how the hell . . .

Suddenly he knew how.

He tore his shirt out of his trousers and ripped off part of it. He wrapped the rag around a stick he found on the ground and tied it. He opened the lid on the can and stuck the cloth into it. It came up dripping wet.

Gasoline!

Quickly he wheeled the bike up close to the truck. Again he dipped the rag into the can and wrung it out over the open fuel tank on the bike. Half a cup. More. He set to work. Dipping and wringing. He felt totally exposed. Any second he expected to hear a shout of alarm. It suddenly struck him that everyone was his enemy. Krauts and Americans alike. Every man, woman, and child—every GI. He was hunted by all. He prayed that Ilse would be able to keep the GI interested and that no one else would show up.

A few minutes later he was done. He estimated he'd wrung out a couple or three pints of gasoline. Enough to get them to Neustadt.

He threw the stick away. His hands reeked of gasoline. He gloried in the stink of it. He wheeled the bike back to the road.

Ilse saw him. Quickly she leaned forward and lightly kissed the GI on the lips. As quickly she drew away and, waving gaily, she ran toward the road.

Woody was waiting for her. She'd done her job well, he thought. But did she have to kiss the damned guy?

It felt good to have her close behind him again, the baskets jutting out from her arms.

He gunned the motorcycle and barreled off toward Neustadt.

Willi looked at his watch. It was past noon. Their transportation would be ready to pick them up at two o'clock, Hacker had told them. They would get to their next stop in Memmingen well before dark.

He looked at Eva. She had regained her composure complete-ly. "We should be getting our things together," he said. "I'll just make a trip downstairs."

Eva stood up. "I'll go with you," she said.

They made their way down the steep stairs from the attic. They could hear Hacker rummaging around for something in his rooms on the second floor. They continued down to the workroom.

Willi was making for the little bathroom when suddenly the heavy portiere in the doorway to the shop was thrown aside and a young woman, a couple of dresses cradled in her arms, came into the workroom.

"Herr Hacker," she called. *"Können Sie . . ."* She stopped short. Her hand flew to her mouth. She stared at Eva.

"Eva!" she exclaimed. *"Du lieber Gott!* Eva Braun!"

19

———◦•◦———

Eva stood transfixed, staring at the girl. Willi at once stepped
up to the young woman. He smiled at her—that special smile with
which a man can tell a woman that she attracts him. "You are
mistaken, *Fräulein*," he said pleasantly, holding her eyes with his.
"My sister's name is Anneliese. Not Eva." His eyes subtly ex-
plored her puzzled face. "A pity all the same," he said regretfully.
"I should have liked you and Anneliese to be friends."

The girl frowned prettily at Eva. "But I . . ."

Hacker came into the room. "Ah! *Fräulein* Damm," he said,
"I see you have brought the dresses. I am certain we can fix them
up for you." He fingered them analytically. "Yes, yes," he nodded. "There are many months of wear left in them." He took her
by the arm and steered her toward the door to the front shop.
"You will try them on, yes? In the dressing room." He turned to
Willi and Eva. "I will be with you in just a few moments," he
said politely. "I have your suit ready, *mein Herr.*"

And he disappeared into the shop with the bewildered girl.

Willi turned to Eva, who stood, ashen-faced, beside him, staring after Hacker and the girl. "Who is she?" he whispered hoarsely,
obviously deeply disturbed. "How does she know who you are?"

"Fannerl Damm," Eva breathed. "She was—my best friend. At
Simbach."

"Simbach?"

Eva nodded. "It—it is only about a hundred kilometers east of
here," she explained. "On the Austrian border. There was a con-
vent school for girls there. It was run by the English sisters. I went

to school there. I was sixteen. Fannerl, she was my best friend." She stood staring at the faded blue portiere seemingly unaware of what she was saying. "It was so strict. Rules and rules. I—I hated it. Only the shows were fun. We—we used to put on shows. Fannerl was always so good."

"Eva," Willi said firmly. He took her by the shoulders and gazed intently into her eyes. "Go to the attic. Wait there. I will talk to your friend. Explain why it is important she does not know you. We have not much time. Go. Now. Please."

Eva nodded. "We were—best friends, Fannerl and I," she whispered. "Best friends . . ."

She started up the stairs.

Willi turned toward the shop. He was profoundly alarmed. The impossible had happened. Eva had been recognized. The danger was enormous. Frightening. He *had* to make sure her friend stayed silent.

He parted the curtains and peered into the shop. Hacker was just taking his leave of the young woman. She stopped in the door and glanced back at the curtained workshop, an expression of excitement and puzzlement on her face.

She left.

Willi hurried into the shop. "Help my travel mate get ready," he said to Hacker. "She is upstairs. I will be back."

Hacker nodded. Willi slipped out of the door into the street. A short distance away he saw Fannerl Damm hurrying across the street.

He followed.

The girl walked rapidly down a side street and entered a small apartment house. Willi ran after her. It was imperative that he get to her before she had a chance to talk to anyone. To gossip about her secret discovery.

He stepped through the front door—just in time to hear a door close on the floor above. He ran up the stairs, two steps at a time. On the door to one of the apartments on the landing was a sign: F. Damm.

He knocked.

Fannerl Damm opened the door. She looked at Willi with astonishment.

"Please, *Fräulein* Damm," he said quickly, "forgive me. I did not want to startle you. But I thought we owed you an explanation. May I come in?"

The young woman regarded him, a strange hopeful, timid, and

appraising look in her eyes. He recognized the look. It dwelled in the eyes of so many young women in Germany. It was the look of loneliness. She held the door open. *"Bitte,"* she said prettily, not unaware that Willi was apparently attracted to her.

He stepped into the room. It was a small, one-room apartment with a kitchen alcove. He took it all in with a single glance. A large bed, neatly made; a threadbare sofa; a table with two straight-backed wooden chairs; a chest of drawers with a pink-patterned porcelain washbowl and pitcher and a mirrored back; a large wardrobe painted with colorful Bavarian ornaments. Fannerl Damn did not live in luxurious surroundings.

"It *is* Eva," she said, looking straight at Willi. "I was certain of it!" She was obviously excited. "When we heard what happened in Berlin, I—I cried." She put her hand on Willi's arm. "We were best friends," she confided. "Many years ago. You understand. I could not be mistaken." She clasped her hands to her chest. "Oh, it is so wonderful she is still alive!"

"Fräulein Damm," Willi said quietly. "There is something I must tell you. Something of great importance." He looked solemnly into her eyes. They were pale blue, almost white, he thought. He placed his hands gently on her shoulders and felt her nearly imperceptible shiver of pleasure. "Will you listen to me?"

"Of course."

"You are aware, now, of Eva's relationship to the Führer?" he asked.

"Of course," Fannerl said, bubbling with the excitement. "It was so—fantastic! I did not know. Not until the announcement came out that she and the Führer were dead. And that Eva had become the Führer's wife!"

Willi nodded grimly. He paced before her. "This brings me to the point I want to discuss with you, *Fräulein* Damm," he said. For a moment he paced in silence, obviously searching for the best way to say what he had to say. He walked behind her chair. "I—I hope you will understand."

She started to turn to him. He touched her hair. "Your hair is very pretty," he said softly. "It has such a lovely shine."

She looked down at her hands. He could see the blush rise on her neck.

"Thank you," she whispered.

The blade sliced across her throat, biting into her white skin as easily as a warm knife into soft butter, severing her jugular vein and cutting her windpipe, instantly choking off any sound. Only a bubbly gurgle frothed in her slashed throat. She wrenched her head around in a final spasm of agony. Her eyes met his in an eternal moment even as they glazed over in death—the astonishment and hurt in them dying with her. The warm blood that welled out over his hands felt silken and slick. He picked her up. He was surprised. In death she was heavier than he had thought she would be. He carried her to the bed and put her down. The bedding would absorb the blood. No need to leave a mess in the room. He poured some water into the porcelain basin and washed the blood from his hands.

He turned the girl over. Only a little blood was still oozing from her throat. Her open eyes stared up at him as if they wanted to commit to a dead memory the image of the man who had robbed her of her life.

Involuntarily he shuddered. He was instantly angry with himself. The primary rule was to sever from yourself all feelings when a disagreeable duty had to be performed. And the girl *had* been a menace. A menace that had to be eradicated. Ruthlessly—and without delay. No regrets. In his mind he heard the Führer's solemn charge: No one must know. The secret must stay with us.

He had only made certain it would.

One more thing.

He did not know the woman's connection with Hacker's tailor shop, but the *Anlaufstelle* had to be protected; no suspicion that would trigger an investigation involving the shop—by either the German or the American authorities—must become a possibility.

He would have to make the killing look like a robbery. No. There was nothing worth taking. It would not make sense. A rape? Possible. Suddenly he had the answer.

Werewolves.

He remembered the lurid warning poster he'd seen tacked up on a fence in Bamberg, addressed "to all traitors and collaborators." In it the Bavarian werewolves threatened death and destruction to all who collaborated with the enemy. *"Unser Rache ist tödlich!*—Our Vengeance is Deadly!—the broadside had stated. And it had been signed *"Der Werwolf'*—"The Werewolf."

It was perfect.

He dipped his finger in the still moist and glistening stain on the bed that had been the life of Eva's best friend. On the mirror he printed in blood: *AMI HURE!*—Ami Whore!

And he signed it, *"Der Werwolf."*

He took a last look at the dead girl.

A word had killed her.

One single word.

Eva.

He glanced at his watch. It was seven minutes to two. He had less then seven minutes to get back to the shop in time for the two o'clock rendezvous with their transportation.

He ran from the room. He bounded down the stairs. He almost collided with an elderly woman entering the downstairs hallway.

"*Heil Hitler!*" he shouted at her.

Startled, she gaped after him as he rushed out of the door and ran down the street.

The soldier sat warily on a slab of broken masonry from a demolished building a few houses down the street from Hacker's tailor shop. His *Wehrmacht* uniform was close to being tattered and there was no way of knowing the rank or service branch of the man. All insignia had been removed. At his feet stood a soiled burlap bag. It probably contained all his worldly belongings. Unshaven, empty-eyed, he looked tired, disillusioned, and dejected.

SS Sturmbannführer Oskar Strelitz had found the disguise as a returning prisoner of war a most effective one. There were thousands of them roaming the roads and streets of postwar Germany trying to make their way home. No one bothered them. The US soldiers looked away, uncomfortably—half guiltily, it seemed. The Germans did not want to get involved; it might mean being asked for food or lodgings. And there was nothing to share. It was exactly what Strelitz wanted. To be left alone. By everyone.

He was watching the tailor shop that served as a *B-B Achse* stop. He had seen Lüttjohann run from the place and hurriedly return. He felt the familiar rushing wariness tingle through him; that faculty of being able to feel trouble in the tips of his fingers, developed through his years of SS investigation—his *Fingerspitzengefühl*. He had long since learned to respect it. It had often saved his life.

He tensed as he saw Eva and Lüttjohann come out of the shop. They were carrying their belongings. They began to walk down the sidewalk toward him. He shrank against the demolished building, melting into the ruins.

Behind the approaching couple he saw a canvas-covered US Army weapons carrier come driving down the road. Eva and Lüttjohann were still about fifty feet from him, when he saw the weapons carrier pass them, abruptly cut to the curb and stop just ahead of them. A big, black sergeant, holding a 30 Ml Carbine, jumped from the cab and barred the way of Eva and her escort.

Tensely Strelitz strained to hear what was said, but they were too far away. He saw the American hold out his hand. He saw the terrified look of alarm in Eva's eyes. He saw Lüttjohann reach into his pocket and hand the Negro sergeant his ID papers.

The big black soldier looked at the papers and gave them back. With his carbine he gruffly motioned them to get into the back of the truck. He followed.

Strelitz stiffened. His hand stole through the front of his tunic to touch the Luger nestled in his belt. Quickly he assessed the situation. When the truck started up and came close, he could pick off the driver. When the black soldier got out to investigate, he would kill him. He then could help Eva and Lüttjohann escape.

He heard the truck start up.

His grip on the Luger tightened, and slowly he began to pull it out. He stood up.

As he did, he was able to look past the driver of the approaching truck, through the open cab into the rear. The back canvas flap was open and he caught a flash image of the three people sitting inside the little truck. All three of them were smiling. The big sergeant was lighting a cigarette for Eva—while Lüttjohann held his carbine!

Strelitz froze, the Luger half out, and the truck came abreast of him. It gathered speed and drove off down the street.

Slowly Strelitz let out his breath. It had been close. It was audacious. Using an American vehicle and what appeared to be American personnel to transport *B-B Achse* fugitives. Was it possible? He had to confirm it. At once.

He picked up his burlap bag and began to shuffle down the street toward Hacker's tailor shop.

Eva drew the smoke from the cigarette into her lungs. She luxuriated the feeling of well-being it created in her. She looked at it. Lucky Strike. It was excellent.

Out of the corners of her eyes she watched the black sergeant. She had never been close to a Negro before, and the man fascinated her. Jet-black, tightly curled hair; a broad nose with flaring nostrils and full lips in a deep brown face. Like chocolate mousse, she thought. She found him primitively attractive. Of course, Adolf had told her the Negro people were *Untermenschen*. Inferior, less than human. Only slightly better than Jews. It had all been scientifically researched and proved, he had told her. She remembered when.

Once, in an amateur show during her school days she had impersonated Al Jolson singing "Sonny Boy." She had told Adolf about it and showed him a snapshot of her in blackface. He had burst out laughing at seeing her disguised as a Jew impersonating a Negro, as he had said. He had asked to be allowed to keep the little photograph, and he had told her about the black people—*Die Schwarze.*

They had left town and were whamming down the country road. Eva shifted on the hard wooden bench. A piece of paper had been caught in a crack. Absentmindedly she pulled it free. She smoothed it out, glanced at it—stiffened.

It was part of a page from the American soliders' paper, the *Stars and Stripes.* Dated May 28, 1945, the headline said:

LUFTWAFFE LEADER COMMITS SUICIDE.

The photograph of Ritter von Greim that had caught her attention showed him in his General's uniform, although the story below it, partly torn away, identified him as Fieldmarshal, the last commander in chief of the Luftwaffe, appointed by Hitler. She read it. Her knowledge of English was good enough so that she could understand the gist of it. Briefly it told of von Greim's distinguished career as a much-decorated pilot in World War I and his command of an air fleet on the Eastern Front until his promotion. Suffering from a wounded foot, which had become infected, the story reported, he was admitted to the hospital in Kitzbühel in Austria, accompanied by the famous test pilot, Hanna Reitsch. On May 24, after the town had been taken by American troops, he took his life.

She bit her lip. She knew Greim had been given a vital mission by the Führer when he left the bunker. She knew he had been told to guard its secret with his life. And she knew how very important Adolf had considered it. He had called it Operation Future.

She wondered if it was to make certain he would not be forced to reveal this, the Führer's final charge, to the enemy, that the *Feldmarschall* had taken his own life.

Did it matter now?

She sat back. She closed her eyes and let the swaying of the truck rock her.

In a couple of hours they would be in Memmingen—at their next stop.

P I N O C C H I O

Woody and Ilse stared at the sign over the little shop on Bodenfelsstrasse 97 in Neustadt, every letter brightly painted in a different color and leaning every which way. In the small display window a generously gilded crèche vied for attention with a boy-sized Pinocchio puppet, surrounded by a clutter of other puppets, marionettes, and carved wooden figurines. Under the playful name of the shop was the legend: *Manfred Moser—Holzschnitzerei.*

Woody looked at the place with a skeptical frown. Could that be the *B-B Achse Anlaufstelle?* It was the address they'd been given. He was sure of it. Both he and Ilse remembered it as Bodenfelsstrasse 97. He had a quick pang of alarm. Had they misheard? Both of them? It was not likely. But—a place full of wooden puppets? Manfred Moser, the sign said, Woodcarving. On the other hand, he thought wryly, what's the difference between Moser's puppets and Zorina's dolls? But he couldn't quite erase the feeling of misgivings from his mind. Had the *Zum Stern* agent given them a bum steer? The man *had* seemed a bit resentful when he, Woody, had insisted on leaving early. And the passwords. *Festhalle*—Banquet Hall, and the countersign, *Mädchenfüralles*–handmaid. Somehow they didn't seem appropriate. How the hell did you work the words *Banquet Hall* into a casual conversation with a damned woodcarver?

He wheeled the motorcycle into a small alley next to the building and put it on the side stand. He and Ilse both took an armful of baskets and entered the woodcarving shop. It was just past noon. They had made excellent time.

A small bell over the door tinkled delicately. No one was to be seen in the shop. Curiously Woody looked around. There were puppets everywhere. Marionettes and half-finished string puppets hanging from the wall; rod puppets, hand puppets, and a couple of ventriloquist dummies propped up wherever there was room; fantoccini, wooden figurines, and severed heads cluttered shelves and tables. And Pinocchios. Every size and shape, with only the long nose in common. At the rear of the shop stood a marionette theater with an ornate proscenium, flanked by heavy draperies. A gaudily clad marionette hung limply over the front of the stage.

Woody and Ilse put down their baskets.

"Hello!" Woody called tentatively. "Anyone here?"

Suddenly a singsong voice rang out:

> *Bitte! Bitte! Bitte!*
> *Was wünschen Sie, mein Herr?*
> If you please! If you please!
> What do you want, good Sir?

Startled they looked toward the voice. The puppet hanging over the front of the marionette theater stage had come to life. He sat on the edge of the stage, cocking his little head at them and waving his hand.

Woody took a step toward the little theater. "Is anyone here?" he asked. As soon as he had said it, he realized how inane it was.

Elaborately the puppet swung around and looked up and down in every direction. "Anyone here?" he sang. "Anyone here?" He leaned forward at an impossible angle and looked directly at Woody. "I see no one. Do you?"

Ilse watched the strutting little puppet with delight, but Woody was not amused. It seemed hardly the time for fun and games. All he wanted, dammit! was the address of the next stop, their papers fixed up, some gasoline—and to be on his way. He was in no mood to hold a conversation with a retarded Mortimer Snerd, for crissake!

The puppet blew kisses at Ilse.

> *Warum, warum, warum,*
> *Ist die Banane krumm?*

He sang with earthy Bavarian peasant humor.

> *Warum ist sie nicht g'rade?*
> *Das ist doch furchtbar schade.*

> Why? Why? Why?
> Is the banana bent?
> Why is he not erect?
> That is a dreadful shame.

"Whoever is back there," Woody said testily, "we only want some information, please. We have just come to town and we wondered if you could recommend a hotel to us. A reasonable place. It need not have a *Festhalle*—a Banquet Hall."

"Hotels are for sleeping," the marionette sang out. "Not for me! Not for me! *I* like to dance." And the puppet launched into an animated jig.

Woody stiffened. The countersign! The puppeteer had not given him the countersign! Had he heard? Could he? Behind those damned draperies?

"Please," he said loudly and firmly, "I should very much like an answer. You are not in a *Festhalle* now, my little friend. So, please stop dancing and give me an answer, if you can."

The puppet stopped. He bowed. "As you wish, *mein Herr*," he said. You might try the *Gasthaus Krüger*. Two streets to your left."

Woody suddenly felt cold. Something was wrong. Very, very wrong. Either they were in the wrong place, or they had been given the wrong passwords. He was suddenly certain of it. An *Anlaufstelle* agent wouldn't make a mockery out of the process of identification, as the puppeteer was doing. The man was just a simple woodcarver. Bavaria was famous for its colorful woodcarvings. There must be thousands of artisans. They had been sent to the wrong place. Deliberately? Had the bastard in Coburg maliciously misled them? Double-crossed them? To show them who was boss? If so, he had only one recourse: Return to Coburg and get the right information. It meant he was dead. As far as the mission was concerned. Dammit all to hell!

"Thank you," he said leadenly.

He started for the door, followed by Ilse. The baskets. They had to hang on to those damned baskets. Come up with some cock-and-bull story of why they were returning to Coburg with them, if they were stopped. He started to pick them up.

Suddenly a door burst open and a woman came hurrying into the shop from a back room.

"Manfred!" she called. "Stop him! Do not let him go!"

At once the puppet on the stage plopped to the floor like a wet rag. The draperies were flung aside—and a man stood facing them.

A steady hand held a Walther 7.65 pointed straight at Woody's guts.

"Stay right where you are," he ordered coldly. "Both of you. Do not make a move!"

20

WOODY GLARED AT THE PUPPETEER. The man was not at all what he had expected. Not the simple, roly-poly and playful Bavarian peasant type, but a man in his fifties, lean to the point of being gaunt, with a deep scar, recent enough still to burn angrily red, running from his left temple to the tip of his chin. Cold, hard eyes bored into them.

Woody drew himself up. "What do you mean by threatening us?" he exclaimed in outrage. "I shall call the police!" He surveyed the man standing before him. His extreme gauntness gouged deep, black hollows under his eyes and in his cheeks. In a flash image Woody saw the faces of the Flossenburg Concentration Camp inmates. Theirs had been the faces of suffering and horror. The face of the man confronting him was the face of ruthlessness and menace.

The woman urgently whispered something in the man's ear. He looked startled. He asked her a question. The woman answered it. Although he tried, Woody could not make out what was being said. The man frowned at him.

"You asked to be directed to a hotel," he said slowly. "What kind of hotel did you say you were looking for?"

"You heard me perfectly well when I asked," Woody snapped angrily. "A reasonable place. Simple. Without luxuries such as a *Festhalle*."

The puppet maker drew a deep breath. "I was—mistaken," he said. "I should not have recommended *Gasthaus Krüger*. There is another place, more suited to your needs. A simple place. With a *Mädchenfüralles* who will take care of you." He lowered the gun.

"What the hell is going on?" Woody asked, exasperated. His fear, only just relieved, still made him sound tense and angry.

"You must forgive us," the man said. "But it is better to be overcautious than not cautious enough." He put away the gun. "My wife just now received the new passwords. Because the Bamberg *Anlaufstelle* had to be closed down temporarily—a matter of possible compromise—all passwords were changed." He looked at Woody. "You were not expected here until tonight. You are early." He eyed him with obvious curiosity.

"We were lucky," Woody shrugged. "We came into possession of a motorcycle. We made good time."

The woodcarver nodded.

"It is still early in the day," Woody went on. "We should like our travel papers brought up to date, including the motorcycle. We need some gasoline—and we shall be on our way to the next *Anlaufstelle*." He looked at the man. "Where is it?"

"In Nördlingen," the man answered. "At a tailor shop." He put out his hand. "May I have your papers?"

Woody handed them to him. He was beginning to relax. "Here," he said, "I am glad I do not have to present them to your puppet."

The man smiled mirthlessly. "You must forgive me my little act," he said, as he examined Woody's papers. "It is my cover. A good cover. Who would consider a simple-minded puppet maker a menace, or an agent of the SS?"

He put Woody's papers in his pocket. He turned to Ilse. "May I have your papers, too," he asked. Ilse gave them to him. "We have a collection point," the man said. "Close by. *Mutti* will take you there. I shall have your papers fixed up—and you can leave for Nördlingen already tomorrow morning."

"We want to leave today," Woody said firmly. "There is still plenty of time to reach Nördlingen."

The woodcarver gave him a quick glance. "That will not be possible," he said.

Woody looked straight at him. Here we go again, he thought. "You owe us," he said quietly. "And everything is possible, if you want it to be." He went on, emphasizing every word. "Besides, I know the comrades in *Die Spinne* will—appreciate your cooperation."

The puppet maker gave Woody a sharp glance at the mention of the powerful, secret SS organization that operated the *B-B Achse*. Woody's veiled hint of the consequences, were he *not* to be cooperative, was not lost on him. He studied the young man. Who was he? Really? And the girl? She was unusual. Only one other woman had passed through his stop. Only days ago. Who were they? There was no way of knowing. It was possible they were nobodies. It was also possible they were not.

"Two hours," he said flatly. Narrow-eyed he looked at Woody. "I will, of course, have to log your request for emergency processing."

"Do that."

The agent turned to his wife. "Give them something to do," he said drily. "They should not be idle if we have visitors." He turned to Woody. "I will bring your travel papers to you here," he said. "In two hours."

He left.

The woman turned to Ilse. "Come with me," she said pleasantly. "I will give you something to do. Sew buttons on a little jacket, perhaps. For Pinocchio. And your young man, I will ask him to repair a broken board in the bridge behind the stage."

They set to work. Woody watched Ilse, as she sewed tiny buttons on a diminutive green Bavarian peasant jacket. She sure is easy on the eyes, he thought. A regular pinup. He wondered about her. Who was she? And how did she come to have the pull she did? He'd tried, in a half-assed way, to draw her out. At first, he thought she'd been friendly, although understandably reticent, but after they'd left Zorina's place she'd seemed withdrawn.

Ilse looked up. She caught him watching her and quickly averted her eyes. Dammit, he thought. What the hell gives?

"Ilse," he said evenly, "you and I are going to have to be together for a long time. Under circumstances that may not always be easy. We will be—damned close. We will have to be able to depend on one another. Trust one another." He looked searchingly at her. "Is there something wrong? If there is, now is the time to . . . to clear the air."

For a moment she sat motionless, without speaking. Only her fingers moved, manipulating the tiny buttons. He did not break in on her silence; she was obviously trying to arrange her thoughts. Her emotions. He could almost see when she reached her decision. When she finally spoke, her voice was low.

"Is it true?" she asked. "Is it true what Madama Zorina said?"

Puzzled, he frowned. It was a totally unexpected question.

"What?" he asked. "Is what true?"

"That you were in charge of the guards—at Flossenburg Concentration Camp?"

A spontaneous denial almost burst from him. He caught himself. It *was* true. Of *SS Hauptsturmsführer* Fritz Diehl, it was true. And he was Fritz Diehl. For now.

"Why?" he asked, playing for time.

"Is it true what—what the Americans say about those camps?" she asked. "The—the terrible things they say went on there?"

It was becoming a conversation of questions, he thought. No answers. Well, dammit! here was one. "Yes!" he snapped vehemently. "Every damned word."

She flinched as if he had hit her. She gave a little sob.

"Is that—what you did?" she breathed.

He was torn. His cover demanded he say yes. But it was obvious that the girl was appalled and revolted at what she had heard. She would reject him totally, if she thought he'd really been part of it. He could not afford that. He also realized that he did not want it. Yet he knew that as a good operative he could not afford to weaken his cover by denying involvement.

"No," he said hoarsely. What the hell was he doing?

She looked up at him. "But—Zorina said . . ."

"Zorina was assuming," he said curtly. "I did not think it necessary to correct her."

"Then, what . . ."

"Ilse," he said earnestly, looking into her face, "accept the fact that I was *not* involved in the horrors of the—the concentration camps. Accept the fact that I abhor what went on there as much as you do. And—accept the fact that the circumstances in which we find ourselves make it impossible to talk freely and openly about everything."

She looked into his eyes. "I want to believe you," she said softly.

"You can."

She nodded. Somehow he knew she did.

"The camps," she whispered. "They were under the control of the *Reichsführer?*"

"Himmler?"

She looked at him, oddly. "Yes. *Reichsführer* Heinrich Himmler."

He nodded. "That's correct."

She bit her lip. "It is—because of him that I am here," she whispered.

Woody was startled "Himmler? Because of Himmler? How?"

"He issued a personal directive to the SS organization in command. He instructed them to—to make certain I was taken to safety."

"Why?" He asked the obvious question with reservations. Did he want to know?

"My mother," Ilse said. "She—she had a position with the SS. She asked the *Reichsführer*. She thought Germany would not be a good place for me. After the war was lost."

"Why did she think that?"

"I do not know."

"Your mother," he said, "what did she do? For the SS?"

"I am not sure," Ilse replied uncertainly. "Something in administration." She sounded almost apologetic. "I was always away. At school. For the last few years I only saw my mother when she came to visit me."

"Where is she now?"

Ilse shook her head. "I do not know." She fell silent, and busied herself with her minuscule buttons. He watched her. Somehow he felt warm and happy.

Ilse looked up. "I know it is not your real name, Hans Bauhacker," she said timidly. "I—I want to call you by a name just for me. When we are—together." She looked up at him, wide-eyed, as if frightened by her own audacity. "Of course," she added quickly. "I will not want to know your *real* name. I . . . ."

"Woody," he blurted out.

"Wu-di?" She frowned prettily.

Shit, he thought, disgusted with himself. Now I've done it! "No, no. *Ru*di. Nickname for Rudolf." He smiled.

She smiled back at him. "Rudi," she said softly, "I am glad they chose you to go with me."

The way she said the name made him wish it really was his.

Willi had wondered how it was possible for two *Ami* soldiers in an American vehicle to transport *B-B Achse* fugitives, the kind of subjects the entire enemy army was searching for, along the SS escape route, until he realized that they had no idea of what they were doing.

They were nothing but black marketeers. Contemptuous parasites, he thought, preying upon both their own and the vanquished.

Assigned to a supply unit they often traveled between towns in their area of occupation, and occasionally—at the request of their "customers" and for a suitable expression of appreciation—they would take along a civilian or two. To visit a sick aunt or something.

They had let him and Eva off at one of the gates in the ancient walls that still partly surrounded the oldest part of this historic town on the Ach River. Memmingen was an important railhead on the Augsburg-Ulm line, Willi knew, and was known for its

[211]

woolen goods, its soaps, and its rope making. Like all the towns in Bavaria it teemed with sad, gray townspeople mingled with enemy occupation troops and a host of discharged prisoners of war and civilian refugees left strewn about the countryside in the tens of thousands.

The Memmingen *Anlaufstelle* was a rope manufacturing plant near the railroad yards; their contact was the plant manager, Heinz Ludwig.

A faded sign on an old red-brick building proclaimed:

RADEMACHER & SOHN
SEILEREI
Gegründet   1888

"We were shut down during the last year of the war," Ludwig explained as they walked down the narrow ropewalk past the massive rope-making machinery. Willi looked around in awe. The building must be at least 250 meters long, he thought.

"We make primarily rope and binder twine here," Ludwig told them. "But we could not get any hard fiber cordage. We had to close down. At a time when our product was most needed by the Reich," he finished bitterly.

He gestured toward several men working on the machinery. "We are in the process of readying the plant to resume production, as you can see."

They walked past the breakers, the spinning devices, the forming and laying machines. At the far end of the ropery was a large storage room. A few old bales of deteriorated fiber and a couple of huge coils of old rope were shoved against the wall; otherwise the place was empty, awaiting new production material. At the far end was a door. Ludwig headed for it.

"We have partitioned off a room from the storage area," he said. "For the use of *Achse* travelers." He smiled, revealing badly decayed teeth. "Ostensibly a rest area for our workers, of course. You will be comfortable there until we are ready to pass you on."

"When?"

Ludwig pursed his lips. "Possibly tomorrow morning."

Willi glanced at Eva. She looked tired. She could do with a good night's rest. The last six weeks had made her condition quite noticeable. It must be a great strain on her. He admired her. She had not complained. But it was obviously becoming difficult, if not impossible, for her to travel any great distances via bicycle or by walking. And they still had a long way to go. The most difficult part. He turned to Ludwig.

"How will we travel?" he asked.

Ludwig shook his head. "I do not know that yet," he said. "I will be informed. Memmingen is a *Verteilerkopf* on the *Achse*—an important distribution center. Other routes branch off here. Travel must be coordinated." He glanced at Eva, not quite able to hide his disapproval. "I shall try to obtain—eh, suitable transportation," he said archly. "By motorcar, perhaps by train."

Willi nodded. "We will wait," he said.

"Excellent," Ludwig agreed. "It is best you remain here. Tomorrow is Sunday. There will be many *Amis* in town. I will have your new Military Government permits for you by then."

"Tomorrow then," Willi said. "Meanwhile, might we have something to eat?"

"Of course. I shall bring you some food." Ludwig left.

Eva sat down on one of the beds. She hoped Ludwig would bring something soft to eat. Like *Leberwurst*. She still had trouble chewing, with those teeth missing in her lower jaw. If only she could have had that bridge put in. She sighed. She was bone tired. Her back—in fact her entire body—ached. She sank back, trying to relax.

Suddenly she felt a tiny movement in her abdomen. A distinct little push. Or kick. All at once she was overwhelmed with tenderness. It was the quickening. She was certain now. A small new life was growing in her—and had made its presence felt. Gently she placed her hands on her beginning swelling. There. Again. A little kick.

She gloried in it, a secret smile illuminating her face. She closed her eyes. In her hands she lovingly cradled the tiny life within her. The life that was part her and part Adolf. A little son, they had told her.

A little boy—in the image of the Führer, Adolf Hitler.

Nördlingen had been left behind a little over half an hour before, and so had the damned baskets, except for one they had tied to the back of the bike as a carry-all. It was only just past 1800 hours and they should have no trouble reaching the Memmingen stop, sixty or sixty-five miles farther, in two and a half hours, before the 2030-hour curfew. Woody wondered what a rope-making joint would be like. He'd never seen one. The little dirt road that led directly south toward Memmingen had been virtually deserted, and they were making excellent time.

Hacker, the tailor who ran the Nördlingen stop, had been only too happy to speed them on their way. It had actually taken him less than an hour to get their forged AMG permits renewed to Memmingen, and hustle up a couple of gallons of black market gasoline for their motorbike. Nervously he'd asked them not to wait in his shop, but to go to a *Gasthaus* nearby to eat and come back for their papers later—on the pretext of picking up Woody's jacket which he left for repair. The man had explained that there was a strong possibility that authorities would come to his shop. He—and the *Anlaufstelle* operation—were in no direct danger, but a customer who had left several items of clothing with him earlier in the day, had been found brutally murdered. By the Werewolves, they said. And investigators might come to his shop to talk to him. He had apparently been the last to see her alive. It was best to take no chances. Woody had agreed.

They were entering a little town called Dillingen on the Danube, when Woody suddenly slowed down.

Ahead a couple of jeeps were parked off the roadway and several GIs and German civilians were gathered in a group.

Woody swore under his breath. He knew at once what it was. A roadblock. A checkpoint for snap security checks. He knew where such checkpoints usually were set up; at bridges, intersections, and railroad stations, and he'd tried to avoid them. As Hacker had said, it was best to take no chances. What the hell was a roadblock doing at the town limits of a two-bit burg?

There was nothing he could do. Slowly he rolled up to the roadblock and came to a halt.

A corporal came over to them. "Off!" he ordered gruffly, gesturing for them to dismount. "Off! *Schnell!*" He pointed to the group of apprehensive German villagers huddled nearby. *"Da. Gehen,"* he said. *"Gehen! Schnell!"*

Woody wheeled his bike over to the group. What the hell was going on? Nobody asked for his ID.

After a short while a sergeant, a big, burly man—looking mean and rough enough, Woody thought, to be picking his damned teeth with a rusty nail—came over to the group. Legs spread, arms akimbo, he glared at them. Brusquely he shouted. *"Mitkommen! Schnell! Alle mitkommen!* Move it!"

The ragged group of uneasy, bewildered Germans followed the noncom as he strode down the road, Woody wheeling his motorbike along. He gave Ilse a reassuring smile. She took hold of his arm.

Presently the sergeant turned off the road and headed for a large barn. Other GIs and German civilians stood outside, and a few

US military vehicles were parked next to the wooden building, among them a self-propelled generator.

And Woody knew what was in store.

Shit!

The German villagers—men, women, and older children—were all herded into the barn. Inside, a large screen had been set up at one end, and a motion picture projector stood at the other. Benches, bales of hay, and planks propped up on bricks served as seating before the screen.

As Woody and Ilse made for a seat, a corpulent burger began to argue with the GI who had directed him to a seat. Red-faced and indignant the man voiced his objections. The big sergeant elbowed his way up to the man. He jutted out his jaw and glared savagely at the German. "Listen, Krauthead," he snarled. "I'll cut your fucking ears off and ram them up your asshole so you can hear me good when I kick your butt! Now—*sit!*"

Woody grinned inwardly. It was kind of good to hear a real GI noncom sound off. He felt downright nostalgic. The German did not understand the words—but he was in no doubt about their meaning. He sat.

A lieutenant stood up before the screen, facing the crowd. The people fell silent. The officer pulled out a piece of paper and began speaking in German with only a trace of an accent.

"Pursuant to AUS directive, MGAF-GO (79)," he intoned, "every German citizen over the age of fourteen, without exception, is required to witness a screening of US Army film, TF-261.9."

He put the paper down. He looked out over the assembled German villagers, his face hard and grim.

"What you will see," he said harshly, "is how your former government dealt with those it considered enemies, unfit, or merely inferior. All the film you will be shown was photographed by your own SS motion picture units and deals with only a fraction of what went on in such concentration camps as Dachau, Buchenwald, and Bergen-Belsen; Auschwitz-Birkenau, Treblinka, and Mathausen; Ravensbrück, Sachsenhausen, Maidenek, and Flossenburg. All in the name of your Führer, Adolf Hitler."

Woody felt Ilse stiffen beside him. He remembered her earlier questions about the camps. She was about to get an answer. In spades. He'd seen the "Mickey Mouse" film before, screened for other such groups. Automatically he took her hand.

The film began. The barn was eerily quiet except for the drowsy whirr of the projector. First there were the usual identifying titles and numbers—and then the shock opening Woody would never forget.

It was another barn: men, women, and children being herded inside, guarded by SS troops, tall and blond and trim in their immaculate, tailored uniforms with the silver ⚡ flashes on the collars; gasoline being poured on the straw, heaped around the wooden structure with its locked and barred doors. And the fire. Flames engulfing everything. And through the flames, through the scorched and burning wood, fire-blackened hands thrusting out through impossibly small openings, clenching and contorting in agony as the flames licked at them, eating away the flesh to expose quickly charred bone. And the head. The terrible head. The head of one desperate man who'd gouged out a big enough hole in the burning planks to force his head through, in a vain attempt to escape the hell inside. Hairless and blistered, his ears and lips charred appendages, his mouth wrenched open in a silent scream, his eyes wide in unspeakable terror—until the searing heat burst them and the hot fluid spurted from them. And through it all, the laughter and merriment, the jeering and derision of the SS guards. It was a sight he would never forget. He knew that neither would the girl who sat stiffly beside him.

And there was more. Much, much more. Narrated by a dispassionate German voice.

The piles of emaciated, white, naked bodies, already drained of blood so they would burn easier, stacked like cordwood at the crematorium ovens; a much more efficient way to dispose of the undesirables than the primitive barn burnings . . . The rows of men, women, and children being herded to the "showers," like cattle to the slaughtering pen; crammed and locked into the common "shower room," to suffer the indescribable agonies of being gassed by Zyklon-B . . . And the rubber-booted, cloth-mask protected men of the *Sonderkommando* who hosed down the hideous tangle of distorted bodies, interlocked by the violent spasms of death, to get rid of the feces and blood that covered them, before wrenching them apart to make room for the next group. The mountains of eyeglasses, shoes, pens, watches, and—most pitiful of all—hair, shorn from the heads of the women . . . .

At Oranienburg Concentration Camp, the voice of the narrator droned on, more than one hundred specially selected inmates of all ages were gassed and the flesh carefully boiled and stripped from their bones in order to provide undamaged skeletons for the collection at Himmler's Institute for Practical Research in Military Science . . . .

Woody could feel Ilse tremble beside him. She clung to his hand. Ilse Gessner, he thought. A few short days ago merely a girl he resented having to drag along. And now someone who looked to him for comfort and strength, whose touch he welcomed.

On the screen a gruesome scene of executions at the site of a mass grave was taking place. Naked men and boys were made to line up at the edge of a huge open pit to be shot from behind by the executioners and conveniently topple directly into the pit on top of the bloody, mangled pile of bodies. Dead—or only near dead. Here and there a groping hand would try to struggle up from beneath the slimy snarl of gory limbs and torsos. The camera moved in on one young man, barely into his teens, kneeling at the edge of the ditch, waiting in stuporous silence for his own death. As his executioner aimed his gun at the back of his head, another stopped him. With a wide grin he pointed to the ground. The executioner fired—the bullet hitting the dirt far from its victim. But, obediently, the young man, unhurt, toppled into the grave. Bewildered he sat up, and looked back up at his killers. He crawled over the bloody bodies—until a bullet fired by the uproariously laughing guard shattered his head.

Woody heard the titters and snickers that rose above the whirr of the projector. He was not surprised. It had happened before at another such screening he had attended. He'd decided it was a nervous reaction. *Nobody* could be that callous. And yet, the screen had just proven him wrong. He gazed around at the villagers, their eyes riveted to the screen. Were they in for the same aftermath as his first "Mickey Mouse" film audience? They had not tittered the next day when they had been forced to exhume and carry the decomposed bodies from a mass grave to a cemetery for decent burial. And they had experienced what was lacking in the film. The stench. The foul odor of suffering, of disease, and decomposition. The smell of death. The stink that had seared their nostrils never to be expunged. As it had his.

And the film went on in relentless horror. There were the women prisoners at Ravensbrück, a concentration camp exclusively for female inmates, who had cancer implanted in the uterus; and the Nazi doctors—wearing earplugs to screen out the screams of pain (anesthetics were reserved for front-line soldiers)—who would remove the womb, piece by piece, to study the effects of the ravaging disease . . . .

A dismal corridor with rows of cadaverously thin children aged one to five, lying naked on bare cots. In a hospital near Munich, the narrator stated, a Dr. Pfannmüller had devised a special way to eliminate inferior children, who in his opinion were nothing but a burden on the Reich. He starved them to death, at no cost to the Fatherland. "Our method is simple and natural," Dr. Pfannmüller boasted . . . .

And there were the guards. The special breed of concentration camp guards. Brutish, demented-looking creatures.

Many of them have become notorious, the narrator said. Ilse Koch, the wife of the commandant, is known as the Bitch of Buchenwald, who scoured the camp for prisoners with interesting tattoos—from which to make lampshades. Or *SS Hauptsturm-führer,* Dr. Josef Mengele, the Auschwitz Angel of Death, who with a flip of his riding crop would decide life or death, while humming music from Wagner. And at the special women's camp, where 92,000 women were put to death, there was the Rat of Ravensbrück, a woman who was particularly fond of flailing luscious young girls with big breasts . . . .

On the screen a group of female guards were throwing the naked, splotched, and half-decomposed bodies from a truckload of cadavers into an open common grave, supervised by a burly headed guard, a woman, wearing high boots and clad in the severe gray skirt and tunic of the KZ women guards. It was the woman known as the Rat of Ravensbrück. She turned and grinned directly into the camera.

Woody felt Ilse convulse. Her nails dug into his hand. He heard her gasp a guttural moan of anguish, as the impersonal narrator continued: This woman's actual name was Klara Gessner, he intoned. She was one of the first Chief Administrators of Guards to reap instant retribution for her evil when the camp was overrun. The surviving inmates rushed her—and literally tore her to pieces while she was still alive.

Woody felt Ilse heave. He heard her retch, and he knew she had vomited. He was horrified. Klara Gessner. Ilse's mother? Was *that* the "administrative job" she had held? Head of the infamous guards at Ravensbrück. He grabbed the girl by the arms as she was about to slide to the floor. He pushed his way to the side, carrying her with him, and started toward the exit. An MP blocked his way.

"Get back there, you lousy Kraut!" he snarled. "You bastards have been dishing it out long enough. Now—eat it!"

Woody shoved him aside. He half carried Ilse out into the open.

The MP was right behind him. He drew his '45 and held it pointed at Woody. "Get your hands up, you fucking Nazi bastard," he snarled in rage. "Now! Or you'll never have another chance."

Filled with blazing fury Woody turned on him. He was about to light into him when the lieutenant came from the barn.

"What's going on here?" he asked sharply.

"That damned Kraut and his broad are ducking out," the MP growled. "Against regulations, Sir. And the bastard is resisting orders."

Woody glared at the lieutenant. *"Herr Leutnant,"* he addressed the officer in German, "the girl is sick. *She* was not responsible for that horror, and she has seen what you wanted her to see." His voice was icy, his angry eyes impaled the officer. "If you force her back in you are no better than the swine on the screen!"

The officer scowled at him. He turned to the MP. "Let them go," he snapped.

Woody found his motorbike. He helped Ilse to mount. She had lapsed into a catatonic silence. She let herself be manipulated with no will of her own.

At the first farm on the other side of Dillingen Woody stopped. At the pump in the farmyard he cleaned the girl. No one was about.

Again he helped her up on the bike, and again they took off down the road.

Already dusk was beginning to tint the countryside with gray. They would not be able to reach Memmingen before curfew.

They passed through the small village of Holzheim where the road ran through a forest. Woody turned off. He followed a path into the woods until he came to a small secluded clearing surrounded by a dense thicket and stopped. He helped Ilse from the motorcycle. She lay down on the grass and pulled her knees up to her chin in a fetal position, enfolding her legs with her arms. She uttered not a word. She only stared vacantly into space.

Woody sat down beside her. "Ilse," he said, "I know it must have been a terrible shock. But you *must* snap out of it."

There was no response. It was as if the girl did not even hear him.

Deeply disturbed, he surveyed her. He made up his mind. The girl would *have* to get herself under control or he would be forced to ditch her. At some farm, perhaps. He would never get her all the way to Memmingen in her state, without being stopped and questioned. And he could not afford that. He frowned. If he did leave her somewhere, would she talk? Would she give away her knowledge of the *B-B Axis?* Touch off an investigation which might spell the ruin of his mission?

He took her by the shoulders. He shook her. "Ilse," he pleaded, "listen to me. Talk to me."

Her head lolled insensibly on her shoulders. She did not respond. He gazed at her. Dammit all to hell, he could not leave her. He wanted desperately to help.

Suddenly he slapped her smartly across her cheek. A hard, stinging blow.

She let out a gasp. Tears welled in her eyes and she stared at him in shock.

Suddenly she broke down. She threw herself into his arms and cried, as her insides exploded with an agony so intense it threatened once again to blot out her mind. Between rending sobs she whimpered: "I did not know. Oh, dear, dear God, I did not know. Mother . . . I—did—not—know . . ."

The grief, the shock, the horror overwhelmed her. She buried her face in his chest. And wept.

Woody held her. He caressed her heaving shoulders. He let her weep—waiting for her trembling to stop, the horror to abate.

It was later. How much later he didn't know. Half an hour? More? It did not matter. Ilse was still huddled in his arms, but her trembling had stopped, her breathing was calm.

The little clearing was getting dark. Night was closing in and the grass and the brush began to release the sweet scents baked into them by the sun during the day. All around them the small, intimate sounds of tiny night creatures murmured to them. Crickets tuning up, a distant throaty frog, the rustling of tiny scurrying feet.

Woody listened to the measured breathing of the girl in his arms. Had she fallen asleep? He knew she must be emotionally exhausted. He looked down at her. Her short, auburn hair seemed to gather the fading colors of the waning day and make them rich and warm. Gently he touched the tousled locks. She stirred, burrowing closer.

He sighed. It was all for nothing, he thought. The ordeal of her flight. Her fear of remaining in Germany. Of being caught. It was all unnecessary. All because of the guilt-born belief, fostered by Goebbels and his damned crew, that the allied conquerors would wreak their terrible vengeance on the families of those they considered war criminals. It was, after all, what they had done in the countries they had enslaved, and would have done, had they been victorious. And, therefore, it was believed. Ilse's mother had believed, although it was totally untrue, that her daughter would be held accountable for *her* deeds, grisly as they were. And in her own way she had wanted to save her.

With some surprise he recognized the depth of his feelings for this frail girl who clung to him. He cared for her—more than he had been willing to admit. The daughter of a monstrous murderess? Part of everything he abhorred? He gazed at her. Was she? Ilse was Ilse, not her mother. She had known nothing of her mother's actions. And she had been appalled at what little she had found out about the atrocities committed by her people; shattered when she'd learned the full truth.

He glanced around the clearing. It was almost completely dark. They would have to spend the night. Gently he began to disentangle himself. Ilse held on to him.

"Please, Rudi," she whispered huskily. "Not yet. Hold me." She lifted her head and gazed up at him. In the dim light her solemn face was pale and her eyes shone darkly.

He looked down at her. He was suddenly overwhelmed by a tenderness so strong that his chest ached. His arms tightened around her slender body. Totally without a will of his own he bent his face down and pressed his lips against hers. She returned the kiss, her full lips opening and yielding to his.

All the horrors, the guilts, the fears were suddenly swept away. Only the now, the two of them, existed. Eagerly, unquestioningly, every motion a caress, they shed the clothing that was keeping them from the closeness they both hungered for. The fresh softness of the grass was cool against their skin as they sank down on the ground. There was no need for words—the little moaning sounds that purred from Ilse spoke a world of want to him.

He kissed her. He kissed the eyes that had seen horror and cried for it; he kissed the ears that had been wounded by words of shocking and cruel revelations; he kissed the lips that had cried out in tormented anguish. And it was all obliterated in his ardor.

He pressed his demanding body against hers. With feline sensuality she kneaded her nails into his back.

He nuzzled into her throat, arched back in ecstasy, and inhaled the exciting fragrance of her skin.

With increasing urgency they moved together in the age-old, ever-new mutual rhythm, each with a fire and a need, aching for release. Locking out the world of violence and evil, each gave, and each took.

He cupped her face in his hands. Her eyes were tightly shut as if trying to prevent the feelings of rapture behind them from escaping. He crushed his lips to hers. Uninhibitedly they strained, one against the other and quickly, bursting with pent-up desire, they silently screamed their ultimate pleasure to one another.

Side by side they lay naked on the grass in the warm summer night. Woody let his eyes rest on the girl cuddled next to him. A pale moon had risen and was shining capriciously though the leafy canopy above them, kaleidoscopically touching her silken, love-moist skin with gleaming silver.

He reached over and touched her, gently stroking her thrusting breasts. The musky scent of love-making was still upon her.

Impossibly, it was even better, more satisfying, the second time. Both were cleansed physically and emotionally of their tensions and free to explore the wonders of one another. Their rhythmic union seemed to throb and last an eternity before they both exploded into exhaustion and well-being.

He was struggling up the hill. The sun beat down upon him in physical torture, searing his eyes. The steep slope was sandy, and he kept sliding down, farther and farther with each agonizing step.

He looked down at the sea of faces below him, faces distorted in anger and lust. Men and women. SS troops and GIs. Young and old. Silently, relentlessly pursuing him with hate, their clutching hands stretched out against him.

The hideous burden he was carrying, the massive iron swastika, increased obscenely in weight with each laborious step he took.

He slipped. He slid down the slope. The massive, twisted burden fell on him and pinned him to the ground. The pressure on his chest became greater and greater until his breathing became impossible and his lungs shrieked for relief.

He felt his rib cage begin to splinter—and with a start he opened his eyes. It was broad daylight. The sun was streaming down through the trees.

The first thing he saw was a dirty, scuffed, hobnailed *Wehrmacht* boot pressing relentlessly down on his chest as he lay supine and naked on the grass. In the next instant he saw it all. The grinning, unshaven face of the man, clad in a tattered *Wehrmacht* uniform without insignia, looming over him; the clothing with which he and Ilse had covered themselves as they slept in each other's arms, tossed aside; the other soldier, sitting on the naked girl; tight grip, her terror-stricken eyes wild above a grimy hand clamped over her mouth, the heavy iron chain from the pouch on his motorbike swinging from the man's other hand. And the P-

38 gun, held by the soldier who stood with his foot on his chest. It was unwaveringly pointed down on his face.

He jerked to sit up. Roughly the man pushed him down with his foot.

"Not so fast, *Kamerad*," he sneered. "You are not going any-where."

He shook his head in wonder. *"Mench!"* he said. "This must be our lucky day. Stumbling upon you, *mein Freund."* He looked around the clearing. "You have much that we can use, Helmuth and me, and use well." A sardonic grin on his unsavory face, he leered down at Woody. "A motorcycle. Good clothes—and money, I should not be surprised." He nodded toward Ilse. "And, of course, *her!"*

21

---◦•◦---

THE SOLDIER SMIRKED at Ilse. "Patience, little *Schatzi,*" he mocked. "We will get to you soon." He nodded to his companion. "Let her scream, Helmuth," he said. "No one will hear her."

The man called Helmuth took his hand from Ilse's mouth. He clamped his arms around her naked waist, obviously enjoying himself. Ilse did not make a sound. She tried to pry herself free, but the man held her in an iron grip. She stopped struggling. She stood motionless, glaring defiantly at the man with the gun.

"You bastard!" Woody growled deep in his throat. *"Verflucht nochmal!* Leave her alone!" He tried to sit up.

The soldier stomped his boot down hard on his chest. "Easy, *Kamerad,*" he warned. "If you want to stay around to watch the cherry picking." Slowly he backed off, his P-38 trained on Woody's gut. "Now. First things first," he said. "We must have proper order in the proceedings, must we not? The little *Schatzi* will be *die Rosine im Wurstende*—the raisin in the end of the sausage." He leered at Ilse. "And a sweet one it will be!"

He gestured at Woody with his gun. "You," he ordered, "get your clothing together. Empty all the pockets. *Los!*" He grinned. "You can leave hers."

Woody did as he was told. Advantage number one, he thought. Up and able to move around, instead of flat on his back. He collected his clothing. He turned all the pockets inside out.

"Put everything in a pile," the soldier ordered. Woody did. Papers. AMG travel permits. I.D., his few personal belongings. And the money he had been given at the last *Achse* stop.

"That nice watch, too," the soldier pointed.

Woody threw it on the pile.

"Excellent," the soldier beamed. "Now—back off!"

Woody did. He watched the soldier closely. The man did not give him a chance. Rummaging through the pile, the soldier pocketed the money and the watch. He left the papers on the ground. He picked up Woody's boots. He felt around inside. "No big bills hidden in the good old *Stiefelbank?*—the good old boot bank?" He found nothing. He tossed the boots at Woody. "Get dressed," he said.

Woody put on his clothes.

"Helmuth," the soldier called. "Throw our cooperative friend that chain." The man tossed the motorcycle security chain to Woody. He caught it. Advantage number two, he thought grimly. A weapon—however awkward.

Never taking his eyes from Woody, the soldier walked to the motorbike. From the tool pouch he fished out the combination padlock. Again he gestured to Woody.

"That tree," he said. *"Los!"*

Woody walked over to the indicated tree. It was a sturdy sapling with a trunk about six inches in diameter.

"Sit," the soldier ordered. "Put the chain around your ankle. Twist it into a figure eight and put the ends around the trunk."

Bleakly Woody obeyed. So much for advantages number one and two, he thought. Back to square one, dammit! He looked toward Ilse. The man holding her was pawing her breasts. Rage boiled in him. He controlled it with an effort. Impulsive action could only get him killed.

The soldier walked behind the tree. He picked up the two ends of the chain, pulled them as tight as he could, drawing Woody's foot up against the tree trunk, held there in the taut loop of the chain. The soldier snapped the lock in place.

"I don't know the combination," Woody growled. "If you lock the damned thing, I'll never get away."

The soldier shook his head in mock sympathy. "Your little *Schatzi* will have to go for help," he sneered. He gave an unpleasantly sharp little laugh. "When she can walk again!" He closed the lock with a snap and twirled the tumblers.

Woody watched him put his gun in his belt and walk toward the other man, still holding the naked Ilse. He turned his back on them. He had only a couple of minutes, he estimated. Three at the most.

Feverishly he unlaced the bootlace from one of his boots. He twisted and ripped off the aglet. He pulled out the wire saw and placed it around one of the chain links.

Twenty seconds gone.

With short, strong pulls he began to saw, bearing down, careful not to telegraph his movements with his shoulders. He listened. He did not turn around to watch.

"Now, little *Schatzi*," he heard the soldier say, the man's voice grating in his ears. "Now we come to you. And *I* am first."

He heard the other man grumble. "Always you first, Felix. To the devil with that! This time it is *me* first! And what about the money? I want half."

"*Schon gut, Helmut, schon gut,*" the soldier placated his companion. "Here. We will divide it."

Woody doubled his efforts. A minute gone. More. He was too keyed up to gauge time. He peered at the chain link. Already a deep groove had been sawed into the metal.

"So," he heard the soldier say, "you got your money. Now, *I* will take the girl."

He heard scuffling sounds. Grunts. A low oath. He expected to hear Ilse scream, but she uttered not a sound.

Two minutes gone.

"*Verdammt nochmal!* Hold her arms, Helmuth!" he heard the soldier pant. "I do not want to have to knock her out. It is no fun that way."

Almost through. The wire bit steadily into the metal. His fingers were bleeding where he gripped the saw, pulling it rapidly back and forth.

He was through. Bless that Limey bastard, Forbes, he thought. With all his might he pulled on the chain—and the link opened up. In seconds he had it unwrapped from his foot and from the tree.

He stood up, the chain and lock dangling from his bloody hand.

He looked. Eyes burning with hate, he looked.

In the little clearing a short distance away Ilse was lying on the ground. Fiercely, silently she was fighting against the soldier who was struggling with her long, naked legs, his own pants bunched around his feet. Savagely Ilse scratched, kicked, and twisted as the other man, kneeling at her head, pinned her arms to the ground. Totally intent upon subduing the girl, they did not notice Woody.

In a few steps he had covered the ground between them. He swung the chain and lock and struck the soldier a vicious blow to the temple. Instantly the man collapsed across the supine girl. Startled, the other man looked up, in time to register his utter astonishment as Woody's boot caught him squarely on the chin.

Woody threw the chain away. He pulled the soldier off Ilse and helped her to her feet. He put his arms around her. For a brief moment they clung to each other.

"Quickly," he breathed, "put your clothes on."

She hurried to comply.

Woody looked at the two unconscious men. They would live. But they would not forget their little encounter in the woods. Not ever. For a moment he was tempted to take the soldier's gun. He thought better of it. He had already once made the decision not to carry a weapon. It was the right one. He picked up the gun and hurled it into the woods as far as he could. He retrieved his watch and his money. He picked up the papers and I.D.

Ilse was dressed. Woody wheeled the motorcycle down to the path—and within a few minutes they were back on the road.

It was 0727 hours when they passed through the village of Schnuttenbach, seventy-five kilometers from Memmingen.

They would be at the *Achse Anlaufstelle* before 1000 hours.

Willi looked at his watch. Again. 0942 hours. The truck was more than an hour late.

The worry had been slow to build, but now it was stiff and taut in him.

They were waiting at a little shed near a row of warehouses at the railroad yard. Obviously their transportation could not pick them up directly at the *Anlaufstelle*. The shed was locked and they had to wait outside. Because it was Sunday there were only a few workers about. All men. It was both a blessing and a curse, Willi thought. A blessing because curious would-be inquisitors were few; a curse because they were dangerously exposed out in the open. Especially with Eva, he felt, a woman and pregnant, sitting on a bench at the shed, sticking out like a coffee bean in a bowl of rice.

Anxiously he searched the road with his eyes.

Nothing.

Scheissdreck! Nothing ever went as planned.

He took a deep breath. Easy. He realized he was becoming edgy. Being shuttled about by a succession of strangers was getting on his nerves. Having to depend blindly on people he knew nothing about. He liked to depend on himself. He had been trained to do so. He was used to it.

Ludwig, the plant manager, had rounded up motor transportation for them, at least. A truck. Delivering the *Ami* newspaper, *Stars and Stripes*. The truck would take them to the next *Anlaufstelle* in Steingaden in the Allgäu, close to the Alps. Willi had raised an eyebrow at this intelligence, but Ludwig had explained to him that, as the *Ami* combat soldiers went home, more and more German drivers were hired by the American Army to drive such nonmilitary assignments. The *Ami* security and screening was so lax, he'd told him, that the *Achse* had been able to place several men, using false names, in such positions. The *Stars and Stripes* trucks could go virtually anywhere, unmolested at checkpoints and by MPs. The driver would simply smile and hand out a few copies of the paper—to be cheerfully waved on by the soldiers, who were blithely unaware that *Achse* travelers were hidden in the back behind the stacked-up bundles of papers. It was foolproof. And not a little ironic.

He frowned. Again he wondered if he should return to the ropery and Ludwig. And run the risk of missing the truck, if it should show up.

He'd give it another five minutes. No more.

He glanced at Eva, sitting quietly on the bench. She seemed composed, patient, as she waited. She was quite a woman, he thought.

Eva hated the waiting. In her mind a problem had the habit of growing in ever greater proportions to the time spent waiting. She felt tense from head to foot. She struggled not to show it. She did not wish to add to Willi's worries. Only once before in her life did she remember a waiting as unbearably strained. It had been during the afternoon of the 20th of July, about a year before.

She and her friend, Herta Schneider, had gone swimming in the Königsee near Berchtesgaden. She had been lying on a wooden raft out in the lake, resting before swimming back to shore, when she suddenly saw one of the Führer's private cars approaching rapidly on the road from the Berghof. She had immediately been filled with a feeling of disaster. She had dived into the water and swum as fast as she could to shore, where a white-faced chauffeur informed her that there had been an attempt to assassinate the Führer at his headquarters at Rastenburg in East Prussia. A bomb. No one knew exactly what had happened, but the Führer was believed to be alive. She had rushed back to the Berghof. She had at once tried to telephone Adolf, but she had not been able to get through. And no one could get any definite information. Wait, they had told her. *Wait* . . .

And she had waited. And the waiting time had conjured up ever more cruel visions of bloodshed, of mutilation and death. The waiting had been the worst.

When finally she did reach Adolf, he had assured her he was safe.

She had been horrified when, a few days later, he had shown her the uniform he had been wearing when the assassin's bomb went off. Bloodstained, tattered, and imbedded with splinters and dirt, it had rekindled her terror.

And she remembered Adolf taking her by her shoulders and gazing into her eyes as he said: "It is by the grace of Providence that I have been spared and chosen to lead my people. This miraculous escape from death more than ever has convinced me that it is my sacred fate to be victorious in the war. And in my mission!"

She sighed. Gently she touched her swollen belly.

The Führer's greater goal would have to be left to his heir.

Her child.

"Eva!" Willi's voice shook her out of her reveries. "Here he comes!"

The truck skidded to a stop at the shed. Quickly Willi strode up to the cab. His eyes flashed at the driver. "What the devil kept you?" he barked.

"*Nur ruhig*—take it easy, *Kamerad*," the driver grinned. A stocky, middle-aged man with a neck that disappeared into his shoulders, he leaned out of the cab window. On his weathered, ruddy face, directly under his nose, a small patch of skin appeared lighter than the rest, where he apparently had shaven off his Hitler mustache. "I did not think you would want to share your trip with an *Ami* sergeant."

Willi gave him a sharp look.

"The *Scheisskerl* bummed a ride," the driver explained. "Just as I was on my way here. I could not turn him down. Had to double back all the way from Woringen. To pick you up. Be glad I am here at all."

He looked around the yard, moving his head stiffly on his thick neck.

"Get in the back," he said. "Behind the bundles. *Los!* We have to be on our way. I have a lot of catching up to do."

Willi helped Eva into the back of the truck, and in less than a minute they were careening down the road toward Steingaden.

They did not see the motorcycle that passed them, with a man and a woman on it, headed for the area near the railroad yards.

If they had, it would have meant nothing to them.

SS Sturmbannführer Oskar Strelitz walked rapidly toward the Memmingen *Anlaufstelle* at *Seilerei Rademacher* near the railroad yards.

He had watched Eva and her companion leave in the *Stars and*

Stripes truck. They were on their way again. Mingling with the railroad workers in the yard, being inconspicuous and seeming to belong at the same time, had not been easy because there were so few men working. But he had busied himself walking along the tracks with a pail picking up stray pieces of coal for salvage, and no one had questioned him. He had been able to keep an eye on Eva and the young SS officer with her.

He had been outraged at the length of time *Frau* Hitler had been forced to wait at the shed. Placing her in that kind of dangerous situation was inexcusable. The agent at the *Anlaufstelle* would be held to account; he would see to that personally.

Ahead he could see the long, narrow building that housed the ropewalk. Although several buildings on the street were damaged, some totally in ruins, the rope manufacturing plant seemed relatively untouched by the shelling. He would get the necessary information from the agent in charge and be on his way, following his wards.

He was about to cross the street when he saw a motorcycle with a young man and woman drive up and come to a halt. He stopped. He watched. The young man inspected the sign on the old red-brick building. He and the woman dismounted and, wheeling his bike, the young man led the girl into the plant yard.

Strelitz frowned. Instinctively he sensed that the two young people were *Achse* travelers. Who were they? They were very close behind *Frau* Hitler and her escort. He knew that when Eva left the Harz hideout there had been no one traveling the escape route behind her at least not within a three-day span. How had *this* couple caught up? And more important, *why?* He felt the familiar tense alertness grow in him. With their own transportation, the couple might easily overtake *Frau* Hitler. At the next *Anflaufstelle*. Is that what they were after? If so, why? He had best find out as much as he could about the young couple. Determine if they might possibly be a threat. He was suspicious. Well and good. It was his business to be. The Führer, himself, had charged him so. It was, of course, possible that the young man was at the plant on business other than the *Achse*. Employment, for instance. But he did not believe it. Even if he did, he would still have to check him out. Thoroughly.

Quickly he decided on his course of action. He would wait. Let the newcomers get settled in, and then confront the agent.

He looked around. He needed a reason for hanging around. Almost directly across from the plant a building lay in ruins with bricks and broken masonry in jumbled piles. He took off his jacket and began to stack the bricks from a crumbled wall. He had a perfect view of the plant gate while he worked.

Twenty minutes he thought. He would wait twenty minutes before going in. He had no idea what would ensue. All he knew was—he could handle it.

Heinz Ludwig sneaked another look at the girl who had given her name as Ilse, as he conducted the newly arrived travelers through the ropery to the room in the back. She was a real *Muckerl*—a real looker—he thought admiringly. Even better looking than the young woman who had just left. Interesting, he mused. Two women. One immediately after the other. The only two he had processed at his stop.

In the room Woody turned to him. "*Herr* Ludwig," he said in a low, confidential voice. "A word with you, if you please." As Ilse, looking pale and exhausted, lay down on one of the beds, Woody took Ludwig aside. He tried to size the man up. How best to get the information he wanted without arousing suspicion.

"*Herr* Ludwig," he said, "when do you think we can be on our way?"

"As early as tomorrow," Ludwig said. "You will be traveling by truck. It leaves the area at half past eight in the morning."

"That would indeed be excellent, *Herr* Ludwig," Woody said. "But we have our own transportation. A motorcycle. All we need is to have our papers fixed up, a little gasoline—and the necessary information to take us to the next *Anlaufstelle* by tonight." He lowered his voice. He gave a quick glance toward the resting Ilse. "You must understand, *Herr* Ludwig," he whispered conspiratorially. "It is not easy to have to travel with a woman. She gets tired. And impatient at the same time. Like a woman, she cannot wait. Everything must turn around *her* wishes. I am sure you understand." He sighed, much put upon. "I have been given responsibility for her. And I should very much like to get her to our destination as quickly as possible. That is what she demands. And I want that, too, before she . . ." He shrugged eloquently. "I should like to leave here as soon as possible, *Herr* Ludwig. I am certain *you* can arrange it."

Ludwig frowned. He would have liked to keep the good-looking woman around. At least for the night. One never knew. He nodded slowly. "It will be arranged," he said.

Woody beamed at him. "I am grateful, *Herr* Ludwig. It *is* a bother, having to drag a woman along. I do not know why I was so singled out."

"If it is any consolation, *Herr* Bauhacker," Ludwig smiled thinly at him. "You are not the only one."

Woody looked at him in surprise. *"Wirklich!"* he exclaimed. "Really! How extraordinary. I cannot for the life of me think of *any* woman who would need to avail herself of the—the special travel accommodations of the *Achse.* Are you certain you are not mistaken?"

"Of course," Ludwig said shortly, a hint of offense in his voice. "There was another couple. They only just left a couple of hours ago."

Woody felt his heart skip a beat. Eva! He grinned crookedly at Ludwig. "I wish the poor dolt good luck," he said fervently. "I know what he must have to put up with." He looked earnestly at Ludwig. "I am grateful," he said. "We shall wait here for our papers."

Ludwig nodded. "It will take an hour," he said. "Perhaps two. It will be no trouble."

He left.

In the ruins outside, opposite the plant, *SS Sturmbannführer* Oskar Strelitz looked at his watch. Twenty minutes.

He placed the brick he held in his hand on a stack. He put on his jacket and briskly walked across the street to *Seilerei Rademacher.*

Plant manager Heinz Ludwig stared at the grim, imposing figure of a man towering over him.

"It is impossible," he said. "In no way can I do what you ask. I do not have the authority. Only in emergency . . ."

"I strongly suggest you take another look at *my* authority," Strelitz interrupted him harshly. "I am certain you recognize the signature on it."

Ludwig obediently looked at the papers the man, identified in them as *SS Sturmbannführer* Oskar Strelitz, had given to him. On special mission for the Führer, Adolf Hitler, he read. Authority not to be questioned. Full cooperation by all officials demanded. No exceptions. He stared at the signature. He nodded.

"The Führer is dead," he said tonelessly.

"As dead as you will be, *Herr* Ludwig," Strelitz said quietly, "if you do not at once comply with my orders." He glared icily at the manager. "Remember, *Herr* Ludwig. The *Brüderschaft*— the Brotherhood—is very much alive. They fully back the Führer's commands. They will not look kindly on any—obstruction."

Ludwig swallowed. "Very well," he agreed. "I will make contact with officials of the *Verteilungsstab*. They will make some calls." He handed the papers back to Strelitz. "I will get you your information."

The cool water soothed the lacerations on Woody's palms, caused by his grip on the wire saw. Ilse looked concerned as she gently bathed the bloody crusts, soaking them off.

"I'll be okay," Woody said. The hands hurt like hell. And gripping the damned handlebars on the motorbike hadn't exactly been therapeutic. If only the cuts didn't get infected.

He glanced at his watch. It had been better than two and a half hours since Ludwig left them. Where the hell was the bastard?

Suddenly the door to the room opened. A stranger—a tall, sturdy man around forty—entered, followed by a cowed-looking Ludwig.

Without a word or a glance at the two people standing at the washstand, the stranger marched to the only table in the room. Woody watched him. Obviously a military man, he thought. Another traveler? Not the way he was taking charge. Who then? What the hell was up? The hackles on the back of his neck itched. Trouble!

The man sat down at the table. Importantly he placed some papers before him. Woody thought he recognized his own among them. He felt Ilse grow rigid beside him.

The stranger turned toward him and fixed him with an icy stare. He pointed to a spot in front of the table. *"Antreten!"* he barked.

Woody bristled. He quickly caught himself. He was in *their* ballpark. He'd better play *their* game. He walked to the indicated spot and snapped to attention. *"Zu Befehl!"* he sang out. "At your orders!"

Strelitz appraised him overtly. Who was this young man? he wondered coldly. From the answers to his inquiries about him and the girl with him he had already made up his mind that his suspicions about them were fully justified. Information had come back from the *Anlaufstellen* at Eisenach, Coburg, Neustadt, and Nördlingen. For some reason he had been informed that prior to the stop at the Harz nothing was available. It had not been needed.

He let his arctic eyes bore into the young man who stood stiffly before him.

"I am *SS Sturmbannführer* Strelitz," he rasped. "I am here to ask you some questions. I am empowered to do so." He held a piece of paper out toward Woody. "Read this."

Woody took the paper. He prayed his hands would not shake. He read. The document was an authorization giving *Sturmbannführer* Oskar Strelitz almost unlimited powers.

"You are familiar with the Führer's signature, no doubt," Strelitz said. It was a statement rather than a question.

Woody looked at the scrawl at the bottom of the page. He had no idea what Hitler's signature looked like. He stared at it.

If that was it, he thought, it sure fit. It was as twisted as the man himself.

"Yes, *Herr Sturmbannführer*," he said, trying to make his voice sound respectful. "Thank you, *Herr Sturmbannführer*."

For a moment Strelitz scowled at him in silence. Woody felt creeping over him the natural, numbing uneasiness common to everyone being questioned by someone in authority. He fought against it. He knew how damaging a guilty appearance could be in an interrogation. Interrogation? If this was to be an interrogation, he was on the wrong side of the table, dammit!

"Your name?" Strelitz suddenly snapped. "Your real name?"

Woody drew himself up. "Bauhacker, Hans," he answered smartly. "*Obergefreiter*. 796822."

His interrogator's cold eyes held him captive. "Look behind you," he said evenly.

Woody turned to look. At the door stood Heinz Ludwig—a Luger pistol in his hand, pointed straight at Woody.

"The next lie you tell . . ." Strelitz's voice whipped through the room like an icy gust of wind. "The next lie—will be your last!"

22

---◆·◆---

WOODY STRUGGLED TO STAY CALM. Despite his efforts, he felt his pulse quicken. His mouth was suddenly dry and his palms felt clammy. He was aware of a tiny muscle at the corner of one eye beginning to twitch. He knew he was exhibiting all the familiar telltale signs of a subject who has something to hide. He could not help it. And he was certain the minute, involuntary signals were not lost on his interrogator. The man was obviously a professional. Good, he thought. His actions would be predictable—up to a point. Images of the countless interrogations he had conducted himself flashed across his mind. It struck him that this time he had to *suppress* the little giveaway signs, not *detect* them. He set his mind in the unwonted role. He knew what he had to do. Give his answers as quickly as he could. Stick as close to the truth as possible. That way he would sound most convincing and there would be less of a chance to get caught in contradictions; less chance to be trapped in Sir Walter Scott's tangled web of deception. He met the steady gaze of *SS Sturmbannführer* Strelitz. He was ready.

Strelitz lazily surveyed the young man standing ramrod straight before him. He was already beginning to display the expected signs of nervousness. Good. But it was not unusual. He would take his time. Give the young man's own mind as much of a chance as possible to reach a full measure of anxiety. Time did that admirably to a guilty mind. Even to a mind free of guilt—if such existed.

Strelitz reviewed for himself the information Ludwig had obtained for him through the *Verteilungsstab*.

His subject had indeed made remarkable speed since leaving the *Anlaufstelle* in Eisenach, where he had teamed up with the girl. The agent in Coburg had been bitterly resentful over the way the traveler, who went by the name Bauhacker, had thrown his weight around. Of course, he mused, that by itself meant nothing. He knew from other information received from the Eisenach *Anlaufstelle* that the man in front of him supposedly was an SS officer. Acting with unquestioned authority would be natural to him. The agent at the Coburg stop had all but recommended the subject be quartered and drawn. Strelitz smiled cynically to himself. That was only wounded pride. He had seen plenty of that before. It was the obvious anxiety by the subject to hurry along the escape route, displayed at every stop, that perturbed him. Why? Through a skillful combination of cajoling and veiled threats, the man had effectively pressured the *Anlaufstelle* agents into sending him and his girl on, ahead of regular scheduling.

He frowned. The man's behavior bore investigating. Especially since intentionally or not, his efforts would soon bring him into striking distance of Eva Braun Hitler.

Deliberately he set his face in the cold, hard mask of a ruthless inquisitor. He would soon learn if the young fellow and his girl were bona fide *Achse* travelers.

Or not.

He would hold off making a decision. Certainly if he had any doubts, it would be better to eliminate one honest SS officer, than to allow the existence of even the possibility of a threat to Eva Braun Hitler.

And her unborn child.

"Your name?" The words rang out like two rapid fire shots and cracked through the room. Woody started. Dammit! It had been too sudden. "Once again, I ask you," Strelitz said ponderously. "What is your name?"

Woody more felt than heard the thin rustle behind him, as Ludwig steadied the gun aimed at his back. He clicked his heels. "Diehl, Fritz," he snapped. *"Hauptsturnführer. SS-Führer-Ausweiss-Nummer 250.252. Partei-Mitglieds-Nummer 3.387.514."* Let the bastard check, he thought defiantly. It was the real Diehl's ID numbers. It buoyed him to be able to rattle them off. And, dammit! he needed all the buoying he could get.

For a long moment Strelitz studied Woody, his eyes hooded. In doubt? Did he know it was the second lie? Woody's self-satisfaction quickly caved in. He could feel the flesh on his back crawl. Any split second a bullet could slam into him. Would he know? Or would he simply cease to exist? He willed himself to meet his interrogator's steady gaze.

Strelitz contemplated him. *Stimmt,* he thought. Correct. The agent at the Eisenach *Anlaufstelle* had been in possession of the man's actual ID cards.

"What were your duties, *Haupsturmführer* Diehl?" he asked.

"*Zu Befehl, Herr Sturmbannführer,* I was in charge of guards," Woody answered. "At Flossenburg."

He was aware of the strangled gasp coming from Ilse. Dammit all to hell! He had assured her he was *not* like her mother. Now he, himself, with his own words, was forced to destroy the trust, the feeling of intimacy that had sprung up between them. He had not wanted her to hear. Not this. But he had no choice. Not if he wanted to stay alive. Bleakly, he knew she would have to hear more. Much, much more. He ached inside.

"Ah, yes," Strelitz said. "I remember the camp, Diehl. I visited there occasionally." He looked sharply at Woody. "I never saw you."

Woody was about to make an apology or an explanation. He caught himself. They would have been lame at best. What was there to say? He would not be drawn into the trap of futile explanations. He knew what it could lead to. Betraying facts that might be damaging. He had used the ploy himself. Often. He stood silent. So what, if they had not run into each other? It was a big camp. Sprawled all over the damned place. He suddenly felt chilled. If Strelitz really knew the camp, he could easily trip him up. He, himself, had been there only once. Desperately he searched his mind for anything he could remember from his visit to the camp. Back in April. After the Death March. Anything he remembered seeing. Any facts he had learned. Any bits of knowledge from his interrogation of the real Fritz Diehl.

His mind was blank. It did not worry him. He knew that a specific question would trigger his recall, now that he had placed himself on the alert. He did not try to force it. He kept his mind clear and receptive.

"An excellent camp," he heard Strelitz comment. "Well kept." The interrogator leaned back in his chair, relaxing, as if wanting to put his subject at ease.

Woody knew at once what the man was doing. It was an old trick. Make the subject feel the worst is over, then catch him with a trick question—and pounce. He steeled himself.

"I was especially impressed with the beautiful little garden just inside the main gate," Strelitz went one. He frowned lightly. "To the right, I believe. At a little white garden house."

Woody's thoughts raced to the memory of the main gate to Flossenburg. "Yes, *Herr Sturmbannführer*," he said. "I remember it well." He saw a hard glint flit through the German's eyes. "But, with the *Herr Sturmbannführer's* permission," he continued, "the garden was *outside* the gate. Not inside."

Strelitz smiled thinly. "Yes. Yes, of course." So, the young man did know the camp. How well?

"You were at the camp to the end, Diehl?" he asked. "Up to the evacuation?"

"I was, *Herr Sturmbannführer*."

"Does the date, April 9, mean anything to you?"

April 9. Woody was blank. He felt himself tense. Easy. Don't panic. April 9? What the hell had happened on April 9? He had no idea.

He shook his head. "No, *Herr Sturmbannführer*," he replied, "I do not recall that date."

"How about the name Canaris?" Strelitz asked.

Of course! That was it. They had told him about it. "*Jawohl, Herr Sturmbannführer*. Admiral Wilhelm Canaris. The Admiral was arrested after the July attempt to assassinate the Führer. He was executed at Flossenburg—a few weeks before the camp was evacuated. In April." He lit up. "Yes, *Herr Sturmbannführer*, April 9!"

"Do you remember anyone else?"

Anyone else? Dammit, what did the bastard mean. "Anyone else, *Herr Surmbannführer*?"

"Executed on that date," Strelitz said impatiently.

Memory clicked. "*Jawohl, Herr Sturmbannführer. General-major* Hans Oster. And one more man. A clergyman. A traitor to the Reich. I do not remember his name. Bauhoffer, I believe."

Strelitz nodded. "Dietrich Bonhoeffer," he said. It was plausible, he thought. The *Kerl* knew. It was quite plausible that he would not remember everything. In fact, too perfect a memory would in itself be suspicious. The days at a concentration camp must have run into one another in dreary sameness. He would try one more question.

"Were you at Flossenburg since the camp was established in 1939, Diehl?"

"No, *Herr Sturmbannführer*. I was assigned to the camp in 1943. And, begging the *Herr Sturmbannführer's* pardon, Flossenburg was established in 1938. In May."

Strelitz nodded. "Of course," he acknowledged. *Schon gut,* he thought. Diehl was Diehl. But—what was his great hurry?

"*Hauptsturmführer* Diehl," he said, "I will be honest with you. There have been certain complaints against you. From the *Anlaufstelle* agents along the route." He looked sternly at Woody. "You insisted on leaving Coburg ahead of schedule, and you arrived at the next stop in Neustadt considerably earlier than expected by the agent there—with consequences which could have become extremely serious. How did you accomplish this?"

"With the *Herr Sturmbannführer*'s permission," Woody answered promptly. He was beginning to feel more confident. The bastard was buying his story. "We were supplied with bicycles for the trip. I—I stole a motorcycle on the way. I thought it would be easier on the *Fräulein* who had been entrusted into my care. And my training, *Herr Sturmbannführer*, in the SS had taught me to use my resources to the fullest."

Strelitz suppressed a sour smile. The little *Gauner*—the little scoundrel—was trying to butter him up. It was not the first time that had been tried. "Why?" he snapped. "Why the great hurry?"

Shit! Here it was, Woody thought. He was stuck with it. He was stuck with what he had told Ludwig earlier. With Ludwig standing right behind him he obviously had to tell his interrogator the same damned thing. He almost glanced toward Ilse, who was sitting in stiff bitterness on the bed. He didn't. What would she do?

"*Herr Sturmbannführer,*" he said earnestly. "I—I thought it best. Under the circumstances. I thought it best to get *Fräulein* Ilse to the port of embarkation as quickly as possible. The *Fräulein* seemed most anxious to get out of Germany. As quickly as possible." He was obviously uncomfortable, but he pressed on. "I—I was not certain the *Fräulein* would bear up under a prolonged journey. And she wanted to—get away from the *Amis.*" That was it. That was what he had already told Ludwig.

He stopped. What would Ilse do? A contradiction. A demurral from her could finish him. Right now. With a bullet in his back.

There was not a sound from the girl.

"Why?" Strelitz shot at him.

"Because of . . ." Woody swallowed. Hard. "Because of her mother."

Strelitz picked up. It was the first really unexpected answer he had received. "Her mother? What the devil has her mother to do with it?"

"Her mother was—Klara Gessner. Head of the Ravensbrück Concentration Camp guards," Woody answered soberly. He saw his interrogator react to the name. He went on. *"She* prevailed upon the *Herr Reichsführer* Heinrich Himmler, personally, to have her daughter evacuated via the *Achse."*

Strelitz threw a quick glance at the girl sitting silently on the bed, staring straight out in front of her. So, she was the daughter of Klara Gessner, he thought, intrigued. *Die Ratte aus Ravensbrück.* He knew of her, of course. Who did not? Naturally, the girl wanted to get away. Especially in view of what had happened to her mother. That last bit of information finished the case. It all made sense. If . . .

"*Fräulein* Gessner," he said. "Is all this correct?"

"It is correct, *Herr Sturmbannführer,"* Ilse said tonelessly.

Strelitz nodded. He returned his attention to Woody. Klara Gessner's daughter, he thought. And a young KZ guard officer. It was plausible. And it could easily be checked.

"Why are *you* so *verdammt* eager to leave, Diehl?" he asked.

Woody drew himself up. "Because of my duties at Flossenburg," he answered. "Carrying out the orders of my superiors and the Führer. Strictly and efficiently, as required. The *Amis* are calling my actions atrocities. I am to be arrested as a war criminal, if apprehended."

It was done. He had destroyed the last vestige of credibility with Ilse. "I abhor what went on in those camps as much as you do," he'd said. "I was *not* involved," he'd told her. It had been the truth. But now, she *had* to believe that his present lie was really the truth.

He only hoped it had saved their lives. He had no doubt that were he to be killed, Ilse would die, too.

Strelitz gathered his papers together. He looked up at Woody. "We will let you proceed on your way," he said. *Schon gut,* he thought. But in no way would he allow them to catch up with Eva Braun Hitler. If they tried, even got close, they would be eliminated. He would see to that.

"Your stolen motorcycle will be confiscated," he continued. "From now on you will go where and when and by whatever means directed by the *Achse* agents. Or we will be forced to terminate your journey right here. Is that fully understood?"

Woody snapped to. *"Jawohl, Herr Sturmbannführer!"*

Jawohl-Jawohl-Jawohl. He was *Jawohling* himself right out of any possibility of success in his mission. Dammit all to hell.

Strelitz stood up. "Ludwig," he called.

The plant manager came up to Woody. He glared at him, animosity in his once friendly eyes.

"You will leave here tomorrow morning," he said. "You will travel by truck to Steingaden. You will be given the necessary papers and instructions before you leave. Meanwhile you will stay here."

He and Strelitz left.

Woody walked over to Ilse. She would not look at him.

"Ilse," he said, "I . . ."

She turned to him. "You saved me in the forest," she said coldly. "I was in your debt." Her eyes blazed anger and contempt at him. "But you lied to me when you denied being a KZ guard. You were! One of the worst." She stopped. She glared at him.

"I despise you!" she spat.

Eva had promptly fallen in love with the little dachshund puppy. The black one with the limpid, brown eyes, the busy tongue and the tireless tail. He was one of a litter of four. He reminded her of Stasi. The mother, a stray, had been brought in by some children. They had found her lying in a gutted, abandoned farmhouse, badly injured and barely alive, with four lusty puppies fighting for her dry teats. She was still alive, although—according to the vet—it was only a matter of time.

The *Anlaufstelle* in Steingaden was a small animal hospital just south of the village, run by the local veterinarian, a man who looked to be in his late fifties, but whom Willi suspected was considerably younger. He limped because all the toes on his right foot had been amputated after they had become frostbitten at the Russian front.

It had been at Stalingrad, he told them, during the bitterly cold winter of '43. He had been a member of the *Veterinärkompanie* attached to the 71st Infantry Division of Fieldmarshal Paulus's 6th Army. On the door, sentimentally painted in black on a circle of carmine, the colors of the Veterinary Corps, was the military symbol denoting a veterinarian hospital: the serpent staff surrounded by a horseshoe.

The veterinarian, Gustav Klingmüller, was outgoing and talkative to the point of being garrulous. Once he had checked their identities to his satisfaction he had told them what pretty nearly amounted to his life's story.

It was a beautiful, sun-filled day—the best of the Bavarian summer—with a few fleecy, white clouds accentuating the brilliant blue of the sky. They were making their way leisurely along a dirt road in a wagon drawn by two horses. Klingmüller had told them they would not be staying overnight at the hospital, but would spend the night in a place which was run by the *Achse.*

"It is a famous place," he said proudly. "You will see. In happier times—may they return, God willing—many tourists came to admire it."

"A famous place," Eva asked, intrigued. "What do you mean?"

"It is a church," Klingmüller answered her. "A glorious work of beauty and splendor for the worship of our Lord. Perhaps you have heard of it. It is the Pilgrimage Church of Our Flagellated Savior. It is called *Die Wies.*"

Eva was delighted. She had heard of *Die Wies.* She had always wanted to see it. But even though she told Klingmüller that she knew about the church and its colorful history, he insisted on telling them all about it. In reverent detail. It took most of the half-hour ride.

They listened to how in 1730 two of God's men from the Premonstratensian Abbey in Steingaden had fashioned a Christ figure from fragments of ancient wooden sculptures of various saints, wrapping the joints in canvas and painting the figure. It showed vividly the bloody violence done to Our Lord and they had called it the Flagellated Savior. They had at first carried it around in processions on Holy Days, but so frightening and ghastly was the image that it aroused too deep a compassion, too great a grief in the faithful, and the figure was put away.

And he told them how it stood, forgotten, for years in the garret of the innkeeper's house in Steingaden, until it was discovered by a peasant woman who took it to her farm, called the Wies Farm, where she prayed to it. And the miracle happened.

He crossed himself.

On June 14, 1738, on the tortured face of the Flagellated Savior, tears could be seen brimming in the eyes!

The pilgrims came, then, to worship the holy image—and from a small rural chapel rose the magnificent church of today.

Even though she knew the story, Eva was moved. Tears, she thought. What tears would the Lord not weep were he to see what had been done to her beautiful, her beloved Bavaria.

"A room has been set up in the crypt under the church," Klingmüller told them. "You will stay there until your transportation is ready. Tomorrow. Only the caretaker knows of the place."

"I suppose he can be trusted," Willi said.

Klingmüller laughed. "No man can be trusted, my friend," he said. "This one no less, no more than others."

He gave Eva a sidelong glance. "Your wife will soon make you a happy man," he said knowingly to Willi.

[242]

"*Die gnädige Frau* is not my wife," Willi said quietly. "I am merely her—protector."

Klingmüller nodded sagely. "So," he said. "The wife of—someone else, then. Someone else who soon will be made proud and happy, not so?"

"*Herr* Klingmüller," Eva said, uneasy with the conversation. "What will happen to the little puppies—after the mother dies?"

The veterinarian shrugged. "Who, these days, can afford to keep a pet that cannot take care of itself?"

Eva fell silent.

The day was all at once less bright.

The road that led through a forest suddenly opened up onto an expanse of green meadows—and there stood the *Wies*. A massive, rather graceless structure, Eva thought, with dark, high-ridged roofs and a single clock tower.

But her sad mood was instantly dispelled when she walked into the church.

Her first impression was of being overwhelmed by light. Then whiteness and gold. And finally a profusion of incredibly elaborate ornamentation and inspiring frescos in glowing colors. It all took her breath away. It was a glorious manifestation, she thought, of the homage Germany and her people offered up to their God. Eight pairs of soaring columns, red, blue, and purple marble, supported the magnificent vault over the choir, and here, above the high altar, set in a gilt-framed encasement, stood the holy figure of the Flagellated Savior.

She let her eyes roam around the bedazzling church in awe and delight, exulting in the intricacies of the capitals and cornices, the sculptured cartouches and carvings. She marveled at the exquisite detailing on the spectacular pulpit with its rich and delicate ornamentation. *Be doers of the word and not hearers only,* read the inscription on the balustrade. Her thoughts went to her Adolf. *He* had been a doer. A doer for the glory of his Fatherland and for his beliefs. Unconsciously she placed her hand on her abdomen. Would his son have the same burning courage and convictions?

The little hidden room in the crypt deep under the church seemed doubly dark and somber after the airy brightness of the nave above.

Eva had a bleak thought of the terrible sewer and the caves at the Harz. Once again she was to be shut away in the dank darkness beneath the surface of the earth. At least, this time, it would be only for one night.

"*Herr* Klingmüller," Willi asked the veterinarian, "how will we travel on the next leg of our journey? I presume it will take us across the Alps?"

"Quite correct," Klingmüller acknowledged. "The next *Anlaufstelle* is in Italy. In the town of Merano. Just south of the Austrian border. Merano is an important collecting point on the route. Three branches of the *Achse* go off from there. One goes to Naples and Rome. One to Genoa. The main one to Bari. You will enter Austria at Scharnitz, pass through Innsbruck, and cross at the Brenner Pass, a beautiful trip this time of year. You will both enjoy it. Then, down to Merano."

"I hope the crossing will not be too strenuous," Willi said, with a glance toward Eva.

"Not at all, my dear fellow," Klingüller assured him expansively. "In fact, I might as well tell you, you and *die gnädige Frau* will travel in style. By the safest, most risk-free and unexpected means possible. You will be above suspicion."

"You intrigue me, Herr Klingmüller."

"Only by intention," the veterinarian laughed. "But I will tell you. You will be travelling as representatives of the International Red Cross."

"The Red Cross!" Willi was astounded.

Klingmüller nodded. "We have a—an excellent working arrangement with certain officials at the Bavarian Red Cross Relief Center in Innsbruck. The mission of the center is to trace missing persons and help to repatriate them whenever possible. They also distribute food parcels. Extensively. We, on our hand, have the means, both the finances and the right connections, to make it attractive for those officials to transport our people to our centers—no questions asked." He grinned with huge self-satisfaction. "I helped set it up," he said. "It is a *prima* arrangement, not so?"

Willi nodded. He was impressed. The organization was even more resourceful than he had imagined. But, then, that was, of course, typical of the SS.

"When you leave here," Klingmüller continued, "it will be in a Red Cross vehicle, flying a Red Cross pennant. No hiding in cramped and dirty quarters. *Die gnädige Frau* will be quite comfortable. You will have special Red Cross passes made out in four languages," he chuckled, "showing that you are transporting food parcels to Red Cross centers in Italy—and you will have a Red Cross armband on your sleeve. You will, as I said, be above suspicion!"

He limped toward the door. He turned. "Should you need assistance with anything while you are down here," he said, "there is a bell next to the door. It rings in the caretaker's rooms. Do not hesitate to use it. His name is Johann. Johann Meister." He grinned at Willi. "Johann *can* be trusted, my friend," he chuckled. "As far as you or I."

And he was gone.

Willi looked after him. He had only wanted a simple answer to his question about transportation, not a lecture on the entire operation of the *Anlaufstelle* and its contacts. Not that it had not been illuminating, he thought wryly.

He wondered vaguely how a man as talkative as Klingmüller could make a reliable *Anlaufstelle* agent.

He shrugged. That, thank Providence, was *not* one of his concerns.

Gustav Klingmüller guided his wagon through the gate into the yard behind the veterinary hospital and pulled the horses to a stop at the stable.

With only slight curiosity did he notice a motorcycle parked near the main building. A customer, no doubt. Someone with a dry cow or an impotent rabbit. Although he could not think of any local who had a *Schnauferl,* as the Bavarians called a motorbike.

The man who had been waiting for him was a stranger. Rugged, with commanding self-assurance, he now stood before him. He had that certain arrogance of a man with power who used it to instill fear in others, Klingmüller thought. He had seen that arrogance before. Often. In the SS officers at the Russian front. Most of them had lost their arrogance—before they lost their lives. He looked with curiosity at the burly man who stood with unbending legs planted solidly on the floor. *The elephant has joints, but none for courtesy.* The phrase whipped through his mind. He smiled to himself. It had been many years since he had read Shakespeare. But phrases that had impressed him still shot up from the depths of his memory when something triggered their release. *Troilus,* was it?

He smiled at the big man. "*Sturmbannführer* Strelitz," he said, "you have impressive credentials." He glanced at the document the man had given him. He had recognized the signature on it at once. He handed the document back to Strelitz. "Yes," he continued, "very impressive. But it will not get you across the border and into Italy, will it?" he chuckled. "No matter. I will have the proper papers for you tomorrow. Meanwhile, I can put you up here at the hospital for the night, and get you on a transport tomorrow. You will be safe here. Of course, we do have another safe house, away from here, but it is occupied by other travelers at the moment."

Strelitz had been about to interrupt the man's long-winded monologue to correct his impression that he was merely another *Achse* traveler. He held off. He had wondered where Eva Hitler and her escort were. He had the feeling that if he just kept quiet, he would find out.

Klingmüller went on. "It is a young couple," he said. "Johann is taking care of them. My comrade, Johann Meister, who operates this *Anlaufstelle* with me." He nodded pensively. "A rather intriguing couple it is, at that," he observed.

Strelitz was instantly alert. He knew, of course, who the couple was that Klingmüller was talking about. But what did the man mean by an intriguing couple?

"Really?" he prompted. "In what way?"

"You will see for yourself tomorrow, my dear Strelitz," Klingmüller answered him. "So I might as well tell you, is that not so? It is a young man and a young woman. She is well along in her pregnancy, six months plus, I should judge. But they are not married."

"Is that unusual?"

"Unusual is, my dear Strelitz, that a woman is traveling the *Achse* at all," Klingmüller said. "She is, in fact, the first female traveler to come through here. Unusual is also that the young man who is no *Lack'l*—not an uncivil fellow—should call himself her protector."

"You think he is the father after all?"

Klingmüller laughed merrily. "Not at all, my dear fellow. There is—something else." He limped over to a large, battered icebox standing in a corner of the room. "Would you like a nice cold beer, Strelitz?" he asked pleasantly. "I can use one myself. It was hot, riding in the sun to the *Wies* and back." He opened the icebox. "We have our own ice plant in Steingaden," he said. "I keep a few bottles of nice Bock beer in the icebox with my laboratory specimens."

"*Bitte*—yes, please," Strelitz said. "A beer would be welcome."

"Would you like a bite to eat? I have some nice *Datschi*—or some *Blun'sn?*" he asked, using the Bavarian dialect words for fruitcake and blood sausage.

"*Danke*—no, thank you. A beer will be fine."

Klingmüller took out two bottles of winter-brewed, dark brown Bock beer. "From the *Bayreuther Bierbrauerei*," he said proudly. "An excellent beer." He opened them.

"You said something else was unusual about that young couple," Strelitz prompted again. He took the beer offered him by the veterinarian. Both men drank straight from their bottles.

"There is," Klingmüller confided. "I find it most interesting that a pregnant woman should travel the *Achse* escape route. With a bodyguard—*protector*. It made me wonder, you can well imagine, Strelitz, it made me wonder *who* she is—and even more, who is the father of the child? Intriguing, not so?"

He took a deep pull on his beer. He wiped his mouth with the back of his hand, a gesture all Bavarian boys seem to have been born with. "I will wager, my dear Strelitz," he said, his voice low and conspiratorial, "I will wager the father is a real *Bonze*—a real big shot in the party! Someone with influence enough to arrange the escape of his girl friend who is no *Flitscherl*—no cheap hussy."

He looked at Strelitz. "Intriguing, is that not so? Trying to deduce who it could be. Who do *you* think it is, my friend? Bormann? Himmler? Keitel?" He gave Strelitz a sidelong, almost mischievous look. "The Führer himself?" He chuckled. "There were enough rumors that he liked the young ladies, not so? Especially the young ladies of the theater. Perhaps our pregnant little girl is a cabaret chorus girl from Berlin, yes?" He shook his head. "It is intriguing, is it not," he chuckled, "to speculate who fathered the child in our mysterious young woman's womb. I must ask Johann; he will have talked to her."

He turned away to put his empty beer bottle on a table.

Strelitz acted. He swung his heavy bottle and struck a crushing blow to the back of Klingmüller's head. He hit him high on the junction of the parietal bones.

The man was unconscious before he hit the floor.

23

---•◆•---

STRELITZ STARED ANGRILY at the unconscious man sprawled on the floor. Klingmüller was a fool, he thought. A dangerous fool. He cursed him for the inconvenience and disruption he had caused and would be causing.

He had had no choice, of course. The idiot sealed his own fate once he started his dangerous guessing game. Obviously an incorrigible *Ausplauderer*—a blab—he had to be silenced, before he started to babble his minacious speculations to anyone who would listen.

It was the kind of situation the Führer in his wisdom had foreseen, he realized, and it had been his privilege to carry out the duty charged him.

Now to finish it.

He had an idea. He looked around the office. A large medicine cabinet with glass doors stood against one wall. He walked over to it. He surveyed the contents. Trays of surgical instruments. Ointments, salves, and lotions. Pills and medicines. A few cans of some sort of powder. He picked up one of them. *Derris Flohpulver*, the label read. It would do. He pocketed it.

He picked up the unconscious veterinarian and carried him to the door that led to the yard. Across the yard was the stable.

He peered out. The place was empty. He hefted his limp burden up over his shoulder and carried it to the stable.

The two horses that had taken Klingmüller and his charges to the *Wies* were in their stalls. Strelitz dumped the comatose man in the nearest one. The horse eyed the prostrate man uneasily, side-stepping skittishly to avoid the motionless body. Nostrils flaring, the animal snorted in nervous confusion.

Strelitz took the can from his pocket. He emptied half of the powder into the palm of his hand. He held it out toward the fretful horse. Curiously, apprehensively, the animal stretched his muzzle to examine the strange offering. On the floor Klingmüller groaned and stirred.

Suddenly Stretlitz blew the powder into the exploring nostrils of the horse.

Instantly, as the strong flea powder burned and seared the sensitive area, the horse whinnied in alarm. He reared up, as the agony in his nostrils worsened, snorting and neighing. As he came down, one hoof crashed into the chest of the man on the stable floor. Strelitz could hear the rib cage crack. Again and again the maddened horse, in a frenzy of torment, reared and kicked and bucked, his iron-shod hoofs stomping down repeatedly on the body at his feet.

Finally the raging of the tortured beast subsided. He stood trembling, his flanks flecked with foam from his mouth, his nostrils flaring.

The straw in his stall was soggy and red with the blood that oozed from the mangled mass at his feet.

Strelitz looked down at the dead agent. He hoped he could be identified. His head had been crushed.

Back in Klingmüller's office Strelitz put the can of flea powder back in the cabinet. He got himself another bottle of beer from the icebox and sat down to take stock.

The mess in the stable would be considered an accident, he was certain. He looked around. There was nothing to betray his presence. He would throw the empty beer bottles in a trash bin he had seen in the yard. All three of them. The vet had obviously gone to the stable for one reason or other—and the horse had gone berserk. Any trace of flea powder found would be natural and would arouse no suspicion. There would be no meticulous investigation that might place the *Anlaufstelle* and the *Achse* in jeopardy.

The danger was in the disarray to the operation itself.

Calmly he examined his options. His first duty was, of course, to the safety of *Frau* Hitler and her companion. He would go to the *Wies* at once and contact Klingmüller's fellow agent there. Then he would have to return to Memmingen and report to the *Verteilungsstab*. Through Ludwig. They would have to make alternate arrangements for the *Anlaufstelle* in Steingaden. It should only be a matter of a day or two.

He glanced at his watch. There would not be enough time to make contact with both Meister in the *Wies* and Ludwig in Memmingen. He obviously could not take the chance of traveling after curfew and being caught as a violator. He would have to remain at the *Wies* until the next morning. He was certain he could do so without being seen by Frau Hitler and the SS officer. He would drive back to Memmingen first thing in the morning as soon as the curfew was lifted. Only one thing disturbed him. With the *Anlaufstelle* schedule thrown out of order by the necessary elimination of Klingmüller, there now was a strong possibility that Diehl and the Gessner woman *would* catch up with *Frau* Hitler. But he was certain he could get to Memmingen before they left at the scheduled hour of 0830 on the *Stars and Stripes* truck, and delay them.

If an encounter did become imminent he would have to terminate the journey of the young SS officer and the daughter of Klara Gessner.

He cursed himself. An urgency, a tightness, a danger had crept into the journey which he had not wanted, not anticipated. It was becoming a race. A race with time—and danger. He should have taken care of the threat posed by Diehl, however tenuous, when he had the opportunity. He had let himself be blinded by the parentage of the girl. He should have realized that something would go wrong along the way. Something always did. That was the reason for contingency planning.

Perhaps it was not too late.

Tomorrow would be soon enough.

SS Sturmbannführer Oskar Strelitz looked at his watch. He felt a pang of nostalgia. The watch was an SS issue; its black dial gleamed fiercely at him. He had no qualms about wearing it. There were enough of them around, adorning the wrists of Germans and *Amis* alike to arouse no suspicion. It was 0627 hours. The motorcycle purred under him. He would be in Memmingen in ample time to take care of Diehl and his girl.

He had spent the night in an empty room in the *Pfarrhaus*— the parsonage—adjoining the *Wies*, without getting near the crypt where Meister had told him the young couple was awaiting transportation.

Johann Meister, a dour, flat-eyed individual, had at once understood the situation. Strelitz was confident the man would be able to follow through, until the organization could put an alternate *Anlaufstelle* into effect. *Frau* Hitler and her escort would be on their way to Merano in two or three hours time, with only a short delay. He would have time enough to dispose of his mission in Memmingen, and get to Merano before nightfall. He estimated the whole trip to be about 250 kilometers, if he took the direct route to the border without detouring to Steingaden and the *Wies*. It was a damned long haul, but he would make it.

He had just passed the little side road that branched off to the village of Burggen from the road to Marktoberdorf, when he saw a dense cloud of black smoke hanging in the clear sky over the road in the distance. The woods lining the road prevented him from seeing what caused it. A fire obviously. A farmhouse? Barn? A haystack? From the sooty color of the smoke, perhaps a vehicle. He drove on.

Quite suddenly, around a bend in the road, the forest gave way to a stretch of cultivated fields, and Strelitz saw what had caused the smoke.

It was not one vehicle, but two.

Two US Army trucks, ditched near a small grove of trees, one overturned, both blackened by fire and still smoldering, their contents of crates and boxes spilled out on the road shoulder and in the ditch. On the road itself at least a dozen US Army jeeps and weapons carriers were haphazardly drawn up, and several *Ami* soldiers were grimly busying themselves around the still smoking trucks. On the road shoulder lay four forms, covered by blankets. A short distance before the site of the burned trucks an *Ami* jeep was halted across the road, blocking it.

An MP sergeant waved Strelitz to a halt with his tommy gun. He had no choice but to obey. It was too late to turn around. The sergeant strode up to him. With unconcealed animosity he glared at him. "Over there!" he snapped angrily. *"Da!"* He pointed. *"Schnell! Schnell! Da!* You wait!"

Strelitz wheeled his motorcycle into a field, joining a small group of anxious Germans who stood around a battered wood-burner truck, two horse-drawn wagons and an old, banged-up Packard touring car.

He walked up to a farmer who stood off by himself, scowling at the scene. In the distance the wail of an approaching ambulance gradually grew louder.

"What happened?" Strelitz asked the farmer.

"What do you want from me?" the man growled.

"Nothing. If you have nothing to say."

The farmer hawked and spat on the ground. "Someone amused himself with a couple of *Ami* trucks," he grumbled.

"Who?"

"See for yourself." The man nodded toward the nearest of the smoldering vehicles.

Strelitz strained to look. On the side of the truck, partly obliterated by soot, something could be seen smeared on in white paint. A swastika. And little by little he could make out the crude writing accompanying it: "Americans! Beware! Before us, men turn into nothing! *Der Werwolf!*"

"They kept their word," the farmer muttered. "I saw them, the four *Amis*. I was one of the first ones here. Their throats were cut." He nodded slowly. "And they were no longer—men."

Strelitz looked at him sharply. "How so?" he asked.

The farmer did not look at him. "Each one," he said, "each one of them had his *Schwanz*—his prick—cut off." He was silent for a brief moment. "And stuck in his mouth," he growled.

Strelitz felt uneasy. He did not care what had happened to the *Amis*. Only that the MPs might take it out on the people they rounded up. In any case, there would be a delay. A delay, before they got around to checking everyone out and sending them on their way. A delay he could not afford. He was not worried that his papers would not stand up to scrutiny by a bunch of MPs. They were the best. But he *had* to reach Memmingen before Diehl left the ropery.

He looked at the scene of bloody and fiery carnage. The words of *Reichsführer* Himmler suddenly rang out in his mind: Ruthless resistance will spring up behind their backs time and time again. Like werewolves, brave as death, the avengers will strike the enemy!

Well and good, he thought. Only, this time, the action of the werewolves might well have struck down a vital friendly mission.

He looked around. Another wagon had joined the group. Perhaps he could double back, find a side road and bypass the scene of the werewolf raid. He started to wheel his bike toward the road.

The MP sergeant stopped him. "Where the hell do you think you're going?" he rasped angrily. "Back. Wait! *Los!*"

Strelitz addressed him in simple German. "I will go back," he explained deferentially. "With your permission, I will try to find another road. It is important I get where I go as quickly as I can." He gestured. "I will go—around."

"The hell you will, you Kraut shithead!" the sergeant spat. "You get your ass back there. You'll wait, you bastard. If it takes all day!"

It was 1142 hours when Strelitz finally pulled up at the ropery in Memmingen. He had seen no *Stars and Stripes* truck on the way. It meant nothing, of course. The truck could have taken any one of the several different roads between Memmingen and Steingaden. There could have been a delay, or a change of transportation. The route was flexible.

Ludwig met him at the gate. He greeted him with a self-satisfied look on his face.

"You will be pleased to know, *Herr Sturmbannführer*," he beamed, "that Diehl and *Fraülein* Gessner left for Steingaden on the *Stars and Stripes* truck—on schedule!"

The light in the confined space behind the bundles of newspapers stacked almost to the roof of the truck was feeble, but Woody—his eyes having grown used to the faint light—could still make out the headlines and some of the body of the stories in the paper he had pulled from one of the bundles. *Stars and Stripes*, Monday, June 11, 1945.

The Allied Control Committee was still trying to hammer out details of the agreement reached in Berlin on June 5 by the four superpowers, represented by Eisenhower, Montgomery, Zhukov, and Tassigny, which divided Germany into four occupation zones with Berlin to be run jointly. Woody hadn't even known of the agreement—let alone the detailed problems it had stirred up . . . Great Britain and the US had made an agreement with Tito for the military administration of Trieste and Venezia Giulia, the region in northeast Italy formed after World War I from ceded territories . . . The point score for enlisted men was about to be lowered again; and the Soviet commander in Vienna had ordered the British military missions to get out.

The Krasnov syndrome on a larger scale, Woody thought wryly. Whenever he thought of the brazenly two-faced Russian liaison bastard, he bristled.

He glanced at Ilse who sat silent and withdrawn, huddled in a corner of the cramped space. Ever since that damned interrogation in Memmingen she had been cool and distant. He knew she felt betrayed and he ached to take her into his confidence and tell her the whole damned truth. Take her in his arms and comfort her; restore her trust in him. And the world around her. He knew he could not, and it was about to tear him apart. But his mission *had* to come before his own personal feelings, so he tried to force himself to ignore his emotions, thereby making the anguish greater. There was nothing he could say, and the silence was bitter. For them both.

He heard the driver tap on the cab window. He peered through it. "Steingaden," the man mouthed at him. He held up two fingers. *"Zwei minuten!"*

Woody turned to Ilse. He touched her shoulder. She stiffened, but she did not move away. There was nowhere to go.

"We are ready to get off," he called to her, over the rumbling of the truck. "Two minutes."

The girl did not look at him. She gathered her belongings together and sat hugging them to her.

The truck came to a stop. Woody heard the cab door slam, and the rear door being opened. Light spilled in trickles through the cracks between the bundles of paper—becoming a torrent as the driver pushed aside the bundles covering their exit.

"Everybody out!" he called cheerfully.

The driver had let them out south of the village. The veterinary hospital which was their destination lay just ahead, around a bend in the road, he'd told them. As they walked along, their bundles slung over their shoulders, Woody looked at his watch. 1147 hours. They had been on the road a good four hours. The driver had had to make an unscheduled detour to Kempten, and the trip had taken almost twice as long as it should. Perhaps there was still a chance they could continue to the next stop that same day anyway, he thought, depending on where it was.

They walked around the bend in the road—and stopped dead.

Ahead they could see what was obviously the hospital. Several vehicles were drawn up on the road before the building. American jeeps, an official-looking German car—and an ambulance.

Woody stared at the unexpected scene. Had the *Anlaufstelle* been blown? What the hell had happened? No matter, he thought grimly. They would have to act as if it did not concern them.

"Ilse," he said tautly, "just walk. Follow me. Pay no attention to anything. Understood?"

She nodded.

They walked on past the hospital. Only one man, sitting in the civilian car, was in evidence. He paid them as little attention as they did him.

Woody was disturbed. He tried not to let it show. He knew Ilse must be afraid. Uncertain. He knew she needed assurance and support. He could not give it, nor would she take it. Dammit all to hell! He cursed the SS officer who had forced that damned interrogation on him.

The sign pointing down the sylvan side road read: *DIE WIES 3 KM*. It was the alternate stop. Ludwig had instructed them to go there in the unlikely case of trouble at the hospital. To look for the caretaker, Johann Meister. And he'd been given alternate passwords.

The road led through a forest, and Woody was glad for the shade. He had begun to sweat. He didn't know if it was because of the hot summer day or the disturbing turn of events. He hoped the first. He was getting thirsty. It had been close and hot in the truck. Memories of the tall glasses of cool iced tea his mother used to serve on hot summer nights back in San Francisco flooded his mind. And, unbidden, the corny joke his father had always told, scandalizing his mother—especially when company was present. The one about the New Mexico Indian who drank forty-seven cups of iced tea on a real hot summer day. And how the next day they'd found him dead in his tepee.

He chuckled to himself. He felt Ilse eye him, strangely. Startled, he realized he had chuckled aloud. What the hell was he doing?

Whatever it was, he felt better.

Suddenly the sound of a motor vehicle could be heard approaching on the road ahead. They walked over to the shoulder, trudging on, single file. The vehicle passed them. It was a truck. It flew a Red Cross flag. Woody thought he could glimpse three people in the cab before the cloud of fine dust stirred up by the truck enveloped him. Dammit! The dust stuck uncomfortably to his sweaty skin. He suddenly didn't know what he wanted more. A cold drink or a shower.

Ludwig had mentioned that the *Wies* was some kind of showcase church, but Woody had not been prepared for the sight that met him when he stepped from the entrance hall into the nave. He stopped dead and stared. He had the feeling he'd walked into a gigantic wedding cake, angels, hearts, and all. Even the gilt was gilded. It was as gaudy and as garish as anything he'd ever seen. He looked around in genuine awe. My God, it's pretentious, he thought.

In the choir at the far end a man was polishing the marble in the base of a tall marble column. Woody and Ilse walked toward him. As they got closer, Woody had another surprise. The marble. It wasn't marble at all. It was painted plaster, for heaven's sake. How kitschy, he thought. He looked at the figure of Christ that stood in a niche above the high altar. A strange, disturbing, marionette-like figure, flecked with painted blood. He chilled. It was the eyes. Haunted. Filled with abysmal suffering. He had seen the same eyes before. In the faces of the Flossenburg Concentration Camp inmates.

The man at the column stopped his work as he saw them approach. "Can I help you?" he asked.

"Yes," Woody said. "I was wondering. Could you tell me, please. *Tempus non erit amplius*—there shall be delay no longer—is it not from Apocalypse 6:10?"

"You are in error, *mein Herr*," the man answered. "It is Apocalypse 10:6." He looked at them. "I am Johann Meister," he said. "Please come with me."

In the crypt room under the church Meister gave Woody and Ilse a surly look. "You have come here at an unfortunate time," he remarked, obviously resenting their presence and the necessity of attending to them at a time when more pressing matters demanded his attention.

Woody nodded. "Apparently so, *Herr* Meister. What happened?"

"An—accident," the caretaker answered evasively. "It is being investigated. By both the *Gemeinde Behörden*—the township authorities—in Steingaden, and the *Amis.*"

"I saw them at the *Anlaufstelle*," Woody acknowledged. He looked worried. "They may come here, too. To investigate. Is that not so?"

"No," Meister snapped, "there is no chance of that." But he did not sound convinced. "I am certain."

"That is not acceptable," Woody said curtly. "I will not risk being caught in a routine accident investigation, because of a stupid mistake on the part of some idiot!" He glared at Meister. "You will have to send us on to the next *Anlaufstelle* immediately!"

"That is impossible," Meister declared.

"Nothing is impossible!" Woody shot back at him.

"If you had arrived this morning," Meister muttered irritably, "you could have left on the Red Cross transport with the other couple." He scowled at Woody. "Now, you will have to wait until tomorrow."

"I will *have* to do nothing!" Woody snapped testily. He was startled. Red Cross! The damned escape route employed Red Cross vehicles. With Red Cross cooperation? It was incredible. But there it was. With a surge of excitement he suddenly realized that that "other couple" of Meister's had to be Eva and her cohort. *They* had been in the Red Cross truck that passed them on the road less than an hour ago! He thought one of the three people he'd glimpsed through the windshield had been a woman. He'd thought nothing of it then because—my God!—Red Cross.

Cold-eyed he glared at the caretaker. Here was his chance. "I am afraid, Herr Meister," he said icily, "I am afraid I do not think that under the uncertain circumstances my companion and I will be safe here overnight." He glowered at the agent. "And neither will you, my good fellow, if you are found here with us." He drew himself haughtily erect. "If you cannot assist us, as required of you, I must attempt to reach the next *Anlaufstelle* on my own. And, of course, give a full report to the Brotherhood." He gave Meister a withering look. "I am certain you understand."

Meister suddenly looked frightened. "I can assure you," he said fervently, "I would like you gone from here as much as you do. I am fully aware of the danger your presence here constitutes at this time."

"Then I suggest you find a way to send us on," Woody snapped.

Meister nodded. "As you say."

"Then do so!"

"There—there is a possibility," the caretaker ventured uncertainly, "a slight possibility that . . ." He stopped. He was obviously thinking.

"I am waiting, Meister!" Woody snapped.

"There is a special Red Cross courier arriving here," Meister said. "He is not supposed to be a transport. He is here to get a full report on the—the accident. And he will have instructions regarding changes in the Red Cross escape route assistance in crossing into Italy. He—he should be here within the hour." He looked at Woody. "I will talk to him. Perhaps . . ."

"We will both talk to him," Woody interrupted firmly. "Where is the next stop?"

"The Red Cross transport goes to the *Achse* collection point in Merano. In Italy," Meister said. "It is at least a five-hour drive."

"Then that is where your courier will take us. Today." Woody's tone of voice precluded any gainsaying. "In one hour. We will have more than enough time to get there, if you, *Herr* Meister, get to work on the necessary documents immediately!"

Willi Lüttjohann was impressed. Both by the magnificent scenery he and Eva had driven through, crossing the Tyrolean Alps, and the ease with which the Red Cross truck, loaded with food parcels, had crossed the border checkpoints. The guards had saluted, counted the number of passengers, and checked the Red Cross manifest, keeping it just long enough to place their stamps on it. He had felt like a tourist, and had thoroughly enjoyed the trip, taking special satisfaction in the obvious pleasure and enthusiasm expressed by Eva.

They had made the trip in just under five hours and had arrived at the *Anlaufstelle* in Merano a little before 1700 hours.

The stop was a small, picturesque inn on the outskirts of town. It was a two-story, ochre-colored building with an attic under a red tile roof. It was covered with vines and had a secluded private garden in back. An open gate led to a walled courtyard in front. Set into the stone wall next to it a shrine with a wooden figure of the Madonna welcomed the travelers who sought the shelter of the inn.

The *Anlaufstelle* was run by an Italian couple named Bazzano, who also ran the inn. *Signore* and *signora* Luigi Bazzano were in the pay of the *Achse*. And according to Meister, pay was the right word. The Brotherhood paid dearly and excessively for their services. Rumor had it, he'd told them, that the Bazzanos had old and close ties to the professional local smugglers and were on as good terms with the local police authorities as well-greased palms could insure. Be that as it may, the Merano collection point was one of the most efficient on the Italian leg of the escape route.

They were greeted with profuse enthusiasm by *Signor* Bazzano, a chubby, animated man who exuded so much sincerity and goodwill that Willi instantly distrusted him. "*Benvenuto,* my friends!" he cried. "Please. Come with me."

Bowing and scraping the innkeeper agent took them to a small room on the second floor, facing the garden. In a mixture of Italian and German and a tarantella of windmill gestures he cautioned them to stay in the room. There were other guests at the inn, he explained, and it was best they were not seen. *Signora* Bazzano would bring them food. Some nice spaghetti, bread and cheese, and a bottle of red wine. He winked at Eva. It looked like *la signora* would welcome it, he observed roguishly. He pointed to a button on the wall next to the door, surrounded by a dirty patch of finger marks on the flowery wallpaper.

"If you want anything," he said, "please ring the bell."

It was two hours later, and dusk was turning the green trees olive drab, when Woody and Ilse walked across the walled courtyard to the inn at Merano.

The Red Cross courier had literally whisked them through Austria, stopping only at the borders and, for a few minutes, on business of his own, at the relief center office in Innsbruck.

Signor Bazzano welcomed them expansively and put them up in a room on the ground floor facing the garden in back. He warned them to stay in their room. Tomorrow, he assured them. Tomorrow he would send them on their way to the *Anlaufstelle* in Bolzano, with new travel papers and a basket with lunch, fixed for them by *Signora* Bazzano herself.

And he left them to rest up after their no doubt exhausting trip.

It was shortly before 2030 hours, the hour of curfew. Ilse was asleep on the bed, and he was dozing in a big chair. Suddenly a noise in the courtyard roused him. It was the sound of a motor. It chugged, sputtered, and died. A motorcycle? It sounded famil- iar. He strained to listen. But he heard nothing. Of course, they were not alone in the inn. There were other guests, Bazzano had told them. Guests? Or *Achse* travelers? Or both? Was Eva among them, or had she gone on immediately after she had arrived, as he had? Bolzano was only about twenty miles to the south, less than an hour's drive. Or, had he caught up with her? Was she in Merano? Bolzano? He was too tired to think straight. He admit- ted, reluctantly, that the constant strain was getting to him. Any- way, there was nothing he could do now. Tomorrow . . .

Slowly he dozed off.

In a room above, *SS Obersturmführer* Willibald Lüttjohann glanced at the sleeping Eva. She did not stir. The sudden motor noise in the courtyard had not disturbed her. He was grateful.

The rigors of the journey were beginning to take their toll. Her strength was being severely tapped. He would have to find a way to make the rest of the trip to Bari less strenuous for her.

Tomorrow . . .

He lay back in the big leather chair and dozed off.

Woody woke with a start. He knew he had had an unpleasant dream and had willed himself to waken from it as he usually did, but it had eluded his conscious mind the instant he woke up. For a split moment he sat motionless, blinking away the sleep from his eyes, trying to remember where he was, and feeling naked be- cause his gun was not in its holster strapped under his shoulder. Then—he knew.

His neck felt stiff from the uncomfortable position in the chair, and one of his legs was asleep. He held his watch to a shaft of pale blue moonlight that slanted into the room. 0307 hours.

He stood up and stretched his legs. He glanced at Ilse, sleeping heavily on the bed, her face turned away from him. He frowned. Dammit! If there was only *something* he could do.

[259]

But there wasn't.

He walked over to the window. Outside, the garden—a mosaic of shadowy and moonlit patches accented by the black silhouettes of trees and shrubs—lay quiet and silent in the beauty of the night. He was just about to turn away when something caught his attention. A movement. Ever so slight. Seen out of the corner of his eye.

He looked, peering into the darkness.

There. Again. Something moved. A figure. The figure of a man.

Instantly he was alert. What would someone be doing at three in the morning outside his window? Who? He didn't know.

But he decided to find out.

Quietly he opened the window. He swung his legs over the sill and silently, catlike, dropped the couple of feet to the soft ground into a flower bed below.

For a moment he stood stock-still, melting into the shadows at the wall.

He listened. He peered at the spot in the shrubbery where he thought he had seen the movement, trying to penetrate the darkness.

He saw nothing.

Suddenly he stiffened. Footsteps. Cautious, clandestine footsteps. Someone was approaching on the path.

In the faint bluish light he saw a man slowly walking down the path. He stopped. He looked around and stepped up to a bush. From his motions it quickly became apparent that he was relieving himself.

Woody felt sheepish standing in the shadows, watching the man. But he could not move without being discovered. And he did not want that to happen.

The man continued to urinate. Woody could hear the thin rustle in the leaves on the ground. Finally the man tucked himself in and buttoned his trousers. He turned to go back the way he'd come. A thorny branch from a rosebush hooked itself to his pants leg and tore at him. The man uttered a low oath. *"Farsholt!—Damn!"*

Woody drew up in astonishment.

The man had cursed in Yiddish!

The man freed himself and walked on. Suddenly Woody heard a low, taut, and raspy command in sharp, guttural German, coming from the black shadows in the brush: *"Stillgestanden!*—Don't move! Don't make a sound!"

[260]

The man on the path stopped dead in his tracks. From the bushes stepped another man. Woody did not recognize him, but even the few steps he took before he planted himself before the first man betrayed his military training. He held one hand in front of him. A split second glint of moonlight on metal was suddenly reflected from the object he held.

A gun.

"What are you doing here?" the man with the gun snarled. "Who are you, *du Judenschwein?*—you Jewish pig?"

The man before him cringed. He began to tremble. "I—I beg your forgiveness. Please!" he mumbled in obvious terror. "There were no—no toilet facilities in the attic. And I—I was . . ."

"*Maulhalten!*—Shut your mouth!" the German snapped. "Do not play games with me. What are you, *du Saujude,* doing here at an *Achse Anlaufstelle?*"

The Jew stared at him. "*Achse?*" he croaked.

The German glared at him, scornfully, triumphantly. "I thought you were a Jew swine when I saw you," he said smugly. "Sneaking out of the house. No Aryan would look like you." His voice grew harsh. "On your knees, you obscene creature!"

The Jew fell to his knees. Woody had the feeling it was not the first time the man had been forced to grovel before a member of the master race. The man wrung his hands. "*Zol Got mir helfn!*" he mumbled.

"Once more, *du Scheisskerl,*" the German snarled. Towering over the kneeling man he pointed his gun deliberately down at his eyes. "What are you doing here?"

"Please! Nothing! Only—we only . . ."

"We," the German interrupted. "There are more of you scum here? *Los!* Out with it. How many *Saujuden* are there?"

"Two—two more," the man stammered.

"In the attic?" The German sounded incredulous.

The man nodded. "We . . ."

"Why?" the German shot at him. "What are you doing there?" He glared at the man on the ground, his eyes narrowed in suspicion. He answered himself. "You are spying on us! You are planning to betray us! Revenge yourselves, you scum!"

"No! No! We . . ."

"Shut up!" the German growled. Slowly, with menacing, measured steps he began to stalk around the kneeling man. "Be quiet! Or you will have shaken that Jewish cock of yours for the last time!"

"Bitte, bitte, Herr Lagerbefehlshaber," the man pleaded, automatically addressing the German as he would a concentration camp officer. "Please. I—I mean no harm."

The German laughed harshly. "No harm, *du Saujude?*" he grated. "To be a stinking Jew is harm enough."

He stopped behind the trembling man on the ground.

Woody watched. Anger and rage were building in him, but he knew he could not interfere. He could do nothing that would jeopardize his mission.

He saw the German switch his gun to his left hand. He saw him reach down toward his boot with his right. In the pale moonlight he saw what he pulled out. A knife.

And he decided.

His eyes flew about for some kind of weapon. A row of slanted bricks formed a border around the flower bed where he was standing. He grabbed one of them. Quickly, keeping to the shadows, he silently skirted the two men on the path, until he was behind the German. The man was intent on the victim kneeling before him, his back turned toward him.

Woody was within a few feet of the man when he saw him draw back his knife arm, aiming the long blade at the back of the Jew's neck.

He rushed the last couple of steps and smashed the brick down on the crown of the German's head.

Without a sound the man collapsed, bowling over the Jew kneeling in front of him.

At once Woody was at his side.

"Quiet!" he whispered urgently. "We don't want to alert the whole damned hornets' nest."

The shaken man stared at the knife fallen on the ground. "He—he would have killed me," he breathed in shock.

Woody helped him to his feet. "You're okay now," he said. "But what the hell *are* you doing here?"

"You—saved my life," the man whispered. *"Got zol dir bentshn!*—May God bless you!"

Woody looked down at the unconscious German. "Help me haul this guy into the bushes," he said. He picked up the man's gun. A Walther 7.65. He hesitated for only a second before he put it in his belt. Together with the Jew he pulled the German off the path. He picked up the knife and threw it next to him.

"Is he dead?" the Jew asked.

"He'll have a bump on his skull the size of a bowling ball and a healthy headache," Woody grunted. "But he'll live." He turned

[262]

to the man. "What the hell *are* you and your friends doing in the damned attic?"

"We are waiting," the man said. "For transportation. We are going to Palestine."

Woody gaped at him. "Palestine? You're illegal emigrants?"

The man nodded. "We are not permitted to go there. By the British. But we go there with the help of *Bricha*."

"*Bricha?*"

"In Hebrew it means escape," the man said. "It is the organization that helps us get to Palestine. We go there by the way of safe houses. Like this one." He glanced fearfully toward the bushes that hid the unconscious German. "I—I did not know there were Nazis here."

"They also have an escape route, my friend."

"The innkeeper told us that there were other guests here. But not—not Nazis." He shuddered.

"The innkeeper is screwing the Golden Calf from both ends," Woody said drily. He was stunned. The *Achse* and *Bricha* using the same safe houses! Nazis in the basement, Jews in the attic. One hell of an arrangement. Ironic. Devilish. But then, as far as *Signor* Luigi Bazzano was concerned, why not? Money is money, whether it comes from Nazis or Jews. He turned to the man.

"Go back to the attic," he said. "And *stay* there. You and your friends will be safe as long as you do. As long as you follow the instructions given you." He nodded toward the German. "That bastard—when he does come to—won't give you any static."

The man nodded. "I will do as you say." He grabbed Woody's hand. "Thank you. And—be blessed by God!"

"*Shalom*," Woody said. He grinned. "And for God's sake, next time you have to take a leak—use your hat!"

The man disappeared into the night shadows. Woody turned back toward the window to his room—and froze.

Clearly seen in the pale blue light from the moon a figure could be made out standing in the window, watching him.

Ilse.

In two strides he was at the window. He looked up at the girl, who stood tensely, staring down at him.

"Who—are you?" she whispered.

Woody stared back at her. How long had she been there? How much had she seen? How much had she heard?

He climbed into the room. He closed the window. He looked searchingly into her face.

"Ilse," he said, "what . . ."

[263]

"I saw it all," the girl whispered. "I heard it all. I—I saw what you did." She lifted her face to him. Her huge, luminous eyes regarded him solemnly.

"Who are you?"

For a long moment Woody stared into the wide, questioning eyes as if trying to read the thoughts hidden behind them.

Then—he told her.

24

WOODY STOPPED THE NERVOUS PACING that had sustained him
during the disclosure of his true identity to Ilse. Gravely he looked
at the girl perched rigidly on the edge of the bed, staring at her
hands that lay clenched in her lap. She was obviously deeply af-
fected, shaken, by what she had heard. She had let him talk, not
once interrupting him.

He was well aware that by telling her what he had, he'd broken every rule in the book—and several that hadn't even been re-
corded. He could have done nothing else. Though neither he nor
she had so chosen, Ilse, for better or for worse, had become part
of his mission, and it was now imperative that there be no reservations, no doubts between them. Ilse had witnessed his interrogation by that *Sturmbannführer* in Memmingen, and she had
just seen him disable what was supposed to be a fellow SS officer
in order to save and aid a Jew! If he had done nothing, it was
quite likely that the girl in her confusion and incertitude might
have sought an explanation elsewhere. And that would have been
his undoing.

There had been no way he could explain his conflicting behavior except by telling her the truth.

"Look, Ilse," he said earnestly, "please understand. I know you
were horrified by what you saw at the atrocity screening, that you
were appalled when you thought *I* had been part of it. I assured
you, I had not, and you believed me—until you heard me admit
such actions to that SS officer in Memmingen. Then you loathed
me. For being what I admitted to being. And for lying to you. But

now you know. I did *not* lie to you. I *do* abhor the horrors that went on in those camps. But I *had* to make that SS officer believe I was part of it. Or I would have been killed. And very likely you, as well. Please understand."

Ilse made no reply. She did not move.

"I cannot tell you any details of what my mission is," he continued. "The knowledge would be too dangerous for you to have. Only this. The operation I am part of is directed against the very forces both you and I abhor. Against the evil that destroyed your country and so many of its people. Against those who would perpetuate it. They cannot be allowed to do so."

"And what now, Rudi—if that is your name?" she whispered bitterly. "What now, that you have told *me* of this mission? Me. A German. The daughter of someone who took a very big part in everything you wish to destroy." There was a catch in her voice, but she went on. "What will you do now? Will you have to—to kill me? To safeguard your secret? Your operation?" She nodded, her eyes bright with unshed tears. "You will, is that not true?"

He stared at her. My God! he thought. She would think that. He was shocked that the idea had not entered his own mind. It was logical. He suddenly realized that his feelings for the girl effectively had blocked the thought. Kill her? To keep her from talking? He knew he could not. His thoughts raced. He would have to trust her. And equally important, she would have to trust him. Now. And hereafter.

How?

"Ilse," he said quietly, "you are right. It would be the easy way out for me. If. If I were just like those I consider my adversaries. But I am not."

He paused. His eyes bored into hers. "There is one way I can win your trust, Ilse. Only one way. I will place *my* life in your hands. Right now. I will leave you here. Alone. For fifteen minutes." He took her gently by the shoulders. "Think of what I have said. What we both believe in. What we have meant to each other—however briefly. What it might mean if the evil of this world remains unchained." He straightened up. "And if you choose to denounce me to the *Achse,* that will be your decision. If not, I will know you trust me, as I trust you."

Abruptly he turned away from her. He walked to the window, opened it, and climbed out into the garden below.

The shadows were deeper and longer among the trees and shrubs. Woody knew his heart was racing in agitation. He could feel it in his throat. He sat down and leaned against a tree. Had he done the right thing? What the hell else could he have done? Shit! He could chuck the whole damned thing. Right now. Take off like a thief in the night and let the damned Krauts do what the hell they wanted to do. All he'd have to do was get to the nearest US Army unit, and he'd be home free.

Even as he allowed himself the luxury of his thoughts, he knew he'd stay in the damned garden, and return to Ilse.

And—to what?

Would she give him away? He thought not.

He could be wrong.

He stood up, too restless to sit. He walked over to the bushes where he'd dumped the SS officer. The man was gone. Back with his friends nursing the bump on his head and trying to explain it away, no doubt.

He looked at his watch. It was difficult to get enough light. Six minutes to go.

What would they do to him, if Ilse blew the whistle on him? They would have to kill him, of course. Unless he could kill them first. He felt for his gun. He carried it in the small of his back. My Dick Tracy comforter, he thought mirthlessly. What if he did do a Prune Face? What if he did cut out. Aborted the damned mission?

What if Ilse did trust him? What would they do to her, if he disappeared?

Again he looked at his watch. Three minutes. He stepped out on the path. He looked toward the window to his room. It was dark. Slowly he walked toward it.

The window was still open, and he climbed in. He looked toward the bed. Ilse was not there.

Suddenly the light went on in the room, a soft glow from a single bulb in a floor lamp. Woody whirled at the sound of the switch.

At the door stood Ilse—and the *Achse* agent, *Signor* Luigi Bazzano.

25

—•◦•—

THE ITALIAN SCOWLED AT WOODY. "I told you, *Signore,* to remain in your room." He sounded aggrieved. "It is not safe for
you to wander around in the garden."

"I could not sleep," Woody said testily. He threw a quick glance
at Ilse. She looked noncommittal. "I needed some fresh air," he
finished.

Again he glanced at Ilse. She stood motionless, staring at nothing, her face pale and pinched. He was bursting to talk to her.
Why was the *Achse* agent there? What had she told him? Imperceptibly he backed away. From both of them. To give himself
room—if he had to act.

Bazzano looked from one to the other. "Please," he said. He
spread his hands in an imploring gesture. "I must ask you to come
with me. *Per favore, Signore.*"

"Why?" Woody asked sharply. He put his right hand on his
hip. He knew he could draw his gun in an instant. "Why?" he
repeated.

The Italian help up a hand. *"Calma, Signore!* There has been
a—disturbing incident," he explained. "One of our guests was attacked. He apparently heard someone trying to break into a ground
floor room. When he went to investigate, he was struck on the
head." He patted himself on the top of his head. "His skull may
be cracked."

"Who did it?" Woody asked.

The innkeeper shrugged elaborately. "I do not know," he said.

"When did it happen?"

"Less than an hour ago."

"I see," Woody said tartly. "And what has that to do with us?"

Bazzano looked anxiously at the two of them. *"Molto, Signore,"* he blurted out. "Very much! There may be a prowler around. *Un ladro*—a robber—perhaps. You may not be safe in this room. *I* will take you to a place where you *will* be safe." He drew himself up and pounded his chest. "Your safety is my duty, *Signore!"*

"Very well," Woody said. "We will get our things together." He looked at Ilse. She met his gaze, her eyes veiled. "Ilse?" he said.

She nodded. "I will get ready," she said tonelessly.

The room the innkeeper took them to was in the basement. It had no windows, but a small grated ventilation shaft. It was spartan, with two cots and a couple of straight-backed chairs. The Italian showed them a heavy dead bolt on the inside of the door. "When I leave," he said. "Bar the door. Open to no one but me. *Capisce?"*

Woody nodded. "And when will you come for us, *Signor* Bazzano," he asked. "When will we be able to continue our journey?"

"In a few hours," the Italian said quickly. "Very soon, *Signore*. About eight in the morning." He bobbed his head, and ducked out the door.

Woody frowned after him. Automatically he tried the door. It was unlocked. He felt uneasy. He did not like the sudden shifty look in the man's close-set eyes, and the way his tongue had flitted out to wet his fleshy lips.

He dismissed it. He could do nothing now, but be on the alert. He turned to Ilse. She was watching him. He went up to her.

"Thank you," he said softly.

Her huge eyes were unnaturally bright as she looked up at him. "I—thought about what you said," she whispered haltingly. "Much of it is true. There has been a terrible evil among us." She gave a little sob. "Perhaps—perhaps I can make up a little for it. For what my mother . . . " Her voice broke.

"Your mother . . ." Woody began.

She interrupted him. "I know about my mother," she breathed in bleak defiance.

He took her shoulders in his hands. A gentle, unconscious gesture of support. "Knowing and accepting are two entirely different things," he said quietly. "It is sometimes difficult to know—

it is always more difficult to accept." He looked down into her upturned face, torn by the look of anguish he saw in it. "You must learn to do that, Ilse. Accept what your mother had become in the course of serving a brutal, inhuman master. Accept that it has absolutely nothing to do with you. You bear no guilt. No shame."

The tears welled in her haunted eyes, clear drops of grief that caught the light and spilled it down her cheeks. Slowly she crept into his arms and laid her head on his chest. She wept silently.

He stroked her short, tousled hair and buried his face in it.

"Hold me," she whispered. "I am so alone . . . "

She sobbed.

He held her tight.

"You are wrong," he said softly.

SS Sturmbannführer Oskar Strelitz looked up as Bazzano entered the room.

"Well?" he snapped.

Bazzano sighed. "It is done," he said. "They are safely in the basement room." He glowered sullenly at the German. "As you requested."

"Perhaps it would be best if we clarified one thing, Bazzano," Strelitz said coldly, his arctic eyes impaling the Italian. "I do not make requests. I give orders. Orders that will be obeyed. By you."

"I am not marching in the German army," Bazzano protested.

"You are in the pay of the *Brüderschaft*," Strelitz countered acidly. "You will do as *they* order. As *I* order. Is that fully understood?"

"It will be much of an expense," Bazzano complained. "It is not within the functions of the *Anlaufstelle*. I do not have such funds."

"You will be adequately compensated," Strelitz snapped contemptuously.

Bazzano licked his lips. "As long as that is understood," he shrugged.

"The man, Diehl, who calls himself Bauhacker, and the woman with him, Ilse Gessner, *must* be eliminated," Strelitz said. He glared at the agent. "I agreed not to take care of the matter myself. Here. Now. Because it might compromise your *Anlaufstelle* and your operation. But only because you, Bazzano, assured me the mission would be carried out once they left here on their way to the *Anlaufstelle* in Bolzano."

The innkeeper nodded vigorously. "My cousin, Pietro, he will take care of them," he said. "They will not reach Bolzano. I, Luigi Bazzano, guarantee it!"

"Indeed you do," Strelitz said coldly. "With your life." He scowled at the Italian. "That attack on the SS officer. Have you any further information?" he asked.

Bazzano shrugged. He gave a sour thought to the painstaking justification he had had to give his SS guests for having Jews at the inn. Protection, he had pleaded. Protection for the important *Achse* travelers. Anyone who might come looking for SS fugitives would be shown the Jews. The SS men had accepted his explanation. Grudgingly. But then—why not? Any time a Jew could be used for the benefit of an SS man, use him. He eyed Strelitz. "No, *Signor ufficiale*," he answered. "Only what the man told us."

"Could Bauhacker, Diehl, have been responsible?"

Again Bazzano shrugged, his palms turned up. "It is possible. It is not for one to know. It is also possible it could have been another guest here. It is even possible that the SS man told us the truth. There are all sorts of *delinquenti* around these days."

He shuffled his feet. He gave Strelitz a calculating, sidelong glance. "There is—another matter," he said. "It is, perhaps, of interest to you."

"What is?" Strelitz snapped impatiently.

"The other couple here," Bazzano said. "She is the pregnant one."

Strelitz looked sharply at the Italian. "What about them?"

"The young man," Bazzano explained, "he is much worried. He worries that his woman may not be able to endure the strain of the traveling to Bari. By the usual *Achse* route. He—he asked me if I could, that is ease their journey. Make it quicker, perhaps? That is what he asked."

Strelitz fixed him with his hard eyes. If the man did not already have a way to do so and had not seen a possibility to enrich himself in the process, he would not have brought it up, he thought. What did he have in mind? He was curious. If anything *could* be done to ease the trip, and the risks, for *Frau* Eva and her child, it must be done. "Can you?" he asked curtly.

Bazzano nodded—reluctantly. "It is possible, *Signor ufficiale*. But it will cost much money."

"What have you in mind?"

"My cousin, Mario, he has a boat," Bazzano said eagerly. "A fine motorboat. He keeps it in Sottomarina. It is a small fishing village south of Venice. In the Golfo di Venezia. I, myself, and my cousin, Pietro, who is a very good driver of automobiles, would take the young people to him. In my own automobile. And he could take them on his fine boat all the way to Bari." He shrugged regretfully. "But, as I told you, it would be much money. It is a long voyage. Many kilometers. Seven hundred kilometers. More perhaps. Much *benzina*—much gasoline. And many hours. Perhaps thirty."

"Arrange it."

The Italian bobbed his head. *"Si, volentieri!"* His eager face suddenly fell. "But," he sighed, "it would be necessary for me first to give money to my cousin with the boat. He will need it."

Strelitz observed the innkeeper scornfully. A slimy little lout, he thought. It was degrading for the *Brüderschaft* to have to deal with the likes of him.

"You will get your money," he said disdainfully.

The Italian licked his lips. "I shall also need to know where in Bari is the *Anlaufstelle*. I only know the next one on the route. In Bolzano."

"I will get the necessary information, and your money, for you," Strelitz said shortly. "By 0800 hours. Be ready to leave by then."

He stood up. "You will take the young woman and her escort to your cousin and instruct him to transport them to Bari on his boat. Understood?"

"Understood, *Signor ufficiale.*"

"And you know your orders regarding the man and the woman in the basement?"

Bazzano nodded. "I do."

"Including the travel papers?"

"Si," Bazzano said. He spread his hands. "But why?" It is much work. And it is not necessary to . . . "

"Just do it!" Strelitz snapped. He smiled nastily at the Italian. "Consider it a safety valve. In case your cousin, Pietro, should happen to bungle the job."

Indignantly Bazzano drew himself up. "Never!" he declared. "Never, *Signor ufficiale. My* cousin would never bungle."

"Good," Strelitz said crisply. "Then you will have no trouble in carrying out my orders without fail." It was dismissal. "I, myself, shall leave here shortly before you do."

"And I, Luigi Bazzano, will obey your commands, *Signor ufficiale.* You may trust me. Implicitly!"

Strelitz regarded the Italian, his lips stretched thin in a little smile of contempt. It was insufferable, he thought, that he and his vital mission had to be degraded by having to rely on such pitiful inferiors. But he had no other recourse. Not in the matter of the Diehl nuisance.

But there were other matters. Matters he would deal with himself. The safety of Eva Braun Hitler and her unborn child.

And Operation Future.

Ilse stirred fitfully as Woody gently disengaged himself, but she did not wake up. She had fallen asleep in his arms as he sat on one of the cots, leaning against the wall. He had always considered it the greatest expression of trust when a dog or a cat fell asleep in his lap, rendering themselves totally vulnerable to him. He looked down at Ilse. Or a girl, he thought. Carefully he lowered her to the cot and stood up. He was stiff. He'd been sitting, holding the exhausted girl, for a long time. He hadn't had the heart to wake her.

The light, coming from a single feeble bulb in the ceiling had been left on. He looked toward the door. The heavy dead bolt was still in place. There was one other door in the room, a smaller one. He hoped it led to where he thought it would. He opened it.

The cubicle behind it was about the size of a shower stall. It was the kind of crude indoor toilet he'd run across occasionally in Europe, especially in France. A cement floor slanted toward a hole in the middle and with two small raised platforms, like tile footprints, to stand on. And a spigot low on the wall. It would do.

Only a trickle of water flowed from the spigot when he turned the handle. He opened it all the way. The performance was not improved. He gave up.

He glanced at his watch. He frowned. It was well past 0730 hours. Where the hell was the damned innkeeper?

He walked to the door. He slid the bolt from its clasp. He tried to open the door.

It was locked.

Someone had locked it while they were resting.

He stared at it. They were locked in. He'd half expected it. The Italian agent seemed about as trustworthy as a nearsighted cobra. He was about to bang on it, when he stopped himself. It would do no good. And he wouldn't give the bastards the satisfaction.

He glared at the closed door.

In time it would open.

To what?

26

———•◦•———

THE BACK OF THE BATTERED LITTLE TRUCK smelled musty and sour with a faint hint of carbolic acid. Pietro, the driver, an acne-scarred young man with two front teeth missing and unkempt black hair, drove like a madman, and the truck bounced and swayed, tossing them around in the empty cargo space.

Woody was furious. For more than twenty-four hours he and Ilse had been cooped up in the damned basement at the Merano inn. *Signora* Bazzano had fed them personally, always accompanied by two silent gorillas with ham-sized fists and no brows. The food had been ample and tasty, and there had been plenty of wine, but the door had been kept locked. The *Signora* had chirped something about emergency measures and her husband being away on some urgent mission or other, all because of a disturbing and unsolved attack on a guest at the inn. All activities related to the *Achse* had therefore come to a standstill, she'd proclaimed.

When Woody complained about being locked in, she'd thrown up her hands melodramatically and cried it was her husband's strict instructions and was all to ensure their own safety. How that worked, she had not explained.

The only good thing about the whole damned mess, he thought, was the fact that both he and Ilse had been able to get more than enough rest, and the rich food had restored their strength. He only wished he could keep such phrases as "fatted calf" and "last meal" from entering his mind.

It was now Wednesday, June 13. He had lost a full day, and had had no chance to learn anything about Eva and her companion, or try to find out if they were at the inn. His only consolation was, that according to *Signora* Bazzano, no one else had left the inn during the last twenty-four hours.

Finally, that morning, Bazzano had shown up, all apologies and unintelligible explanations. They would be leaving immediately, he'd announced. For the *Anlaufstelle* in Bolzano. His cousin, a clever boy who could be trusted as if he were Luigi Bazzano himself, would drive them there on his way to pick up supplies for the inn, which he always did on Wednesday mornings. Hurriedly he'd given them the address of the stop in Bolzano and the passwords to use, and he'd stuffed their new travel papers in Woody's breast pocket.

He felt for them. He'd not even had a chance to examine them.

He fished them out. He held them to one of the streaks of yellow light that lanced into the truck through numerous cracks.

He froze.

The travel permit, for him and Ilse, gave them permission to travel by whatever means at their disposal, private or public, to the city of Rome.

Rome. Not Bari!

He stared at it. Was it a mistake? Deliberate? To keep him from getting to Bari? If so, why? Who had issued the orders? Why Rome? He cursed. He should have realized there would be other escape route branches fanning out once the *B-B Achse* line reached Italy. But, even if he had, how could he have insisted that *he* be sent to Bari? He had been lulled into a false sense of security, he realized, by the name *B-B Achse.* Bremen—*Bari,* dammit! Not Bremen-Bari-Genoa-Leghorn-Naples or whatever other damned Italian seaports the bastards could think of.

He calmed down. Excuses weren't going to get him anywhere. He took stock. He had lost a full day—and he was on his way to a totally different place from where he wanted to go. If he hoped ever to catch up with Eva.

Eva? Wait a minute. Had she, in fact, been sent to Bari? Or to Rome? Or to some other Godforsaken place? Who the hell knew? He suddenly felt utterly defeated. He had no possible way of knowing. Or finding out.

Even if he in some way could change his destination once he arrived in Bolzano—and he had not the foggiest notion of how to pull off that little trick—but even if he could, how could he know he wasn't just scratching his ass on the wrong cheek? The damned mission was closer to coming to a head in time than ever before—and further away in realization than when he started.

If he could change his route; if he selected the correct seaport; if he could get there in time; and if he could spot Eva before she boarded her ship for Africa or for South America or wherever she was headed. If . . .

Dammit! The whole mission had become a forest of *ifs*.

For a moment he toyed with the idea of going for assistance to the local CIC in Bolzano. If there was a CIC office in the town. Another damned if! But what could they do? Trample around in the forest of *ifs*, and drive his quarry deeper underground than ever. Apparently the slightest sign of anything unusual sent the *Achse* operatives into a flurry of security measures. Look at what had happened at the Merano inn. All because he'd tapped some stupid bastard on the head.

No. There was nothing to be gained by involving the local CIC. Not now.

He was on his own. He'd have to stay that way.

With a problem that had just grown tenfold larger.

They had been driving for about half an hour when Woody felt the truck slow down. It made a sharp turn to the right, obviously on to a rutted dirt path off the main road. He was at once on the alert.

After a few minutes the truck came to a stop, and he heard Pietro get out of the cab. What was up? Rest stop? Hardly. Not after only half an hour.

He heard Pietro pull the latch on the back door to the truck. The door opened a crack and stopped, standing ajar.

Woody stepped up to the partly open door. He pushed it.

The truck was parked on a dirt path in a forest. A few feet behind it stood Pietro, a thin, unpleasant grin on his acne-scarred face—and an old Glisenti 1910, 9 mm pistol in his hand stretched out before him. It was aimed carefully at Woody.

"You will come down from the truck," the Italian ordered. "You, *Signore*, and the *Signorina*."

Woody at once grasped the situation. Somewhere along the line he'd been blown, and his elimination ordered. His—and Ilse's. How? How had they penetrated his cover? What mistake had he made? Never mind. It was immaterial. Now. Everything was, except staying alive. Within the span of a few heartbeats a plan swept into his mind. Instantly he decided to act upon it. Adrenalin surged to support it.

"Stay back in the truck!" he whispered over his shoulder to Ilse. "As far as you can. Do not move until I tell you!" He heard the girl scramble to obey, then turned his full attention to the Italian. Fearfully he stared at him. The man held the pistol at arm's length in one hand pointing it at him as if pointing with a finger. Good. He was not a professional. He could be rattled.

"Please," he cried in his best Italian, his voice unsteady with apprehension, "please do not shoot!"

He surveyed the Italian. The man stood ten to twelve feet behind the truck. It might work. With a little luck. Anyway, whether it would or not, it was the only game in town.

"I will do as you say," he croaked. "Please do not kill me!"

Pietro shrugged. He seemed to enjoy the feeling of being in complete command. "I have my orders, *Signore,*" he said. "I must follow them. As a soldier, you will understand."

Woody jumped down from the back of the truck, clumsy in his apparent fear. He landed off balance and struggled to catch himself. He reached a half-crouched position—when he suddenly let out a bloodcurdling scream. In the same instant he made a quick feint to his right, immediately reversing himself and, still roaring in fury, has face fiercely distorted in raging frenzy, he catapulted himself at the Italian.

Pietro started violently, shocked at the sudden, unexpected scream. With instinctive reflex he fired in the direction of Woody's feint, just missing him, as Woody made his countermove. At once he swung the pistol back but it was impossible for him to check the swing of the gun held in one hand and the second shot went wild. Before he was able to bring the pistol back and fire point-blank, Woody hit him in a hard, low tackle which knocked the wind out of him and sent his Glisenti pistol flying.

When he picked himself up, he found himself staring into Woody's Walther.

"Don't bother to get up, Pietro, my boy." Woody grinned at him, his bantering tone of voice and choice of words somehow more menacing than cold threats. "Just stay right where you are. Make yourself comfortable. You'll stay there for a while. Perhaps—forever."

He planted himself solidly before the frightened Italian, sprawled awkwardly on the ground. "Now," he said pleasantly, "you and I are going to have a little talk." His voice suddenly grew hard. "Who told you to kill us?" he barked.

Pietro stared at him, his eyes dark with terror. He made no reply.

"Why?" Woody shot at him.

[277]

Pietro just stared. Woody sighed audibly. "Do you have a knife, Pietro?" he asked. "All good little Italians seem to have one. At least a penknife. Do you?"

Pietro sat as if petrified. He made no sound. But his pants darkened in front of him as he lost control of his bladder.

"Come now, Pietro, my boy," Woody coaxed good-naturedly. "I can easily find out. Although, if I have to, it might be less pleasant for you. So, how about it?"

Without taking his eyes from Woody, the Italian dug into his soggy pocket and brought out a folding knife.

"Fine," Woody approved. "Throw it over here."

Pietro did. The wet knife landed at Woody's feet. He worried it with the toe of his boot.

"Now, then, Pietro," he said, "you and I have a decision to make. I have some questions. You know some answers to them, and I want those answers. Are you going to give them to me, Pietro?"

The Italian stared at him. He swallowed. But he said nothing.

"Very well." Again Woody sighed with resignation. "The hard way, then."

He nudged the knife with his boot. "I can stick the blade of this little knife under your fingernails, Pietro, and slit them open to the quick. I can split your nostrils—and I can even cut off your balls! But I am sure you will have told me what I want to know long before I get to that part of the ritual. What do you think?"

Carefully he bent down and picked up the knife.

"Or you can, of course, decide to talk *before* you lose a few fingernails. Or your balls." His voice grew harsh. "Who ordered you to kill us?"

Pietro looked panic-stricken. He licked his dry lips with an equally dry tongue. His face glistened with the sweat of fear. "My—my cousin," he whispered hoarsely. *"Signor* Bazzano."

"That's much better," Woody said. He made a show of pocketing the knife. "Why?"

"There was an SS officer," Pietro said. "From the *Brüderschaft,* he said he was. A *Sturmbannführer.* He told my cousin to do it."

"When did *he* get to Merano?"

"The same night you did, *Signore.*"

Strelitz! His interrogator. Woody had an instant mental picture of him. The bastard *was* out to stop him. Prevent him from catching up with Eva. The man found out that he, Woody, against his explicit orders had pressured the *Achse* operator at the *Wies*

[278]

to send him on his way at once. How much else had he found out? The guy was cute, he thought wryly. Real cute. Putting locks on all the back doors. Like giving him papers that would shunt him off to Rome—in case Pietro should strike out. As he just had. He felt a grudging respect for the man's professionalism. "What exactly were your orders?" he demanded.

"I—I was to—to leave you here," Pietro stammered. "Hidden in the bushes. No one would miss you. And when they found you, they would think perhaps—partisans . . . And then—then I was to pick up the supplies in Bolzano and return home. As I always do."

Woody nodded. It made sense. But something was still nagging him. "Why this whole production?" he asked. "Bazzano could have gotten rid of us long ago. At the inn."

Pietro shook his head. Now that he had begun to talk he seemed eager to give information.

"My cousin does not want trouble," he said. "Not at the inn. That would not make him feel safe. He would not allow the German SS officer to do anything. At the inn. And he wanted to be sure, and to send you off himself, and get you away from the inn, before . . . " He let the sentence die.

"Why wait?" Woody asked. "Why did he not get rid of us yesterday, instead of having us sit in the damned basement?"

"He was away," Pietro said. "We had to go to Sottomarina. By automobile. I was driving."

"Sottomarina?"

"It is a fishing village. On the Adriatic coast. Near Venice."

"What did you have to do there?"

"We took a couple of guests there. To my cousin, Mario."

Woody tensed. He felt the familiar surge of excitement that came with the first hint of a real clue in a case.

"Describe the couple," he snapped. He hoped he had not betrayed his eagerness.

"A man and a woman, *Signore*," Pietro answered. "Germans."

"Describe the woman."

"She was—pretty. Blond. Maybe she had thirty years. Maybe more. One finds it difficult to tell with a woman."

"Do you know who she was?"

Pietro shook his head. "I only heard the man talk to her. Once. He was solicitous. He called her Eva. But this I know . . . " He showed the gap where his missing teeth used to be. "She was big." He held his hands in front of his stomach. "With child."

Woody stared at him. With his last two words the man had

given him the key. The key to the whole damned case. It instantly opened a floodgate, and understanding cascaded in on him. It was the key to why Eva had to be saved and spirited out of Germany. The key to why her travel along the escape route had been so vigilantly guarded. The key to the whole elaborate Berlin charade!

Eva Braun Hitler was carrying the Führer's heir!

He was stunned at his realization. "Why did you take them to Sottomarina?" he snapped.

"We took them there because Mario has a boat. A fishing boat."

"Were they going on the boat?"

"Yes."

"Where was he taking them?"

"To Bari."

"Where in Bari?"

Pietro shrugged. "Some *cantiere-riparazioni battelli*—some boat works."

Woody fixed the Italian with a burning stare. "Think, Pietro," he said. "Think hard. Did they mention the name of this boat works?"

Pietro frowned. He shook his head. "I do not remember," he said. His eyes flitted away from Woody.

"Listen, Pietro, and listen good," Woody said, his voice ominously low. "I'll give you a choice. You remember the name of that damned boat works and you'll live. If you don't you will be the one they'll find hidden in the bushes. Dead!"

Pietro stared at him. "If I—if I remember," he whispered, "you will not hurt me?"

"Remember, dammit!" Woody snarled.

Pietro flinched. "It was—it is called *Cantiere-riparazioni Battelli di Benjamino Montesano*," he breathed.

Woody let out his breath. How long had he held it? There it was.

The final stop. The point of embarkation from Bari.

And Eva was already on her way there.

At once a plan began to take shape in his head. "Listen carefully, Pietro," he said. "I promised you I'd let you live—and I will. More than that. I'll save your ass for you with Bazzano for having botched the job."

Pietro looked up, eagerly.

"You do exactly as I tell you," Woody continued, "and you will come out of this smelling like a rose."

"*Grazie, Signore,*" Pietro exclaimed effusively. "I will do what you say. Exactly what you say. *Lo prometterò, Signore!*"

"First," Woody said, "how were you to prove to old Bazzano that you had in fact done away with me? I'm sure the bastard wouldn't be satisfied with just your word."

Pietro nodded vigorously. "That is true, *Signore*. I was to bring back your papers to him."

Woody nodded. "I will give them to you," he said. "And you will give me whatever identification you have." Pietro looked startled. "You can always say you lost them and have them replaced," Woody finished. "That's your problem."

Pietro nodded.

"Here's what you'll do," Woody went on. "You will take us to Bolzano in the truck and let us out where I say. You will finish your business in town and drive back to the inn. You will tell Bazzano that you did your job and got rid of us, and you will give him my papers as proof. Do you understand?"

Pietro nodded eagerly.

"If you do not do what I am telling you to do, the *Brüderschaft* will find out, and I don't have to tell you what the consequences will be for you. On the other hand, do what I say, and you'll be a damned hero."

Without taking his eyes off the Italian he called, "Ilse! Come on out now."

Ilse appeared at the back of the truck. She climbed down and joined Woody. She looked at Pietro as if seeing him for the first time.

"There's a gun lying somewhere over there," Woody said, nodding toward some bushes. "Would you find it and bring it to me?"

Ilse walked over to the spot indicated. Almost at once she bent down and picked up Pietro's Glisenti pistol. She brought it to Woody. Pietro was watching, apprehension once again growing in his eyes.

Woody checked the gun. Six rounds left, including one in the chamber. He switched it to his right hand. He contemplated the Italian, who sat watching him wide-eyed.

Suddenly he fired. He emptied the clip.

Pietro threw himself flat on the ground, clamping his hands over his head.

"What's the matter, Pietro?" Woody grinned. "Afraid of loud noises?" He threw the empty pistol to him. "You might as well show cousin Luigi that you did a thorough job." With his own Walther he gestured. "Pick it up. And let's get going. We will ride with you in the cab this time."

He followed the Italian to the truck, Ilse beside him. He was encouraged. Perhaps he did have a chance of pulling everything off okay after all. He was certain Pietro would jump at the chance of saving his own skin and do as he had been instructed. That meant Bazzano, and Strelitz for that matter, would be off his back. He'd learned where the Bari *Anlaufstelle* was and that Eva was on her way there, and not to some other port of embarkation. And he had found out exactly how to identify her. After all, how many pregnant women could there be who traveled the *Achse* escape route?

His remaining problem was how to get to Bari before Eva left.

He had an idea. It was risky. But, hell, the time for taking real risks had come.

27

——●·●——

Pietro considered himself lucky. *Molto fortunato.* He would do exactly as the German had instructed him. He was very clever, that German. No one would know the truth. And what did it matter that another couple of Nazis escaped from the Allies in *Germania,* eh? *Niente!* He would describe to Luigi how he had shot them. Both of them. Killed them. How they had pleaded for their lives, and how he, Pietro, had been determined and unyielding, deaf to their begging. He would show where he had shot them, each of them many times to be certain, and he would show his empty pistol. He would show how they had died. He looked forward to it. Luigi would believe him, and there would be no trouble for him. He even had the German's papers to prove he was telling the truth. *Benissimo!*

He gave a quick, sidelong glance at the man sitting next to him. He had said not a word since they left the forest, and they would be in Bolzano in a few minutes. He shrugged. *Non importa.* The man would tell him where and when he wanted to be let off.

Woody nearly had his plan of action formulated. Everything had changed so suddenly, and he was forced to play it by ear. However, he did want to have an overall game plan. He thought he did.

He peered through the dirty windshield. Ahead, on the horizon, he could see the town of Bolzano, the center of the German-speaking population of the Italian Tyrol, situated on the Isarco River. He knew little about the town. Only that it had been of some strategic importance during the war as the hub of the Brenner Pass railroad and highway as they dipped down from the Alps. That, and the steelworks located in the town, had been enough to invite severe Allied air strikes, and the city of 75,000 souls had been extensively damaged.

In his mind he went over his immediate problems once more. How to get to Bari. He had that one licked . . . How to pass as Italian, which he had to be able to do if he used Pietro's I.D. cards. He was grateful for the Italian he'd learned at school in Switzerland. It was adequate for him to get along, but it was not good enough for him to pass as a native, even a native of another province. He thought he'd figured out how to get around that difficulty, too. He'd have to remember to look in the truck's toolkit before he sent Pietro on his way . . . And there was Ilse. He had no choice but to rely on her. He hoped he could. He thought so. Perhaps it was only wishful thinking. He would give her his instructions once they got rid of the Italian . . . The CIC. He'd wrestled with that one. At first he'd thought that now was the time to enlist the aid of the locals. It had been a tempting thought. He could easily have passed the buck. But the more he'd examined the consequences he knew would result if he did, the more he'd realized it would not work. By the time he would be able to establish who and what he was; by the time he could convince a local CIC officer of high enough rank to take action; by the time his story could be verified and he'd get permission to operate in Italy, and the necessary cooperation; by the time a mission to Bari could be mounted that'd have even half a chance of succeeding, Eva would be halfway to Argentina.

Dammit! He was still on his own.

They had reached the outskirts of town. The ravages of war were evident everywhere: in the empty ruins that lined the streets, and on the equally empty faces of the people who walked them.

They passed what had apparently been a little park, now an open, crater-dotted expanse of rubble with a tangle of scorched, uprooted trees.

"Stop here," he ordered.

Pietro brought the truck to a sputtering halt.

"Do you have a toolbox in the truck?" Woody asked him.

Puzzled, the Italian looked at him. What now? he thought. What did this *ragazzo pazzo*—this crazy fellow—want now? He nodded. "In the back," he said.

"Out!" Woody snapped. "I want to take a look at it."

The toolbox contained a jumble of rusty bolts and nails, wadded-up lengths of wire, and an assortment of black, greasy hand tools. Woody rummaged around in the mess and selected a pair of pliers. He put them in his pocket. He turned to Pietro. "Okay," he said curtly, "get going. And if you want to save your dumb ass, do exactly as I told you."

"*Si, Signore,*" Pietro affirmed, bobbing his head fervently. "I will do exactly as you said." He hurried to the cab of the truck, and in no time he was barreling down the suburban street into town.

Woody looked at Ilse. "Come, Ilse," he said. He started to walk into the empty lot.

Ilse followed. She looked up at him, a puzzled expression on her face. "But this is not the *Anlaufstelle,*" she said. "I thought *Signor* Bazzano told us it was at a Franciscan monastery."

"It is," he said. "But we are not going there. I'm changing the plans."

"But—I . . . "

"Please, Ilse. I'll tell you about it in just a minute."

They walked to the far side of the leveled park. Woody looked back. He had a clear view of the street, and close behind him stood a row of gutted houses. He sat down on a fallen tree trunk. Ilse sat next to him.

Gravely he looked into her eyes. "Ilse," he said, "we have to separate."

Shocked, she began to protest.

"Hear me out," he said solemnly. "I have to get to Bari. As quickly as I can. It will be difficult. And dangerous. I just can't take you along."

"But what am I to do?" she exclaimed, alarm and fear darkening her eyes. "Why can I not go with you? I will not delay you." She grabbed his arm with both her hands. "Please," she beseeched him, "do not leave me here!"

He took her hands in his. "Ilse," he said soberly, "I can't tell you *why* it is impossible for me to take you along. Not now. Some day, I will, I promise you." She started to protest. Gently he silenced her. "Listen to me, Ilse," he said solemnly. "I once asked you to trust me. You did. And even though for a while you thought I had lied to you, you know now that I didn't. And you know why I could not tell you everything right away. This is like that, Ilse. Once again I ask you to trust me."

She looked at him, her eyes veiled. She said nothing.

"I am asking you to help me," Woody continued quietly.

"Help you?"

"Yes. It is important. I want you to listen to me, Ilse. Very closely. Remember everything I say. Will you do that?"

"I will listen."

For the next few minutes he spoke to her, earnestly, urgently, while she listened in wide-eyed, apprehensive silence. Finally he was done.

"Do you understand, Ilse?" he asked her solemnly. "You know what you must do?"

She nodded.

"Repeat it to me. Everything I told you."

She did.

"Will you do it?" he asked.

For a long moment she sat in silence, staring down at her hands, clenched in her lap. Then slowly she nodded her head. "I will do it," she whispered.

He took a deep breath. He put his hands on her shoulders. He gazed into her sober, pale face, desperately trying to read the thoughts hidden behind her brooding eyes. Did she agree because she believed him? Because she *wanted* to help him? Or because she could do nothing else? Because it was expedient? He ached with the need to know.

"One more thing," he said. "I want you to do one more thing for me before we part."

She looked up at him. "What is it?"

He pulled the pliers he'd taken from Pietro's toolbox from his pocket. He had given it a lot of thought. He would make the sacrifice, but he'd be damned if he'd ruin his looks. Even for a short while. The first lower left bicuspid had been his choice.

"I want you to pull one of my teeth," he said. "I can't do it myself. I can't get the right leverage."

Startled she stared at him. "You—have a toothache?"

He laughed. "No," he said, "I just want to improve my Italian."

She shook her head. "I do not understand," she said.

"I've got to pass for Italian," he explained. "But my Italian isn't good enough. If I have a swollen jaw and a fresh hole where my tooth used to be, it won't seem funny if my speech is a little slurred and thick, and if my pronunciation of certain words is a little strange, or if I use as few of them as possible. You see?"

"I—I do not know if I can," she remonstrated.

"Sure you can. It won't hurt you a bit!"

She frowned at him. "How can you make a joke?" she chided him. "It is serious. I would give you much pain."

"If you don't, my chances wouldn't be worth a plug nickel."

She shook her head. "What is—plug nickel?"

He grinned. "Let's just say, if *you* don't pull the tooth I'll have to do it myself. I'll have to wriggle it loose. Wrench it out. And, believe me, that's a hell of a lot more painful."

She shuddered. "Show me how."

He put the serrated jaws of the pliers around his lower bicuspid. He grabbed the handles. He squeezed them together as hard as he could.

" 'ust 'eeze eh 'andles 'n 'ull," he mumbled.

Puzzled she looked at him. "What?"

He took the pliers out of his mouth. "Put the jaws of the pliers around the tooth so you have a firm grip," he instructed her. "Then squeeze the handles together as hard as you can. Use both hands. I'll sit on the log, you stand in front of me. Put one foot on the log for leverage, and pull as hard as you can. The tooth will come out."

She nodded, her face grim. "I will do it," she said.

She positioned herself. She placed the pliers around the tooth. Involuntarily Woody tensed. The little tool suddenly felt like a bulldozer in his mouth. He grabbed hold of the tree trunk with both hands and held on.

" 'ull!" he said.

Ilse pulled.

The pliers slipped off the tooth, and Woody nearly fell backwards off the log.

"Again," he said, sitting back up. "And Ilse, you must not be afraid to hurt me. It will never work if you are. And, dammit, it *has* to!"

She nodded, her face pale. Little beads of moisture gleamed on her forehead. Again she placed the pliers around the tooth. With both her hands she pressed the handles together. She leaned back, placed one foot on the log—and pulled.

A sudden, sharp pain shot through him. He felt as if his entire jaw was about to be torn off. He clung to the log. The pain stabbed up through his face in a quick succession of agonizing waves which quickly became one searing lance of liquid fire. A hideous, grinding sound grated through his bones, reverberating in his skull, sending billows of nausea through him. The pain exploded in a blinding blast in his head, and with a thousand fiery fingers it clawed at the back of his eyes trying to escape.

Suddenly there was a sickening, moist, and tearing sound, and the tremendous pressure and pull on his jaw let up in a paroxysm of white-hot pain. The warm blood welled in his mouth. He swallowed it.

He looked at Ilse. In astonishment she stood staring at the bloody tooth held in the pliers, which she still gripped in both hands with white-knuckle tension.

Gingerly he felt the tender hole with the tip of his tongue. It seemed enormous. Big enough to hide a baseball. As big as a catcher's mitt! Pain was still throbbing from it with every beat of his heart, but the excruciating sharpness of it had disappeared.

"Thank you," he said thickly. He was gratified to note that he didn't have to fake his slurred speech.

Ilse dropped the pliers, and the tooth. She looked at Woody, her face drawn. "Are you in much pain?" she asked.

"No, I'm fine." He grinned. "And my Italian has been vastly improved. It will be as good as the next guy's who's just had a session with his dentist. Or a doorknob." He grew sober. He looked at her. "It is time, now, Ilse," he said. "You must be on your way, and so must I. Is everything clear?"

She nodded.

"Be off, then," he said softly. "It won't be long, and we'll see each other again."

She looked long and searchingly at him. Suddenly she went to him and put her arms around him. For a moment they clung to each other. Then, without a word, the girl turned and walked away.

He watched her, picking her way through the rubble, not looking back. Had her goodby been a goodby forever? Would he really see her again? This girl he had come to care about, perhaps more than he was willing to admit? A girl who had been born and brought up in Nazi Germany? A girl who was the daughter of a woman who was the embodiment of everything he abhorred, everything he had fought against? Very possibly he had placed his life in her hands.

What would she do with it?

His jaw ached. He spat a mouthful of saliva and blood on the ground. He turned away, and resolutely he walked off into the abandoned ruins.

The main railroad station at Bolzano was unexpectedly busy with travelers. Badly damaged during the air raids, the building itself and the track system had been repaired to some extent, and the station was able to function at better than half capacity.

Woody made his way to the ticket counter. From behind a small, open window a bald, sour-looking ticket agent peered at him over the rim of his glasses.

"*Vorrei un biglietto per Bari,*" Woody said, deliberately making his speech almost unintelligible.

The ticket agent glared at him. "*Cosa dice?*" he snapped. "*Non capisco.*"

"*Scusi,*" Woody said. "*Mi fanno male le gengive*—my gums hurt." He pulled down his lip exposing the fresh hole in his lower gum. "*Mal di denti,*" he mumbled.

The man gave him a churlish look. "*Che cosa vuole?*—What do you want?" he growled.

"I want a ticket to Bari," Woody said, his speech still thick, but intelligible. "On the next available train."

The ticket agent pulled a small cardboard ticket from a grimy wooden rack. Woody paid for it with the money he'd received at the Merano *Anlaufstelle*. "*Devo cambiar di treno?*" he asked.

"Yes. Change trains at Bologna. This one goes to Rome. The train to Bari leaves from Bologna."

"*Grazie,*" Woody muttered. "*Da che binario parte il treno per Bologna?*"

"*Binario numero sette*—track number seven," the agent said.

"*A che ora parte il treno?*"

"At three-fifteen."

"Will it be on time?"

The surly ticket agent glared at him. "*Il Duce* is dead," he grumbled. "You still want the trains to run on time?"

Woody walked toward Track #7. He still had quite a bit of time before the train was supposed to leave, but he preferred to know exactly where he was going and what the layout of the place was, before sitting down somewhere to wait.

He was pleased with himself. His Italian had passed muster swimmingly.

In a short while he'd be on his way to Bari.

He might still make it.

Fighting the nausea had quickly become her sole concern. It had started less than an hour after they had left the harbor of Sottomarina, when the boat had begun to pitch and roll in the choppy sea. Eva had never been seasick before. The feeling was not anything like the nausea she had occasionally felt when she had eaten something that disagreed with her, or the morning sickness she had experienced in her early pregnancy. It was a feeling all its own, a feeling of utter misery.

At first she had loved the boat. Gaily painted in red, green, and blue it had a motor and one mast. It was broad in the beam and had looked very romantic to her. Like the boats in the picture postcards she had seen from Venice and Naples. And the prospect of going by boat instead of in a succession of smelly, jolting trucks had seemed exciting. But now she hated it. She could hardly wait for the voyage to be over, although she knew it had barely begun. She did not know how she would be able to stand the feeling of constant dizziness and being on the edge of vomiting for another twenty-four hours or longer. She worried if she would have to feel that way during the entire voyage to South America. She would just never live through it.

Mario, the Italian captain of the boat, had laughed at her. She would soon get her sea legs, he had said. And then she would never want to leave his beautiful boat, the most beautiful one on the whole Adriatic Sea. There were two other crew members on board. A small, wiry, swarthy man with a bushy, black mustache and a big, strapping fellow with muscles like cords. Both of them had seemed studiously to ignore her, but somehow her discomfort with them had been assuaged knowing they were among the people protecting her. If only she could feel better.

Wretchedly she looked around the cluttered cabin, the only one on the boat. Baskets, netting, coiled ropes, and oilcloth storm gear hung in disarray on hooks and nails. She was lying in one of the four wooden bunks. A couple of soiled, once brightly colored curtains were hooked up on a sturdy line stretched in front of the bunk. They were pushed to one end. In the middle of the cabin a table, painted red, was bolted to the deck. It had a raised edge so it looked like a tiny red field with a red fence around it, she thought. A lone, penned-in earthenware bowl was sliding back and forth on it.

The cabin smelled of fuel oil and old sweat, mingled with garlic and paint. She longed for the fresh air on deck, or in the open wheelhouse, but she had not the courage to leave the bunk.

Willi would be in the wheelhouse, she thought. With the captain. Mario. It was there he had discovered the gun carelessly hidden behind a panel which had been standing ajar. He had taken it out. He had admired it. It was a Beretta 1938A, he had told her, while he had caressed the weapon. Italian made. One of the best submachine guns of all times. He had showed her the wooden stock, the perforated barrel jacket, the bayonet mount, and the box magazine that would hold forty 9mm rounds. He had given it to her to hold. It had been cold to the touch. She had felt a chill run through her.

Suddenly she felt a feeble kick in her stomach. Gently she put her hands across the swelling.

She wondered if the little one was seasick, too.

She sighed.

All would be well once they reached Bari.

Bologna had long since been left behind. There had been no difficulties in changing trains, but there had been an hour's delay.

Woody scrunched down in the corner of his seat next to the window. It was getting late. Already darkness was obliterating the countryside. It had been a long day, and he wanted to try to get some rest before hitting Bari the next day.

It would not be easy. The wooden bench was uncomfortably hard; the old rolling stock jolted along rails that attested to the fact that the roadbed had not seen adequate maintenance for a long time; the air in the railroad car was stifling and foul-smelling— apparently the Italians preferred their cars hermetically sealed, and to top it all, his damned gum hurt like the devil. Besides, he admitted ruefully to himself, he missed Ilse. For a fleeting instant he wondered what she had done after they separated; then he swept it from his mind. It was no good to start speculating. Tomorrow he would be in Bari. Tomorrow would be the day.

He was suddenly aware of a commotion at the far end of the car. He looked—and sat up with a start.

At the door, having just entered the car, stood an MP and a *carabiniere*—an Italian policeman.

Automatically Woody's hand touched the pocket where he kept his travel permit and identity papers. Or rather, Pietro's ID papers. He glanced toward the two men. They were going from seat to seat, examining the papers of every traveller.

His mind raced. He had not had to show Pietro's papers to anyone as yet. Would he get away with it? It was quite possible. But the travel permit, the only one he had, the one given him by Bazzano, was a different story. It permitted him to go to Rome. *Rome*—not down the Adriatic Coast to Bari!

What could he do?

Not show the permit at all? They'd kick him off the train, take him into custody. Bluff it out? Fat chance. Claim he'd gotten on the wrong train by mistake and would switch as soon as he could? Sure, and they'd see to it he did just that.

Whatever he decided to do, he would never get to Bari.

Dammit, there *had* to be another way!

He strained to think. His mind was blank.

The two men were almost upon him. The MP turned to the man next to him.

"*Permesso per viaggiare,*" he demanded gruffly. "Travel permit."

Woody closed his eyes.

It would be his turn next.

28

—•◦•—

SUDDENLY HE HAD AN IDEA. It was crazy, but with a little luck it might work. Anyway, it was all he could come up with.

He put his left hand to his cheek and stuck his right index finger into his mouth. A quick, sharp rake with his nail opened the healing hole in his gum. The pain that knifed through him almost made him cry out, but only a soft moan escaped him. The blood was instantly oily and warm in his mouth.

He kept his eyes shut, his left hand to his cheek, and leaned into the corner.

He felt a hand shake him.

"*Svegliati!*" he heard the MP call. "Wake up!"

Groggily he opened his eyes and turned toward the man, keeping his hand to his cheek.

"*Permesso per viaggiare,*" the MP barked.

Woody nodded his head. With his right hand he fished out his travel permit from his inside jacket pocket. He shook it open.

A sudden coughing spasm overtook him. Blood spewed from his mouth, splattering on the paper and trickling down his chin.

"*Diavolo!*" he mumbled in confusion. "*Mi dispiace*—I'm sorry." He removed his left hand from his cheek and tried to wipe the blood off the paper, effectively smearing it all over. He pulled down his lip and opened his bloody mouth. "*Ho perduto un dente,*" he snuffled. "I lost a tooth."

He held out the soggy, blood-stained paper toward the MP. "*Eccolo,*" he said thickly. "Here it is."

The MP peered distastefully at the blood-smudged paper. Only the official printed heading and the dated stamp were clearly readable. The rest was largely obscured by the blood smears. The MP did not touch the permit.

"Okay," he snapped. He turned away.

Woody pocketed the permit. With his tongue he gingerly probed the reopened wound in his jaw. Shit! It had just begun to heal. Still, he grinned to himself, his ass had been saved by a hole in his mouth. Some trick!

He sent a fleeting thought to Bernie Haskins. It was just as well that the Corps HQ yank artist had the reputation of being a crackerjack dentist.

He shifted painfully on the rock-hard bench. As if the ditch in his mouth wasn't enough, he thought, he'd have calluses up to his damned neck by the time he got to Bari.

It was late in the afternoon of Thursday, June 14 when *Signor* Bazzano's cousin, Mario, piloted his colorful boat into the placid waters of the harbor at Bari.

Willi and Eva, along with the two crew members, were on deck watching the approach. Although Eva never had found her sea legs she felt much better now that the sea was calm, and she was excited at finally reaching their port of embarkation.

She glanced at the two crewmen. They stood apart. She wondered about that. She had thought there would be more of a comradeship between them, working closely together on a small boat as they did. Or perhaps too much familiarity did indeed breed contempt. She had been aware of the big man watching her. She had never actually caught him doing it, but intuitively she had known. It had made her slightly uncomfortable, although with Willi constantly near her, she had felt safe.

The boat chugged through the channel in the breakwater. On the promontory to their right lay the remains of the old city. Willi surveyed it with interest. He had made it a point to find out a little about the place, once he had learned it was their destination. Built by the ancient Illyrians and Greeks and already an important center of the Byzantine rule in southern Italy in the ninth century, it had been cruelly damaged—in fact all but wiped out—in the German air raid on the harbor in December of 1943. At the base of the promontory he could see the big sports stadium presented to the city of Bari by Mussolini as a reward for having had more babies born there than in any other town its size in Italy. Naturally it had been named Bambino Stadium. Ahead on their left, opposite the old city, was the main inner harbor with its wharfs and piers along the east jetty.

It was still a little too early for the lighthouse on the tip of the jetty to be operating. Or perhaps it was still out of commission.

He observed the harbor scene with the greatest interest. There was still much evidence of the brilliantly executed air raid against the Allied shipping in Bari harbor ordered by *Feldmarschall* Kesselring: sunken ships sticking up out of the oily water like the tips of rusty icebergs; demolished warehouses and buildings in ruins; and newly repaired docks and piers. He remembered with pride the accounts of the raid that had filled the front page of every newspaper in Germany. Bari had been the most important Allied seaport in southern Europe. Tankers, ships loaded with ammunition and supplies for the Allied armies, had been piled up in the harbor like flies on a piece of flypaper, moored at the berths at the east jetty, against the breakwater and lying at anchor around the Vito Mole and scattered throughout the harbor waters.

At 1930 hours on December 2, 1943, about thirty JU-88s of *Feldmarschall* Freiherr von Richthofen's *Luftflotte II* had struck. When the lightning air raid was over half an hour later, seventeen Allied ships—American, British, Norwegian, Italian, and Polish— had been sunk, and eight more severely damaged. The town had been destroyed and the harbor blocked and rendered totally useless. Over a thousand Allied military personnel had been killed outright, and an even greater number of Italian civilians who had been cooperating with them. The raid had all but stopped the advance of Montgomery's Eighth Army up from the toe of Italy, exactly as *Feldmarschall* Kesselring had planned it. It had been a glorious operation, the most successful air strike against Allied shipping since the triumphant attack by Japan on Pearl Harbor.

Once inside the breakwater Mario navigated his boat toward the old harbor where the fishing fleet was tied up. Here, too, was the boat works they were headed for, the *Cantiere-riparazioni Battelli di Benjamino Montesano*. Willi wondered how long they would be there before boarding their ship for Buenos Aires. At least long enough to get their final papers, he thought, and the medical certificates required by the Argentine immigration authorities.

He heard Mario shout orders to the two crewmen to make ready for the approach to the pier at the marine railway at the boat works, and he watched them begin to position coiled ropes along the starboard side of the boat.

SS Sturmbannführer Oskar Strelitz had enjoyed his brief stint as a member of Mario's crew. It had been a welcome change of pace, and he had been able inconspicuously to keep an eye on his charges. He had enjoyed working with his hands and putting his back into the chores aboard the boat.

It had not been difficult for him to persuade Mario to take him on for the trip—and to keep his mouth shut. His motorcycle— the one he had confiscated from that fellow Diehl—had changed hands in the process. Even now it was securely lashed to the mast of the boat. Mario was not a man to take any chances.

They were coming down to the wire. Once Eva and her escort were aboard the ship that was to take them to Argentina, the first part of his duties was done. Phase I of his assignment in Operation Future.

Ahead was Phase II, the distribution and administration of the funds the Führer had deposited in the Swiss banks.

As he hauled the coiled ropes into place he chuckled to himself. Listening to the Führer regaling Bormann in the Bunker with tales of the enormous sums of money that would be available to him *only* if he brought *Frau* Eva to safety, he had almost been able to see the man drool with greed. As the Führer had known he would. He had been afraid the Führer had been overdoing it, but he had quickly realized that the Führer's truism—people will believe a big lie sooner than a little one—was quite correct. That idiot, Bormann, had eagerly swallowed the bait, no matter that it barely covered the hook. And of course, when the hour of need arose he had traitorously betrayed the Führer's trust to save his own miserable skin.

There were, of course, funds available in Switzerland, huge funds, and he, *SS Sturmbannführer* Oskar Strelitz, had the key to them. Not Eva Braun Hitler! She had no inkling they even existed, much less how to gain access to them. That had been the lie. That, and the outrageous size of the funds the Führer had dangled before Bormann. A fully justified lie of expedience by the Führer, of course, to ensure his own perpetuation and that of his beliefs. A big lie.

The last big lie of the Führer, Adolf Hitler.

The funds would be used for the purpose for which they were intended: Operation Future, providing assurance that the Führer's heir one day would rule Germany in the image of his father and once again bring the ideals of his father to the world. This time to triumph.

He looked toward shore. They were approaching the boat

works, and Mario was throttling down. Soon they would be safely in the boatyard. Soon *Frau* Eva would be on her way to Argentina and total safety for her and for her child. There was nothing to stop her now—nor to stop the far-reaching plans of Adolf Hitler.

Nothing!

Mario shut the engine down. Slowly the boat drifted toward the pier and the massive marine railway. The railway was hinged down, and the cradle on the solid hauling platform was visible in the water, its two rows of angled, slender supports reaching up patiently from a sturdy base. Like a giant dead crab, Strelitz thought, lying on its back, its legs pointing up lifelessly.

Four or five boatyard workers stood ready to assist in guiding the boat onto the cradle. It had been decided to go all the way and actually haul the boat up into the yard, rather than simply discharge passengers. The closer to routine the arrival of Mario's boat at the boat works was, the less risk of anyone becoming curious.

Slowly, carefully the boat was guided onto the cradle and secured. The operator in the winch house up on land beyond the turntable pit started the winch. The thick cables grew taut, and slowly the railway rose and the hauling platform with the boat gripped in its cradle moved out of the water toward the turntable.

The massive wooden beams at the ends of the turntable and the hauling platform slipped steadily, inexorably closer and closer until they met over the pulley pit with a resounding thud.

The cradled boat on the platform was hauled onto the turntable, the oil-soaked landing was rotated in the pit to line up with an empty rail spur, and presently Mario's colorful boat had joined others in Benjamino Montesano's boat works, resting inconspicuously in the shadow of a huge crane.

Willi and Eva had arrived at their final destination on the *B-B Achse*. Within hours they would leave war-torn, enemy-occupied Europe and safely embark on a new era, an era that in time would see the rebirth of all that had been lost.

For now.

The railroad station had been a treasure trove of information. In a dog-eared, grease-spotted telephone directory borrowed from the stationmaster's office after much dickering and the passing of a few lire, Woody had found the address of the *Cantiere-riparazioni-Battelli di Benjamino Montesano* in the old harbor. Part of a torn and soiled city plan tacked up behind the shattered glass of a display case had, as luck would have it, included the area he sought, but the section of town where the railroad station itself was located was ripped away. However, the San Nicola Basilica in the heart of the old town, where the fishermen and their families lived, was on the remaining part, and he'd had no trouble finding that. The Bari citizens had been helpful—and cluckingly solicitous when he showed them his mutilated mouth.

The old town was heavily damaged, but Woody was awed by the way the resourceful inhabitants had made makeshift repairs and somehow managed to make the ruins habitable. The place was teeming with people. Barefooted children played in the rubble-strewn streets, and black-haired women were busy hauling in the colorful wash that had been strung out to dry between the windows in the building walls still standing.

It was beginning to grow dark as Woody walked past the San Nicola Basilica. Though battle-scarred and shrapnel-pitted the famous Apulian Romanesque monument miraculously was still standing, a testament to survival. He looked at the imposing structure.

The North Pole, Woody thought. This war-scorched, battle-marred edifice was a far cry from the pristine, white wilderness where Santa Claus was supposed to reside. Yet, here he was. Really. At least his bones. It had been one of the first childhood illusions, he recalled with bittersweet remembrance, that had been shattered by his insatiable thirst for knowledge. Santa Claus. In reality, he had found out, his favorite was a fourth-century Bishop of Myra in Asia Minor, a kindly man who became the patron saint of merchants, mariners, and especially children: Saint Nicholas. Some seven centuries after his death, he had read, a band of sailors from Bari stole the saint's remains and spirited them to their hometown where in time the San Nicola Basilica was erected to house the relics. And here, in the crypt under the very building he was walking by, the sacred bones of Saint Nicholas, patron saint of children, were laid to rest. For a fleeting instant all his present problems and perils vanished, and his childhood disappointment at learning the truth flitted through his mind. He remembered reading how the fame and legend of Saint Nick had swept through Europe, and that in Holland he was known as Sint Niklaas, or as the children would say, Sinter Klaas. It was the early Dutch settlers in New York who brought the name and the gift-giving tradition to the new world, and Sinter Klaas in the cauldron of New World languages was soon corrupted to Santa

[298]

Claus, the Father Christmas of today. He had felt betrayed. It was the first time he'd realized that sometimes knowledge can inflict hurt.

When he had first heard the story, he remembered, he had been told that good old Saint Nick was often represented with three golden balls. He'd wondered mightily how a man could have three balls, especially golden ones. He'd even tried to picture himself so endowed, but he'd been left only to speculate. And he'd been too embarrassed to ask. Only much later had he learned that the three golden balls were the symbol of the medieval merchants' guild, and since the merchants of necessity also were moneylenders, the three balls became the sign of the pawnbroker. How quickly tales of romance and mysticism turn mundane, he mused.

He looked around as he hurried through the devastated old town. Santa Claus must have been sound asleep, he thought, the day the Nazis rained their special gifts from the sky down upon the harbor of Bari.

It was a good two hours later when Woody finally made his move from his place of hiding at a derailed flatcar lying on a railroad siding inland from the Benjamino Montesano Boat Works. The yard was dead and apparently deserted, but not entirely dark. There was still a partial moon in the cloudless sky and the boat works were sparsely illuminated by the pitiless glare from occasional naked light bulbs hanging on tall poles throughout the place, creating feeble pools of pale light beneath them. He had long since gotten his night vision and was able to see quite well. In turn he stretched and flexed each muscle in his body to limber them up after his hours of cramped immobility. Absentmindedly he tongued the hole in his jaw. It was beginning to heal again.

Stealthily, silently, keeping to the shadows as much as possible and avoiding any quick motions, he made his way to the tall fence, part wooden, part wire, that surrounded the boat works. A large, wrought iron double gate big enough to accommodate two trucks driving abreast gave access to the yard. A big sign painted in black letters had been affixed to it: *VIETATO L'INGRESSO!*—No Trespassing! And to make doubly sure a sturdy padlock effectively barred unwelcome visitors. But in the wooden fence adjoining the gate was a small door, also locked. It took Woody less than thirty seconds to pick it.

Automatically he checked the Walther 7.65 he'd taken from the SS officer in Merano and eased it into his belt on his left. He stepped inside, closing the door softly behind him.

For a while he stood motionless, listening to the night noises and getting his bearings. Directly in front of him loomed a huge semicircular ship saw, a pile of heavy timbers stacked nearby. The area was in deep shadow from a water tower rising from sturdy iron supports next to the saw housing. Cautiously he slipped from the door in the fence to the pool of blackness beneath the tower.

He peered into the gloom surrounding him. A weather-beaten wooden building stretched before him. He could make out a door, and beside it a window, its panes almost opaque with grime. But a faint, distant light shone behind them. Carefully he tried the door. It was unlocked. It opened at his first push. Quietly he stepped inside.

He found himself in a large plant, the combination joinery and machine shop of the boat works. In the middle of the spacious area stood a single work light, its caged bulb totally unable to reach the far corners of the cavernous hall. The big shop was cluttered with boxes and benches, crates and casks, and rolls of cordage and canvas. The place was deserted, but only by humans. Spaced throughout the shop stood massive pieces of machinery poised like menacing, misshapen sentries of age-tempered steel; black-silhouetted planers, caulkers, sanders, and shapers seemed to watch his every step malevolently as he slowly made his way through the area; lathes and broachers, milling machines and compressors seemed to lie in wait for his slightest misstep.

His heartbeat was rapid and loud in his head. He knew he was letting the eerie atmosphere of the damned place get to him. He took a deep breath and willed himself to ignore it. Dammit!—it was nothing but a bunch of dirty and decayed machinery.

But sometimes death does hide in dirt and decay.

At the far end of the shop area he came to another door, leading to the outside. For a moment he listened, then—slowly—he pushed it open.

Before him, bathed in the pale light from the moon and the feeble spots hanging high on the naked poles, lay the yard area of Benjamino Montesano's Boat Works. Dominated by a great, circular turntable pit from which radiated more than a dozen rail spurs like spokes from the hub of a gigantic wheel, the yard was a jungle of shapes and shadows. On the spurs, ringing the turntable pit, wedged in their squat, iron-wheeled cradles, stood a conglomeration of boats in various stages of breakdown and repair, like skeletal behemoths huddled around a dry watering hole, each tethered to an A-shaped scaffolding stand. And keeping them in check, positioned around the periphery of the yard, he could glimpse several stacks of drums and barrels, empty cradles, broken scaffolding, and a few shacks and sheds, lorded over by a tall crane.

Woody stood statue-still, breathing shallowly through his mouth so he would be able to hear the slightest noise. The only sound that reached him was the ripple of the wavelets slapping at the piers and the floating docks at the water edge to his right. With his eyes he made a thorough search of the area lying before him, picking a spot, studying it until he knew it in detail and moving on to the next, until he had surveyed the entire yard. He had seen no movement at all, nothing out of keeping.

The massive landing in the turntable pit was empty, forming a solid bridge between the marine railway and the winch house, but there was a six-foot gap between the landing and the hauling platform which had not been pulled all the way up, to leave room for repair or maintenance work in the pulley shaft. It showed up as a pitch-black hole in the ground, and puzzled Woody until he figured out what it was. Over the door to the ramshackle shed that housed the winch machinery was painted in big, black letters: *PERICOLO!*—Danger! He could not make out the legend written beneath, although a little blue light bulb, fixed over the open doorway, spilled a puddle of pale light on the oil-soaked ground outside which glistened with a septic, iridescent shimmer.

Danger!

The hackles rose on the back of his neck. He felt the familiar tightening sensation in the pit of his stomach. That gut feeling that had become so familiar to him since he had first felt it, how long ago? When for the first time he had stood in the dark outside a barred door, gun in sweaty hand, ready to break in and grab a cornered enemy agent.

It was here, he thought. Here in the gloom and clutter and filth of a two-bit, run-down boatyard; here amid the stench of machine oil and tar and soggy rot. It was here he would finally end his quest.

Win—or lose.

Cautiously, keeping to the deepest shadows, he started into the yard, making his way from boat to boat. He looked back toward the building from which he had come. It was a two-story affair. Above the workshop a row of windows, all dark, indicated the existence of offices or rooms. The building on the side facing the yard had been freshly painted. Light blue with white trim. An outside staircase with a white handrail led to the upper story.

He was coming upon a boat, pinioned in its cradle. Broad-beamed, it was gaily painted in red, blue, and green. It had a single mast and a rust-pitted screw.

He stopped. The cradle was still wet, and so was the ground around the rails on which it stood. The boat had only recently been hauled from the harbor waters.

Warily he climbed up the A-shaped scaffolding standing next to the boat. For a moment he stood still, etching the layout of the boatyard on his mind.

Ahead of him gaped the black circular hole of the turntable with the waterfront and the marine railway with its hauling platform on the right, and the winch house on his left. Beyond the turntable pit he could make out the big crane and a few dark sheds. To his right stood the main building and, surrounding him, on the other rail spurs radiating from the pit, were other cradles, some empty, some with boats.

He took one more step up the ladder. He peered over the railing of the boat—and froze.

Lashed to the mast was a motorcycle. *His* Belgian motorbike. The one he had stolen at the inn, *Zum Grünen Kranze*. The one that had been taken from him by the *Achse* agents in Memmingen. *His,* dammit! There was no doubt. One of the damned baskets he'd been saddled with in Coburg was still tied to the back of the bike as a baggage rack!

He stared at the motorcycle. He craned to look.

Suddenly there was the sound of a door being opened, coming from the building.

At once he went rigid.

Clinging to the rickety scaffolding, he turned toward the sound.

29

―――•❖•―――

In THE DIM LIGHT he could see three figures walking down the stairs on the side of the building. A portly, elderly man whose left sleeve was pinned to the shoulder of his jacket as was the custom of amputees in Europe. Especially the war-wounded. A young man who, with obvious familiarity, cradled a submachine gun in his arms. Woody thought he recognized it as the distinctive Italian Beretta. And a woman. A woman, blond, and unmistakably pregnant, who made her way down the wooden stairs holding on to the railing, carefully peering over her swollen belly.

Eva!

Woody hardly dared breathe as he clung to the scaffolding. Even though he knew there was no way he could be seen by the people on the stairs as long as he kept still, he felt nakedly exposed, hanging on to the spindly wooden frame. He stared.

Eva. Pregnant as life. About to carry the Führer's heir to a safe haven, God knows where. And to a future which was planned to hold—what? Unleashing another Adolf Hitler on the world? Possible.

Unless she was stopped.

Now!

The three people paused at the bottom of the stairs. Eerily detached, their voices drifted across the darkened boatyard.

"The truck is parked in the shed over there," the portly, one-armed man said. "The keys are in it." He pointed to one of the shacks standing beyond the turntable pit at the far end of the yard. "I will go and open the gate."

"Grazie, Signor Montesano." It was the young man who spoke.

"Remember. Your ship leaves at midnight. From Pier 87. On the east jetty. A Portuguese merchant ship. It is called the *Estrela.* The captain's name is Arnaldo Caldeira. You will give the passage money to him personally."

"I will remember."

"In bocca al lupo!—Good luck!"

"Thank you, *Signore.*"

Montesano disappeared around the building in the direction of the big iron gates. The young man turned to the woman.

"Wait here, Eva," he said. "I will get the truck and pick you up."

She shook her head. "No, Willi," she said. "I do not want to stay here. Alone. I will go with you."

He nodded. He took her arm. "I will help you," he said. "The footing is treacherous."

They began to walk toward the turntable pit, skirting it at the waterfront side.

Woody's thoughts raced. He would have to act. And act now! Or it would be too late. He'd give the crippled boat works owner time to get as far away as possible. He'd wait until Eva's companion, the man she had called Willi, was out in the open, presenting a good target. If he could incapacitate the guy, if he could grab Eva and get her aboard the truck, there was a bare chance he could barrel out of the damned place. Shit! He was writing himself into a kiddie matinee serial.

There had to be a way.

The ship! The *Estrela.* If he could beat them to the pier, a chance to stop them there might present itself. There were bound to be MPs on the docks. Any commotion would do. And, dammit! A commotion was something he most certainly could cause.

He shifted his weight on the scaffolding. The rung on which he stood protested with a sudden grating creak.

In the quiet of the darkened boatyard it sounded like an explosion.

Instantly the young man with the submachine gun whirled toward the noise.

And Woody.

Woody swore. He had no choice. He was committed.

"Drop your gun!" he shouted. "Put your hands on your head! You are covered!" He hoped his voice conveyed a confidence he did not feel.

The man was good. The echo of Woody's call had not died

down when he dropped to one knee and fired a burst from his submachine gun at the sound of Woody's voice.

Woody heard the bullets slam into the hull of the boat. He was showered with multicolored splinters that bit into his face where they hit. He saw Eva throw her hands to her face. He knew she screamed, but he heard no sound.

Willi was fully alert. And furious. They had been betrayed! By whom? No matter. His eyes flew around the yard. How many were there? Only one had made himself known. One? There was still a chance to get Eva to safety. He thought he knew exactly where the ambusher was.

Tensely Woody watched the young man Eva had called Willi, squatting near the pit, almost invisible in the murky gloom, presenting an impossible target. He saw him raise his submachine gun once again. He tried to shrink into himself as he stared at Death, squatting on the stinking, oil-slimy ground of a crummy boatyard at the edge of nowhere. Stiffly he waited for the next burst from the gun. As long as he kept perfectly still the man might not see him. There was nothing else he could do. He was far outmatched in firepower.

The seconds were eternal. Any split instant he would see the fiery muzzle flares from the deadly submachine gun.

It might be the last thing he'd ever see.

Suddenly a booming voice rang out through the yard. He whipped his head toward the sound. Standing squarely in the doorway to the winch house was a big man—a Luger in his hand gleaming harshly in the faint blue light.

"Stay quite still!" he called, his voice the voice of command. "Or you are dead!"

Woody was stunned. He knew the man! It was his interrogator. His nemesis. The big German—*SS Sturmbannführer* Oskar Strelitz!

Willi also whirled toward the sound of the commanding voice. Sudden rage flooded him. He, too, recognized the big man. He was one of the sailors on Mario's boat! It was *he* who had betrayed them! He whipped his submachine gun into position.

The bullets slammed into the big man's body. In shock his head spun around to stare at his assailant, the man he had sworn to give his life to protect. His mouth gaped open in an expression of utter astonishment—an expression that disintegrated into a splatter of crimson as the second burst from Willi's vengeful submachine gun struck.

Heavily he fell back into the winch house. His lifeless body struck a lever before crashing to the floor, and suddenly the winch machinery rumbled to life. The heavy cables snapped taut, and with a jolt the massive hauling platform began to inch its way toward its impact mating with the turntable landing, slowly, irresistibly, inch by inch closing the gap over the pulley shaft.

Woody had jumped from the scaffolding. He stood at the edge of the boat cradle, feet slightly apart, his Walther 7.65 held in both hands extended before him. He had not the firepower of his enemy. He had to rely on accuracy. He was dimly aware of other shadowy figures moving furtively in the gloom around him, converging on him. Montesano's men. With a conscious effort he forced himself to ignore this new menace.

He saw Willi swing his submachine gun toward him. He saw him rise up slightly to get better aim. He saw the muzzle flash as the burst was fired. He felt a lance of fire rip along his hip. He stood his ground.

Now!

He fired. Three fast rounds.

He saw Willi flinch and stagger. His gun jerked up and the last burst went wild, thudding into the deck and the mast of the boat above his head.

All of a sudden there was a thunderous explosion, and flames shot from the deck of Mario's boat high into the night air.

The motorcycle! The thought tore through Woody's mind even as he once again took deliberate aim at his enemy. The gas tank had been hit!

Willi had felt the bullets tear into his chest. Two of them. He felt no pain, but he knew he was dead.

With terrible, haunted eyes he turned to Eva. She stood transfixed, eerily bathed in the flickering light from the burning boat, staring at the terror of a nightmare that suddenly had become reality.

And he knew.

He knew he had to carry out the Führer's final command.

He lifted his submachine gun. He aimed it straight at the gently rounded swelling on Eva's young body.

He pulled the trigger.

The offspring of the Führer, Adolf Hitler, his son and heir, would not be born in enemy hands.

Better not be born at all.

It had been the Führer's final wish.

The empty gun fell from his hands. Dimly he was aware of a

figure running toward him. And—all at once—lights. Blinding white lights. And the sound of motors. Rumbling and roaring. And voices. Shouting in English. In Italian. Figures. Figures of men all running toward him.

His instincts etched into his mind from time primordial shrieked to him to run. To hide. To flee. He had not the strength.

Suddenly a thunderous blast rocked the yard. Flames shot into the air like fingers of liquid fire greedily probing toward the dark sky. Dimly he realized what had happened. Burning debris from the blazing boat must have fallen to the ground and set fire to a drum or drums of oil or paint, exploding them. Already several other boats were ablaze.

The Montesano boatyard was turning into a howling, crackling inferno.

He stumbled back. The ground under him moved as the heavy hauling platform rumbled on to lock in place. He lost his footing, and tumbled down into the narrow pulley shaft. He struggled to his feet. There was barely room for him to stand. His head and shoulders were level with the ground. Dully, incomprehensibly he stared at the massive, monstrous platform, oil-smeared and work-scarred, inches from his face, inexorably closing in.

The scream of utter terror that started to explode from his throat was crushed from him, as the hauling platform, carrying the lifeless body of Eva and her child with it, labored to meet its mate, fighting the obstruction that sought to keep it from reaching its goal. A different, a sickening, crunching sound joined the steady rumble of the machinery. The mammoth beams of the platform had barely inches to go when the winch mechanism finally cut out.

Woody stood staring in heart-stopping horror down at the bullet-riddled body of the young woman sprawled obscenely on the hauling platform.

Eva. Eva Braun Hitler. The Führer's wife.

Willi's submachine gun burst had ripped viciously across her belly, obliterating her womb and what it had sheltered. Mercifully the flickering fire from the blazing boats and the glaring beams from the headlights and searchlights did not reveal the full horror of the abomination huddled at his feet, crimsonly oozing out over the time-gouged wood to mix with the oily black scum that covered it.

Mesmerized, he stared at the gruesome sight. He thought he could see what had been the unborn Hitler child reaching toward

[307]

him with a tiny, bloody, still unformed arm. The bile rose burning in his throat. He turned away. He kept his eyes averted from the pulley shaft.

All around him flames were licking avidly at the sky. The roar of the fire was punctuated with explosions as motorboat fuel tanks and oil drums detonated in the searing heat. The conflagration, fed by the incendiary fuels, was consuming the boat works, devouring timbers, buckling metal, scorching the very air. Through the flame-washed smoke ghostly figures leaped from the blaze like tormented souls in the depths of hell itself.

He was conscious of someone putting a steadying hand on his arm. He turned. It was his C.O. It was Major Mortimer L. Hall.

He blinked himself back from the brink of the hell that had threatened to engulf him. He looked around. All through the boat yard MPs and *carabinieri* were rounding up men. The crew from the boat works. Montesano. Mario.

He looked at Hall, his eyes bleak.

"What the hell kept you?" he mumbled.

PART III

———•◆•———

20 June, 1945

30

THE HEADLINES ON THE FRONT PAGE of *Stars and Stripes*, June 20, 1945, heralded Ike's triumphant return to the States and the fabulous hero's welcome, complete with ticker-tape parade up Broadway in New York City, given him the day before by four million cheering New Yorkers. It had been a reception that dwarfed the memories of those accorded Charles Lindbergh and Admiral Byrd.

The paper was lying front page up on the desk of Brigadier General Irwin Buter, Chief of Staff, XII Corps, but the four men assembled in his office at Corps HQ in Regensburg paid it no heed. They were listening attentively to the General.

Buter looked at Colonel Streeter and Major Hall. "Dick," he said. "Mort. I want you both to place yourselves completely at the disposal of the undersecretary while he is here at Corps. Any information he wants, you give him."

The two officers nodded their agreement at the only civilian present.

Undersecretary of State David Rosenfeld turned to Buter. "Thank you, General," he said. "I am sure I shall have several questions that need clearing up, once I digest this—this extraordinary turn of events." He looked at Woody. "I congratulate you, Lieutenant Ward," he said. "On a job well done. You have indeed shown resourcefulness and courage well beyond the normal call of duty."

"Thank you, Sir," Woody said smartly. Why did that kind of "official" talk always sound so damned pompous, he thought. He shifted uncomfortably on his chair. He still hadn't gotten used to being called Lieutenant. The new gold bars on his shoulders still seemed to belong to some other guy. But Mort had put him in for the field commission and Buter had promptly approved it and had, in fact, made it a point to assure him that the promotion in no way would interfere with his being sent home to the States as soon as he desired. With points to spare!

Rosenfeld turned to Buter. "Just let me get this one thing straight," he said. "This escape route. The B-B Axis, I believe Lieutenant Ward called it. All the—the stops along the route pinpointed by the lieutenant were raided, were they not?"

"That is correct, Sir," Buter acknowledged.

"And all were found to be abandoned?"

Buter nodded. "The people manning them had all flown the respective coops," he conceded. "Apparently alerted immediately after the raid on the Bari embarkation point. Their communication network appears to be excellent." He looked grimly at the undersecretary. "But I do not for a second believe the Nazi escape operation has been destroyed, Sir. I am certain other routes will be found—if they are not already in operation."

Rosenfeld nodded. "I dare say you are right, General," he agreed.

"Only at one stop on the route were the people caught with their pants—eh, caught unaware," Major Hall interjected. "At an inn in the Italian town of Merano. It seems that the escape route agent who operated the stop, the innkeeper, Bazzano, was laboring under the impression of some sort of false security."

Woody grinned to himself. Pimple-face Pietro had saved his own hide—and put his uncle's ass in a sling.

"The main question remaining," Rosenfeld frowned, "is how to handle the whole sensitive situation with Eva Braun Hitler. We know now why the Nazis wanted the world to think she had died in the Bunker in Berlin, and the Russians undoubtedly are perpetuating the myth because they cannot get themselves to admit that they bungled in the first place. Of course, that's par for the course." He looked at Buter. "From what we know now, it seems certain, however, that Hitler himself did indeed die by his own hand. And was subsequently cremated."

Buter nodded. "I agree."

Rosenfeld sighed. "I shall prepare my report, General. Make my recommendations. I should appreciate your comments when I have done so. And, of course," he added soberly, "everything said here and done here must remain top secret."

"Of course."

"It seems to me, Sir . . . Woody ventured. "It seems to me that the best thing to do is just to leave well enough alone. Let everyone think Eva died in the Bunker." He looked from one to the other of the officers in the room. "She and Adolf are just as dead."

Rosenfeld stared at him. A slow smile of amusement crinkled his face. "Young man," he said, "I think you have the answer. We just—keep our mouths shut!" He nodded to himself. "That, I think, is exactly what I shall recommend to the President."

Woody and Hall were walking back toward the CIC office. Hall gave Woody a sidelong glance. "That was one hell of a female bombshell you let loose on the poor bastards at the Bolzano CIC," he commented.

"I wasn't even sure she'd go there," Woody said. But she had, he thought. She had. And he was grateful.

"She moved heaven and earth, and what's more the whole damned CIC outfit in town to get me on the horn. And she sure hit me with a big enough two-by-four to get my attention. I was in Bolzano practically before the phone connection was broken."

"She saved my ass," Woody said.

"By the way," Hall continued. "She's a bright cookie. We offered her a job. As one of our civilian CIC employees. She took it."

Woody stopped dead in his tracks. He stared at Hall. "She—took it!" he exclaimed. "She's here? At Corps?"

"Sure," Hall grinned. "As a matter of fact, she's waiting in my office."

The last couple of words were delivered into thin air. Woody was already halfway down the corridor.

She was standing at the window when he burst into the office. She turned. He'd never really seen her in a simple, feminine dress. She looked beautiful. In two steps he was at her side. He folded her in his arms.

"Ilse," he whispered.

For a moment they held on to one another. Then Ilse gently freed herself. She looked up into his face, an enigmatic expression in her eyes.

"I—I did what you asked," she whispered. "I went to the Americans."

"I know," he said. "I know. Oh, God, do I know!"

"I know everything now," she said soberly. "I know what you were doing. All the time. With me. With everything."

He studied her face. Suddenly he was in no hurry to get on a damned boat and go back home. There were other matters to settle first.

He tried to read the thoughts behind her solemn eyes. He could not be sure.

What he wanted, what he needed, was her understanding. Her trust. At least—for a starter. Was it there? Was it there in the big luminously liquid eyes regarding him?

He did not know.

But he knew it would come. It would take time, but it would come.

It would come . . .

Appendix

———— •◦•— ————

In July of 1981 the world press carried a startling report by Professor Reidar F. Sognnaes, founding dean and professor emeritus of anatomy and oral biology at the UCLA School of Dentistry and one of the scientists who worked on the identification of the burned bodies of Adolf Hitler and Eva Braun, a report that raised valid and serious doubts about the true identity of the woman whose body was found with Hitler's.

It was *not* Eva Braun.

The charred body, which was discovered in the Chancellery garden by SMERSH, the Russian counterintelligence, and identified as that of Eva Braun, was most probably that of someone else.

Professor Sognnaes pointed out that one of the pieces of evidence by which Eva supposedly was positively identified was a certain dental bridge with white plastic teeth. But despite the fact that the woman's cranio-facial bones were burned beyond recognition by the searing fire, this crucial piece of dental evidence used by the Russians to identify the body as that of Eva Braun was claimed by them to have been found with the remains, intact and undamaged.

DOCUMENT NO. 13 of the Forensic-Medical Commission to the Soviet Army, dated 8 May, 1945, Berlin-Buch, Mortuary, Field Hospital for Surgery No. 496, describes how Eva's cranium was literally consumed by the heat and flames with only a few charred remains of the lower left facial bones and a few teeth found. Yet the autopsy report states that the dental bridge survived: "On the metal plate of the bridge the first and second artificial white molars are attached in front; their appearance is almost undistinguishable from natural teeth."

But, had this bridge actually been on the body when it was being consumed by the flames, the metal plate would have melted, the plastic facings on the teeth would have exploded, and the bridge would have been destroyed. However, the bridge was *not* on the body; for some undisclosed reason it was added to the remains later. According to the dental assistant who was to have fitted Eva Braun with the bridge, this fitting never took place, and the bridge was still in the files of the Berlin workshop when Eva Braun supposedly died in the flames. It was later seized at this workshop by the Russians and added to the unrecognizable remains of the woman burned with Adolf Hitler.

Professor Sognnaes considers it quite likely that the body found in the Chancellery garden was not Eva Braun but a substitute. If Eva did *not* die in the Bunker, someone else died in her place and was burned in the fire pit.

It would have been relatively easy to make such a substitution. The actual facts surrounding the suicides of Adolf Hitler and Eva Braun Hitler will probably never be known. Although several eyewitnesses were questioned exhaustively by many interrogators, their accounts of the same event were all different and contradictory. Principal among these witnesses were SS *Standartenführer* (Colonel) Erick Kempka, Hitler's personal chauffeur; SS *Standartenführer* Heinz Linge, Hitler's valet; SS *Sturmbannführer* (Major) Otto Günsche, Hitler's Senior SS Adjutant, and Artur Axmann, the Hitler Youth Leader.

All of them gave conflicting reports of the same events. In fact, thirty years after his original testimony, Kempka admitted that at the time he had simply told his interrogators what he thought they wanted to hear. Originally he had testified that he heard the shot that killed Hitler; in truth he was not even present in the Bunker below, but was still in the garden above!

Each man who entered Hitler's room and saw the bodies saw something different and at times gave conflicting reports. Günsche at first said he saw the bodies sitting next to each other on the sofa, but later he said Hitler was sitting in a chair and Eva was lying in another chair. Linge saw them both lying on the sofa, and Kempka, when he did arrive, saw Hitler lying and Eva sitting. Kempka saw the entry of the bullet into Hitler as being through the mouth, while Günsche saw the same wound in the right temple, and Linge saw it in the left!—a statement he later changed to the right.

Even the few minutes of the commonly shared experience of waiting for Hitler and Eva to take their own lives were reported in totally different versions.

Kempka and Linge reported that they heard the shot that killed Hitler; Axmann said that no shot was heard at all. And it has been established that no shot could possibly have been heard through the heavy door.

According to Günsche there were at least seven people directly outside the door. They were Goebbels, Bormann, Linge, General Krebs, General Burgdorf, Axmann, Günsche himself, and a couple of SS officers. According to him, he, Linge, Goebbels, and Axmann entered the room behind Bormann. According to Linge, however, he smelled gunpowder in the corridor and then fetched Bormann, and the two of them entered the room. And other reports state that Bormann arrived after everyone else was already inside Hitler's room! The picture is totally confusing. And when the reports by the various chroniclers of the events—Shirer, Trevor-Roper, Ryan, Fest, Payne, Goldson, Irving, Boldt, O'Donnell, et al—are added, the picture becomes even more confused and contradictory.

The only thing on which they all seem to be in agreement is the fact that the bodies were wrapped in blankets as they were carried up to the Chancellery garden to be cremated, making identification difficult if not impossible.

One of the most knowledgeable of the chroniclers of Eva Braun, war correspondent Nerin E. Gun, states: "The fate of Eva Braun's corpse, or of her ashes if her body was completely cremated, remains a mystery." He notes that the German General, Hans Krebs, at his urgently requested meeting on May 1, 1945 with the Russian Field Marshal Vassili Chuikov, informed him of Hitler's suicide and the cremation of his body in detail, without mentioning a word about the death of Eva Braun, a fact, which under the circumstances, seems highly suspicious to Mr. Gun. And he wonders why the Soviets waited more than twenty years to make public the report of their findings regarding the bodies of Adolf and Eva, arguing that there was no real evidence to support the death claim of Eva Braun, and—citing the weight of contradictory statements—he considers what really happened on Monday, April 30, 1945 "one of the great enigmas of contemporary history."

In the months that followed the defeat of Germany and the collapse of the Third Reich several reports from different European sources claimed that Eva Braun Hitler had been seen in various parts of Europe. The reports ceased after several months.

As for the abortive breakout of Martin Bormann and the various versions of his death, they are matched only by the many versions of his successful escape to South America, and both are far outdistanced by the reports of subsequent Bormann sightings in many places both in Europe and in South America. The facts will undoubtedly never be known.

However, there were in existence several more or less effective organizations that assisted thousands of high-ranking Nazis and war criminals in escaping from Germany, and helped them find concealment and refuge abroad, especially in South America. Of them the three most important and best known were ODESSA, *Die Spinne* (The Spider), and *Die Schleusse* (The Lock-Gate).

All of these escape organizations had their beginnings during the final months of the war and shortly thereafter. Through the years they were aided by many other more or less clandestine organizations and societies which sprang into being throughout Germany and the rest of the world. These organizations included General von Manteuffel's *Brüderschaft* (Brotherhood); *Der Rudel Klub,* originally founded in Argentina by Hans Ulrich Rudel, a Luftwaffe ace; HIAG—*Hilfe und Interessengemeinschaft der Ehemalige Angehörigen der Waffen SS* (Aid and Mutual Interest Society of Ex-Waffen SS Members); *Stille Hilfe* (Silent Aid); *Evangelische Hilfswerk* (Evangelical Aid Work) in Hamburg; the notorious *Vatikanische Hilfslinie* (The Vatican Aid Line) between Austria and Rome, one of the best-organized and safest escape routes also known as The Monastery Route because the escape route safe houses were run by religious orders and ended in the Collegia Teutonica di Santa Maria dell' Anima in Rome, in the charge of Monsignor Alois Hudal, a Croatian nationalist, Bishop of Eila; *Der Salzberger Zirkel* (The Salzburg Circle); St. Martin's Fonds in Belgium; HINAC in Holland; KABSZ (Comradeship of Fighters on the Eastern Front) in Hungary, believed to have been founded by one Karoly Ney under the direction of Otto Skorzeny; *Hjelporganisasjonen for Krigskadede* (Aid Organization for War Wounded) in Norway; *Dansk Frontkämpfer Forbundet* (The League of Danish Frontline Fighters) in Denmark; and *Kameradschaft IV* in Austria, as well as many others.

The secret escape routes operated along similar lines. All had organizational headquarters in various major German cities and branch offices located wherever necessary, and they were financed by the numerous hidden Nazi accounts and funds, as well as with large caches of money and looted valuables within Germany itself, or secretly transferred to neutral foreign countries well in advance of the contemplated escape operations.

Along the escape route was a series of "stops" or "safe houses"—*Anlaufstellen*—spaced every forty or fifty miles, staffed by from one to five loyal members who knew only one other stop on each side of their own. They provided the "travelers" with money, transportation, safety, and new identification papers made out in false names, if needed.

Die Schleusse (The Lock-Gate) was one of the first major escape routes to be organized. As early as the fall of 1944, selected high Nazi officials had received their false papers—passport, identity *Kennkarte,* birth certificate, marriage license, work permit, and other applicable documents, prepared by the special bureau of the Gestapo, set up for the purpose, or by such operations as *Aktion Birkenbaum* (Operation Birch Tree), which was created to manufacture such false documents for the use of the future escape route travelers. The main routes of *Die Schleusse* were the Northern Route: Hamburg, Kiel, Schleswig, Flensburg, into Denmark and on to South America; and the Southern Route: Austria to Italy and Spain as the gateways to the Middle East and South America.

Die Spinne (The Spider) was, at war's end, undoubtedly the main secret underground escape route, its network covering Germany, Austria, and Italy. Known in France as *L'Araignée* and in Spain as *La Araña,* the organization was headed for a while by General Paul Hausser, a co-founder of the Waffen SS. With headquarters in Augsburg or Stuttgart, and a *Verteilerkopf*—a distribution center—at Memmingen, *Die Spinne* operated the successful *B-B Achse* (B-B Axis), a main north-south route using the Bs from Bremen in northern Germany and Bari, its final destination on the southern tip of Italy on the Adriatic Sea, in its code name. The escapees traveling the *Achse* were, in fact, often aided by some religious orders and by certain Red Cross officials who smuggled the fugitives across the borders disguised as Red Cross couriers taking food parcels to refugee camps or shepherding groups of DPs—displaced persons. Trucks, driven by German drivers, hauling the *Stars and Stripes* were, in fact, often used to transport *Achse* travelers, and Jewish illegal emigrants being smuggled to Palestine by the Jewish refugee organization, *Bricha,* occasionally did share a safe house with fleeing Nazis, such as at the inn at Merano. Apparently discontinued, or sharply curtailed, shortly after the war, *Die Spinne* formed the foundation for the largest and most efficient of the escape routes, ODESSA.

ODESSA—*Organisation der Ehemalige SS Angehörigen* (Organization of Ex-SS Members)—had its headquarters—*Verteilungskopf* (Allocation Center)—in Munich, after being controlled from Augsburg and Stuttgart during its earlier period of operation. It had branches all over Germany and Austria as well as in South America. ODESSA operated two main southern escape routes—from Bremen to Rome, and from Bremen to Genoa—and a northern route through the Flensburg escape hatch into Denmark. Many knowledgeable historians are convinced that Martin Bormann fled Germany via one of these ODESSA escape routes along with such others as Otto Skorzeny, Franz Stangl, and Adolf Eichmann, all of whom did.

Mystery still surrounds the fates of both Eva Braun and Martin Bormann. It is almost as if a carefully orchestrated scheme to mislead and deceive took place.

Did it?

When all the reports are considered, including the statements by Professor Sognnaes; when all is said and done, we know only one thing for sure:

We will never know the truth.

List of Abbreviations

———••———

AMERICAN

AAF	Army Air Force
AC of S	Assistant Chief of Staff
AIC	Army Interrogation Center
AMG	American Military Government
APO	Army Post Office
AUS	Army of the United States
CIC	Counter Intelligence Corps
CID	Criminal Investigation Department
CO	Commanding Officer
Co	Company
CP	Command Post
DC	Dental Corps
EM	Enlisted man (men)
ETO	European Theatre of Operations
G-2	Military Intelligence
GI	General Issue; Infantry man
GSC	General Staff Corps
HQ	Headquarters
ID	Identification
IPW	Interrogator of Prisoners of War
MG	Military Government
OIC	Officer in Charge
R&R	Rest and Rotation; Rest and Recreation
SOP	Standard Operating Procedure
TDY	Temporary Duty

TM	Training Manual
T.S.	Tough Shit
USO	United Service Organization

GERMAN

BMW	Bavarian Motor Works
Km	Kilometer
KZ (KL)	Concentration Camp
SS	Schutz Staffel (Elite Corps)
UFA	Berlin Film Atelier

BRITISH

SOE	Special Operations Executive

Bibliography

In addition to the author's personal records and several works in foreign languages, the following English-language books have furnished authentication and facts for *Eva:*

Bar Zohar, Michael. *The Avengers: The Story of the Hunt for Nazi Criminals*. Arthur Baker, Ltd. London, 1968.

Bezymenski, Lev. *The Death of Adolf Hitler*. Harcourt, Brace & World. New York, 1968.

Boldt, Gerhard. *Hitler: The Last Ten Days*. Coward, McCann & Geohegan. New York, 1947.

Bullock, Alan. *Hitler: A Study in Tyranny*. Harper & Row. New York, 1962.

Delarue, Jacques. *The Gestapo: A History of Horror*. Macdonald & Co. New York, 1964.

Dollinger, Hans. *The Decline & Fall of Nazi Germany & Imperial Japan*. Bonanza Books, New York, 1962.

Dyer, George, Lt. Col. *XII Corps: Spearhead of Patton's Third Army*. XII Corps History Association, Washington D. C., 1947.

Farago, Ladislas. *Aftermath*. Simon & Schuster, New York, 1974.

Fest, Joachim. *Hitler*. Harcourt, Brace, Jovanovich, New York, 1973.

Foley, Charles. *Commando Extraordinary*. G. P. Putnam, New York, 1967.

Goldstone, Robert. *The Life and Death of Nazi Germany*. The Bobbs-Merrill Co. New York, 1967.

Gun, Nerin E. *Eva Braun: Hitler's Mistress*. Meredith Press, New York, 1968.

Hanfstaengl, Max. *Hitler: The Missing Years*. Eyre & Spottiswoode, London, 1957.

Heiden, Conrad. *Der Führer: Hitler's Rise to Power*. Houghton Mifflin Co., Boston, 1944.

Hitler, Adolf. *Mein Kampf*. Houghton Mifflin Co. Boston, 1943.

Hutton, Clayton. *Official Secret*. Crown Publishers, New York, 1961.

Infield, Glenn B. *Disaster at Bari*. The Macmillan Co. New York, 1971.

—— *Eva and Adolf*. Grosset & Dunlap, New York, 1974.

—— *Skorzeny: Hitler's Commado*. St. Martin's Press, New York, 1981.

Irving, David. *Hitler's War*. The Viking Press, New York, 1977.

—— *The Rise and Fall of the Luftwaffe*. Little, Brown & Co. Boston, 1973.

—— *The Secret Diaries of Hitler's Doctor*. Macmillan Publishing Co. New York. 1983.

Koch, H. W. *The Hitler Youth*. Ballantine Books, Inc. New York, 1972.

Langer, Walter C. *The Mind of Adolf Hitler: The Secret Wartime Report*. Basic Books, New York and London, 1972.

Modern Military Branch, National Archives. *The Hitler Source Book*. Washington, D. C., Unclassified 1968.

O'Donnell, James P. *The Bunker*. Houghton Mifflin Co. Boston, 1978.

Parrish, Thomas, Ed. *Encyclopedia of World War II*. Simon & Schuster. New York, 1978.

Payne, Robert. *The Life and Death of Adolf Hitler*. Praeger Publishers. New York, 1973.

Pia, Jack. *Nazi Regalia*. Ballantine Books, Inc. New York, 1971.

Pridham, Geoffrey. *Hitler's Rise to Power: The Nazi Movement in Bavaria*. Harper & Row. New York, 1973.

Reitsch, Hanna. *Flying Is My Life*. G P. Putnam. New York, 1954.

Ryan, Cornelius. *The Last Battle*. Simon & Schuster. New York, 1966.

Satzger, Alfons. *Wies Church*. Verlag Wallfahrtskuratie, Wies bei Steingaden, New York, (n.d.)

Shirer, William L. *The Rise and Fall of the Third Reich*. Simon & Schuster. New York, 1959.

Smith, Bradley F. *Adolf Hitler*. Hoover Institution Press. Stanford, 1967.

Speer, Albert. *Inside the Third Reich*. The Macmillan Co., New York, 1970.

Tabori, Paul, Ed. *The Private Life of Adolf Hitler: Notes and Diaries of Eva Braun*. Aldus Publications, London, 1949.

Toland, John. *Adolf Hitler*. Doubleday and Co. New York, 1976.

Trevor-Roper, H.R. *The Last Days of Hitler*. Macmillan Publishing Co. New York, 1947.

Whiting, Charles. *Skorzeny*. Ballantine Books. New York, 1972.

———— *The Hunt for Martin Bormann*. Ballantine Books. New York, 1973.

———— *Hitler's Werewolves*. Stein and Day, New York, 1972.

Wiesenthal, Simon. *The Murderers Among Us*. McGraw-Hill Book Co. New York, 1967.

Wighton, Charles. *Eichmann, His Career and Crimes*. Odham Press, Ltd., Eastbourne, 1961.

Zink, Harold. *American Military Government in Germany*. The Macmillan Co. New York, 1947.

About the Author

————— ◆•◆ —————

Ib Melchior, as well as being a best-selling author, is also a motion picture writer-director-producer in Hollywood with some twelve feature films and numerous TV shows to his credit.

He was born and educated in Denmark and graduated from the University of Copenhagen, majoring in literature and languages. He then joined a British theatrical company, The English Players, headquartered in Paris, France, as an actor and toured Europe with this troupe, becoming stage manager and co-director of the company. Just prior to the outbreak of World War II in Europe he came to the United States with this company to do a Broadway show.

Then followed a stint in the stage-managing department of Radio City Music Hall and the Center Theater Ice Shows in New York, and when Pearl Harbor was attacked he volunteered his services to the U.S. Armed Forces. He served with the "cloak-and-dagger" OSS for a while and was then transferred to the U.S. Military Intelligence Service. He spent two years in the European Theater of War as a Military Intelligence Investigator attached to the Counter Intelligence Corps. For his work in the ETO he was decorated by the U.S. Army as well as by the King of Denmark, and subsequently awarded the Knight Commander Cross of the Militant Order of St. Brigitte of Sweden.

After the war he became active in television and also began his writing career. He has directed some five-hundred television shows both live and filmed, ranging from the musical *The Perry Como Show* on CBS-TV, on which he served as director for three and a half years, to the dramatic documentary, *The March of Medicine* on NBC-TV. He has also functioned as director or in a production capacity on eight motion picture features in Hollywood, including AIP's unusual *The Time Travelers,* which he also wrote.

Besides this extensive career as a director, Ib Melchior's background as an author and writer includes numerous stories and articles published in many national magazines including *Life,* as well as in several European periodicals, some of which have been included in anthologies. He has also written a couple of legitimate plays for the stage, one being *Hour of Vengeance,* a dramatization of the ancient Amleth legend that was the original source for Shakespeare's *Hamlet.* This play was produced at the Globe Playhouse in Los Angeles, and the Shakespeare Society of America and the Hamlet Society International jointly awarded Melchior the "Hamlet Award," 1982, for excellence in playwriting.

Melchior has won several national awards for television and documentary film shorts that he wrote, directed, and produced, and he has written several scripts for various TV series including *Men Into Space* and *The Outer Limits.* Among his feature motion pictures are such films as *Ambush Bay,* a film with a World War II background filmed in the Philippines for United Artists, as well as the notable *Robinson Crusoe on Mars* for Paramount and several other films with a science fiction theme. In 1976 he was awarded the Golden Scroll by the Academy of Science Fiction for best writing.

Ib Melchior is the author of the best-selling, critically acclaimed novels based on his own experiences as a CIC agent, *Order of Battle, Sleeper Agent,* and *The Haigerloch Project,* as well as *The Watchdogs of Abaddon, The Marcus Device,* and *The Tombstone Cipher.* His novels are now published in twenty-five countries.

Ib Melchior lives in a two-story, Mediterranean-style home in the Hollywood Hills. He is an avid collector of historical documents and military miniatures. He is married to the designer, Cleo Baldon, and has two sons. He is the son of the late Wagnerian tenor, Lauritz Melchior.